LION ON THE HEARTH

Books by John Ehle

FICTION

Move Over, Mountain
Kingstree Island
Lion on the Hearth
The Land Breakers
The Road
Time of Drums
The Journey of August King
The Changing of the Guard
The Winter People
The Widow's Trial
Last One Home

NONFICTION

The Survivor: The Story of Eddy Hukov
*Shepherd of the Streets: The Story of the Reverend
    James A. Gusweller and His Crusade on the New
    York West Side*
The Free Men
*The Cheeses and Wines of England and France, with
    Notes on Irish Whiskey*
Trail of Tears: The Rise and Fall of the Cherokee Nation
Dr. Frank: Life with Frank Porter Graham

Lion

on the

Hearth

JOHN EHLE

Press 53
Winston-Salem

PRESS 53
PO Box 30314
Winston-Salem, NC 27130

PRESS 53 *Classics*

Lion on the Hearth

First Edition

This Press 53 *Classsics* edition is scanned
from the original 1961 First Edition,
with new front matter and author biography page.

Printed on acid-free paper

ISBN 978-1-941209-30-1

To Samuel Selden

*For every family
there is a lion on the hearth.*
A FOLK SAYING

PART ONE

1

THE HOUSE WAS SOMBER WHEN CALEB KING GOT home, for most of the sunlight had gone for the day and there weren't many windows in the rooms, and none in the hall where he stood now. The house was overly quiet, too, or so it seemed to him after the daylong noises of the store, where people sought him out and asked favors and traded. The house was usually noisy when he got home because the boys were there, talking among themselves and with Beth, and carrying on and arguing, but he was the first one home tonight.

"Lotti," he called.

The word was hollow in the hall. It reverberated there, imprisoned by the wooden walls. He heard no answer. He took his hat off, a Western type of hat, and smoothed his hair down, then smoothed his mustache at the edges. He walked through the hall to the dining-room and pushed it open. "Lotti?"

She was bound to know he had come home early in order to talk to her. "Where are you?" He heard nothing.

The table was set for supper, he noticed. He pushed open the kitchen door and she was there, standing at the sink, washing dishes.

3

She didn't look up, even when he entered.

"Lotti, I reckon you're feeling well," he said gently. She still didn't answer or look at him. "It's not bothered you yet, has it?"

She began to hum, a low moaning sound. "No, it's not," she said.

"The boys will raise the devil, of course. But you know that." There was suffering in her voice, he could tell, though not, he guessed, from body pain. "God knows, though," he said, "we got to live each person his own life."

She went back to her work. She just wouldn't talk about it, seemed like. A woman of fifty had no business showing secret manners around her husband, he thought, but she had been that way all her life, always private and overanxious about herself. Not that he had complaints. The two of them had got along all right. Almost thirty years married, a long time.

"Well, I hope you feel all right," he said. When she didn't answer him, he stepped out onto the back porch and let her be. No doubt she would use her own ways to deal with the problem. That's what she wanted.

He smiled suddenly, for he saw Kin, his youngest. Kin was coming up the path from the chicken lot, a big basket of eggs in his hands, much too big a basket for a five-year-old boy; he was jumping from one yard board to another, even though the ground was dry—not that he would have used the boards if the ground were wet, Cal realized, for he got muddy whenever he wanted to. "Hey, Kin, get on in here," he called.

Kin looked up, surprised to see his father home, then he began to run toward the porch as fast as he could. Cal held the porch gate open for him. "You go to the chicken pound and it takes you half a lifetime to get back. Never get to Liverpool that way."

He took the basket of eggs as Kin came up the steps, just in time, too, because the boy almost fell. He was looking up at his father, proud of the attention he was getting and of the good feeling in his father's voice.

"Look a' there," Cal said, licking his lips as if he had road dust on them. He started counting the eggs as the screen gate slapped

4

shut. "Got a lot of eggs here, boy. Let's see, got thirteen."

"Got fourteen," Kin said.

Cal considered that, studying the boy seriously; then he started counting the eggs again. His hand moved slowly among them. He had big hands, coarse and tough, but they were gentle in what they did now. "Got thirteen, Kin," he said.

Kin peered over the rim of the basket and began counting them again. Cal waited, not moving or saying anything, just looked down at the towhead of the boy as he worried over the problem.

Kin finished counting. He backed off and studied his father.

"Got thirteen," Cal said quietly.

"Got fourteen," the boy said.

A glint came into Cal's eyes, though the other features of his face changed not at all. He shook his head, as if disappointed in the boy, but abruptly he chuckled deep inside his chest, and he ran his hand fondly through the boy's hair. "Going to rise in this world, going to do well if you hold to your own mind like that. Do you hear me?"

"Yes, sir."

"You hold to yourself and you'll do all right. My, how I wish I had it to do, to start out afresh."

A somberness came over him, an anxiousness. He turned from the boy and looked out at the sheds and the chicken house and the family garden spot. "You go into the kitchen and get washed, Kin," he said, and he walked out into the back yard and moved around the new room he had just built onto the rear of the house; he was always building, changing, and he walked down the driveway toward the front yard, thinking about his youth, back before he came to the city, when he had lived on a mountain farm near Asheville, one of the farms which huddled in the valleys and coves of the Blue Ridge and the Black and the Smoky Mountains, the mighty chains of tree-covered mountains with spring water pouring from them twelve months of the year. He had moved to Asheville in 1913, just ten years before. He had been forty and had decided that there was no hope for progress on the farm. He had packed his belongings, his wife, his three sons, and a niece, Beth, into wagons and had driven down the Cole Mountain Road. He sold his land and stock to his brother, and with that money he made a down payment on six acres of open land on the south side of the business section of Asheville. The bottom third of the land he set aside for a house or two and a garden. Through the middle of the upper two thirds, with the same team which had pulled one of his three wagons to town, he plowed and harrowed in a road, connecting it at the uphill end, the south end, to Market Street, which until that time had been the place farmers had traded, where they had been fleeced for a hundred years. He made his road into two blocks and sold off lots on the upper one to people who wanted to open shops. The lower block he set aside for the farmers and for himself. On the right side as one faced uphill was a market place for them, which they could use to show their goods. On the other side he built the King Store, adding to it year by year as he gained means, until now it covered almost an acre and contained everything the country people needed. Caleb King was a man of wealth now, but sometimes he got to thinking about the late start he had taken on his life.

Lotti had heard him on the porch talking to the boy, and she heard Kin come into the kitchen. "Get your hands washed," she said. She didn't look at him. Until a few months before, Kin had been her favorite; she would tell the others of her children to leave him be, that he was for the Lord's service. But of late she had stopped concerning herself with him, for she had come to see that he had the same traits as the rest, the marks of Cain, she called them.

She put a rusty-bottomed pan under the waterspout and worked the pump handle, moving it jerkily, as she always did when she was upset. Water spouted out, and she set the half-full basin on the oilcloth-covered table near the sink and put a cup of soft soap next to it.

He was just like his brothers; she had given up on him, as she had on Paul and Collins and Matthew before him. The family

6

shouldn't have left the farm, she thought; that was one fact of the matter, for the city tainted the heart. On the farm health and contentment had come from the buds and the breaking of ground, the nourishing of seeds and the green growth, the cold water from the rocks and the ever-present looming dark mountains close on all sides (except down the cove where the school was, and where the store and the bridge were). A person could more easily keep perspective if he were close to nature. But in bargaining and loaning and paying, of that nobody ever had enough, and nothing was natural about it.

"Where you been, boy?" she asked.

"Getting the eggs." He moved his hands in the soapy water.

"Lord, boy, you been gone an hour. You're a strange one, all right." She dried her own hands on her apron, a frayed piece of cloth cut from a flour sack, just as her aprons had been made from flour sacks when she had lived in the country and was poor. She rubbed her face, getting the circulation back into the skin. She was pale, though her cheeks were always pink; she had a long face with thin lips, which had been pretty once and now was stark-looking. "Law, boy, I thought you would turn out to be like your grandfather Juniper. He was a dreamer, too, but what he dreamed about was human kindness. He had thousands of dollars, for everybody handed him money for his churches and his work, but he gave it away to the needy. So he never had nothing left for any of us except love and gentleness. I can hear him now singing—" She stared at the blank wall in front of her, where the smooth plaster was cracked, and she seemed to be listening to her father sing, back in the old days. "When he died, I wasn't yet marryin' age, and it was a blow so deep—" Tears welled up into her eyes, as they often did when she talked about her father. "He was a dreamer," she said, pumping water over the pans in the sink, "not one given over to buying and selling."

He listened to her, quiet and apprehensive, standing as if ready to flee should there be a need to.

Abruptly she looked down at him. "What you think about down

7

at the chicken pound? I seen you the other day climbing through the fence to get over to the Tumpkins place, and no doubt you went on to your father's street. Is that it?"

He twisted before her. "No, Mama."

"Just as close as you could get, to see the trading, is that it?"

His lips trembled, but he stiffened them. He laid the washrag aside and drew back from her, but his eyes didn't leave her face.

She turned from him. "You go on, boy. Go away. Set at the table till your father and brothers are ready to eat."

He moved sideways out of the nook, where he was caught between her and the coal stove, where the corn bread was baking in heavy black frying pans.

The marks of Cain, she thought.

She had borne eight children in all. Two had died at birth and two others in childhood. Of the four who were alive, all fell short of her need. Kin was the youngest, and Paul was the oldest. Paul, born in 1896, she had named after the New Testament saint and had dedicated at birth to God's service, but now, at twenty-seven, he worked at his father's store and had no interest in spiritual matters. He was a bachelor; often he went with girls, but usually with the fast type, Lotti suspected, the ones who didn't expect marriage. He had no time for long-range contracts. A big man, both large of bone and heavy, he was given over to the burning ambitions of the Kings, but he tried fitfully to keep his feelings inside himself.

Collins, born four years later, in 1900, was now twenty-three. He was his father's chosen boy from the beginning and was named by him, the only one of the eight who didn't receive a Bible name. Collins had been intended for farming and trading, but two years after the family reached the city, he ran away. He was found and brought back home, but two years later, when he was seventeen, he left again. He had come back once for a visit. Now he wrote but seldom, and his letters never revealed anything about himself, but they were good to receive, Lotti admitted. "To my dear mama Lotti," they would start, "the dearest sweetest little mama in all the world."

Lotti's third son, Matthew, was now a handsome, loose-tongued

8

boy of fourteen. She had been convinced she had a perfect servant of the Lord in him, but before he was half grown, he revealed his true nature, so she had gone about praying for Kin, whom she named John, which when translated means "beloved of God." Her preacher had told her that. She tended to Kin prayerfully, keeping him isolated from the others as best she could, but by the time he was turning five years of age, it had become clear that he also tended toward his father's ways, not hers. She stopped objecting when Beth and the others called him Kin, instead of John. This nickname had been started by Paul, who had often said, "Well, he's holy and not one of us, but anyway he's kin." But he was one of them, Lotti had decided, as day after day she watched him listening to the words of business that were said on the porch and in the parlor, as he watched his brothers enviously and waited for his father's kind words, as he sneaked out to the back of the lot behind the chicken house and crawled under the wire fence and looked at the street, which rose for two blocks before him, with the farmers' market so close he could hear some of the words that were spoken there. He would, Lotti knew, look at the street hungrily, taking in the color and the sights, the masses of overall-clad farmers and their gingham-clad women and girls, coming into town for business and Lord knows what other pleasures.

Well, they had taken Kin from her. She didn't think of him as being called John now herself. Kin was what he was; he was just like the rest.

She swished the wash water from the pan she had given him into the sink.

Beth came into the kitchen as Kin was leaving, and she caught him in her arms and squeezed him tightly against her breasts. Beth smelled of perfume, he noticed. His mother smelled of soap, his father of tobacco, and Beth of perfume.

She pulled at Kin's ears playfully. "Where do you think you're going?" she asked, and he giggled.

She was about eighteen and was pretty in a natural way. There

9

was nothing flashy about her. Many men passing her on the street wouldn't realize that she was pretty at all, and only a few would notice her. She never fixed herself up, that was the trouble, rarely wore makeup because Mama Lotti didn't like it. She stayed at the house and took care of things, as she had done since Caleb had brought her to the city with his family.

She backed Kin into a corner, growling at him, and he began once more to giggle.

"Leave him alone," Lotti said, speaking out of her irritation with the day's worry. "Are the boys home? Is Paul here yet?"

"Yes. On the porch." She grabbed Kin's arm and started to pull him to her again, and he came willingly. She pulled him into her arms and against the softness of herself, but Lotti spoke out more sharply, so Beth released him, then winked at him. She shoved him gently through the dining-room door. "Matthew's here, too," she said. "Seems like word has gotten out."

"Nothing to be done about that," Lotti said, pursing her lips. "No apologies to be made for what's natural."

Beth closed the door.

Kin sat down at the dining-room table and tried to listen, but he couldn't hear what they were saying, so he got up and went out into the wide hallway, where a single light bulb hung from a worn black cord, dangled at head height for a tall man. The bulb didn't give out much light; it was the smallest one Lotti had been able to find anywhere, and such light as it had to offer was soaked up by the brown paneling of the walls and ceiling. The only piece of furniture was a massive halltree, a hickory coat rack, never used, which rested like ribs of dark bone against the south wall. It faced the sinewy banister rail and the stairway, and the flower-print curtain which sealed off the space under the stairs, so that trunks and coverlets could be properly stored there. Kin didn't like to stay long in the hallway.

Paul and Matthew were on the porch. They were rocking back and forth, somewhat irritably, and Caleb was sitting comfortably in the swing, looking about contentedly, as if being home early for supper were a natural occurrence. Kin went out and sat down in the swing beside him.

"What you going to do?" Paul asked his father.

Cal cleared his throat and peered across the wide porch and out over the yard and the narrow dirt trail. "It's her business, seems to me."

"Must be partwise your business, too," Paul said, arching his back as if to relieve the tension in it.

Matthew, the fourteen-year-old, said, "Going to be a laughing subject by Monday. It's embarrassing." He picked at his thin cheeks. He was a frail boy when compared with Paul, but was just as handsome and seemed to have much appeal for women, even at his young age.

Paul adjusted his big body to the wicker rocker. "It's damn near a miracle this time."

Beth came through the hallway and told them to come in to eat. They got up slowly and stretched, each one holding to his thoughts, and filed through the hallway to the dining room and sat down around the oval table, which was lit by a light bulb shaded by folds of newspaper Lotti had tied to the cord. Supper consisted of corn bread and buttermilk, a two-quart bowl of string beans heated over from dinner, which was the main meal of the day, coffee, syrup for those who wanted sweetening on their bread, and cold apple pie for dessert. As a rule the family ate in silence, unless Matthew wanted to start one kind of devilment or another. He was a great one for that, either for taking advantage of Paul's highly emotional nature by poking him into anger, or for joking his mother into speech. But often, since he quit school and went to work full time, he ate at the store, cutting open a can of fish and eating out of the can, or ate at one of the restaurants up the street. Matthew ate most of the time, that was the truth of the matter, but he didn't always get home for meals. Beth said it was because he didn't want to miss a trade.

But Matthew was present tonight and he ate quietly, glancing curiously from time to time at his mother, and at Beth, who was scowling at him, defying him to say what was on his mind.

When everybody was through eating, the father and Paul went

into the parlor, which was down the hall to the right at the front of the house. They closed the door. Rarely was the door closed in summertime, and when it was, it meant that a serious conference was being held.

Matthew sneaked down the hall and entered uninvited.

Beth nervously got up from the table, brushed down her apron smoothly in front, and began gathering up the dishes. "I'll do that, baby," Lotti said lethargically, but Beth went on working. Lotti sat at the table, crumbling corn bread into milk and stirring it around, then eating the mixture with a spoon, but it was evident that she wasn't thinking about what she was doing. Once she started humming a sad song, one of the old hymns, something about a beautiful morning which the Lord had given.

The voices of the men in the parlor rose. "Well, when the hell is she going to stop?" Paul was saying. "This can't go on and on, can it?"

Lotti hummed a little louder, but she didn't try to drown out the sound of her sons' voices.

Paul was shouting now. "Doc LeClair was laughing so hard when he told me that he couldn't hardly get it out. Everybody knows she's anxious for a preacher. Well, what's wrong with Kin?"

Kin stared through the door at the hallway. Beth, mumbling something under her breath, started down the hall. Her aunt called to her, but she went on, went right into the parlor. "You're a fine group, shouting at the top of your voices," she said angrily, speaking as loud as Paul had spoken and acting as if she were a close member of the family. "You sit in here talking as if a crime has been committed."

"You'll have to admit it's a damn miracle, Beth," Matthew said whining, as he sometimes did around her.

"You hush up. What's wrong with her having a child?"

"Well, Beth," Paul said heavily, "she's had eight, for God's sake."

"And one more means somebody else to inherit, is that what worries you? Yes, that's what worries you and Matthew. Your mama having another child is poor business. Well, that's too bad."

12

"Oh, be quiet, Beth," Paul said wearily.

"That's your mother in there," Beth said. "Don't you know that? Doesn't it mean anything to you?"

There was no answer for a minute, then Paul spoke, breathing deeply, as if tired of the arguments. "Papa, she's too old to have it lost for her by a doctor, ain't she?"

Beth stormed out of the parlor. She came to the dining room, her face flushed and her small fists clenched. "They're animals," she said. She took Kin by one arm, dragged him into the kitchen, and slammed the door after them. "Your brothers are animals," she said, lecturing him fiercely. "They'll eat their own kind. They want to kill the baby. And your father is sitting in there looking at them as if he never saw such impertinence, but saying not a word to criticize. The kind judge, he sees himself as. My lord!"

Kin drew away from her and sat down in a straight-back chair near the kitchen table, in the corner near the door, and leaned his cheek against the cold enameled top. They could hear the voices from the parlor, but couldn't make out much of anything. Then they heard Matthew let out a laugh, a cackle that penetrated all the barriers. Paul told him to shut up, but Matthew went on laughing. "Gonna be another little one," he said, bellowing. "Fifty years of age and she's not through yet!"

Beth stormed back down the hall to the parlor.

Kin went to the doorway to the dining room. Lotti was sitting at the table alone, just sitting there stirring her milk and corn bread and looking at the tablecloth, her lips moving as if she were putting thoughts into words. He went to her and slid onto a chair next to her. She wasn't eating. She was just sitting there and maybe was listening to the voices of her sons. She wasn't crying, but her eyes were damp.

He pushed a dish out of the way and leaned his head forward on the table. She said nothing to him. She stared before her, her face set. There was nothing weak about her, and there never was any doubt but that she knew what she was about and had the will to carry it through.

"Mama, I'm going to be a preacher," he said.

She took another bite of the corn bread.

"Mama—"

From the living room, Paul was heard to say, "Well, let's hope it's the last one. My God! When are we going to come to an ending of childbirths around this house and settle for what we've got?"

Beth was heard to say, "Keep your voices down."

"Mama—" Kin said.

"It's like a disease," Lotti said, "eating out their souls. It's taken all my boys. It's made them unfeeling."

Kin grasped her hand. "Mama—"

"They got no human understanding," she said.

2

THE DOCTOR, OLD MAN LeClair, HAD NEVER DELIVERED a woman of fifty, and he was more than mildly interested in the event. When Matthew, breathing heavily from his run, brought word to the house one noontime that his mother was "paining," LeClair got his arms through his black coat at once and hurried upstairs to get his bag. He found it beside his bed, where he had gone a bit earlier in the day to give himself a shot, a little something to keep going on, he had told himself.

The streets were almost empty as he drove his car into the Square, a treeless, hilltop space hemmed in by three- and four-story brick buildings. Several people were standing near the motion-picture house, and another group stood outside the Langren Hotel, an eight-story, square white building which glistened now in the sunlight. It was large and fine, though not as fine as the George Vanderbilt or the Battery Park, and certainly not as fine as the lordly Grove Park Inn, which was located three miles from the center of the city.

"Progress, we've got progress here now, Matthew," LeClair said, as he stopped the car at a red light.

"Yes, sir," Matthew agreed emphatically. "Greatest little city in the country."

"It's going to be a big place before long, all these rich people coming in here. How much money your father worth now?"

Matthew shook his head. "Worth a fortune, I guess."

"You guess?" He turned left at Market Street. "Hell, you know he is." He slowed down at King, turned right, and before him was the long street, with shops and houses, and, below that, the market and the store, all of it jammed now with cars and wagons, and with the mountain people. LeClair slowed his car to a crawl, so as not to hit anybody. "King Street," he murmured.

Matthew grinned at him, a glint in his eye, one of pride mostly.

"My lord," LeClair murmured, driving carefully. Muddy-wheeled trucks coughed and backed into place at the curb. The air was vibrant with talk and laughter. A street preacher was pouring out the news that Jesus was coming again. "Hear me, hear me, hear me, Jesus, Jesus is coming down from the peaks, atrailing cloud wisps. . . ."

LeClair stopped at the end of the first block and let a family get across in front of him. To his left was the market area, an open space, marked off in stalls, where mountain people sold and traded their own merchandise. Two scraggy farmers, arguing over a stall, began to fight, kicking at one another, scratching and gouging and biting. One was knocked against a horse, so frightening the animal that she broke a trace.

Across the street from them was the store, a huge, low, wood building. Women stood in front of it, pulling shawls around themselves to fend off the fall coolness. The air was lively with the sound of the bargaining and the bawling voices of the Negroes, employees of the store, who were helping to unload crates of vegetables and baskets of apples, intended for hotels and restaurants uptown, where the rich tourists were. Inside one of the great, open doors, a woman sat in a wicker-bottomed chair and nursed her baby at her breast. At another door a Negro moved crocks of sauerkraut out of the sun. Townspeople were walking about, buying chickens ready-dressed, suckling pigs, new hides, or whatever else they wanted, for the store had everything. The store had progress, LeClair knew, not the clean progress of the rest of town, but the rough and tumble progress of the mountain world itself.

"Life," he said, nodding to Matthew. "That's what King Street is."

Matthew hunched his shoulders and belched. "You can buy it, I'll bet," he said, casting a sharp glance at LeClair, "for a million dollars."

LeClair parked the car near an oak tree at the corner of the Kings' porch and let himself in at the front door. He greeted Beth cheerily, ignoring her fretful expression. "Which place is she using for this one?" he asked.

The middle bedroom, the one off the parlor, downstairs," she said.

He struggled out of his heavy coat, Matthew helping him. "Does it have a big bed?"

"It's the one Mama and Papa King always sleep in."

"Is it a strong bed?" He flung the coat upon the halltree, and a puff of dust came up from it.

"Yes, sir."

"The Irvin Wilson woman was bearing three days ago, and the slats give way. It takes good slats and plenty of room to bear a baby, even for a woman of your aunt's experience." He wiped his nose with a handkerchief and moved into the parlor, where a bright coal fire was burning in the grate. "Just think of her age," he said respectfully.

"Yes, sir," Beth said.

He backed up to the fire and clasped his hands behind his back to warm them. "Many a woman that old would give anything to have a chance at another one."

"That so?" Matthew said, grinning.

Cal and Paul filed into the room, pulled rockers up to the fireplace and sat down. Kin followed them to the door.

"Now, you men will want to keep out of the way," LeClair said. "But you can come with me, Beth, if you want to. Maybe you can help a little." He rocked back and forth on his toes for a while longer, and when his hands were warm, he led the way into the bedroom just off the parlor, the first in a series of three bedrooms which had been built onto the house, and closed the door.

"I hope she comes through," Caleb said. He took out a package of tobacco and bit off a piece. "What if Lotti dies?"

Matthew considered that speculatively, but Kin looked up, at once alerted. Lotti, his mother, die? He had seen chickens die. He had seen dead animals on the road. He had watched his father bury a dead cat and put a rock on top of the grave. He knew a little something about death, but he had not known his mother could die.

"You take care of the boy, Matthew," Cal said.

"Let him take care of himself."

"You do it," Cal said.

Matthew scratched at his cheek and looked at Kin. "Hell," he said. He got up from his rocker. "Come on," he said.

He took Kin out into the hallway and around the staircase to the flower-print curtain. "You can go out into the yard, if you want to."

Kin didn't move.

"Come on in here with me then, damn you." He opened the curtain and moved inside. He grabbed the boy's arm and pulled him in, too. Then he closed the curtain carefully. "You make a sound and I'll brain you."

Through a crack in the wall Kin saw his mother lying on the bed, a sheet over most of her body, her face and shoulders wet with perspiration. The doctor was beside her, holding her hand and talking to her about something, and Beth was standing to one side, in front of the clothes rack. The doctor whispered to Beth and she went into the next bedroom, from which she could go on through to the back porch if she wanted to, and so reach the kitchen that way.

A spasm of pain came over Lotti. She looked to Kin as if something were torturing her, and he almost cried out.

"Stop squirming," Matthew said to him.

He heard somebody in the kitchen and he guessed it was Beth, and for a moment he wanted to run to Beth and cling to her, but he didn't want to move, either. He was deep-scared. He wanted to huddle where he was, because at least he was safe there, and stay there until the calamity was over and his mother was dead, or, if she were not dead, then the danger was gone.

His mother said, "Nothing is to happen to this birth."

"Lie quiet, Mama Lotti," Beth said.

Beth was back in the room, and Kin felt better. Beth was strong and kind and would do all that could be done, he knew.

"Nothing is to happen, you hear me, Beth?" Lotti said.

The doctor rolled up his sleeves. He selected an apron from beside a basin of water Beth had brought in and tied it around his waist. He was chewing tobacco.

"I can get you a thick apron out of the chest," Beth said. "Mama Lotti has good aprons." She dug around inside a chest and came out with two new, heavy aprons, both pink, one of which she gave the doctor.

"Nothing's to happen to this child," Lotti said. "Doctor, do you promise?"

"I don't lose many," he said.

"If one of us is to go, I know it's my time. But my boy's work is to do. You hear me?"

LeClair opened his bag. "Just lie quiet, Lotti," he said.

"You do as I tell you."

"You shut up, Lotti. If you want to be the doctor and have me be the patient, we can talk about changing places." He winked at Beth, then moved to the window, opened it, and spat into the yard.

When he came back to the bed, Lotti was in the grip of another spasm. He laid his hand on her chest and felt of her heart, then he laid the back of his hand against her forehead. "You don't want no dope, Lotti?"

"No."

"Here, Beth," he said, "you get a rag and keep the sweat wiped off of her. She's drenching the bed."

Beth approached the bed slowly.

"Here, get on up to the job at hand," he said. "Stop holding back. Better to see this one pop into the world than be surprised to find your own coming out between your legs." He cleared his throat with a retch and put his handkerchief to his mouth. "Ever one of us comes from the same narrow opening, each in his time." He scratched at his back with his long, lean fingers. There were round sweat patches circling his armpits. "Course, a hot room ain't the best place for it."

He peered down at Lotti, then he felt her forehead, then her cheek and chin, and the flesh under her chin. He felt her pulse, too, and held his finger on her neck. "You bring me my bag, Beth."

Lotti spoke out shrilly. "I don't want help from that needle."

He filled the hypodermic.

"Now, I'll not have it," she said, rising to one elbow. Sweat stood out on her face and shoulders. "I've borne eight, and not even the first did I have a needle, and I'll not have one now." She pushed her head into the pillows as a pain began to build inside her.

LeClair took hold of her arm and turned the blue vein up to view, but she pulled her arm free sharply and slapped at him. He stepped back and watched her critically, grimly. He laid the hypodermic needle on the trunktop.

"You just get this baby born," she said. "I don't mind bearing pain for this baby. I don't mind if pain soaks me up for this baby. He's the one I'm counting on, and I don't want no drugs to be between me and him, you hear?"

LeClair hunched his shoulders. "You're a woman of your own mind, that's evident." He lifted the edge of the wet sheet and peered at her twitching flesh, then turned the sheet down and tossed it toward the wall at the back of the room.

Kin saw the huge protrusion on his mother, a bulbous growth on her belly or inside her belly. He stared incredulously at the watery surface of her flesh.

20

"Jesus," Matthew whispered. Matthew was strained and awkward of face, too, as if the monstrous awesomeness of the occurrence had penetrated through to him. He no longer could watch the birth with clinical, cynical interest.

The protrusion on her body moved, as if it were alive. "Jesus Christ," he whispered, and flattened his hand against the wall, pressed his face close to it. He was breathing deeply, and there was a huskiness, a denseness to his breath.

The doctor folded a clean sheet and put it under Lotti's legs. "Now you go on about your business, Lotti," he said. Kin felt sick on his stomach. Something shuddering and awful was about to happen, something which had frightened his father and for the first time shattered the tough cynicism of Matthew. It was going to happen. He had caused it, he knew, but he didn't know how, or what it was.

Beth backed off from the bed, the wet cloth still in her hand.

"You always bear healthy ones, Lotti, as I recall," LeClair said, "except them two in a row that died."

Lotti clutched the metal rung of the bed.

"Well, it's beginning to appear," LeClair said.

Pain swept through her and her mouth opened to scream, but she didn't make a sound. Pain swept high and her muscles tightened hard as wood.

"He's got his head in sight," LeClair said.

Kin stared horrified at a mass of watery, curly hair, appearing, then disappearing into the body of his mother, as if possessing life of its own. It was as if a sound were heard whenever the body appeared, for the sight pulsated like a heartbeat.

"It looks all right so far," LeClair said, and touched the slippery head. "It's not as big as most of yours were, but sometimes the strong, fat ones get the croup, same as the little fellows."

Lotti's eyes were wide and anguished.

"Lotti, you want a shot?"

She shook her head fiercely.

"The pain is heavy, ain't it? Women say they can feel it coming on them, like a person approaching; they can just about see it rising, and it keeps coming until it don't never stop."

A spasm grew as he spoke, took hold of her, and the head of the baby pulsated, more of it coming out of her now.

The pain slacked off. She began to pray and weep.

LeClair moved to the head of the bed and felt her pulse again. "Well, I hope this is your last one," he said. "You're getting too far in age to be carrying on with a thing like this. After all, years weaken us. If you watch a little child run around in the yard, you can see that, all the energy he has—well, a grown person don't have it. And you're fifty."

She cried out. The sound seemed to echo the event itself and to carry the terror of the sight of the hung head of the baby and the clenched white fists of the woman. Kin shook with fear.

"Jesus," Matthew whispered. "Jesus, Jesus," as if the word had a tang of comfort for him.

"It has to be a boy," Lotti said. "I need a man for the service. I've gone through so much pain before, I've borne eight, but I've got not a one."

"Oh, honey, listen," LeClair said, "Let's try to let this one free and worry about the rest of your problems when we have a quiet time."

"I've prayed so."

Beth began to sob.

"It has to be a boy," Lotti said. "I've got no other chance."

"Boy or girl," he said kindly, "It's what God wants you to have. The baby's organs are done made. You can't change what's there, not by waiting, and your heart's none too young for this as it is. Come on now, Lotti."

"Mama Lotti, can I do anything?" Beth asked.

"Get back from here," LeClair said. "What the hell you reckon you can do? Lotti, come on now."

Lotti lunged, her muscles contracted. LeClair sprang to the foot of the bed, tried to get his fingers under the baby's chin. "That was a good one, Lotti."

"Tend to your business," she said heatedly.

22

"Don't you worry about me."

She was sweat-covered.

"Come on, Lotti," he said.

She lunged, and he bent to his work. The muscles of her body hardened. Blood flowed into her face and neck, but her belly and thighs were gray-white.

"His head is through, Lotti, that's fine. Just fine."

Kin, trembling, stared dazedly at the face of a baby.

"Jesus," Matthew whispered, his breathing more raspy still.

"Ah, God," Lotti wept. "Oh, God."

"You got a small one, Lotti." He went on working, sweat dripping from his nose and from the point of his chin. He worked the baby free, and it began to bawl.

"Look at that, will you?" he said. He held it up. "A boy."

Only when the bed was clean and neat did he give the new child to Lotti. She grabbed him, awkward in her haste, and fastened his little mouth over the tip of one of her breasts. He began to suck, his mouth smacking and making popping sounds. She closed her eyes. Her lips moved in thankful prayer.

"What's his name to be, Lotti?" the doctor asked.

"John," she said.

Beth came to the bed. "Aunt Lotti, you've got one named John. What's this one's name?"

"His name is John."

"Mama Lotti, you don't know what you're saying—"

"I know what I'm saying. I know his name." She laid her hand on his naked back and rubbed his skin. "Little John, beloved of God," she said.

When the bedroom was opened to the family, Matthew crept from his hiding place. He stood in the dark hallway, collecting his thoughts, getting hold of his emotions, until he heard Paul approaching, cursing, mumbling obscenities, then he moved quickly onto the front porch, but Paul came out there, too. Paul kicked a rocker into place and sat down, his big body hunched over, his face caught in a fit of anguish—hatred for the new baby, Matthew guessed. Matthew went down the steps at once and around the house to get away from him.

Paul watched him go. "God damn you, too," he murmured. He breathed deeply, sighed as he exhaled. He clenched his big hands together. They were flabby but tough. He ran one hand over his face, rubbed his mouth, drying the slobber off of it. He closed his eyes tightly. The family had been in order, he had known what the situation was, where each person's loyalties were, but now the new baby threw everything off balance again. It left him dangling, that was it, and brought back to him a feeling he had suffered when as a boy he had sought some hand to care for him, some face to be near his, some arms to be around him, some words of affection, had sought in vain, had sought pitifully. The unknown, that was it, the unknown brought back the feeling. The unknown was a slippery walk on which he might fall again into old fears and dreams. He feared even an unknown caller on a telephone, an unknown writer of a letter, a stranger from far away. He feared the smile of his mother when he had not expected it and could not explain the reason for it. He trembled before a softly spoken word from Beth; it always sent a shiver through him, shaking him, as if it, too, came from some far-back moment. And now this, the unknown brother. The new element in the family, which jarred the family loose from its moorings, gripped him.

He crunched his big hands together till the knuckles popped. Sweat dripped down his face, glistened on his flesh. He smelled of sweat. He smelled his sweat and cursed softly, obscenities flowing out steadily from him, as he rocked, his eyes still closed.

"Can't you say anything with a clean mouth?" Beth said from the door.

He stiffened and was quiet. He heard the screen open and she came out onto the porch. She stood beside him. "You talk filthy, Paul. That little baby's not going to hurt you."

"Leave me alone, Beth," he said grimly.

"Well, don't be so touchy, Paul."

24

"Shut up, Beth. Get on. Get on. God damn it, let me be."

She touched his shoulder, and he pulled away from her. "Beth, get on."

"You don't seem to like anybody, Paul. I worry about you."

Tenderly she spoke, caring about him, she spoke that way, and it went through him like a hot blade touching him. He got up and stomped away, heavy on the steps, his strong body leaving, as if propelled away from her. "Go to hell," he said, "will you, God damn it." He moved up the lane toward the great store.

She turned, swung around angrily, went into the hall, and closed the door. She leaned back against it, breathing heavily. So abrupt he was, so callous, yet not callous, either. She couldn't understand him, but she knew he was dangerous to himself and to all he loved, that his big hands were cruel wanting to be gentle, for they could not stand to be gentle.

Cal came into the hall. "What you out here in the dark for?" he said.

"It's Paul. He's upset again. More than I've seen him before."

"Is he?" Cal said. He paused, as if studying about that. He cared, all right. Beth knew, but he rarely interfered in another man's world. "Has he gone to the store?" he asked.

"He always goes to the store when he leaves here, doesn't he?"

"I don't know about that," Cal said simply. He sighed, a heavy, weary sound.

"The baby make you nervous, too, Papa King?"

He scratched at his face. She could see him easily now, even in the dim hall, his brown, tough skin, his eyes light blue and keen, his lips working slowly as he moistened a piece of tobacco in his mouth. "It's her baby. I told her she could raise him."

"You're not going to let her take Kin's name, are you?"

"I told her just now to do what she wanted. She's near crazy about him. She won't hear reason."

"But it's Kin's name!"

"Yes. But in my opinion, Kin's a better name than John, anyway." He walked on down the hall.

"Papa King," she called out after him.

He didn't stop or answer her.

"Well," she said softly, a sigh, little more than that, one of defeat more than anything.

"Beth," somebody said softly. Then she heard a whimper.

She moved slowly to the curtain that closed off the space bneath the stairs and opened it, and she saw him as he looked up at her. "Kin, honey, come out of there." She took his arm and pulled him to her. "Kin, you didn't watch it?"

The whimper was all the answer he made. She knelt down beside him. He was trembling and he had a fever. "You saw it?"

He nodded, trying to hold back the tears.

"Well, who took you in there—that Matthew?"

He nodded.

"Make a little boy watch a birth," she said angrily. She ran her hand comfortingly over his forehead and face. "But don't tell on him, Kin honey, for it would make your mother sick to know it. We'll find a way to get even with him."

Kin closed his eyes. Whatever she said was all right with him. He loved Beth. He loved Beth, as he had loved his mother. He loved Beth and his mother, but his mother had become a long way off to him. He was lonely for the hands and arms of his mother, except when he was with Beth.

"Honey, you're trembling so," she said.

He held to her.

"Now, don't you worry about all this. I'll stay with you till you stop thinking about it. Let her have her new baby, and let the others have the store and the street. Let them tear one another apart. I'll watch out for you."

Tears ran down his cheeks. She kissed his cheeks. "Little boy, honey," she whispered. "You're my little boy."

"Beth," he said.

"Yes, honey, yes," she said, rocking him back and forth in her arms. She kissed his cheeks. "Ah, Kin," she said, holding him to her breast. "We neither of us has anybody except the other."

26

He closed his eyes tightly. "I didn't mean to hurt Mama."

She rocked him back and forth. "Hush. You didn't hurt her. You're not to blame. Hush."

He tried to speak, but words choked in his throat. And it didn't matter so much to understand anyway, now that Beth was holding him. He felt her cold hand on his forehead again, and suddenly he grabbed her hand and squeezed it and kissed her hand, and the tears rolled freely down his face.

3

THE NEW BABY GREW LIKE A WEED PLANTED IN STRONG earth; his button mouth was always framed for the nipple. Lotti watched over him day and night, and slept in the middle bedroom, so that she could be beside him. She was jealous of everybody who came into his presence and didn't want members of the family to pick him up, talk to him, touch him, or come into his room if she could keep them out of it. Even Cal was told to leave him alone.

She bathed him daily and oiled his flesh with pure olive oil, so that when he lay in the crib naked, or with just a diaper on, he had a glow. Month after month, into the second year, she oiled his flesh.

Kin feared the baby and hated him. He listened eagerly to words of criticism of him.

"He's too quiet," Beth said. "He never cries."

"Mama said God had him born for a purpose," Matthew said playfully, frowning at Beth, waiting for her reply.

"Maybe God did have something to do with him," Beth said doubtfully, "but his little eyes peering out—well I'm not so sure."

"He's getting damn fat for a saint," Paul said.

28

When he was two, the baby caught his first cold, and LeClair was at the house so often Matthew claimed he was a boarder. "He's just got the sniffles, Lotti," LeClair said.

"You never can be sure what they've got till they're well," Lotti said.

"I'm trained to know what they got. He's not sick bad."

"Didn't I lose four, and two of them about his age, and they had a nose condition."

"Lotti, your two died o' pneumonia, didn't they?"

"Nobody knows what a baby dies from if they can't talk."

LeClair frowned at her and thought about that. "Well, I declare," he said, shaking his head, lost to the wonders of her argument and to the fact that she believed it. "Now, this baby here has the sniffles, Lotti," he said firmly, "and not much of that, and it might come from the overdose of grease you've been using on him. He looks like a sultan now, all brown and shiny. And look at the rings on that boy's belly. You ought to cut down."

He rubbed his fingers against the stomach of the child. "Goochy goo," he said, poking his forefinger down into the flesh. "That boy could go till spring without a bite," he said. He straightened stiffly, clasped his hands behind his back. "He looks to me to be a picture of a healthy child with a runny nose, Lotti."

Kin listened whenever the doctor came. He was alive to all the news about the boy, the "angel boy" as Paul called him. He told nobody about what the doctor said; he didn't dote on stories about the baby because he liked to tell them to others. He kept everything to himself and brooded over it.

He would watch the boy as he would go to his mother, even at three years of age, and fumble at her dress buttons. She would open her dress and he would suck, loudly smacking his lips and tongue, and his mother would close her eyes and a sense of peace would come over her. She would sit there like that, almost as if in a trance, until the child's stomach was filled.

Kin would watch her, pitifully revolted, not by the boy or his mother, but by the relationship they shared of spirit and body. One

29

afternoon while she nursed the boy, he touched her arm, and she started so suddenly and looked at him so strangely that at once he stumbled away, frightened and hurt, pained so severely that he would not even tell Beth. He closed the door of his upstairs room and lay on the bed in misery.

When he came downstairs he heard his mother talking in the kitchen. He went into the parlor, then into the room where the boy was playing. He knelt beside him. The child peered back at him; in his lap was a color book of Bible characters, a crayon was in his hand.

"What you doing?" Kin said.

The boy stared at him as if Kin had no right to be there, as if his brother were a stranger, belonging to the world of the dining room, the kitchen, the hallway, the porch.

"You want me to show you how to color the pictures?"

The boy stared at him.

"You little devil," Kin said, hurt by the rejection.

The boy stared at him, even when Kin held out his hand for the crayon.

"Are you going to stay in here all your life? Won't she let you go outdoors?"

There was no answer.

"You can talk. You talk to her. You can talk as well as I can. Say something."

The child stared at him.

Kin slapped him in the face, then froze in sharp pain because of it. "You little devil," he whispered, backing off from him. The child watched, saying nothing, his lips pouted, as if he might cry, but he didn't cry.

"You devil," Kin said, stopping at the door, staring back at him.

He stayed out of the house whenever he could. In school he buried himself in learning. On the street, the bawling, brawling street, where his father was king, he soaked up all the wonders of the store and of the mountain people.

30

He learned to trade before he was twelve. He learned the value of a dozen eggs or twelve hundred, of fryers and broilers and hens, of salt-cured and sugar-cured hams, of celery stalks and cucumbers, either by the pound or by the bushel, of asparagus, of quarts of sourwood honey in yellow and white combs, of canned blackberries put up and sweetened by a countrywoman's hand, of canned pears and peaches and apples, of corn whiskey and apple brandy, of beans, fruit, Burley tobacco, cabbage heads, pelts, turnips and turnip greens, lettuce in head and leaf, tow sacks, paper pokes, and the quart-size bottle of stomach remedy. He learned to test a mule and estimate its strength and disposition.

He met the farmers and learned ways to remember their names and to find out their nicknames as soon as he could. And they came to know him. "Young King," they called him. And the girls would flash smiles at him, and he would smile back, as if he knew what life was all about. He knew nothing, actually, except where babies came from. He knew that common fact. But he didn't know how they got there.

He listened to Paul trade, swiftly judging a salesman or buyer, judging to the cent and minute how far he could go, how much he could get. He watched Matthew gleefully talk, distract the attention of even the most skillful trader as he closed in to make a deal. He watched his father humorlessly, honestly consider every business transaction. He lived in a world of worn overalls and gingham dresses and the blond hair of the mountain people, who were Protestant and, on the whole, Republican and fiercely proud.

Sometimes he would go up to the second block of King Street, which his father did not control, where the taverns and cheap restaurants were (chicken and dumplings, with coffee and hot bread for fifteen cents), and where three two-story houses, in which only women lived, stood side by side. The women could be seen of a Monday morning flopping mattresses over the sills of the east windows in order to dry out the sweat and dampness. "Hello, young King," some of them would call to him, twisting their bodies provocatively, shifting their hips, jangling copper and silver jewelry.

"He's going to be bigger than Paul or Matt," they would say. "Look at his innocent face."

He would not turn away from them, or blush or feel ashamed of his ignorance. Nor was he ashamed of the rising interest inside his body. He knew there were secrets unknown to him, but that they were natural secrets. He would know them in time. He knew someday he would have a woman of his own, as his father had, or many women, as had Matthew and Paul.

"You come to me first, boy," Helen, a bright-eyed woman of thirty, who ran the second house up the hill, told him. She winked and told him that. "You will, won't you?"

He nooded simply, and Helen laughed, a good laugh, and Kin watched her with the steady, bargaining eyes of the Kings.

Sometimes he would go into one of the cafés to watch the men eat their meals. They would eat, then sit around the tables and listen to music. A woman named Mrs. Jasper ran one of the restaurants, and every night about seven she would go to the upright piano and limber up her fingers with scale exercises, then she would play hymns. She could play almost any hymn anybody asked for, and she knew a few popular songs, too, such as "Redwing" and "Indian Love Call," and "Little Gray Home in the West." The men would lean on the tables and pick their teeth and listen. This was in early evening, before they went back down to the farmers' field or went to one of the three beer taverns, which operated steadily in spite of prohibition, or to one of the houses, or to get their wagons and start a nighttime trip home.

Often of a day Kin would go into one of the gunsmith shops and look at the black weapons, shotguns and pistols mostly, but rifles, too, and at the shiny cartridges and red-cased shells. Malcolm Finletter ran one of the shops, and he liked to have Kin come around. "Going to be borrowing money from you when I get old," he would say, though he was old then; he was probably seventy. He would stoop his shoulders and study a thin metal scythe. He had ruined his sight in the work in that dark place, but he carried on. "This scythe is what the devil carries when he comes to get you," he would

32

say, and his red eyes would gleam and his lips would part to show his teeth. "Cut you off at your knees and carry you off to the grave," he would say.

But he didn't frighten Kin, who knew full well that he would never die. Only old people died, and Kin knew he would never be old. He had been trying to get grown for years and couldn't even get there. Before him lay a vast number of years which he could not hope to live out.

Sometimes Malcolm would put aside his work and get out his guitar. "Oh, Caleb King was a mountain man, sing lo, sing lo," he would sing in his gravelly voice, "and he had five sons, sing lo." He was always making up songs, and he would put "sing lo" at the end of the lines, so that he wouldn't have to worry about rhyming the words.

There was an herb shop on the second block, too, run by a man named Porter, a huge fellow with a great belly. Some said he had the biggest belly in western North Carolina, and there was much speculating among the farmers about how Porter could possibly manage to have intercourse with his wife. "You know what this is, young King?" Porter asked Kin one afternoon, holding up a piece of a root. "That's ginseng root. The Chinese think it gives you back your powers. Now, this piece is shaped like a man's arm, you see, so if you have arm trouble and you're a Chinaman, you drink tea made out of this piece." He held up a hand-sized piece shaped like the lower half of a man's body. "What you suppose they'll use that for?"

"Leg trouble," Kin suggested.

"Yes," Porter said. "What else?"

Kin studied the root. "Stomach trouble."

"Might help," Porter said. "What else?" The grin on his face got wider as he watched the boy.

"I dunno."

Porter laughed out. "Yes, you do. Hell, you never did get to the big reason that piece of ginseng will bring five dollars an ounce in China. The pecker, boy. The pecker!" And the laugh came out of him again.

Sometimes Porter would talk to Kin about his daughters. "I want you to take your pick, young King." And once in a while one of them, a pretty, well-formed, brown-haired girl named Cynthia, who was a year older than Kin, would be in the shop helping out. Porter had seven daughters (he had no sons at all), and Cynthia, the youngest, was like her sisters in that she liked men. It was as if Porter had served all his girls a cup of ginseng tea daily from birth on. Cynthia often would try to get Kin to help her as she sorted through the clean, dry, blue cohosh roots, or the boneset herb ("Don't put in those large stems, Kin"), the peppermint leaves and life roots, the jasmine and the spearmint leaves, the sumac-root bark and the white-oak bark, which had been rossed and dried. She would brush up against him as they worked and joke with him so freely that he would sometimes become embarrassed.

"Down here life is raw," Kin's father would tell him. "Hope it don't choke you, boy."

Kin would shake his head, trying to hide the doubts he did feel. There was something cheap about King Street, all right, but it was natural, like a birth, and was life-bearing.

"These are my people," Cal King would say, looking about him. Over to one side of the doorway two old people were sitting on casks and peering through age-blue eyes at the passers-by; nearby Matthew was talking in a low voice to a girl who had come into town without any money. Cal's weathered face seemed never to quiver with interest at anything he saw. Often he and Kin would cross the street to the big public farmers' yard and move among the wagons and trucks and crudely built display stalls, pushing their way among the farmers and customers. Everywhere they went, the farmers made way for them and welcomed them. "Mr. King," they said, as if announcing Cal's arrival. "Morning. Mornin', young King." Cal and Kin would answer with a nod or a wink. As they moved on, a woman might say, "There go the Kings, children. Remember them."

"These are my people, Kin," Cal would say over and over, as if it were a refrain Kin must learn, and he would spend hours talking to them, men and women and their young from the troughs of the valleys and from the lower mountainsides, with slender limbs and frank gazes and faces washed in cold spring water.

"Every smart one and every damn fool," he would say. "Every decent one and every no-count one. Don't you think you're better than the best of them, either. I come from the same place, back in the hills. I grew up just twenty steps from an outhouse on the edge of our cabbage patch, just like them. And you're of me, boy. You're one of them."

"Yes," Kin would say, welcoming the words.

"I know what it is to break mountain rocks and clay, to dig a living out of the ground, with the rains washing away the earth and the bugs coming and the blights and storms, and the women getting wrinkled on the skin by the time they're forty, and the men getting feeble in their backs from daytime labor and straining and cutting wood and dragging logs and burning stumps and working the animals, trying to make do, and the children coming on so fast that a man can't feed their open mouths, can't do nothing, damn it, but count 'em and try to remember their names, and yet he loves every one with a passion till they get old enough to show their natural dispositions and kick up their heels to him. Yes, hell, I know. And maybe now I live easy, Kin," he would say, placing his hand on Kin's shoulder, "but we're still from them; out of their bodies we come." He would turn his eyes toward the top of King Street, where the fine businesses and shopping stores were. "And not from them," he would say, and his jaw would set. "Not, damn them, from them."

Kin learned from him. Let the city people think as they pleased and go their way; let them look down on King Street if they wanted to, and many of them did. He didn't care. He was one of the mountain people and proud of it. From Mitchell and Starnes coves. From Smith Ridge and Yancey County. From Bent Creek and Collins Road, which was no more than a footpath kept cleared by five generations of Collins men so that they could get to market. He would look off at the tree-coated tops of the mountains and breathe the cool air they sent down. He was of the blue peaks and ridges, which gathered clouds and bathed in rain and grew green plants the year round. He was of their hard ground. And nobody could rightly look down on a mountain man.

"My brother's living back in there still," Caleb told him one day. They were sitting at one of the doors of the store, watching the store attendants haul and sort. "Beth's father's back there. He wants Beth to come home."

"No," Kin said, the word bursting out of him.

Cal was surprised by the boy. "Don't fret," he said, "I'm not going to send her back." He spat on the ground and crossed his legs contentedly. "Beth has been in the city too long to take to country life again." He rubbed his coarse hands together. "But Clarence is ailing. He worked on his chicken coop and got a nail in his foot, and that festered. I sent him some purifier, but it didn't cure him. And now he's got a strain in his back." He bit off a new twist of tobacco. "Well, what do you think of our steet today, Kin?"

Our street, Kin thought. He loved it, as he loved his father.

"It's got a strong smell sometimes, don't it?" Cal chewed and spat and chewed. "But most of the stock trading is shifting to the railroad yards, and I expect it all will someday."

A little girl, her pigtails flying, came running up, bringing a basket of big blackberries which she nervously handed to him. Cal thanked her with his country kindness and courtesy. She was flustered with blushing and good feeling as she ran back to her mother, who was watching. "That's a pretty little girl, ma'am," Cal said to the mother.

Whenever he could, after school and on Saturdays, as a rule, Kin followed his father around the lot. Once he watched him trade two mules for a wagonload of Burley tobacco in half a minute. Another time, Cal spent an hour wrangling over the trade of five quarts of canned apples for five yards of muslin. But if anybody ever got the better of him, Kin didn't know it—unless his father wanted to do a man a favor, as he sometimes did, most often a man in trouble. He would grow thoughtful then, as if he were in church and were contemplating doing something for the Lord.

Kin and Matthew understood this quality in their father, but

36

Paul did not. He became upset if Cal made a poor trade and carried on as if the foundations of the business were being weakened. But Cal didn't pay any attention to what he wanted to ignore. He helped those he wanted to. If a man's wife had recently died, that man could count on a good trade for shoes for his children, or something of the sort. It was Cal's way of giving sympathy and redressing wrongs. Kin understood that.

"Young King," they called him on the street, his father's street. The city now kept it in repair and ran the farmers' field, regulating the use of the stalls, but it was Caleb King's, for he had put it in with his hands, he had given the mountain people this place off to themselves, where they were welcome.

Now it was Kin's place, too. His father's and his.

And of an evening, toward sundown, he would watch with regret, with a sense of the shuttering of his hopes, as the great wooden doors were moved, a hollow rumble going out over the street as each one closed. Finletter would close his gun shop, Porter would close his herb shop, all the shops would empty. Farmers in the market place would say, "Well, that's it for now," and get ready to go home or to the houses or the restaurants, often laughing, talking loud. "Going to get me a mess of beans tonight; I'm hungry as a bear." Get their horses hitched to wagons, get their Fords cranked up. Go home. Men and women and their children, talking loud.

"Come on, Kin. I'll see you at the house," his father would say and go down the street. Paul would walk past him as if he didn't see him. Paul never seemed to see him. Matthew came by. "What you waiting on, boy?" he would say. Almost every night he would say the same words: "Ain't you coming home?"

He kept a journal in which he put down his thoughts. He wrote about school and the store. And sometimes about Beth, about how she would help him around the family, would notice him when nobody else seemed to, for even his father didn't pay him or anybody much mind at home. At home Cal seemed always to be observing, and resting.

37

He would write about Beth, but not about his loneliness, for he didn't know quite what loneliness was; he didn't know how to say loneliness, for the word didn't say it, and so far as he knew everybody at home had the same feeling, a trouble, as if he had been forgotten, dropped and not cared for, and maybe not wanted. Only Beth was different.

He read a good deal, too. He poured over history, read novels and the like, rarely reading all of a book, taking parts of it and catching hold of them, setting the book aside, returning to it, until a stack of books reminded him that he must return them to the library. Almost every night after supper he went to his room to read, but he would keep his mind on Paul, too, and on Beth. Sometimes he would hear Paul in his room pacing, the floor creaking under him, or he would hear him move across to Beth's door and stop there, never knocking, never speaking, then go back to his room or go heavily down the stairs to the porch or to the dining room, where he might find her. Kin would go downstairs then and stay close to her, too. "You go on," Paul would tell him. "Get the hell gone."

But he would stay close by.

One night he was reading, and it seemed that Paul was more anxious than ever. Kin followed him downstairs, but Beth wasn't in the dining room, or anywhere around. Paul moved to the porch and peered off up the street, as if lost in thought. Kin went up to Beth's room and looked in there.

When he got back downstairs, Paul was standing in the front yard, still looking up toward town, his shoulders hunched, a scowl on his big face. He peered back at Kin, then, without saying a word to him, started up the lane toward the foot of King Street.

"Where is she?" Kin called, but not loud enough to be heard, he guessed. He never asked Paul anything; he wasn't used to calling to him.

He sat down on the porch. Cal and Lotti were in bed. Matthew was up the street somewhere. The porch was dark as the night, and he sat in the dark, a frenzy rising in his thoughts. Where is she? Where is she?

He got up and went into the parlor and, without turning on the light, looked at his father's clock. It was almost ten. He went back to the porch. Soon he went up to her room to look in there again. He stopped by at his room, sat on the bed, and tried to read. He went to the back window and looked through the branches of the sycamore toward the sheds and garden spot, seeking in what was known and unchanging an assurance that Beth was not gone.

He took out his journal and wrote in it, across one page, If she is gone, I will be lonely. He underlined the word. Lonely, lonely, he wrote at the bottom of the page, for he knew what it meant if she were gone.

Almost an hour went by. He heard nothing. Paul was still looking for her, he guessed. He went back downstairs and stood at the screen door to the porch.

Almost at once he sensed that she was on the porch. He saw her then, sitting with somebody, a strange man, older than she, perhaps thirty or thirty-five. They were sitting in the swing. The man put his arm around her shoulders and drew her to him.

"Beth," Kin said, the word bursting out of him.

She stood. "Kin, is that you?" she said, her voice husky as if it had too much breath in it.

He stepped out onto the porch.

"Kin?"

"Yes," he said, staring at her, not able to stop staring at her.

"You go on back to bed," she said.

"No," he said, a sigh, a moan. He would not leave her; not even with a weapon could she drive him away now.

"I'm sorry, Morris," she said softly.

The man stood. "I understand," he said. "Good night."

"Good night," she said.

He left, and there was quiet for a long moment; then Beth came to Kin, moving faster as she walked, grabbed him and shook him hard. "Don't ever do that again!" she said.

He freed himself, not mindful that she shook him, and went to

39

the steps. He looked off into the darkness, toward where the man was walking. "Are you going to leave me?" he said.

"Now—listen to you."

"I don't dare."

"Kin, I don't want to leave you. You know I don't."

"Do you know him?"

"Of course I know him. What sort of question is that? Just because you don't know him doesn't mean I don't. I met him one Sunday when I was going to church. He was opening wood crates in his new tailor shop, and I heard somebody talking away in a foreign tongue. I stopped at the open door, and when he saw me, he became nervous, because, I suppose, he had been cursing and he didn't know I didn't speak German. So we met that way. Each Sunday morning I go by and we talk. Tonight he took me to the motion pictures."

"What's his name?"

"What do you care about his name? Now, I don't want you to take this as a personal matter, or for Paul—"

"I don't care what his name is," Kin said.

She went to him, looked down at him. She touched him, put her hand on his shoulder. He pulled away from her.

"His name is Morris Kraft," she said.

"I told you I didn't care."

He went to his room and closed the door. He sat on the edge of the bed and tried not to cry. He lay down and covered his face in his pillow, then got up, went to the window, and looked down at the moonlighted sheds and the garden, but all he could think of was Morris Kraft, Morris Kraft, and being in the house if she left, lonely.

4

THE DEPRESSION OF OCTOBER, 1929, STRUCK WITH THE
suddenness of an autumn storm and brought a gift of misery. It roared
in out of the North, and Asheville, which now had a population of
over forty thousand, rocked and shivered from it. The city's boom
ended in a moment. Rich and poor, startled and stunned, found fear
in their beds. Hunger touched the bellies of the young. Bread lines
formed. It was the beginning of a long misery.

Nearby in the mountains, the farm people tightened their belts
and told each other they would have to "make do." That was the
motto of years past. "Make do or do without." Don't buy anything.
Use what you have. Make it last. When it breaks, mend it. Strap
it up and make do. Make do in Stevens Cove. Make do in every
barn and house and field in Yancey County. Make do along the
banks of the French Broad River, up the valleys to the coves, and
up the coves to the headwaters of the branches.

Caleb King watched the depression with the disgust of a farmer
who sees the results of city planning. This, as he analyzed it, was
the return on the lazy notion that a man can work only with paper
and be productive. He had never believed it.

His own wealth had been invested in land and a few town houses. He had had only seven thousand dollars in the banks when they closed. That money was lost, and, of course, the value of the land and houses had decreased, but the land was still there and its value would come back in time. He had been through depressions before, and they had always lasted for a year or a year and a half, then the climb upward had started. But for that period, conditions would be torturous.

Those farmers who came to trade or borrow pleaded for good terms. Cal did what he could for them. Not so with Paul. His eyes were blind to suffering. "Take my price or carry your goods back home," he would tell them. He meant it, too.

Matthew was easier, except when Paul was around. The truth was, Matthew knew the future of the family, and his future at the store, was more likely to depend on Paul than on his father, who was willing to let things take their natural course. To keep his place on King Street and the assurance of someday owning a part of the store, he was willing to trade tough or even unfairly, if that was what Paul wanted. Matthew, now twenty years old, had little confidence in himself, that was part of the trouble. Paul had never let him feel that he had done anything well; Paul's shadow had shaded him.

Only Kin rejected Paul's orders. He was really too young to trade for big lots of merchandise, but he traded with the lesser farmers. When Paul objected, he kept right on doing it, and Cal finally told Paul to mind his own business.

"This is my business," Paul shouted.

Cal waved him aside. "Not while I live," he said. "I built this place for all my boys."

But it was Paul who kept the books. He had a little office in the back, and only he ever went in there. In fact, Paul kept all his father's accounts and records—those Cal didn't keep in his head. And whenever Caleb traded liberally, Paul would moan in distress about what the books showed. "Papa, you're killing the store and your holdings." When these announcements brought no result, he would recite his personal hurt and losses. "I've worked my bones sore in this store. My God in heaven, to see it go! While him"—he pointed at Kin—"he's not done a thing till here lately, and all of it has been to hurt us."

Kin watched him warily, but traded generously, as before.

"They come creepin' in here from the valleys, begging leniency," Paul delared. "Well, what produce company is giving us lenience? They won't even pay their bills, those that ain't already declared they're bankrupt. Where we going to sell all these God-damn hams you're buying? I never seen so many hams. We're ass-deep in hams in this store, and that boy"—he pointed at Kin—"come dragging in another half a dozen today that he must have sought for."

"Never mind," Cal would say. "The depression is just here for a few months. And we have plenty."

Paul would shake his head. It was not in his power to accept as true anything which was not known, and the length of the depression had not been determined.

Cal had to acknowledge that the store was overstocked. He gave much of the food away, mostly in colored town, which was hardest hit by the job layoffs, but part of it he sent by truck to Greensboro and Winston-Salem, trying to sell it. His truck kept going down the mountains, loaded with food, and chugging back up the Old Fort road, its engine steaming. "We did what we could, Mr. King," the drivers, two store assistants Cal trusted, would tell him. But they never seemed to do very well.

Cal sent his truck to Raleigh and Durham, seeking markets. As the depression lengthened, he sent his truck to Fayetteville. As it grew still deeper and harder, he sent his truck all the way to Wilmington, where the drivers traded for fish. He turned a small profit on that trip, and at once started trading heavily with Wilmington, Morehead City, and other coastal places.

A wave of illness swept through the mountains. The farmers dug for roots and cut bark and made tea. The houses in the second block of King Street had to turn away women trying to get work. Many of them took to the streets. They hadn't done that before.

43

It wasn't right; it was a form of begging, but they did it. "A dollar?" they asked. "Fifty cents?"

Cal's world shook. "What did they do to cause all this? What closed all the businesses?" he demanded. He hired new men to tend the store, though he had thirty on hire already. Paul tried to keep others away from him. "You go on," he told them when he caught them hanging around. They were Negro and white, boys and men, ill-clothed, as a rule, and lean of frame. "Get gone."

They came back, sometimes alone, sometimes in packs, wanting work, wanting food. Paul would see them hanging around at the doors looking for Caleb, and he would chase them away. "I'll take a horsewhip to you," he would say.

They left, but they came back.

"God damn you," Paul said. "God damn you, you're out to wreck us."

He told the store attendants to carry sticks and keep them out.

Then one afternoon, two Negroes, little more than boys, were caught stealing a chicken, and Prime, a big Negro man, got hold of both of them and held them down on the sawdust until two other Negro attendants got hold of them, too. The men pushed them forward until they stood before Paul, who was balanced on both legs, watching, his great body relaxed but his face muscles working spasmodically, his lips pressed tightly together. "You thieves?" he said. "Say you're thieves."

"We ain't stealing," one of the boys said.

"He was stealing a chicken," Prime said.

"No, suh." Both boys shook their heads. One said, "We was going to clean it."

"Clean it alive?"

"We was going to help."

Paul caught one of the boys by the front of his shirt and shook him. "You come in here and steal. Say the truth. Say it."

The boy was choking. "I steal," he said.

Paul released him, threw him back. "Take them to the police," he said.

44

"Let them be," Kin said.

The words fell like a stone hammer falling on the ground. The thud shuddered through them all. The Negro boys flashed their attention to him, to a boy, also standing balanced on both feet, looking not at the Negro boys or at Prime, but at Paul. "Let them go, Prime," he said.

Prime and the other big Negroes released the boys and slowly stepped back, watching not the boys now or Kin, but Paul, where a scowl as dark as pitch had settled.

"You better get out of here," a farmer said to the two boys.

They didn't move. One of them looked around at the grown Negroes, seeking assurance and permission.

"Get out," Kin said to them, and as if they had been released, as if a rope had broken, they dashed from the store.

Paul lifted a hand slowly and scratched his face. His big shoulders were hunched, his palms were flat, as if ready to strike. "You and Papa," he said softly, "you cross me again. You better not, not in my store."

Kin felt a tremble come to his legs. His store, his store. He shook his head, rejecting what Paul said, but turned and went outside, where he stood near the door; then he went up the street, walking fast, not fleeing from Paul but not wanting to see him again right now, proud of himself but afraid, too.

He could not match Paul, he knew that.

Later, when he dared go back to the store, he saw his father standing near a counter where shoes were sold, over which oiled brown boots hung, and Paul was close beside him, talking in a stiff tone. "They come in here to steal; we can't protect what we have from thieves. You and him give away all we have, or let them take it. You hire the thieves and pay out all the savings. I'll stand for not another damn bit of it. This can't go on."

Cal seemed not to hear. He saw Kin, and a flickering smile touched his eyes, then he turned away. He walked to another counter, but Paul followed.

45

"That woman in here this morning, you give her money. My God in heaven, what are you going to do when you run out?"

"Paul, they look to me."

"You've not got it, damn it. You've sold most of your land now, and you've not got it."

Cal moved away from him, but he followed, persisted, arguing grimly. Cal turned to him. "You shut up," he said.

Paul flinched, but quickly recovered. "No, you're going to listen to me this time. I ain't no child. You'll listen to me and not to that boy, you hear—"

Cal's hand darted out, and, except for a reflex action, it would have struck him. It did not, but the intent was known, both the intent to strike and the will which held him back from striking, both were seen by Paul and Kin. The action came as a choice, as a decision more sharp and painful than a slap, and Paul stumbled back as if he had been hit by a powerful man. His mouth opened, his eyes bleared, and a choking sound came to his throat. "Ah, Papa," he said. "Papa."

"I—didn't mean that," Cal said.

"Papa, what did you do that for?"

"I didn't mean nothing, Paul," Cal said, and sought an explanation. "I'm not against you, boy, you know I'm not. But they press in on me, wanting food, work, stealing, wanting to get to be whores, anything. Well, they press in on me. Now, you got to understand how it is."

"You choose, Papa."

"I don't choose. Don't weaken me like that." He glanced at Kin, who was concentrating on every word. "He's just a boy, Paul."

Paul backed away from him. "Well, that's a sight," he said, his voice choked up. "That's a sight, ain't it? How many years I put in here, and now it's a choice—"

"God damn it, Paul, don't talk like that."

"Yeah," Paul said. He looked over at Kin, blinked. He wet his lips and backed off again. He suddenly, more quickly, moved past four stunned store attendants and sought the back room, his office.

46

where he closed himself in and began cursing, pacing.

For hours he was in there. Kin saw that once or twice Cal went to the door and started to go in, but he didn't go in. Once he said to Kin, "I wasn't going to hit him. He knows that." Later he said, "He's got so much emotion in him, and he's afraid of it, and most anything gets him disturbed."

The sound of the cursing, the pacing, the feel of the restless anger flowed through the walls of the back room.

"Paul don't change; he don't know about change," Cal said to Kin. "He thinks the world has a set pattern, and when it changes from it, it's sinned. He don't seem to know that it won't never go back like it was."

"Won't it stop, Papa, the depression?"

"It'll stop, but not where it started." He looked back at the door of Paul's room. They could hear Paul walking, his weight heavy on the earthen floor. They could hear him cursing on and on. Matthew and several attendants stood at the other end of the store from him, watching that door, as if the door might open and pour forth a burst of power. Paul was powerful, all right, they knew that. And smart. He was a machine, and he and the store were belted together, one moving with the other.

"What you think we ought to do, Kin?" Cal said softly. "You think I better give in to him for a while?"

"Don't give in," Kin said pleadingly.

"You don't understand, boy," he said. He reached over and touched Kin, not looking at him. "Go on outside."

"Papa."

Cal shook his head. "Go on."

Kin slowly went to the big door and stood there looking out. He knew his father was walking to the door of the back room. A moment later he heard him knock, then he heard him say, "Paul, let's talk, you and me, and see if we can work out a way."

Kin looked back. He saw the store attendants nod to each other, as if they had predicted this. He saw the door open at the back and his father go inside. The door closed. There was no pacing

47

now; the danger of the power bursting through was gone. Matthew sighed in relief and went to work waiting on a customer, who didn't understand the strange quiet of the place.

The poor were turned away now. Cal refused to see what was happening. "It has to be this way," he told Kin. "He's right about our losing out. We can't supply the countryside."

But as the second Saturday came upon him, as hundreds crowded in on the street to sell and only a few came to buy, he left the store and the street, unable to stand the strain and bitterness of distress all around him.

Kin found him an hour later, sitting in the parlor, huddled in a rocker staring at the coal fire, a sweat on his face as if the fire were hot. It was worry sweat. Kin knew.

Kin sat down on a cot near the window and watched him. His father had seen him come in, he knew, but he didn't mention anything to him. "How much more land do you own, Papa?" Kin asked.

"Fifteen thousand acres of timberland." Cal paused until the words fell quiet. "Two thousand acres of valley land." He paused again. "The store. These two houses. And mortgages in eighteen counties."

Kin waited. He let the silence settle around his father again. "You're a rich man yet, Papa."

Cal nodded slowly. "I know."

"Can you sell some of it?"

"If I can find a buyer. It takes a man who has money left."

He stood suddenly, irritably. "I can strip myself, is that what you mean?" He looked down at Kin. "You want that?"

Kin blanched before him. "Yes, sir."

"Do you?" Cal said, vaguely, wonderingly. He turned away, moved into his bedroom, just beyond the parlor, and slammed closed a chest drawer. "Well, I don't know," he said.

"Is that you, Cal?" Lotti called from the room beyond.

He opened the door to her room. "Who do you reckon it is?"

"You're home."

48

"I know I'm home. Ay, God, I can't live in the store no longer, do you know it? They come in like flies. And I got Paul on one side, moaning defeat. Ay, God," he said fiercely. Then abruptly, seeking something to attack, he said, "What you got that boy still locked up all the time for? He's not going to know what a bird is till he's grown."

"Why, you leave him alone," Lotti said, rising defiantly.

"When's he going to school? Ain't he past six?"

"You hush, you hear?"

"God knows he can't learn all there is to know at his mother's knee."

"He's not ready to go out with the others yet. Maybe if I can send him to Miss Lucy Tyson's private school—"

"And spend money on that, too—"

"Don't talk to me about money. You've got more'n anybody has a need for. I've never asked for much, but I want my youngest to have proper training."

"You get his tail washed and get him in school, then." He swung away and came back through his bedroom to the parlor. He called back. "Kin'll be in the seventh grade, and this one's not took his first look at a speller."

"Well—well, you stop yelling at me."

"On Monday, Kin," he said, turning to him, standing tall above him, "we'll go uptown and sell my land."

He stood looking down for a while longer, almost as if he had forgotten Kin. Then he left; he went out quickly, and Kin saw him a moment later moving with big steps across the lawn, back toward the street.

The idea of Johnny going to school didn't terrify Lotti, but Cal's attitude did. He had stayed away from the boy, as he had promised on the day the boy was born, and this was the first order he had given her concerning him. Out of the side window she watched him walk up the lane, and she told herself if he tried to take this one, too, she would fight him.

He had the other children. A time or two she had told Paul he ought to get out and get married, but Cal had shushed her, told her to let Paul be. She had told Matthew to stop going up the street every night, but Cal had shushed her on that, too, had said Matthew was old enough to do his own governing. She had told Beth she shouldn't go to the movies so much with that foreign man, but Cal had let her go. For every attitude she had, Cal had a different one.

She didn't even talk to him about Kin. He had taken over Kin entirely, he and Beth. Beth had even walked Kin to her friend's tailor shop and had him fitted for school clothes, as if what he had from last year wouldn't go another round. "Going to school matters so much to a boy his age," she had told Lotti.

Lotti had her own ideas about that, too. It probably meant too much to Kin. Mind was all right, and everybody should have enough to carry on his business, but some of the smartest people she had known had not loved the Lord. Oh, they were smart, they could master books, but when it came to praying through to God, or discerning words of truth in the Bible, they were ignorant. It seemed to her that the world would be better off if everybody had less education and acted a little less smart, and more people humbled themselves, for the ones who kept coming out of the schools weren't the ones who could lead in hopeful prayers.

"Better not to know too much," she had once told Kin. And his pleasure over his good marks in school had vanished in a wink. Well, that wouldn't hurt him, for he was always peering into a book as if it contained a secret; he read too much. She had never read but one book in her life, yet she found in it more knowledge about natural and unnatural things than could be put in all the other books of the world. And she had told Kin that, too. It was necessary for a mother to instruct her child.

She heard him now in the parlor, rocking in a chair. He coughed once. She opened the door and saw him. She went into the room. "Where's your father?" she said.

"Up at the store."

50

"Well, why ain't you up there? Ain't that the place you like the best? I never see you around the house."

He looked up at her, hurt. "I don't know, Mama."

"Him come in here, start talking about my boy going to school, as if school was a magic. I read him Bible books. Why don't you ever read in the Bible? There's one right in my bedroom you can borrow, or you can read the one in the sickroom, or read Johnny's."

"I don't want to read now, Mama."

"Seems to me we got plenty of Bibles around this house."

"Yes, Mama."

He went out into the hall, went on upstairs, and she felt miserable about the way she had talked to him, but Cal had criticized her about Johnny.

She went to the hall and called up toward his room. "Come out and be a part of the family life around the home. It's not right for a child to withdraw himself."

She waited, but there was no answer.

She went back into the parlor, irritated, sick with worry and bitterness. She went into Johnny's room and sat down near him. He was looking down at his Bible-story book, as if he hadn't noticed the commotion.

"When I was little," she told him, "when your grandfather was alive—" and she stopped and thought about him, tears in her eyes. "Of an evening, all of us would gather in the parlor and he would pray, and each one would offer up a little prayer beside of his'n. Then we would make confessions of our sins. Mama would come in late, for she never seemed to take to the confessing; she would come in, kitchen sweat on her face, and say a word or two before he said a-men."

Her soft words tumbled over one another without emphasis, as if she had related this many times before and wanted it called forth now again as a refrain, an assurance.

"And what has replaced all the good work and prayers? Rich men sitting on hotel porches studying their losses. My boys and husband trading all day. Matthew up the street. Paul in the store.

He ain't married, doesn't even have a marryin' girl. He stays up there close to your father, poring over ledgers. He's hiding in that store like he used to hide in the barn back home—get up in the loft, and nobody could find him, but I knew where he was. He had a little play place up there, off alone. That's where he went to get away from Collins, for Collins used to tell him what to do and where to do it. Collins was a strong-willed boy. But Collins has not done nothing for himself, neither. Where is he now? Only the Lord knows. When's he coming home?"

Her voice stopped, as if it had come of its own to a question it didn't want to leave. She sat, staring at the floor, then got up slowly, shook her head. She went into the parlor and sat down near the fire and thought about Collins. He had been to Oklahoma. Been to Oregon. Another time he had written her from Alaska. What was he doing in all those places? Only once had he come back to her since he left, telling big stories about the world out there, and people on the street had followed him around. "There are mountains out West that tower over ours," he had said. Everybody listened. Of course, when they found out the truth, it was that nobody could live on the ones out West and grow a crop, and that the water wasn't fit tasting. But he just told what he wanted to, and the rest had to be dragged out of him by questions. Still they followed him, and one night when Paul went up the street, he reported that Collins had seven women gathered around him at one of the taverns, and he was telling them stories such as nobody has a right to know about, and those sinful seven were giggling over every word.

Well, it was to Paul's credit that he had got angry. There were things that should embarrass anybody. Paul reported that Collins got to singing in that big bass voice of his and reciting yarns about the Mexican women and the way they are made different from the Texas women, and how the Eskimo women have flaps on their stomachs. "What do they need flaps for?" Paul had demanded, and Collins had said it was to keep the change in that the men gave them.

52

Lotti had to smile, thinking about the flaps on the Eskimo women, even though she knew it was wrong to think about such things. Ah, that Collins was a quick-minded man, and when would he be home again? "My dear sweet precious mama Lotti—" The words warmed her whenever she thought of them.

She cast off the questions. She got up, stood unsteadily, dizzy with thoughts. She went back into the middle bedroom and looked down at Johnny. A beautiful child. Her chief hope and joy. She sat down on the bed and leaned far over and put her arm around him awkwardly. "You're Mama's baby," she said.

He looked up at her, fondly, she thought, contentedly.

"I won't let your papa steal you away."

He looked at her so compassionately; he was a dear child, and was for God, she knew.

"You're going to be the strong one. Like young David of old, you'll go out from the Valley of Elah to face Goliath of Gath, and you'll be strong with the power of God," she said.

He looked up at her with such trust.

After dinner on Monday, Caleb talked to Paul in the parlor. Kin and Matthew sat at the table and waited. They could hear the talk, about money and land and the poor. Paul got excited, and Cal began to talk loud, too. "I'll not let them go by, not while I have a bite of food to give them," he said. He came bursting out of the room and sought out Kin. "Come along," he said, and was off at once, walking heavily through the hall, throwing open the front door.

Kin ran after him.

"He thinks if he don't give in to the depression, it'll go away, as if you can punish a depression. My God. Let them starve, he says."

Kin hurried along beside him.

They walked up King Street, Cal shaking his head like a great wounded animal to those who sought to stop him. He moved past shop after shop on upper King Street, many of them closed. Porter

53

came to the door of his herb shop to watch him. Malcolm set aside the shotgun he was working on and peered at him through the cleaned-off place on his front window. "What's he doing up here?" he said.

They turned up Market Street, and near the intersection of King and Market they stopped at a furniture and hardware store, a small place which had such dirty windows that Kin had often wondered if it was open for business. Over the door, as he saw now, was a foot-long metal plate bearing the single word "Fulcher."

Cal paused before it as if estimating his strength; then slowly, calmly he pushed open the door. A bell jangled, setting Kin's nerves on edge.

The store was so dark Kin couldn't make out anything except the clutter of items near the door. There were bedposts and awnings, coal buckets and horn-speaker radios stacked side by side and on top of one another. As his eyes grew accustomed to the dimness of the place, he saw that the whole store was stacked full of merchandise, dusty and, in some cases, broken.

He decided that nobody was in the store. Then a small voice said, "Well, well," and he saw Fulcher sitting at a roll-top desk at the back of the room. He was a slight, drably dressed man with a few strands of white hair left on his head, and a peaked, red face. He waited for them to approach, not rising, not even moving, but sitting calmly in his swivel chair. His thin hands were clasped together as if in prayer. There was nothing rough about them, Kin noticed. They looked like city women's hands.

"I was saying to one of my friends the other day," Fulcher said, "how is Cal King coming along with his work?" He massaged one hand slowly. "And they told me you was doing well."

"I didn't get hurt too bad in the fall," Cal said. "But this lingering is hurting many."

Kin was relieved to find that his father's voice was natural and firm. No doubt his father was tense, but there was no sign of it.

"Sit down, sit down," Fulcher said.

Little space was left for chairs, even near the desk, but one fold-

54

ing chair was leaning against a wall and Cal pushed it into place. Kin backed off a pace or two and watched.

"That your boy?" Fulcher asked.

"One of them."

Fulcher nodded. His tongue worked with a tooth that was bothering him. "Is he the smart one in school?"

Cal frowned, drew his shoulders in. He didn't know much about Kin's schoolwork. "They're all smart, all my boys," he said.

"Yes, but is he the one named Kin?"

Kin was as surprised as his father. He had done well in school and the other students knew it, but he hadn't thought anybody in town would know, and certainly not a man whose name he had not even known until a few minutes before.

Fulcher stared at Kin, and Kin stared back. After a moment, Fulcher turned away, rested his white hands contentedly on his belly. "I keep a check on some of the boys coming along," he said. He rubbed his brow with the heel of one hand. He never used his fingers much if he could help it, Kin noticed.

"I'm here on business," Cal said.

Fulcher nodded. "I've been expecting you. How much can you let me have?"

Cal crossed his legs. "I'm looking for money."

"You're not borrowing, surely."

"Somebody has to sell or borrow, if the farmers get help."

"Yes. Well, I've done all I can do for them." He coughed as he squirmed in his chair. "Not that as many call on me since they stopped using my store and services. That would be—let's see— that would be starting about the time you plowed in your road and took my business to the foot of the hill with you."

There was bitterness in his voice, all right; it lay just behind the gently said words. But there was not a frown line in his face; he seemed to be relaxed, idly considering the matter at hand, which, one might think, didn't concern him very much.

The bell jangled and a customer came in. When he appeared in the aisle, Kin saw that he was only a boy. "I need a caster," the boy said self-consciously. "One like this." He handed Fulcher a caster. "Need it for a bed."

"Uh-huh," Fulcher said.

Kin expected him to tell the boy to come down later, or to look down the street for one.

"You looking for one just like this?" Fulcher asked, taking the caster.

"One that will fit the same size."

"Uh-huh." Fulcher sat there studying the caster. With a lazy motion he let it slide from his palm onto the desk. "Wait here, boy," he said.

He moved to the top of a narrow set of stairs, took from a nail a pair of work gloves, which he pulled on, and went down the stairs, walking slowly, for they were steep and narrow. Kin heard him rummaging about in the basement, from which a moldy odor came. He came back upstairs, moving even more cautiously. When he got to the narrow doorway, Kin saw that he was carrying a trunk, and this he set down on the floor beside his desk. He opened the lid and began taking items out of it—wheels and gaskets and leather belts which had been collected over the years. The floor near his desk soon was littered with the merchandise, and he worked without speaking, or even noticing the Kings, until he found four casters which had been wired together.

He removed them from the wire and compared them with the caster the boy had brought in, selecting one of them as a fit. He laid it on his desk, then returned the junk to the trunk, which he closed. "I believe you'll find this caster here is just the thing." He handed it to the boy.

Without another word he took the trunk back down the stairway and came back up. He removed the gloves and hung them on the nail, and returned slowly to his chair, where he paused to get his breath.

The boy studied him thoughtfully. "How much do I owe you, sir?" he asked. He dug a worn purse from his pocket.

"Oh," Fulcher said, inhaling deeply to fill his lung. "That'll be two cents."

The boy stared at him for a moment longer before he quickly selected two pennies and laid them on the corner of the desk.

"I thank you," Fulcher said.

"Yes, sir," the boy said, backing away. He turned and hurried out. The nervous bell jangled for a few minutes after the door closed.

"Yes, yes." Fulcher sighed. "Ah-h-h," he said. He winked at Kin and fixed him with his gaze. "You see there, boy," he said, "it pays to save things."

The words stunned Kin, he was dizzy with them. The world of Market Street, of Fulcher's musty store, pressed in around him. The words took on the dryness of the place; the dust-lined walls and the words came together, as if the words were made of the old wood, as if the walls were as hard and straight as the meaning of the words.

Fulcher belched. "You're looking for money, you say, Caleb?" He belched again. "You borrowing on the store?"

"I'm borrowing on my house."

Fulcher shook his head. "I can buy houses for next to nothing."

"Not made of white-oak timbers, like mine."

"No. I don't want to gamble on getting a house. But I'll loan forty-five thousand on the deed to the store."

The offer seemed to hold a place of its own in the room. Forty-five thousand dollars. Here in this rumpled store in which only one sale had been made of late, and that for two cents, what a world of money was forty-five thousand dollars!

"How much you give me for the sale of ten thousand acres of timberland?" Cal asked.

Fulcher chewed on his lower lip. "People have been in here four, five times this week asking that. I can buy timberland at five dollars an acre, but it's not worth it. The truth is, I need all the sorry little bit of money I've put by."

Cal smiled. "I've heard you're a wealthy man, Fulcher."

57

"Huh? Me? I don't know who you talked to, but I just make out like everybody. There's a plenty of folks in this world who begrudge a man living, you know."

Cal's grin broadened. "That's so." He tapped his knee with his long fingers. He got up slowly, shook his shoulders free of tension. "You come down and see us whenever you can, Fulcher. You haven't been down there in all these years."

"I don't often get out of the store, except to go home."

"How is your wife?"

"Well, she's ailing, but they're all of them old complaints."

"You have a daughter, don't you?"

Fulcher nodded. "Florence is all right, though she's never seemed to fill out much. She's peaked and pale yet."

"Somebody said you were going to leave that big house of yours in Biltmore Forest and move back to the country."

"No, but I've missed the country, Caleb. My wife does. She likes to have living things scratching around in the yard. Last year I bought her some chickens, but the neighbors complained about them running loose. I told them they could pale their flower beds in bresh if they valued flowers higher than life, but they said I was to fence my hens or suffer the law. I bought her a cow the other day; got one for four dollars."

Cal considered that. "You pasturing a cow in Biltmore Forest?"

Fulcher nodded slowly. "There's not a law pertaining to cows." His sharp eyes suddenly peered up at Cal, then over at Kin, and Kin saw the secret laugh there. Then abruptly Fulcher grew serious. "My wife likes to milk is the truth of the matter. She'd get to heaven easy if she had ten cows to milk a day." Once more he smiled, and once more, just as abruptly, the smile closed. "Fifty-five thousand on the store."

Cal shoved his hand deep down in his pants pocket, pulled out a handkerchief, and noisily blew his nose. "A man can't hardly lose much on a four-dollar cow," he said. He shoved the handkerchief back into his pocket. "We'll get on back down the street, Kin boy." He winked at Fulcher. "See you."

58

Cal led the way down the aisle. As they reached the door, Fulcher's voice snapped out again. "Sixty-five thousand on the store."

Cal stopped. "No, I don't want to put my store at stake," he said. "I just want to sell a little timberland."

"Well, I hope you'll tell me if you find a man with funds. I'd like to get some money in, myself."

Cal opened the door. The bell tinkled as they left, and they could hear it as they started along Market Street. "I'll go up to the bank tomorrow," Cal said, his voice heavy. "Maybe I can borrow a little something on the land, though not as much. I'd rather have sold it."

"Would he have loaned more on the store, Papa?"

"I can get a fortune on the store; more than he said. But I don't want to lose it.

"No," Kin said anxiously. "Don't lose it."

"They'll go hungry till their bellies are gaunt before I lose the store."

5

Morris Kraft, who was small of build and handsome, had been born in Germany thirty-four years before. He had lived there during the First World War and remembered the hunger and the lack of care for the ill, and the suffering of his father and finally his father's death, which came about just before Morris, at twenty-five, crossed into Switzerland. From there he made his way to New York and later came on down to Pennsylvania, where he apprenticed himself to a tailor. After three years, he moved south and arrived at last in the mountains of North Carolina, which reminded him of home. Now he was a tailor in his own right, with his own shop; and though it was small and as yet yielded scarcely enough to live on, it was his own and was a start.

He was a gentle man who disliked struggle and pain, and who in America had acquired a love of books.

Usually when he came for Beth, the two of them would go off at once, with only the glowering eyes of Kin to trouble them, but one night Cal met Morris as he came up the walk, and they sat down on the front porch, Cal assuming a pontifical air because of his embarrassment. "Young man, I want you to know that I have watched the interest you have shown my niece."

Morris sat on the edge of a porch rocker, ill at ease, especially so when Kin came out and stood at the banister rail not five feet away and glared at him. "Hello, Kin," he said hesitantly.

Kin said nothing.

"Is Beth ready?"

"I don't know."

Morris smiled uncomfortably and knitted his small hands together.

Cal King watched him closely, judging his value. "Perhaps you would come and spend some time with us, visit us one day, so we can get acquainted."

Morris shifted position on the edge of the chair. "That would be a delight," he said.

Cal frowned, unhappy with the choice of words. He had not heard a man use the word "delight" before, but he supposed in learning a foreign language a person must be permitted errors. "We would want you to come maybe to dinner. You could come to dinner on a Sunday, this coming Sunday. Go to church with Beth, then come here and eat a bite with us, and we'll get to talk to one another."

"Sir—" Morris said uncomfortably, "I—sir, after church on Sunday, I will meet Beth and come here, and that will be fine, and I thank you."

Cal considered the slight evasion. He moved the chew of tobaccco from one cheek to the other. "What's wrong with church, Mr. Kraft?" he asked. He seldom went to church himself, but he felt church attendance was good for a young man. "Don't you go to church?"

Morris glanced at him self-consciously. "I'm a Roman Catholic, Mr. King."

"Ah, Jesus Christ," Cal whispered, turning his eyes toward heaven, as if seeking relief from the burden that was laid as added weight on all the rest.

"I'm not a practicing Roman Catholic," Morris said, "but I was reared in the Roman Church and I would as soon not attend a Protestant service." He saw that this did little to alleviate Cal King's discomfort. "The truth, Mr. King, is that once I came to question the existence of a God at all."

"Well, that makes a good Catholic, does it?"

"No, sir. The Church would be displeased."

"I hope it would."

"But in the war we had a great deal of wreckage in my family, and after the war I had a period of doubt. Have you ever been in a war, Mr. King?"

"Not till here lately," Cal said, wiping his mouth and clearing his throat.

"But I believe in a God, in my own way, Mr. King. I have come to that."

Morris was growing more desperate, but he might as well be talking to himself now, because Cal King had given up on him. Cal didn't care what a man's belief was so long as he was a Protestant. He would give a man the widest possible margin. A man could be an agnostic, so far as Cal was concerned, so long as he was a Protestant agnostic. But this man was a Roman Catholic.

Cal became more upset as he thought about it. He swung back and forth, the swing creaking threateningly, and glared out at the lane and didn't listen to anything Morris Kraft was trying to explain to him. And Morris became more agitated. Fortunately Beth came out.

"Let's go," Morris said, taking her arm at once and hurrying her away.

When they were gone, Matthew, who had been listening from the hallway, stepped out onto the porch and sat down in the rocker Morris had left. He lighted a cigar and puffed on it heavily, much like Paul did, then blew the smoke toward Kin, grinning at him. "What do you think of your prospective cousin-in-law?" he asked him.

Kin turned away from him. "He's not your business."

"He's a real prize, ain't he?" Matthew puffed at the cigar and blew smoke. "He's what I call a dy-na-mic fellow." He turned in his chair and peered at his father. "What do you think about him, Papa?"

"I don't think too highly of him," Cal said.

"How'd you like to get him in a trade?" Matthew puffed on the cigar and laughed, but when Paul came out on the porch, he became quiet. Paul pulled a chair up to the porch rail, adjusted his big body to it, and stared out into the night as if dissatisfied with it.

Nobody said anything to him and he said not a word. Matthew, who never could stand the suspense of silence, soon got up. "Want to come up the street with me, Kin?"

Kin drew back from him.

"I'll show you something you never have seen before."

Kin shook his head. He remembered seeing the birth; that was something he never had seen before, and he didn't want to see it again. He wished he had never seen it at all. Sometimes he would wake up at night in a sweat and realize that he had been dreaming about the birth.

Matthew went on down the steps and across the yard, walking with a loose stride, apparently none too anxious to get anywhere. Paul watched him till he was out of sight, then he leaned far forward and broke a stem from a bush. He took out a pocketknife and began to skin away the green bark. "I don't think she ought to be allowed to go out with that man," he said, "no matter what has to be done to stop it."

"You just leave her alone," Cal said easily. "It's none of your business."

Kin, scowling at Paul, moved around Paul to the swing and sat down next to his father.

"She's too nice of a girl to go out with him," Paul said. "She's done more work for the family than any other person in it." He hesitated, as if the kind thought embarrassed him. He worked on the stem, hunched over, concentrating on it. "Somebody has to take care of her."

"I told you to let her be."

63

"I'm her cousin, so it's my business."

"She's my closer kin, and I'm telling you to leave her alone."

"I can't help worrying about my cousin."

Cal flared up suddenly, but he caught control of himself. He glared at Paul, who wasn't looking at him; then he laid his arm across the back of the swing and spoke gently but firmly. "How's your brother Matthew doing up the street?"

Paul glanced warily at him. "You see him working at the store. He trades all right. He's a tough trader."

"I mean up at the beer halls and the women houses. How's he holding out?"

Paul shrugged. "Don't ask me."

"He must spend a fortune up there. He doesn't seem to never tire of women and whisky. Is that so?"

"I don't know," Paul said.

"They tell me he sometimes spends over twenty dollars a night, that he's a big spender. Women like that, seems like."

Paul shrugged.

"You don't care, Paul?"

Paul glanced at him again. "He's not my concern."

"When it comes to relatives, you're just concerned about your cousins, is that right?"

Paul's eyes narrowed and he flinched. He studied his father. "He's your business, I said."

"Your brother spends half his time here lately pickling himself with whisky and it's not your business, is it? It takes money to be a drunk. I don't pay him a big salary. Do you pay his whisky and gambling and women bills, Paul?"

Angrily Paul got up. "You say to let everybody take his own way. Well, that's all I've done. He's your boy, not mine."

"Seems to me, just looking on, that you don't care if he wrecks himself, Paul."

"Now, let's not talk like that, Papa."

"I don't aim to talk any more about it. I've said what I have to say. But that doesn't answer my question. Why is it you don't care if your brother Matthew eats himself away, and you can't stand the thought of your cousin Beth going up the street with a strange man?"

Paul slammed his hand against a porch pillar. "You twist things, you hear me?" He stomped down the steps and crossed the lawn with long strides, his big body responding to his hurt and irritation, his shoulders hunched, his head low. He seemed to radiate power as he moved; physical strength covered him over.

When he was gone, Cal crossed his legs and smiled. He sat back in the swing, relaxed and kindly now. "Huh," he said. "He loves that girl."

Kin looked up at him. "Who?"

"Beth, of course. Paul loves her."

A sweat covered Kin in an instant. Not Paul. Not Paul with Beth.

"I thought he might," Cal said. "He loves Beth, but I think he'd just as soon destroy his brother." The swing creaked as he idly pushed it back and forth. "Matthew's steadier than he appears, though."

Never Paul with Beth, Kin thought.

"He's not a deep man, but he's got a stiff backbone to him. He won't give, if he ever gets his footing."

Never with Beth . . .

The interest of the family in Beth's romance was almost over-shadowed by Johnny's first day in school. There was much activity around the house for a week preceding the event, Lotti occupying the boy's attention with instructions about how he was to act toward his teacher and his classmates. She bought a large quantity of clothes for him and altered them to fit. Most of them had to be let out, for Johnny was overweight. He was round-chested and round-bottomed, and his legs and arms were beefy, too. He had been stuffed with food almost every minute of his life, and given medicine and otherwise protected, and never had he been permitted to run or jump or play for fear of injury. Of course, he played gentle games sometimes, usually with his mother in the house; if not there,

65

then on a grassy spot in the front yard.

Lotti dressed him for school in a blue sailor suit with ducks in the print, but she changed her mind and decided on a white-and-blue suit she had made for him the week before. Once that was on him, however, she changed her mind again, and the child became worn out from her frenzied changing and unchanging of his clothes. It was not his nature, however, to complain. He continued to survey the world with a stony objectivity.

He ended up in navy-blue pants with a white shirt. There was a little dog embroidered on the shirt pocket, and the collar had a ruffle to it, just enough to set off the full face of the child and his long curls of blond hair.

Matthew drove them to the private school, then came on back to the store. He told Paul that he should have seen Lotti sniffing and smelling as she approached the place, as if testing the air to see if it were going to be pure enough for her boy. "She said she would walk him home or get him back in a ca-ab," he said, drawling the word as if imitating her. "Oh, God, she helped the little devil over a puddle no bigger'n a dog pisses," he said, giggling and laughing and shaking his head in wonder.

Cal was irritated by it all. "Well, he's a smart one, you'll have to admit that. He's not to blame for his mother fondling him like he's a hound pup. She's done taught him to read."

"He might be able to read as far as Genesis 1:1," Paul said, getting up from the barrel where he was sitting and moving to the patent-medicine counter, where he made a cash sale to a customer. "Unless you get a wad of them curls cut off his head, Papa," he said, coming back to the stove-heated place, "he's going to be marked down as a fairy before he even gets both feet out of the cradle."

"Now, hold your tongue," Cal said. That suggestion annoyed him considerably; his greatest fear for the boy was that he was likely to develop less masculinity than he would need to get along.

"Going to be wagging his big ass up and down King Street," Paul predicted, "with even the mules braying after him when he comes

66

by. Going to be a laughingstock in every house and stable in the district."

Cal kicked at the wood box and retreated behind a counter stacked with brogans. He called an attendant over to straighten out that place, fussed at him sternly, taking out on him his irritation with Paul; then he wandered on past three waiting customers to the tin-bucket counter, where he called another attendant over and cussed him out.

"I'm going to buy him a cross before long," Paul said to Matthew, "and see if he can tote it up King Street. Going to make him practice with it."

All morning they talked about the little fellow, entertaining each other with ideas and stories. "He smells like a pint of Spanish olives by the time she gets done with his cleaning," Paul said. "He's got such a glimmer on him he shames the fireplace."

"She was trying to get him to read a picture book last month," Matthew said, "and she told him what a dog was, and a cat, and a cow. He's a smart little cuss, you know, and he had those words right on damn near ever page. But Mama didn't like the way he said 'horse.' You know, it sounded like 'whores,' and there are some words that irritate Mama that don't irritate nobody else in the world, and she was trying to get him to twist his mouth around differently. So she'd say, 'Horse, Johnny,' and he'd say, 'Whores, Mama,' ever time."

"I wish I'd a been there," Paul said, "when he was learning about the ash tree."

Cal overheard that, and he commenced to laugh. He didn't laugh often, and when he did, it was a good, warm moment in the store, and even the customers were delighted. He and the two boys and the customers broke out laughing, though only Cal and the two boys had a clear idea of what they were laughing at.

That afternoon Kin came to the store and traded for a while. He had been assigned to Miss Martingale for his seventh-grade home-room and history teacher, in spite of his best hopes. She had taught in the school ("held out at the same stump," she termed it) for thirty years, and she was much feared by thousands of students who had gone through her classroom. Two hundred and twelve pounds of quivering flesh, she put up with no nonsense, and she worked according to a firm theory that nobody ever got educated in the schools of North Carolina. Should a brilliant student put the theory to the test, she would swamp him with heavy assignments, trying, as the student knew, to force him to concede.

She had opened the class that morning by asking each student questions about the previous year's work. "Something I can test your ignorance by," she told them. Nobody dared to answer the questions correctly. When she got to Kin, she paused and considered him thoughtfully. "You aren't related to Matthew King, are you?" she asked.

"Yes, ma'am," Kin said.

A groan came out of Miss Martingale. Somewhere deep inside the mountains of flesh, a wobbly sound originated.

Kin had planned to miss his question, but the groan seemed to be an insult to his family, so he answered correctly. When he did, another groan, one of even deeper weariness, emanated from her. "I suppose anyone will run across a bit of knowledge, even in school," she said. "Let me ask you this, Kin King; who was President Tyler's Secretary of State?"

Kin stared back at the tiny, gleaming eyes. He remembered almost everything he ever read. "Daniel Webster," he said.

The small eyes closed as Miss Martingale flinched, then she smiled faintly as if listening to music. "And I believe if you were to study your history thoroughly, you would find that he was also Secretary of State under President Harrison."

"Yes, ma'am," he said. He watched her for a moment, then quietly said, "And also under President Fillmore."

The class gasped. The smile faded slowly from Miss Martingale's face. She sat back, shuddering, and it was a minute or so before she was prepared to go on to the next child.

Kin said nothing to Matthew or his father about the incident.

68

It had gone down in the school as a major victory in the thirty-year war between students and Miss Martingale, and he had found himself much discussed at recess, but the world of school and the world of King Street were so different that it never occurred to him that what happened in one place would be of value or interest in the other.

He did tell Beth when he got home. She was asking and laughing about what he said when they heard a car door slam, and both of them raced through the hallway to the front door, for they knew it would be Lotti. She had just left a taxi, they found, and she and Johnny were coming up the walk. On his first day in school, the boy seemed to have wilted. His white collar, so nicely stiff in ruffles that morning, was limp and awry. His pants had a mud smear from one knee down to the cuff. There was a red mark on his cheek where he had scratched himself.

Lotti held one of his fat little hands. "Well, I tell you," she said, leading him up the porch steps, "I hope I never have to go through another day like this one."

Johnny nudged her to get free, and she released him. Pouting, he marched past Beth and Kin and went into the bedroom, and on through that one to his own room, slamming doors as he went.

Lotti sank back into a parlor rocker and spread her legs out stiffly before her. "Well, I don't know," she said wearily, "I suppose maybe I shouldn't have stayed with him all day, but I wasn't the only one, don't you think I was. There was six of us mothers there."

Beth sat down on the cot next to the window, near Kin.

"I told the teacher when I got there that Johnny was a special child, and she nodded. She really was a sweet woman, name of Tyson. We had some Tysons back in the hills, and they was good people. Strong of character, and they worked like dogs. Nothing weak about the Tysons. And I told her what the situation was, and she showed understanding. Then I took a seat at the back of the room where the other mothers was. Miss Tyson got the children quiet and she commenced to call the roll. Well, ever child said something to his name being called, till she got to Johnny. She said, 'John King,' and he sat there at his desk and stared at her. 'John King,' she said. Johnny held silent, so I spoke up and said, 'Well, you can see he's here, can't you?' I mean, it was so clear that he was present, there was no point in repeating the name over and over. She went on with the roll, and then she come to questioning the children, and she asked Johnny how old he was. He didn't say a word. He just sat there and looked at her. She come down the aisle to him and said, 'How old are you, Johnny?' He just looked at her in that way he's got."

For the first time in Beth's recollection, Lotti seemed to be disappointed in the boy, even critical of the solemn, studious look with which he would study every irritation.

"Course, he knew he was seven, but he didn't say the number. And finally Miss Tyson turned around and went back to her desk, not giving a glance toward where I was."

Lotti studied the floor, silent now, and Beth waited thoughtfully, not knowing what to say to her. Lotti was disturbed, all right. She was disappointed in her boy and didn't know how to justify his poor showing. For a long while she sat there.

"I know his father is going to insist on him going to a school," she said.

Beth wanted to tell her not to think about it, to let the worry pass, for she couldn't stand to see Lotti lose her last big hope, but she didn't know how to approach the subject.

Suddenly Lotti sat up, as if new life had come to her. Her face stiffened and strength seemed to flow back into her. "Beth, I tell you what I think," she said, and nodded emphatically. "I think that Tyson woman ain't got Johnny buffaloed, not a bit."

6

As the depression lengthened, Paul, with the rights of a successful prophet, made even more frequent and distressing predictions about the store, and took on even more authority. On the whole Cal had always permitted his boys to assume as much control of the store as they thought they could handle, anyway, believing that they should extend their talents to the limit and develop along natural lines. Exactly what "natural" meant wasn't clear, but he used the word often. If two of his boys got into an argument, he stayed out of it. This argument was part of the "natural" development of the boys. If one boy wanted to order a new brand of merchandise, he didn't interfere, and if the goods didn't sell well once they were in stock, he didn't mention it. This also was part of the natural development of the boys. If Paul wanted to handle the books, that was all right with Cal. If another boy wanted to handle the books, he would have to wrench control away from Paul.

A son exerting his energies, Cal felt, would develop his strength; a son who had his problems solved or adjusted for him by his father would develop unsteady powers of his own.

Paul gained so much authority that he even told his father one afternoon that he should get off King Street "or you'll bankrupt us yet." The suggestion that Cal King get off King Street came as a surprise to those who overheard it.

Kin fretted about Paul's growing control. He made notes in his journal, predicting Paul's next move. His frenzied writing about the store and his worries added to his intense feelings, until one idle afternoon he found that he had courage enough to sneak into the back-room office, Paul's room, to see what he could find out.

The door was unlocked. He slipped through and closed it quietly.

The room was narrow, only seven feet wide, and was no more than twelve feet long. In it were a rickety table and, on the other side of the table, a chair. The table had a drawer across the front, but most of the office supplies were stored in a wall bookcase. That was where several gray ledgers were. Kin took them down, put them on the table, and opened one. He discovered an array of numbers, every page full of figuring.

He opened another ledger, and it, too, was crammed with carefully drawn figures, each centered in its blue-lined box, no figure touching any of the lines.

He opened another book. This was Paul's journal, in which he recorded his observations about incidents at home and the store. "Today I told Helen not to come around me any more if she had nothing to offer," Kin read, and he wondered if this was the Helen who had worked in one of the restaurants for a while. He read several references to the family in the book, and one about himself. "Kin traded poorly on ten bushels of string beans today. Loss 50¢. Papa said nothing to him. He always trades poorly, won't try to learn."

Kin totaled one column of figures in one of the store's ledgers and found that the addition was off ninety cents. He added the next page and found that it was off thirty cents, but this error partially corrected the one of the day before. He added four more columns and found that only one page was added accurately. Everything was neatly, even artistically done; the bookkeeping showed dutiful attention, but it was unreliable.

He studied the listings themselves to see if every item had been entered, but he couldn't tell about that. The trades were not entered at all; only major cash transactions were, only the money that went out and came in. Within the store itself, merchandise was continuously changing because of the trades, and these were not itemized, and, indeed, they could not be. So it was difficult to tell the amount of profit or loss, even over a long period. There was much room for mismanagement here, Kin saw, and even for theft.

He found his father's loanbook and noticed that most of the people who owed his father money hadn't been making payments. Most of them hadn't paid much of anything since the close of 1929.

He searched through the table drawer. He found no record to indicate the size of Paul's savings, but he did find notes for personal loans which Paul had made to mountain men, with land as security. He also found in the drawer a letter-sized leather case, which was strapped and tightly tied. He couldn't get the knot loose at first and started to put it back, but he kept at it, and finally it was open. Inside was a paper, which he unfolded.

He saw that it was a certificate for twenty per cent of the King store, a gift to Paul King, made out two months before and signed by his father.

Kin dropped the paper to the tabletop and sat back in the chair, his body trembling.

He heard Paul outside in the main room of the store, coming toward the office. He sat immobile in the chair.

Paul stopped. "Matthew, that fellow Turner brought in another truckload of half-green apples, all crated with ripe apples on the top, and by God I won't do business with him or his family again. He's out there loading them back."

Slowly Kin folded the certificate and put it in its case and tied the cord and returned it to the drawer.

He leaned back once again in the chair. Twenty per cent gone, twenty per cent Paul's, the store that was his and his father's.

Paul said, "When the bastard drove up, I knew what he'd done. Him and his brother both are crooked as laurel trunks. But I said, 'Hell, yes, unload 'em; we buy good apples, you know that.' So he unloaded all them bushel baskets, and then I went down the line kicking over one after another to show the green apples underneath, and him and his two boys are out there gathering apples from the gutter right now, the son of a bitch. Does he think I just got started storekeeping?"

Kin heard Paul's heavy footsteps again. He was coming toward the room. "Son of a bitch," Paul was saying, mumbling, as he often mumbled.

He came through the doorway, his head down, still talking. Then he stopped. He stared at Kin, his mouth open, his jaw moving but no words coming out now. His face showed fear as well as anger and embarrassment. And maybe hate. "Papa," he said huskily, then louder. "Papa."

Cal King heard him and recognized pain in his voice and hurried to the room. "What you want?" he said. Then he saw Kin sitting at the table in the chair.

As if his father's entrance had unleashed him, Paul advanced on Kin, grabbed the boy by the front of his shirt and jerked him away from the chair, shoved him against the wall. Kin didn't fight him; he did nothing, actually, except watch the bitterness explode inside him.

Cal pulled Paul away. "What the hell is going on?"

Paul swung away from his father and sought the desk, his eyes misty, and began slamming ledgers closed and shoving them back on their shelves, getting pages folded and not caring. He swung once more on Kin. "Get out of here."

"Don't yell at me," Kin said, speaking firmly, but his body was trembling and the nerves at the back of his neck twitched.

Paul grabbed him and shoved him toward the door.

"Let him be, damn it," Cal said.

"I'll kill him," Paul said, trying to swallow. "Papa, I'll kill him."

74

"Kin, did you get into Paul's things?"

"Paul's things?" Kin said. "Paul's things?"

He turned from his father and stumbled past Matthew at the door, and past several store attendants who had come because of the shouting, and went out into the cavernous, dim main room of the store.

Cal caught him and pulled him around to face him. "I said what were you doing in there?"

"I was reading, Papa. The books."

"You better keep him out of here, Papa, by God!"

Cal's gaze stayed on Kin. "What did you see, Kin?"

"Twenty per cent," Kin said, his throat choked.

Cal nodded slowly, absorbing that and its meaning, deeply considering the worry the discovery might cause the family, trying to penetrate, too, into the exact nature of the boy's painful concern. "I'll—ask you to stay out of my business," he said.

Paul slammed the door of his office. The lock turned. They heard him cursing, the obscenities pouring out steadily.

"You just get him excited. You make things worse, you hear me?" Cal said.

Kin swung away from him and sought the street outside.

He stood on the street, dizzy from deep troubles and the sudden sunlight. Matthew was beside him, shaking his arm. "What did you see? What's in there, Kin?"

"Twenty per cent," Kin said. "Ask Paul." He pulled away and crossed the street to the farmers' yard and lost himself in the crowd. "Young King," somebody said, but he moved on.

Twenty per cent his, twenty per cent Paul's.

He walked up the street. Cynthia Porter, who at seventeen liked to be called Cyn, was standing in the doorway of her father's herb shop. "Where you going, Kin?" she asked.

He went on by. He didn't want to go home; he wanted to get away from home and the street.

He walked until late in the afternoon and found himself at the school. He was in the classroom, Miss Martingale's old classroom.

He was standing at the door. Some need inside him had brought him there. He moved to his desk and sat down.

He had always held his father in such high esteem, but his father had rebuffed him, even though he rarely interfered in a dispute at all; his father had favored Paul, had even given Paul part of the store which was Kin's, which Kin wanted as he wanted the love of his father. His father had been the strong one, whom he could count on to govern wisely, but his father had weaknesses like everybody else.

He realized somebody was standing beside his desk, he looked up to see Miss Martingale. Perhaps she had been there for some time; he didn't know. She had always been tough on him in class, but now the scowl was gone and she was looking at him kindly.

She touched him. He had never known her to touch anybody before. She touched his shoulder, then her fingers rested on his face. "What did you discover?" she asked.

It was such a beautiful question that it moved him. How did she know?

"It will all clear up in time," she said. "You'll see. Only fears that you don't now dream of won't pass away."

"What do you mean?" he asked, whispering.

"You'll see." She touched his shoulder. "Do you want to tell me about it?" she asked. She squeezed his shoulder gently.

"No, ma'am," he said, although he did. But he couldn't tell her about his father.

"I want to tell you something," she said.

He couldn't take his eyes off of the huge face, the mass of flesh from which her small eyes peered, now so compassionately.

"In my years of teaching, I've known many bright students. But none has been brighter than you." Pain seemed to move through her, as if the statement had wrenched her. "If you ever need help," she said, speaking slowly and with difficulty, "anything at all—" She glanced away from him. Once more she squeezed his shoulder, then went on down the aisle, her head lowered, her great body knocking against the school desks.

76

He wanted to cry. He was so moved, so deeply moved. He lowered his head to the desk and wept, soft sobs breaking through him. He wept for himself, and her, and for his father.

He arrived home late to dinner and nobody said anything to him about it. He could tell that a change had come over the family. He ate his food and didn't look at Beth or ask her anything while she served him. His mother was in the parlor. He could hear her talking. "When you give one boy something," she was saying feverishly, "I have to ask you what my Johnny's going to get."

Beth brought in a pot of hot coffee and sat down across the table. "Matthew came home early and said Paul owned part of the store now. Is that true?"

Kin nodded.

"Matthew packed his bags and left home, Kin."

Kin looked up at her, studying her, trying to figure out his own thoughts. "Left?" He had been jealous of Paul, but he hadn't known Matthew was. He had always thought Matthew was an ally of Paul's. "Where did he go?"

She stirred cream into the coffee. "Nobody knows where. And I'll ask you something: Do you hear anybody else asking where he went? It's a strange family," she said. "They don't care."

"But you're worried about him, aren't you, Beth?"

She sniffed, as if bothered with a cold. "I worry about anybody who's in suffering, don't you?" She took a sip of the steaming coffee. "When I first came here, he was a little boy, and I was just four years older. We liked one another very well. I've cared for all the Kings, Kin. Every single one. Sometimes I think I'm a member of this family, too." She smiled, but it was a tentative smile which vanished quickly, as if it pained her. "I guess everybody wants to be part of the family she lives with." She set the coffee aside suddenly, and her anger flared. "Sometimes I think I'm the only one who really cares about the members of this household, who can see them as people." And with that she got up and went into the kitchen.

Paul came into the dining room a few minutes later. "Do you know where Matthew went?" he asked.

Kin shook his head.

"Can't you speak?"

"I'll speak if I want to."

"You know where he is?"

Kin shook his head. Paul laid a palm on the table and leaned over, so that his face was close to Kin's. "I know you know where he is. The two of you are together, trying to interrupt things. Where is he?"

Kin looked straight ahead. He could hear the raspy inner breathing of the big man, and could smell the sweat of him. Out of the corner of his eye he saw him watching, staring, waiting.

Slowly Paul straightened. Kin heard him moving down the hall. "I'm going up the street to find him, Papa," Kin heard him say.

Beth came back into the dining room, carrying a cup of coffee. "Was he looking for Matthew?"

"I think so."

"He thinks he's in charge of the family now. He owns the store, so he thinks he owns us, too." She frowned and grunted deprecatingly. "He's a big ox," she said, sitting down, stirring the coffee with the spoon from the sugar bowl. "Always feeling everything so deeply. He wants people to like him so much."

"Paul?"

"Yes."

"Nobody likes Paul. Not even up the street."

She looked off vacantly, scratching at her neck absent-mindedly. "I know," she said.

He left her in the dining room and went into the parlor. Cal was there winding the clock. It was a wood-works clock which his father had imported from Connecticut in 1833. He wound it slowly, so as not to break teeth off the maple gears, then closed the glass and locked it. There was a painting on the glass of a textile factory and a street.

78

"Hello, Kin," Cal said simply, slipping the key onto the high chest. "It's been a big day, for you, for Paul." He looked about, irritated with the feeling he had. "I was talking to a man from Morehead City once, and he said ocean waves are usually little, but sometimes a big one comes in and, smack, it knocks people over. You reckon that's so?"

"I guess it is."

"It's so with days, anyway. You sure hit us today, boy." He shook his head wearily, untied his tie, went into his bedroom, leaving the door open. He began to undress for bed.

In an hour, Paul was back, Matthew, drunk, in tow. "You get to bed," Paul told him. Matthew went up the steps to his room without a word.

Lotti came out of her room. "Was that him?" she asked.

"He's back," Paul said, pleased with his work. "I got him."

"Well, I'll sleep better knowing he's come home. Was he in a hotel?"

"He was in the Langren. He just wanted to be come for."

"Well, you did well to get him, Paul."

"Uh-huh." He looked at her, studied her in the pursed-lip way he had of working out his problems. "Mama, I want you to start bringing that little boy to the table to eat when the rest of us eat."

She looked up at him sharply, searchingly. "I don't know what you're talking about. I'll feed him after the rest have gone."

"Are we going to contaminate the boy, is that it? Can't he eat at the same table with us?"

"With Matthew in there cussing, with you in there running things, is that what you mean? You leave my boy be, or you'll run into me, not your father. Maybe you can push around your father, but you don't do it to me, you hear?"

Paul's face twitched with nervousness. He tapped a fist into his big open palm. "We're going to have things done right from now on, Mama," he said firmly.

Lotti, white-faced, abruptly left the hall and went to her room. She closed the door and locked it.

The next day she fed her boy separately, as before, but she was careful to stay out of Paul's way.

Two nights later, when Morris Kraft came to the house, Paul met him on the porch, and Morris perhaps expected to be challenged, for he stopped at the edge of the porch and stared at the big man.

"You come for Beth?"

"Yes," he said firmly.

"She's not going to see you."

Morris moved toward the front door, but Paul caught him, held him tightly, so tightly that Morris winced and almost cried out, and on Paul's face came a look of hate so fierce and full that Morris gasped when he saw it. Paul released him and turned from him and sought a chair. He sank down in it, as if he had forgotten Morris, as if his hate of Morris had overcome him, and now it was the hate that troubled him, not Morris at all.

Morris straightened his shirt. He knocked on the door and stood, stiffly, waiting. Beth come at once, and when she saw Paul, she realized what had happened.

Paul turned to her. "Beth, don't go," he said, pleading with her more than ordering her.

She took Morris's arm. "I'm going to the moving pictures, Paul."

"I'll have him run out of town, Beth."

"No. You don't dare do that."

"Dare? Dare him?"

"Dare me," she said. "I can hurt you as bad as you can hurt me. I can hurt you worse, Paul."

He murmured an oath and turned from her.

After that, Morris didn't come to the house. Kin thought Beth might have stopped seeing him, but one night she went uptown soon after supper, sneaked away, and when she came home, at ten o'clock, Kin, who was reading in his room, heard Paul speak to her as she came across the yard to the house, speak to her about Morris. "I told you to leave that man alone, and you sneaked off to see

80

him." His voice showed hurt and his words tumbled over one another, as if his emotions confused him. "What's he got that you can't leave alone?"

Kin heard Paul slap a porch pillar with the flat of his hand, as he often did when he became irritated. "I don't care what Papa said," he shouted.

Kin closed his book, placed it on the chair, and opened his door. He wasn't going to stand for much more from Paul, he told himself, not where Beth was concerned.

"I asked you to go to the pictures, didn't I?" Paul said. "I asked you, but then you go traipsing off to his place."

The front screen door opened and Beth came running up the stairs. She passed Kin, trying not to let him see her face, and a pang of pain went through him.

Paul slammed the front door and charged up the stairs after her. "I followed you tonight, by God," he said, not paying any attention to Kin. "You went into his shop at eight o'clock, and if there was a light on in there all night, I didn't see it." He went right on into Beth's room.

Beth said something, but she wasn't speaking defiantly, as Kin expected, but in a low, almost apologetic voice.

"Now don't tell me you have to give him cooking lessons in the dark," Paul said.

"We were back in the kitchen," Beth answered heatedly. "It's in the back, the last of three rooms."

From below Cal King called up. "Let's settle down and keep more quiet up there."

Paul lowered his voice. "I'm thinking about right and wrong," he said. "Somebody has to talk to you about this thing."

"Not you," Beth said, but she wasn't angry, and Kin was dismayed by the thought that perhaps she welcomed even Paul's concern for her.

"Beth, I worry about you something terrible," Kin heard Paul say. He had never known such tenderness in Paul. "Beth, I went stumbling up the street, following you like a schoolboy. Now, Beth, we've got to come to an understanding."

"No, you get on away, Paul."

Kin stood motionless.

"Paul, let me go. Paul."

Kin waited.

"I said let me go," she said, at last defiantly, and instantly Kin dashed down the hall.

Paul was holding her, he saw, embracing her. "Beth, Beth—" Paul was saying, his breathing heavy, "don't turn away from me, Beth." Beth was trying to pull away.

"All right, Paul," Kin said.

Paul's hands fell sharply away from her. He turned stiffly to Kin, incredulous. He seemed to be unable to accept the fact that Kin was there. "Who are you?" he said, forming the words singly and with difficulty. "Who the hell are you? You keep popping up."

Beth backed toward the bed and sank down on it. "You go on, Kin," she said, biting at her hand. "Please, Kin—"

He didn't move.

Paul advanced on him, the big lumbering body too big for his feet. He hovered over him. His fist suddenly struck out, but Kin had been waiting and ducked and threw his own weight behind a blow to Paul's big belly. The blow landed solid and he heard a grunt, then he felt a blow to his head and he reeled across the wide hallway and bounced against the door of Matthew's room. He felt the tough, flabby fist again. He heard Beth scream and Paul clutched at him, but he escaped. His father was on the steps and the lights were on and Beth's arms were around him. His head throbbed and he was dizzy, but he could see Beth and smell the perfume she had on. "It's all right," she was saying, "It's all right."

Kin saw his father. He was facing Paul. This was the moment, Kin knew, when his father would put Paul in his place. Now his father would speak out and make known who was head of the family, right now.

"We'd better all go to our rooms," his father said. That was all.

Kin wanted to shout out at him, tell him to speak out bluntly. But he was too sick, and he said nothing; he was too discouraged now. Beth released him and he stumbled down the two steps to the landing and went into his room and closed the door.

He heard his mother call from downstairs. "What is it, Cal? What's going on?"

"You go on back to your boy, Lotti," Cal answered. "It's all over now."

It's not over, Kin thought. It never will end like this.

"We heard a big commotion. It woke Johnny and me up."

"It's over, Lotti. Go to sleep."

Kin heard his mother close the door.

"Now let's all get back to bed," Cal said. "Paul, Beth—"

Not a word was said. Kin heard the two doors close. Then he heard a door open. "Hey, papa, did they fight?" Matthew asked.

"Just a flare-up," Cal said. "Good night, Matthew."

"Sounded like a fight."

Kin stretched out on his cot. He felt his face where Paul had hit him. It was sore and his nose was bleeding. He wiped away the blood. He tasted blood in his mouth. A tooth was loose maybe. He felt his teeth with his tongue, and he couldn't tell where the blood was coming from. Maybe it was a cut. He was still dizzy from the impact of the flabby fists. But he had hit Paul one solid blow. He had hit Paul once, anyway.

Cal came down the two steps to the landing and stopped. Kin watched his door. Slowly it was pushed open and Cal, a sadness resting on him, stood in the doorway and looked down at him. "You take Paul on in a fight?" he asked quietly.

"Yes," Kin said.

The old smile, the one Kin hadn't seen in weeks, crept into the corners of his eyes. "How old are you?"

"Fifteen."

"And he's thirty-six, and a big man, too." He closed the door and pulled up the chair. He brushed the book out from under him and it landed open on the floor. "You all right?"

83

"I think so."

"It's an amazing thing, boy. Paul shouldn't have hit you like he done. He's—he's not able to control himself. I keep hoping he'll improve. But—what can anybody do? I used to think a man could take an ornery mule and train him to act proper, but I never have heard tell of it being done. You just have to learn to accept the mule you've got."

Kin watched him. "Yes, sir," he said simply, wondering about him.

"I fought my own brother once, boy. This brings it back to me. He was always worrying about whether my papa liked me better, and whether he would get a share of the farm. There were two of us boys and four girls, all the girls living in Tennessee and Virginia now, married off." He wiped his mouth with the sleeve of his worn robe. "Anyway, one December my brother and me was drivers on a bear hunt, way back in the hills, and we unleashed five dogs at the mouth of a valley and moved into it, making noise, so that the bears would run toward the high ground, as they will, where the hunters were stationed, my father among them. A bear often heads for the crossovers to the next valley, Kin."

"Yes, sir," Kin said, watching him. His father was speaking slowly, as if he didn't care how long he took. He seemed to be content just to be there.

"It was a fall day, none too warm, just right for hunting, and we were in high spirits, but just when we got to the first creek crossing, little more than a branch, Clarence slipped and fell, and somehow he thought I enjoyed his falling. This angered him, and he said something or other about it. We went on, and he was climbing over a fallen chestnut trunk when a birch limb swung back and struck him full in the face, and he saw me looking at him. Well, hell, I didn't do it, but I was looking at him, so he blamed it on me. We went on, and we got to the place where Great-Grandpa King built the first cabin, and where my grandpa lived in his life. Why my great-grandfather built way back up there, I don't know, except maybe back then everywhere was way back up there, no

84

matter where you were. Anyway, an old pit about twenty feet deep with smooth clay and rock walls was in that place. Maybe once it had had an outhouse on it, or maybe one of them had dug for water when a spring dried. Anyway, I saw Clarence was walking toward it, and naturally I called out. Well, sir, he turned on me and said, 'Yes, I can't even make my own way through the woods without your help, can I?' And he come at me with killing in his face, grabbed hold of me and threw me down, and the first thing I knowed the hole was at my head and I was on my back with my brother on top of me. And I said, 'No, Clarence, don't kill me.' "

He paused. He could see it clearly in his mind, Kin realized, the slick shaft below him, and could feel the horror he had felt then. He could hear his brother breathing.

"Then Clarence seemed to understand. He realized where we were. I saw something flash across his eyes, as if a film was pulled away, and I took account of that moment to grab hold and get a grip on him, because I knew he was considering what was right, but I didn't trust his judgment. So we wrestled there, and soon we both was about to fall in. We stopped fighting then, but neither would let go of the other. Neither dared to. Then I let up a little, and he did. A little more. Gradually we released one another, and we drew back and got up."

Cal thought about it, nodding slowly. He took out a piece of tobacco and stuck it in his cheek, moistening it. "Brother agin brother," he said, chewing on the tobacco to get the juice started. He chewed for a while. "Clarence is ailin' now, you know. I had a doctor from Candler go up to look at him, and seems like he's got more pains than he can name, or that the doctor can name, either. He's got a stomach condition and a back condition. Don't look like the farm is doing him much good, even now that he owns all of it."

"Does he own all of it?" Kin asked.

Cal nodded. "I sold him my part when I come to Asheville. He has it all. But it's not helped him any. He still holds off from me, especially since I come to town and made money. And Beth's with me and not with him. He's all alone out there. He's still envious of me." He chewed and thought. "I expect envy is one reason your brother Collins first run away from home, his envy of Paul and Paul's envy of him. He's a big, strong man, your brother Collins is, Kin."

"Yes, sir," Kin said quietly.

"Wherever he goes, people follow Collins. In any town he lives in, everybody knows who Collins is. He lives in hotels, always in the finest, travels first-class on the trains. He does enough trading to make a profit to live well on. Money seems to flow easy to Collins."

"Where is he now?" Kin asked.

"San Francisco is the center of his travels. He's there more often than he is anywhere else."

"I don't remember him very well, except his singing to me."

"Yes, he would bounce you on his knee and sing. That was the time he come back from Texas. He's been to Alaska. Been to Mexico. Been to Canada, Montana, Nevada, ever'where. Your mama hears from him now and then."

"Yes, sir."

Cal felt of Kin's jaw. "Sore?"

"A little bit."

He felt of Kin's nose. "It's not broke, is it?"

"I don't think so. I think I have a mouth-cut, though."

"You go to the doctor tomorrow and see if you have. Tell him to let me know how much it costs."

"All right."

"And don't you worry about things around here, boy. I'm fifty-eight. No, I'm fifty-nine. I've been living a long time, and I know a lot about mules."

He left quietly, and Kin lay in bed thinking about him and what he had said, and about Paul, and about Collins, who was way off in San Francisco.

He murmured the golden words: Collins King, San Francisco.

He lay there thinking about him and how Collins had been such a happy man, with the strong good odor of tobacco about him and of shaving lotion, sweet-smelling and nose-tingling. He wondered how it would be to see Collins again, to see him there in the house.

Paul would have to leave Beth alone then. He would have to find his proper place again, Kin thought. For Collins was a powerful man.

And it would be good to have his laughter in the house. Kin remembered his smile and his laugh. He wanted to see him, this strong, happy man, the second son.

He crept from the bed and got his school notebook. He took out a sheet of lined paper and his pencil. He laid the paper on the seat of the chair and wrote his words clearly, block printing the letters so that there would be no mistake about them.

> *Dear Collins,*
> *Papa is in trouble and needs you,*
> *and I need you too. Please come home.*
> *Your brother,*
> *Kin (Johnny)*

7

IT WAS NOT UNTIL THE FOLLOWING SPRING THAT THE answer came.

My dear precious mamma Lotti,
 I think about you and dear papa all the time, and about my fine brothers and cute little cousin Beth, and I was just thinking that maybe the depression has caused suffering in Asheville, as it has here in the big, fine city of San Francisco, and I said to myself that I ought to go home and see my family once again. So I am coming to see you, sweet dear mamma Lotti, and will arrive on the mid-day train, the last Thursday of May, nine days from now.

Across the bottom of the page, Collins had written his name.

The letter came as a wondrous sweet balm to Lotti, as a promise of good times and deliverance. She vowed that, except for little Johnny, Collins was the best son she ever had, and she read the letter over and over, murmuring the words to herself or reading them aloud to anybody who would listen. "My boy is coming to see me," she would say. "Beth, where is San Francisco?"

But the letter fell like a life blow to Paul. A deep distress affecting all that he did seemed to deaden his mind, so that he couldn't get organized as well as before. He seemed not to hear much that was said to him; at the store he lost track of orders, forgot what he was doing; then he would indulge himself in a tirade against some store employee. At night he would go up the street; he stayed up the street even more than Matthew. He would come home early in the morning, drunk and cursing and talking about Collins. "Handsome, made like a damn god, ain't he?" he would proclaim outside Beth's closed door. "Like a young lord, he's coming home." He would lean over the banister rail and call downstairs, "Just three more days, Mama!"

One night he called downstairs. "I'm going away; did you know that? Didn't I tell you? I'm going off. You got me in prison in this place."

Each night he would come home drunk, rude with his criticisms of Collins and the family, but in the morning he would be solicitous, anxious to find some way to please them, as if he were looking toward the time when he might need their help.

Kin was in a daze. He couldn't study, he couldn't even think straight. He could remember being bounced on Collins' knee, and he could even remember the texture of Collins' voice, deep and vibrant, as Collins sang to him. And the eyes, often winking at him. And the smile. And how everybody on the street would follow Collins around, and how people said women sought after him. Kin remembered hearing his father say that parents used to hurry their daughters home after church meetings whenever Collins was there, and they would lock their girls in the house if he set foot in their yard. Once he stole every chicken in Lotti's henhouse and sold them so that he could buy a gift for a girl he loved at the moment.

Such talk impressed Beth immensely. She was twenty-five, and even yet men to her were a mystery. She saw herself waiting for a Prince Charming to come and carry her off; her dreams were like that. She didn't see him as being Morris, and not as being Paul, either, whom she loved in the way that she might come to love anybody with whom she lived and who needed love so much. She knew Paul's good side and his bad. He was a man of deep feelings, deeper than hers or than anybody else's in the family. He was easily hurt, he carried a grudge for a long time, he responded awkwardly and sometimes profanely to a show of kindness. But he needed sympathy and care more than most, and he sought sympathy, in his way. He was a strong man, too; there was nothing squeamish or silly about him; even his ruthlessness and his emotionalism were part of the vibrant male animal that he was.

She knew that. On the other hand, Morris Kraft was shy and competent, well able to hold his emotions in control or to subjugate them almost entirely. He was prim and neat and kind. He wasn't nearly as self-centered as Paul; he didn't see the happenings of the world only in terms of their importance to him and his hungers. He was interested in the world for the wonder of it, and in people and books. He was a faithful subscriber to the *National Geographic Magazine,* which he bound in semiannual volumes and which he shelved on display in his tailor shop. He bought books from every book salesman who came through town, and the more expensive a set's binding, the more anxious he was to purchase it.

He was honest. He operated on a predictable schedule; every hour was accounted for, but he was rarely in a rush. He was almost never confused, although sometimes he became frustrated.

If she had to choose between the two men, she would choose Morris. That choice was safe. But she suspected that in the chilly house he would keep, where love would be held in restraint, she would regret her choice occasionally and would wonder what life would have been like had she submitted herself to Paul.

At the moment she held off from both, unwilling yet to yield to either or to accept love from either, though both had mentioned the matter, each in his way, Paul with such deep feeling that he could not control his voice or keep his hands from seeking to touch her, and Morris with objective argument—polite incidental statements which she could continue for a while to ignore. But she didn't really want to ignore them. That is, the suggestions did interest her; they rested on her mind almost constantly now. She wanted with deep passion to shed her ignorance and yield up herself and her own secrets.

One night she and Morris had been in his kitchen talking, sitting close together. He had his arm around her and one hand had come to touch her right breast. She had not pushed his hand away. But when his hand touched her thigh, she got up suddenly and left the room, swept on by anger and embarrassment and fear.

The room next in line, between the kitchen and his glass-fronted shop, was the small, crowded room in which he slept. She stopped there and slumped down on the bed to regain control of herself. Evidently he took this as a sign that she would yield to him. Whether she would have or not under other circumstances she didn't know, but when she looked up and saw that he was undressing, his lack of courtship, his hasty, blunt assumption, irritated her so much that she left his apartment at once and would not talk with him about the incident, even when he next came to the house, except to tell him that she was through seeing him.

But within a month she longed to see him again. She missed his gentle comments and his doelike, mournful manner. She found herself, too, thinking with longing about the dark room in which she had waited quietly, and of the bed on which she might have found with him some satisfaction for the questions which troubled her, and some relief from the emotions which were increasing inside her. Sometimes at night her thoughts would excite her, and her longing would threaten her and grow inside her like a hungry plant, and she would fret on the edge of sleep, then would fall asleep and dream erotically, and would wake up tired, weary to death but satisfied, though still unknowing, wondering.

But the dreams were not of Morris. Only one of them was of Paul, and it shamed her to think back on it. The dreams most often were of a handsome man of strong arms whom she had not met in real life, who took her to himself and whispered to her and made her feel important to him. To him she gave herself, unashamedly she gave herself, and the movements of her body on her bed as she loved him warmed her.

Such dreams came more often. She sought them and feared them. She told herself she should marry Morris and be done with it, that she would find with him satisfaction, she would find relief from this ever-present tension. With any man she would, she told herself. She said to herself that she was getting too old to dream like an eighteen-year-old girl anyway, that she should sever herself from the fairy tales she had heard as a girl, that there was to be no handsome knight to come to the room where she was sleeping and run his hand through her long soft hair, there was to be no gentle kiss, no soft touch at her throat, no slow untying of the bodice of her gown, that she must accept as true and so, a fact as sure as ice and rain, that the world was hard and for her offered no heroes, but only Paul in a room across the hall, a deep-feeling man but one not fully accountable and one who had little patience with niceties and politeness, and Morris Kraft, a patient and kind person who loved her with a passion he could all too easily control. She would be denied, she assured herself, the privilege of loving anybody to the extent that control of her own actions would be lost to her, for love in her world would not sweep her out of the reality of a Monday, Tuesday, Wednesday.

She told herself this, but she did not believe it. The longing for the gentle knight was more beautiful and soul-feeding than the coldness of her house. She didn't believe it, and she looked forward to the arrival of Collins with a longing which closer and closer brought her to anxiety. What would he look like now? What would she look like to him? What would he say to her? What would she think of to say to him?

He had sometimes embraced her, she remembered. She had been twelve and he seventeen. He had pecked kisses on her cheek and laughed at her shyness, and once or twice had held her close in fondness.

Then he had left. At twenty-one he had come home again, and she at sixteen had thought him grand and handsome. But within a month he was gone and her heart broke for longing. He had left a note for Lotti on the dining-room table. Beth couldn't read it, couldn't bear to think of it. She had seen it lying there, open, and through the paper on which the lines were written Collins had stuck the stem of a single flower.

All the stories told about Collins, his experiences on the farm and in town, were not true, Paul insisted, and since the stories grew in number as Matthew and Kin thought up new ones to plague him with, he found himself spending the dinner hour each day refuting them. "Collins was thirteen when we left the country for town," he stormed out at one meal, "and you people act like he was sleeping with every farm woman in Buncombe County."

Lotti blushed, as she always did when intimate matters were discussed. "Well, you'll have to admit, the girls in town and country both all did like Collins."

Paul cursed in agony.

He and Collins had fought since Collins had been big enough to walk across the room to strike him. Collins had taken a dislike to him in the crib, so far as Paul could determine. And he had to admit to himself that he had taken a dislike to Collins the moment he heard that he was born. It was a strong animosity, nourished in jealousy, for the love his mother had once given him went entirely to the new child. His father had shown no interest in either boy until both were able to talk with him. Cal was interested in conversation, but wasn't much caught up by baby talk, and he hadn't fondled and played with his babies an average of half an hour apiece. So Paul had been left alone to toddle around the droughty farmhouse and around the farmyard, fending for himself, stepping in chicken manure and sitting down in it while trying to get it off his feet, falling into the cold creek and getting out by himself, hoping always for help, seeking someone to help him, and failing to find help because of Collins. He had hated Collins with such passion that once on finding a dead wildcat in the woods, one which his father or another hunter and shot through the head, Paul had stomped the cat and beat it and poked it with sticks, telling himself all the while that

93

this was what he would someday do to Collins. He had worked himself up to such a passion with his kicking and punching and sticking of the body of the animal that he had quite lost control of his senses.

From that time—he was eleven years old then—his hatred of Collins had been tempered by his fear of that hatred. The hatred had come so close to overcoming him that he, from that moment of excess, drew fearfully inside himself whenever he considered Collins. He held himself back, permitting himself only slight pleasure, partaking slowly, bit by bit, of his hatred of the younger boy, never releasing himself again to the full fury of his passions; it was almost as if he had been defeated by Collins, as if his hatred had grown so great he could no longer trust himself with it.

It was not made more gentle by the fact that Collins came to ignore him. Rarely did Collins utter even a contemptuous word of Paul. Collins was so handsome, so well formed, and life came to him with such ease that he assumed command of his older brother evidently without intent or serious consideration. He commanded not because he sought command but because he was a person to whom command came naturally. And Paul found himself looking to his younger brother, four years his junior, for permission and help, even when Paul knew more than Collins did about the work on the farm. Grave and serious and withdrawn, Paul looked at those around him from behind the wall of his damaged feelings, while Collins was open and free with everybody.

When Collins, at fifteen, ran away from home, Paul took it as the first kind service God and the other powers had arranged for him in his life. When Collins was found two weeks later and brought back, Paul became ill. The doctor said he had a "stomach croup."

Collins left again at seventeen, but when he came home for the visit four years later, Paul's sense of personal security was shattered again.

Collins left once more. Gradually Paul permitted himself to believe it; then even to believe that Collins this time would not come back at all. A year passed. Two years. Paul began to dare to be himself.

Whenever a letter from Collins arrived, Paul would study it closely for any clue as to Collins's intentions; the farther away Collins was, the better Paul felt. The only time he ever went to the Asheville public library was to find out just how far it was from Asheville to San Francisco.

And now Collins was on the train coming home again.

On the Thursday when Collins was to arrive, Kin asked his father at breakfast if he could go with him to meet Collins at the station. Cal grunted and avoided the question, and cast a worried look toward Paul, who was glowering at his food.

"You go along and get him," Cal said finally.

"You're not going?" Kin asked.

Cal fretted about it. He studied Paul again, then shook his head. "I'll stay at the store," he said.

Paul smiled, a grim, small smile. "Nobody should go," he said, "if you ask me. Run off from home. Never let anybody know where he was or where he was going. Come back like he's somebody." Irritably he ran a hand over his face. "You'll find he's been starving to death most likely and now wants a decent meal from those of us who've been left here to work."

Kin left the house right after breakfast and walked up King Street. He told several of the shopkeepers that there was going to be a fine surprise on King Street that afternoon. When he told Mr. Everett Fitzpatrick, who ran a clothing shop, that Collins was coming home, the old Irishman let out a giggle and ran to his cash register to see how much money he had. "Wealth'll be flowin' before long with him in town."

Kin reached the Square, where workmen were putting in a water fountain for lilies and goldfish, and he wanted to tell even them that his big brother was coming home. He saw Dr. LeClair and hurried across the street to tell him.

LeClair rocked up on his toes, then back on his heels and thought about it, a big grin coming over his face. "Would you think of that?" he said. "I remember, I remember."

There was such fondness in his voice that Kin glowed with good feeling.

"I made the rounds with him one night, and before I knowed it, I was young again. He had found two strong women, and I weren't too old back then." He grinned slyly at Kin, and winked. "I'm not too old today, either, though I won't tell you what my age is. You can try to guess it, though, if you want to."

"Sixty-one," Kin said.

"Sixty-one, you say? Well, that's right," LeClair said, surprised, "you guessed it." He winked at Kin again. "But I have my powers yet, though they don't get overused much for the lack of chances." He laughed low and sniffed of the spring air, which was light and carried a hint of flowers. "Did, uh, did Collins ever pay your pa back all that money he took from him to run away from home?"

"Collins? Stole money?"

"Stole it clean out. When he left—that was when he was a boy— he took all the cash money your pa had, and when the government brought him back to town, he had done spent four hundred dollars of it."

"How did he get it?"

"He knew where your pa hid his money in the house. I don't know where. The next time he left home he was still a young fellow, and he just took half your pa's money, took about two thousand dollars in cash."

Kin stared openmouthed at the doctor.

"But he doubtless paid it back when he returned a while later for a visit, for he had it to pay, I'll tell you that. He had a diamond ring on his hand worth ever bit that much. Did you ever see your brother take a hand in a poker game?"

"No, sir." Kin was wrapped up in his attention. There were a thousand wonders to Collins King.

"He gets to talking so high and fine that a man might get to betting all he owns. I seen a poker game at the Battery Park Hotel going along with four, five dollars being put down for a hand, and Collins come in. First thing you knowed, the game had upped itself and some of those rich men were damn near mortgaging themselves. Collins thinks big; there's just nothing small about him. And the people losing their money seemed to be all glad to meet him."

Shortly after ten o'clock, Kin took the streetcar at the Square and rode down Patton Avenue past the fancy stores where the nicely dressed women and the suit-clothed men shopped and worked. The wheels rolling on the track seemed to say "Collins, Collins." And he thought, Collins with the soul of gold, coming home. Coming home. Coming home.

The streetcar turned left at the foot of Patton Avenue and slid and scraped its way down the steep hill to the river. Kin thought about what he would say to Collins when he met him. After the greeting he would tell him about Paul, then tell him that Matthew had run away from home and come back, and that he wasn't doing well and was spending too much time up the street of a night. He would tell him about the angel boy and his mother's hopes and the way she excluded everybody else from her affection. And about his father's problems with the depression and the family, and about how Paul was trying to take control of everything. He would tell him about Beth and Morris Kraft. He would pour the chronicle of the family's recent struggle into the sympathetic ears of the big man, the powerful Collins King.

Think of it, Kin thought, he had just mailed a letter to Collins King, San Francisco, California, and it had been delivered months later when Collins had returned there. And Collins had been wise in his reply not even to mention Kin's letter. Collins had been all over the country; he knew how to do things.

The car came to a halt at the foot of the Patton Avenue hill, and Kin asked the conductor, a sour-faced man who had long since grown tired of streetcar tending, where the train station was.

"You get off here and walk down to the station, or you transfer to the Valley line."

Kin had ridden the streetcar only once before; he and Beth had ridden up and down Patton Avenue, sightseeing, peering at the buildings, especially at the Battery Park Hotel, which looked down on the more common world from its high site. They had ridden up and down the avenue a time or two, and had ridden down the hill and back once, noticing the wonders of colored town. But he knew nothing about streetcars or how to transfer to the valley cars, so he got off and set to walking toward the station, which he decided must be the big brick building about a quarter of a mile away, the one which had a dome on it.

He stopped only once, and that was at a hand laundry where he saw one of the long dogs like Miss Martingale had, a dachshund, though he didn't know what the breed was called. Its legs were so short that he couldn't see how it could scratch fleas on most of itself. He patted the dog's head and talked to it, and a man in shirt sleeves came to the door of the shop and proudly watched them.

"One of my teachers had one of these sausage dogs," Kin said.

"That so?"

Kin patted the dog until the man took it inside to feed it, then he hurried on. He had seen Miss Martingale with her dog two or three times up on the Square. Probably that was all Miss Martingale had to keep her company at home, a little sausage dog.

He had regretted graduating from her class. It wasn't just leaving her; in fact, he had been so loaded down with work he sighed with relief to be gone. But he had been separated from a girl he liked. She had sat right beside him in that class. "Mary Lou," he said, whispering her name to himself. He often spoke her name, and sometimes at night he dreamed about her, or, as was true more often, he would lie on the cot and think about her. And the life force would rise in him and he would feel guilty, especially when he thought of Mary Lou naked. He would often promise God not to think about her any more, for he knew it wasn't right to think about Mary Lou like that. With the girls in the houses up the street, maybe it wasn't wrong no matter what one thought—at least, he had heard men say that one could do whatever he pleased with them. This made them all the less appealing to Kin, who wasn't too clear about any single action one might take with them, much less a variety, and who preferred to think of being with somebody equally modest or unknowing.

He preferred to think about Mary Lou, and his body would react in ready anticipation. He never even told Beth about it. He started to tell her once, but Beth probably guessed what he was going to say and became flustered. She didn't want to hear about it, he guessed.

A streetcar passed going north, away from the station. He would have had to wait all that time for it, so it was a good thing he had walked. He had to hurry to get to the station and meet Collins. Like a knight in armor, Collins was coming home. Now let Paul find his proper place. Let the smile come back to his father. Let the country people take hope. Collins King was home.

Kin approached the towering brick wall of the station house. Think of men building that; he could scarcely consider it. Brick on brick. And two feet thick in the walls. A million bricks, maybe. A church for the railroad, that's what it was, built by businessmen who worshipped the rolling trains.

He stood beneath the great tiled dome and stared up at it. The waiting-room seats, set in three formal rows, were of polished oak and their bases were of marble. Two neatly dressed clerks waited behind gleaming counters, ready to be of service, even though not a customer was in the building at the moment. About the room was a hush and the smell of smoke; it was a place of worship, all right.

"Is the train from the West on time?" Kin asked.

"It might nigh is," the taller of the two clerks said. "It'll be along by twelve-thirty."

"What time is it now?"

"Not quite eleven."

Kin sat down on one of the benches and wondered how in the world he was going to wait more than an hour and a half. He had been so anxious to meet Collins that he had got to the station way ahead of time. Of course, he guessed it was just as well to wait here as at the store or the Square, though his excitement had reached such a peak he didn't see how he could wait all that time anywhere.

Huge doors opened from the station house onto the platform, where the trains rolled in. He went out there and peered up the sets of track.

"Hello, young King," a big Negro porter said. Another porter stood nearby, a smaller, square-shouldered man of forty-five.

"How are you, Seth?" Kin said. He knew the big porter's name, for he had once worked on King Street and for a few days had worked in the store, helping unload for the farmers.

"What do you think about all this here de-pression, young Mr. King?"

Kin shook his head. "It's nothing that started on King Street," he said, quoting his father.

Both Negroes laughed and nodded appreciatively. Kin peered off toward the west, wondering if the train were in North Carolina yet or if it were still rolling through Tennessee. "Does it get held up much by the mountains?" he asked Seth.

"No, not coming from that way. It's a slow rise alongside the river. But from the other way, it comes up hard out of the hill country. They lost a lot o' men buildin' it to the east."

"Lost them?" Kin said.

"Yes, they had to blast out a path right up the mountainside, and loop it around to get as near a level bed as they could, and make tunnels. And the rocks fell on 'em, and the slides come and buried 'em, and the dynamite blew them up, and the illness laid them by, and in one field out there near the crest they buried four hundred men who died of sickness."

"I never heard about it before," Kin said wonderingly. "I read in a book about the man who designed it all, though."

"Yes, suh," Seth said softly.

There was something lurking behind the words, Kin felt, something not yet said, which maybe Seth was afraid to say. Kin looked up at the tall, broad-shouldered man. "Who did all that work, Seth?" he asked.

Seth stared out at the black and dreary train yard. The other Negro turned away, as if to disassociate himself from him. Seth kept looking straight out, and then he said, quietly, as if the thought were his own and he didn't seek to share it, quietly to himself he said, "Didn't you know it was the niggers that built the railroad?"

Kin guessed he would wake up years later and lie in bed wondering what he had heard in his sleep and would remember what he had heard so softly said, so cautiously uttered by a man lonely in his pride, afraid even to claim credit for work done, and in the words he would sense then, as he did now, the existence of an unwritten history, carried one man to another, here and there, stories of the hard work done but not recorded except in the work itself, of brick on brick, rail on rail, of heavy ties falling into place, and of the graves of the dead. The words were the lonely utterance of workers who had heard, for somebody had told them; yes, out of the past they had heard of the clearing and cutting and of black-skinned men and their watery white sweat, of brutal toil of a daylong and troubled sleep of a night, of animal work and a foreman with a callous will, and of wood and leather and rock and clay and making a roadbed through the hills with picks and shovels and oxen, they and the foreman and death. With pride only of a night, stolen for themselves and repeated while the children listened, black men saying to their young, "Listen to what I tell you: it was the niggers that built the railroad."

Kin walked on down to the roundhouse, a brick building with a giant steel turntable in the center. An engine was being rolled from the turntable onto one of the sets of track which radiated outward from it like spokes of a wheel. White mechanics worked on the engines, repairing and cleaning and oiling, and all the time there was the racket of the place, echoing in the covered building. Two of the engines were steaming from their run up the mountains.

He was back at the station house by twelve-fifteen. At twelve-twenty, he went to the platform and looked anxiously up the track, but he saw not a single wisp of smoke. At twelve-thirty he came back inside, and the tall clerk assured him that the train had passed Marshall on schedule and would be into the yard directly.

He went back to the platform and sat down on the edge of it, but he got up so that he could see the train better. He went down the platform to where Seth was standing. "Is it coming?" he asked him.

Seth smiled. "Can't you feel it?"

"No, I don't feel it."

"The ground shakes with it, it quivers some. You don't feel it?"

"No."

"You will when it gets this side the bridge. The air feels it, too, as well as the ground. Can't you feel it yet?"

Kin shook his head. "I can almost feel it."

"It's in your bones you feel it. It's not in your head. It hits your bones."

"I think I feel it."

"The whole valley wakes up to it. It comes in like that. It moves the rocks and the air, you see. It rushes in like that and it gets to you."

"There she comes," the other Negro said.

Kin strained to see. His body was alive to the arrival of the train.

"Makes you proud when you see it," Seth said.

Kin saw her then. Out of the northwest she came, rushing against the body of the wind, smoke rising from her funnels and a blast of steam. She sounded a cry as she challenged the first crossing and rolled across the river bridge, clanging on the tracks, a black giant trailing a gray plume. All the way from California, he thought. All the way from where the gold miners once were and along the trails the wagon trains left, from St. Louis and Denver and other towns of the far-flung land. There she was, shiny and gasping and bolting, twin-engined now, making her unchallenged way.

The engineer leaned out of the first engine. "Get back," he called to Kin, "stand back, I say."

But Kin stood close. The pistons swept near him, clanging sound against him, their hammering roared in him, and the engineer grinned and shook his head, for he knew how it had been for him years ago when he had watched the trains come in.

The brakes swished heavily. Steam poured from the engine, as if it were bleeding steam from open wounds. Porters raced toward her from the station house. The clerks came to the windows. Passengers rose from the oak seats and moved expectantly to the open doorways.

Passengers aboard the train looked out with prideful indifference at the people watching.

Porters opened the car doors and lowered the steps. "Asheville," Seth called proudly.

"Asheville," another porter called.

All the way from California, Kin thought. All the way to Asheville.

Several passengers got off. Kin scanned their faces. There were three or four young men among them, and he picked out the best-dressed one and rushed up to him. "Collins?"

The man shook his head and bobbed away.

Kin turned to another man. The man shook his head.

A third man, not well dressed, a poor man, stopped and looked at Kin. "Collins?" Kin said slowly.

The man frowned. "Who'd you say?" Then he turned and went on into the station house.

Where is he, Kin thought. Where is he?

He turned to the station house and went inside the big room. People were greeting one another, or hustling toward the train, following porters.

He went back to the platform. A porter swung off the train just then, and Kin started toward him, but the porter turned away. "Right this way, suh," he said to somebody following him. "Yes, suh, Asheville, that's your stop."

A passenger stepped down from the train, and Kin's breath caught in his throat. He was a big man, about six feet tall, slender, and he wore a Western hat, a Western coat, and a black string tie. He was a powerful man and his lips were fixed in a smile, a questioning sort of tentative smile as if he weren't sure but that any minute he would laugh. His shoes were dark brown and brightly polished, his shirt was white silk. And his eyes were the eyes of the Kings.

Kin wanted to sink down on the platform, he was so relieved and glad, so sure now of the goodness of his deeds.

The porter ran on ahead. "I'll get your bags, suh, yes, suh," he called back. The big man started after him.

"Collins," Kin said, but his voice was hoarse and not much sound came out. "Collins," he said, but still not loud enough, for Collins was entering the station house already and Kin had to run to catch up.

"Right here, suh," the porter said, setting down two yellow solid-leather bags, both bulging with goods. Collins handed him a bill.

"Yes, suh, yes, suh—"

"Collins," Kin said.

The big man turned. The blue eyes were a deep blue now. The smile on his face wrinkled and opened. "Yes, sir?" he said.

"I'm Kin."

"Kin? Kin o' me?"

"I'm your brother. I wrote you."

"Did you? You the one named Johnny?"

"I once was."

"Once was, you say?" He laughed. "Well, Kin, where's Papa?"

"Up at the store."

The smile slowly faded from his face and something close to anger rested there. Then he nodded, ever so slightly. "I thought he might come to meet me." He shrugged his shoulders. "Well, let's go see the big town."

Kin rushed to pick up one of the suitcases, but Collins got them both. Kin ran to the door to open it, proud to bursting. People were looking at Collins. The clerks behind the counter were staring at him, as if they were glad to see him stopping at the Asheville depot. Just as Kin's father had said, everybody seemed to know him, even though they might not know his name. He carried the air of the world with him—the whole wide world.

"We—got to take a streetcar," Kin said, panting.

"Where do we catch it?"

"We wait for one, and it'll take us down three blocks to the switching place, where we change over to one going up the hill."

"We can walk to that one, can't we? Stretch our legs. I've been on that train for four days and nights, rolling on, state after state. I tell you, it was a roaring thing."

"Yes, I saw it come in."

"It climbed through the Rockies with a bellow and a puff. It come across Wyoming and the flatlands of Kansas." He started walking along the cobblestones, Kin running behind him. Kin remembered all the things he had decided to tell Collins, but he knew he wasn't going to tell him now. There was no need. Collins knew. Collins knew everything.

They left the sidewalk and walked in the street. Soon they were out in the middle of the street, walking down the center of the street-car tracks, Collins carrying his heavy bags as if they weighed nothing.

"Collins," Kin said, panting, for they were moving fast.

"Yes, sir, kin o' mine?"

"Why we walking down the middle of the street? They have a sidewalk over there."

"Have they?" Collins smiled again, and it warmed Kin and pleased him wonderfully. "I've always liked the wide road," Collins said.

PART TWO

8

THAT NIGHT AT SUPPER KIN ATE MORE THAN HE HAD
ever eaten at a meal in his life. Usually at night the family didn't
have freshly cooked food; they ate what was left over from dinner,
but the women knew just by looking at Collins that he wouldn't be
satisfied with corn bread, milk, and beans. So Beth and Lotti set to
work baking two six-and-a-half-pound hens, making dumplings and
dressing, opening jars of canned vegetables and fruit. There was food
for everybody, and talk.

"Come through sleet in Kansas, thick as window glass, and the
wheels slid on the tracks. Come down rain for thirty hours out on
the plains. When we come into a station the porters would be hugging
themselves under their black capes, their black faces sticking out and
nothing showing except their eyes and white teeth, and the yellow
lights behind them in the station house. The country passed like
the flat of a man's hand, then rose in the hill country, with trees and
creeks and curving dirt roads into the farmlands; and the train kept
coming, never giving out of land to pass through. I tell you, nothing's
as great as this country."

"That's right," Cal said. He had always been proud of America, though he had not seen much of it. He watched Collins with pride as he talked and ate. Only Paul was resentful and wary.

"Passed by telephone lines and telegraph lines, with the poles straight and pointing upward, and the lonesome cattle on so many acres that never could a million men eat all that beef. I saw a forest fire that covered a county, the trees going up to heaven, and I thought what a loss, but this country can stand a thousand more fires like that one and not make a difference in a board or plank."

"Yes," Cal said. "Yes, that's so."

"Plenty. That's what we've got here. Plenty and power. Who talks about a depression in a country as great as this one?"

Cal grinned and peered around at his other boys, and at Lotti, who was listening, fascinated by the words of her next to oldest. And Beth stood in the doorway, ready to bring more food when it was needed, her eyes on Collins.

"The people are strong, have you noticed that? And the women are so pretty I wanted to get off the train at every mile of track. Handsome, strong people, that's what we've got here."

Kin had never heard such wonderful talk. It was a marvel just to see Collins sitting there at the table, wiping his mouth with his napkin and cutting big pieces off a hen and stuffing them down, pouring steaming gravy on hot dressing, and staring at Beth as she came in and out of the room, his eyes roving over her, then to his father and to Paul and his mother. He seemed to want to know and devour everything that came in sight.

"Mama Lotti," he said, "Mama, you're prettier than you were when I last left home. You're getting younger, Mama."

"Lord a' mercy, listen to that, would you?" Lotti said, almost beyond herself with pleasure.

"Look at the pink in her cheeks, Papa. How old are you now, Mama—thirty-eight?"

"Lord," she said, breaking into a laugh. "Thirty-eight! Listen to him!"

"Did I guess it wrong?" He sopped a biscuit in gravy. "Look just like a fresh young girl in California to me, Mama. Why, you were looking middle-aged last time I saw you, but now seems like you're slipping back to being a young thing again."

Lotti peered at the other members of her family, unable to conceal her fine feelings.

"Well, there's no better mama at any age. Nobody deserves her youth more than Mama Lotti. I tell you, nobody ever said how fine a mother she's been to me."

Kin was embarrassed, and so was Paul, who was almost as flushed as his mother, and Cal King and Matthew glanced at one another and tended to their eating. Collins hacked off another quarter of a pound of chicken and slid it onto his plate. "Never heard her complain about being put upon. Never heard her complain about her work, did you, Papa?"

Cal cleared his throat self-consciously. "Can't say as I have." He glanced uncomfortably at Collins.

"Just like the old song, 'My Mother Is Like the Flower That Blooms by the Garden There.'" He grinned at Lotti.

"Well, I never claimed to be all that," she said, beaming. "I declare, Collins, there's no accounting for the way you talk."

"You remember that song, Matthew—'Mother Is Like a Flower?'"

Matthew grinned from ear to ear. "I've heard it."

For a second it looked as if Collins would break out with the lyrics. "Got a fine batch of children here, Mama. You and Papa ought to be proud. And I'm not speaking of myself, either. But your boy Paul here—"

Paul strangled on a bite of food.

"He's the oldest and I'll bet he's the best. Look at the fine figure on that man, and the sharp cut of his features. Look at that head of hair. You see those gray eyes? Have you ever seen their match? Why, any parent would be proud to have Paul sitting at the table. And Matthew here cuts a handsome figure, got spice to his manner. Can't tell me he won't go far. And Kin, bright boy. You can look at Kin's face and tell he's got big plans going for him. You've got three winners right here at the table, Papa."

Cal wiped his mouth with the back of his hand and cleared his throat. "I think so," he said.

"And Beth, look at her standing there at the doorway, pretty as a picture of a maiden in the springtime with a rosebud in her hair waiting for her lover to come up the path—"

Beth's eyes widened and her face got red.

"Perfect family," Collins declared, pulling off a chicken wing and sucking on it. "Brothers and cousins and parents. And Papa here, always the quiet one. But he knows. He knows everything that goes on, keeping an eye out, knowing how to speak sharply but kindly, and for the good of all. And look at the provisions on this table. Prosperity, in a time of hunger, some say. That's this country!"

Boy, he could talk, he could go, and Kin could hardly keep up with him just listening. The idea of anybody saying all those things! Kin blinked up at Beth proudly. She was staring at Collins as if she had never seen a man before in her life. Kin wanted to reach out himself and put his arm around Collins. He was the finest man he had ever seen.

"Well, I tell you what I think," Lotti said, flushed with pride and overwrought. "We don't all count our blessings enough. It's not right to let what God gives us go by without thanksgiving for it."

"That's right, Mama," Collins said.

"We get to biting at one another, not trusting one another."

"You're saying it right, Mama."

"We don't count our blessings near enough. Don't see the blue for the clouds."

"I believe it."

"But you always was one of the best, Collins."

"Now, Mama," Collins said, swallowing a mouthful of dressing, "don't tell me about myself."

"You were a fine boy, my best boy, in many ways, though you was a prize one for devilment. And you left me when you wasn't hardly full grown—"

"I know it, Mama, but I just had a hot mind back then."

"Went traipsing away, and nobody knowed where you was."

"I didn't go far, Mama, without thinking of you and Papa, and my brothers and little Beth there, so pretty—"

"Well, you was a prize and I know it," Lotti said, "but now you listen to me. There's somebody I want to show you, and I think you'll appreciate him as much as I do." She pushed back her chair.

"Where you going, Mama Lotti?" Collins asked, surprised. "We haven't finished eating, have we?"

"I have somebody to show you." She left through the kitchen, and the family knew where she was going. The angel boy. She was going to get him. Collins hadn't seen him, hadn't even heard about him, most likely, for he had fooled around up the street all afternoon, telling stories about new farming methods he had heard about in Arkansas and a woman who had a forty-six-inch bust in New Mexico.

"Where's she going?" Collins asked his father.

Cal cleared his throat and tried to decide how best to approach the answer, but before he got started, he heard Lotti coming back. She came in, the boy with her. His curly hair fell to his shoulders, and he was dressed in a blue suit with flowers on it. He was as pretty as a painting, the last word in boys on this earth.

"Well, who's this?" Collins asked, beaming.

The little fellow stood as straight as a soldier, looking at Collins with big, trustful eyes.

"He's John," Lotti said.

"You say he is? You one of the neighbor's little children, are you?"

"He's mine," Lotti said. "He's your new brother."

Collins froze. Even the smile on his face stuck in place. Everybody was quiet and still and watchful as they waited for his reaction, and no doubt Collins knew this, but he had no sure reaction at hand. He looked up at his mother, then at his father, who was busy folding his handkerchief and awkwardly stuffing it into his pocket. Slowly he turned back to Johnny. "Well, you're a fine little boy," he said.

Paul, who was irritated aplenty, reached halfway across the table and got the coffeepot. He poured himself a steaming cupful and dumped a tablespoonful of sugar in it. Beth stood in the kitchen doorway, drying her hands on her apron and watching worriedly.

113

"Ain't he a beauty?" Lotti asked, running her hands through his silky hair.

Collins nodded dumbly. Then a grin opened on his face and a chuckle started far down in his throat. "Well, it sure gives me hope," he said, peering about at the brothers. "Don't it give you hope, boys?"

Matthew laughed raucously.

Collins grinned at Beth, then at his father, then back at the little boy. He held out his hand to him, but Johnny stood back, pressing against his mother's legs. Collins reached out and caught his arm, brought him to him.

But the little boy pulled away, almost violently. Collins blinked in surprise.

"He stays off to himself mostly," Lotti said.

"I see he does." Collins winked at the boy, who was staring back at him. "Oh, I'll bring you a stick o' candy," he sang softly, "next time I go to town." He stopped, because he wasn't getting any reaction at all, except the steady stare from the beautiful little face. "You don't like candy, boy?"

"I give him quite a bit in his room," Lotti said.

"Uh-huh," Collins said, glancing uneasily toward his father. He cleared his throat and leaned back in the chair. "Sure is a fine surprise, Mama Lotti," he said. "That's as fine a boy as I ever saw."

Lotti knelt down and took Johnny in her arms, squeezed him ever so tightly, and he responded not at all. His little hands were clenched and his eyes stayed on Collins.

Collins shifted uneasily in his chair. "Yes, he's all right. I can see that." He looked questioningly at Beth, who was peering suspiciously at the child.

Paul, irritated to the limit of his patience, suddenly pushed back his chair. "Mama, get that angel boy out of here."

Lotti swung toward him with a fury. "After all was so content and polite tonight, you have to blurt out, do you? Don't you be telling me what to do again, and don't you refer to him no more in those tones, or by that name, either. Who do you think you are around here, anyway? I've heard from you till I'm sick of it, so you understand me! I'm tired of looking at you, hearing from you! Get out and get a woman and marry and start a business of your own, instead of stealing your father's!"

Paul was aghast. Kin felt magnificent elation; he wanted to shout out. Cal stared at his plate, all the blood gone from his face.

Lotti stood before Paul, her fists clenched and with not a sign of fear. Then suddenly she grabbed Johnny's arm and rushed out with him.

"Ah-h-h," Paul said, a moan, seeking words for his stunned hurt. "Ah-h-h, did you—hear that?" He appealed to the family. "Ah, lord. Turned on me like that. My own mother." He was floundering, agonized to the edge of his senses.

Collins shook his head sadly. "It's a shame," he said. He mixed gravy with a new helping of dressing, filled up his coffee mug, and drained it. Beth, anxious to leave the room to collect her thoughts, took the coffeepot out to the kitchen to refill it.

Paul pushed back his chair from the table but kept his seat. His mouth was open, as if he had forgotten to close it. "My own mother," he said. "Well, what is there left, when your own mother . . ." He stared at the table, at the bleeding remains of the food.

"Beth, did you hear what Mama Lotti said to Paul?" Collins asked her as she came back into the room. "She really spoke out, said her piece. It's too bad, Paul."

"My own mama." Paul was stung deeply, all right. He wasn't even listening to Collins or noticing Beth's concern, though she'd come over to stand next to his chair. He didn't notice anybody. He sat there on the edge of the chair, his mouth open.

"Now, I—suppose we're done in here," Cal said uneasily. "Let's go out on the porch."

He started to get up, but Paul suddenly said, "No, we can set in here and talk business."

Cal clouded over like a storm and almost blurted out at him. But he restrained himself and sat back down.

Collins cleared his throat. "Beth, this has been fine. You must have come from heaven to this house, Beth."

Paul said, "Kin, you get out of here, so we can talk to Collins, see what he's come home for. Go on."

Kin kept his seat.

"Kin," Paul said, warning him.

Kin sat there, his gaze on the empty, dirty plate before him, where the broken half of a breastbone remained. Beth suddenly took his arm and ushered him into the kitchen and closed the door.

"Did you see that girl move, did you?" they heard Collins say. "Spunk."

"Beth's all right," they heard Cal say. Then the voices dropped and they couldn't make out what was being said.

Beth started working the pump handle at the sink. "You're not grown yet, did you think you were? No use of you sitting in there with them, a boy fifteen. I'm glad you don't have to."

"You had no business pulling me out of there like that," he said, his feelings hurt. "You sprained my shoulder blade."

"I would have pulled you out by your hair if you'd planned to sit in there and take part."

They heard Paul's voice rise in anger. "I'm the one who saved the store through this depression. Papa would have give it away to the beggars, like he did all his land and money. I'm the one who has kept it going. I don't expect thanks for it, but I don't want blame, neither. And where were you, Collins, while this was going on—out whoring around with the Eskimos! Now you come in here asking about how the store's doing and how much profit it's made and who owns the store. What the hell business is it of yours?"

Beth grasped Kin's arm and pulled him onto the back porch and closed the kitchen door. "You shouldn't hear all that," she said breathlessly.

But they could still hear Paul when he spoke. He was loud and unrelenting. "If Papa wants to give me twenty per cent of the store, or forty per cent of the store, it would be only fair for the work I've done. I have a right to forty or fifty per cent right now for saving the store. I've sweated and—"

This voice rose still higher, until suddenly there was a shout and

116

a window shattered. Beth ran back into the kitchen and threw open the dining-room door. Kin rushed in after her.

Paul, white-faced, was standing at his place at the table, looking toward the open hallway door and rubbing one side of his face, where a swelling was already forming. "He's come back to get me, Papa," he said.

Matthew had pressed himself back into one corner. Collins had left the room.

"You've got to help me, Papa," Paul said. "He always has been out to get me since he was born. You know that."

The window behind Paul had been broken and the bottom half of a chair was caught in the splintered frame. It was Collins' chair. Collins had thrown it at him.

"Papa, you and me have got to work the store problem out together, see the tail end of this depression through together, just as in the past." Paul was trembling. "I won't have him down there, snooping around in my business, looking over my shoulder at every move." Paul looked piteously at his father. "You've got to help me, Papa."

"I try to help all my children," Cal said.

Paul slammed his hand on the table. "That's no answer. You hear me? That's no answer. I need help and you talk easy." He slammed his hand down again and a plate bounced to the floor. "He comes home to get me, and all of you kill the fatted calf for him. Never did the same for those who stood loyal to the family and the store. You've strung up a feast for him. You cook fat hens for Collins. You've cooked and made welcome for him." He stumbled almost blindly to the door, but turned once more to face them, sweat on his face, his eyes glazed over, not seeing them clearly for the sweat and the despair and anguish. "You've all done it, ever one of you is guilty!"

Just then, out on the porch, Collins laughed, and Paul stopped in place, and everybody stood still and quiet as the laughter rolled through the house. Then they heard his deep voice, still chuckling, say, "No, Mama Lotti. It's on the lower part of their belly that they got the pouch."

9

COLLINS HAD HIS SERIOUS MOMENTS. IN FACT, ALL OF Collins' moments were serious, in that each one was intense. He was always involved in getting all he could out of life and never ceased to be astonished by what he discovered. To the worrier who maintained that life wasn't worth living, he offered no argument because he couldn't accept the premise seriously. Evil there was in the world, and suffering, he didn't deny that, but those who dwelled on such considerations seemed to him to be part of the problem they were analyzing. Death existed, he knew, but those who had a fear of it so pitiful and powerful that it marred their lives were playing Death's part in the play. The fear he had of life was not that it would someday be taken away from him but that he would not make the most out of it while he could, and all arguments which underscored the heavy aspects of life seemed frivolous to him in that they were needless and pointless. To Collins important considerations revolved around the laughter of somebody; how he liked good laughter! And women, any woman; evidently he loved all women. And earthy stories; they fed his exuberance, and when he told them, he occupied himself completely, building for the approaching moment of wit, when he would roar with pleasure. Haw, haw, haw, he would laugh, holding his arms out as if opening himself to the wonders of the story and to all around him. Haw, haw, haw.

He was not a student of philosophy. He had no use for thoughts about thoughts. He had no interest in gaining perspective on the foibles of nations or the development of the human race. He lived from day to day, triumphantly he was alive. And since the moment was so important, and since action was the vehicle and substance of his life, his life took on the nature of his surroundings. If he found himself in a distressing situation which he could not correct and could not escape, his whole being would suffer dreadfully. He had been frustrated even on the train coming east, simply because the direction seemed to him to be wrong. By going east, he seemed to be going backward. The buildings were older at the depots, there was more smoke, more heat blistering around the smokestacks of the factories, less expectancy as the porters announced the towns they were approaching. Every mile of track and every place had come to be examined so many times that proof beyond doubt existed that no miracle was to be found ahead, no strange shape or object. Each mile the train rolled made new discovery less and less likely, and sameness more and more routine.

How much better was the booming West, he felt, for the West was the unknown and the new and the just starting, a place of imagination where no idea was too different, no plan beyond consideration; in the West life was lived high and with vigor. Traveling through the West renewed Collins, for the open unused land cried out its need for people and development. On the first day of his trip east he had sat at his drawing-room window, his feet up on the footstool, and had scanned the passing marvels of the great California valley and the scraggly mountains of the High Sierras. It was all vital and exhilarating to him. Only one place in all that country ever gave him a moment of distress—Donner Pass, in the High Sierras, a spot of death where the first pioneers were snowbound for a winter and died most horribly. He had read about it; he had talked to Californians about it. There was a death home for people of the pioneer spirit, the spirit Collins loved. Whenever his train moved upward through the tunnels and crept across that pass, he would feel a shudder of death remembered. But there only, one place only in the West, the golden land.

The depression of the eastbound journey lifted somewhat as his train entered Newport, Tennessee, and moved along the main street of town, stopping momentarily for a few passengers, then entered the narrow French Broad River valley. The train rolled alongside the gushing, foamy waters into the mountains of North Carolina, and Collins yielded to good spirits once more, for this high world, though old, and heavily used in part, was full of unexplored crevices and valleys, and because of its isolation was charm-protected; its blond people, separated from the rest of the South by the barriers of mountains, had retained their own qualities. To the east lay the piedmont hills, which graduated down to flat plantation lands. To the south lay the plantation areas of South Carolina, Georgia, and Mississippi. To the west was Tennessee and to the north was Virginia. All around them were these old places, stricken with the slave disease. But this mountain land was isolated, elevated, free. The people still held to the way of their ancestors, who had come from Ulster, England, Scotland, and the Ruhr. They were, as Collins saw them, quaint and earthy and full of good, strong life forces. They were no man's master and no man's servant, these planters of corn and millers of flour, hunters of bear and beaver and raccoon, tanners of hides, storytellers around the fires, never to go out, of ten thousand mountain cabins, sons of the men of the long rifle who had fought only one battle, that in late autumn after the crops were in, when they walked and rode tough horses to a lowland place, a hill which was called a mountain, though there wasn't much mountain to it, they felt, where a British general, his army around him, felt secure, and they walked up the hill and killed him. They even killed his redheaded mistress, which some said was a waste. They left his body naked in the field and sent word to George Washington, who was, they had been told by somebody, a tidewater Virginian; they sent word to him, anyway, at Valley Forge that a victory was won. Actually, it wasn't just a victory; an army had been annihilated. Then they went back home, walking and riding and talking and shooting off their guns at squirrels and crows—and sometimes at one another.

Men and women with their children watched Collins' train as it snaked its way alongside the broad river. Mountain men walked along the tracks, loose-jointed walking, with the loping strides of the woodsman, as if they, too, were just getting back from the lowlands and Kings Mountain. They turned their heads to smile with quizzical pride at the thundering monster passing close by. Mothers waved their babies' hands at the train. Old men chewed and considered thoughtfully the marvels of the outside world.

Collins got off the train at Marshall and spoke to a family in order to hear again the dignified manner of a mountain man's reply. He spoke to the woman and heard once more the sad, sad lilt of her voice and noticed the quiet manner of her delivery and the frank appraisal of the world which marked her face. What sadness, what a sense of self-appointed nobility these isolated people had, how unlike the flatland Southerners with their animosities and their sense of loss, and how unlike, too, the rambling searchers of the West and the beat-'em-if-you-can inhabitants of the North. How unimpressed these people were by what was foreign to them, and content and friendly they seemed to be in the high world of their own ways.

By the time the train reached Asheville, Collins had thrown off his last worry. He was home, and the anticipation of a happy meeting carried him forth. He wanted to see home again. The street, the store, the house of his parents. His chest swelled with pride when he considered the success of his family. He had come back to this mountain island, to his own sweet, lost, never-to-be-found-again childhood home.

The first night he spent up the street talking to mountain men and drinking whisky and beer. He slept late into the following day, and that afternoon he devoted to his mother, listening to stories about the angel boy and laughing with her at the wonders she claimed for him. When Johnny got home from school, he played with him, tried to break through his hidebound exclusiveness, and managed to get a giggle out of him at last.

Beth had a surprise, her breath was taken away, soon after supper when Collins sneaked up behind her in the kitchen while she was washing dishes and put his arms around her. She jumped from fright and wiggled free, wide-eyed and instantly alert, only to see a playful grin on his face which denied her the right to be angry. "Come on, Beth," he said, "we ought to go up the street tonight and see how many laughs they have."

"Why—what makes you think—" She halted nervously. "I declare, I haven't planned to go out tonight, Collins."

He took her hand. "Come on and get ready. Come on, will you?" he said, leading her from the kitchen.

She followed, frightened and a bit confused, and happy. He stopped in the dining room and told Lotti he was taking Beth with him up the street. Lotti looked up from watching Johnny eat. "Beth? Beth going with you, you say?"

"We're going to throw off some of these mortal cares," he said, winking at his mother, then running his hand through the hair of the angel boy so that he laughed. "Going to have to finish those dishes up someday; might need 'em again."

He led Beth down the hall. "Let's hurry, Beth," he said. "We're cheating ourselves out of a good time now." And with a gentle shove he started her up the stairs. When she looked back, he was leaning on the stairway post, smiling up at her, looking at her so kindly that she almost stumbled.

In her room, she got out a stick of lipstick, which she hadn't used enough off of to notice, and a packet of rouge. She slipped on her Sunday dress, abandoning herself slowly to her excitement now, here in the privacy of her room. It was true—true and wonderful.

She came out of her room just as Kin came upstairs, laughing at something Cal had said on the porch. He stopped and stared at her. "Beth, for goodness' sakes," he said. Then he said, and the words gave her confidence, "Beth, you sure are pretty."

122

"Well, I don't know whether I'm pretty or not, Kin. I do feel foolish, dressing up so on a Friday."

"You—going out with somebody?"

"Collins asked me."

Kin's eyes opened wide in surprise.

"You don't mind, do you, Kin?"

He considered it. Huskily he said, "He's all right, Collins is."

"I know. He just sweeps his way through life, taking what's good, doesn't he? I—I guess that's the best way, isn't it?"

"He's the best man to eat supper with that I ever saw."

"Yes."

"Did you hear him tonight talking to Mama about how he had never eaten food better fixed?"

"Lord knows, we ate ever bite on the table." She laughed. "Now I've got to hurry. Where's Paul?"

"On the porch."

Kin caught himself, a worry coming over him. Beth was frowning, too. "I guess I can't sneak out the back with Collins, can I? That wouldn't do any good."

"No," he said. He came close to her, still looking at her as if he treasured the sight of her, and he took one of her hands. "I hope Paul dies the minute he sees you," he said. Then, blushing, he stepped back out of her way.

She went down the stairs slowly, savoring the goodness of her rich, tumbling feelings, and stood at the screen door for a moment, wondering about making her entrance before the four men on the porch. She opened the screen as quietly as she could.

Matthew saw her first. He was leaning back against the porch rail, and he stood up stiffly and stared at her. Cal stopped swinging and stared. Then Collins saw her, and a big grin came over his face, and he spoke as if to the other men, but he meant the words for her. "Not but one girl as pretty as this one was ever born, and I never was fortunate enough to find out her name." He stood as he spoke, got up from the rocking chair, and came to her, impressed—sincerely impressed, it seemed to her—and ever so kind, and he took her arm.

But she stiffened when she saw Paul. Collins noticed it and turned to look at him. Paul, glowering, had risen from his rocker and his face was shadowed by anger. "Where you going?" he said to her.

"Up the street."

"Up King Street?"

"That's right."

"With him?"

Cal got up from the swing, which creaked as it trembled on its chains. "Paul, I believe you and me better talk tonight about the monthly statements for the store."

"Hell," Paul said. He kept looking at Beth. "You're going with him?"

Cal said firmly, "Paul, you and me have work to do, do you hear me?" He opened the screen door, held it open for Paul, but Paul didn't move.

Collins took Beth's arm. "Come on, Beth," he said. "No need to waste time with this." He led her to the steps.

Paul watched them, his gaze on them fiercely. "Beth, you come back here," he suddenly called out.

Cal, standing in the doorway, said, "Paul, come on in here; don't make a public display."

Paul moved down the porch steps and stood in the front yard, staring at Collins and Beth as they walked up through the grove of sycamores, past the Tumpkin's rented house, toward the store.

Cal said, "He won't harm her, Paul. Come here. I want to ask you about some things."

Paul moved across the yard to the lane. Then he started walking toward King Street.

"Paul!" Cal shouted, moving to the edge of the porch. "Paul, damn it, come here!"

But Paul went on, hurrying.

Kin came out onto the porch. Cal slumped down in the swing and sighed, so deeply he sounded ill, and shook his head. "I have three children up the street," he said, "for I think of Beth as close as my own, and ever one is a problem, ain't that so?" He shook his head

124

again, as if in pain, and it was a while before a smile crept back to his face. "Say, Kin," he said, "you don't suppose your cousin Beth thinks she can snare Collins, do you?"

There were three beer halls on the upper block of King Street, and at night they accommodated the bulk of activity and furnished most of the street light, too, since the women houses were somber-looking on the outside and the shops and restaurants were closed. One of the beer halls was named Jacob's, and it was here that most of the farmers assembled, because Jacob, who had migrated southward eight years before from New York City, offered credit to the farmers. He was one of the few Jews in Asheville, the only one on King Street, and he was a curiosity piece for the mountain people. They showed him to their children in connection with Old Testament stories, and generally evidenced a high regard for him, for the Bible clearly indicated to them that the Jews were selected by God and that anybody who harmed one was courting God's anger. This attitude gave Jacob a hold on life somewhat different from any he had had before, and he freely enjoyed the pleasures which come to one who finds he is considered to be a minor prophet.

He knew every customer's debt to him and he made demands for payment repeatedly. He made collections occasionally, when crops came in, or when a man sold stock or herbs. But often he had to collect by letting the fellow work off the debt in the beer hall itself. This accounted for the fact that there were always too many waiters in Jacob's and that the waiters were awkward and ungainly. The mountain people objected to submitting themselves to any form of servitude, and they made irritable servants, unless accepted as members of the family. "Bring me a beer," if said to one of Jacob's waiters, might bring the customer the astonishing reply "Who do you think you're ordering around, God damn you?"

It was to Jacob's, about halfway up the block, that Collins brought Beth, and Jacob went out of his way to welcome them. He escorted them past bottle-laden tables and slouching, resentful waiters to the back of the smoke-laden narrow room. One of the more gangly of the waiters moved in to see if maybe he could help wipe the oilcloth, but Jacob did it all and brushed off a chair for Beth. He was about to take the order himself when he noticed two men sneaking out the front door. "Here, here," he called, hurrying to reach his cashbox.

The men, grinning, waited for him. "We thought you was busy," one of them explained.

Jacob whipped out a blue-back pad in which he kept his records and marked down the men for the beers due.

"That's right, just put it on the tab," the other one said.

Beth tasted her first beer that night and found it bitter. Collins laughed about that. She listened as he told her he didn't care for beer as a steady drink himself, but her attention was on the sidewalk out front, where Paul had stopped. Paul kept looking in at her and Collins. She wanted to tell Collins about it, but she decided not to worry him and perhaps start a fight, and almost certainly dampen his enthusiasm for the evening.

Collins began to talk about his travels, and soon she was caught up in the stories. Jacob returned to the table, and he joined the conversation, too. He called over a friend of his, who traveled buying herbs and medicines in Yancey and Madison Counties, to hear the wonderful flow of words, and one of the waiters, tired of bothering with customers, sat down next to Jacob to listen. Eleven people, by Beth's count, had soon gathered around the table, and Collins was inquiring into the health and manner of each one, and was talking about himself and his friends, talking with grace and gusto, always ending a story with a boisterous laugh that was contagious and which attracted others. Soon the beer hall was filled with people. A woman, or really she was only a girl, started singing a happy song which had ribald lyrics, and Beth felt that the world was opening its happiest face to her at last.

When they left Jacob's, the cool air of the street refreshed her, and the street seemed quiet after the noisy beer hall. "I want to take you to another place," he said, "one where we can talk. It suddenly grew crowded in that one." He led her across the street to a larger beer hall run by a woman named Mrs. Walker, who didn't give credit even to her sons (who usually could be found at Jacob's). She was a sweaty, large-boned woman who kept perfect order in her place.

Collins found a table in one corner. He asked Beth about herself, and she told him about the farm where she had lived for a few years, and about leaving her father, and about going back to visit him only once. "He's out there by himself," she said. "My mother died when I was less than two years old. He's out there alone, farming and cooking for himself."

"Maybe we ought to take you by to visit him again, Beth."

She had argued bitterly with her father on her one visit, and she didn't like the idea of going back, but she did like the idea of visiting there with Collins, of being with him. "Maybe so," she said. "Of course, he'll just get to talking about my staying with him."

"Does he ever come to town?"

"No. He doesn't like Papa King. He doesn't like King Street, he says."

Collins thought about that. "Life gets deep sometimes, you know it," he said, "if we let it." He ordered beer and got to talking to the waiter, asking who he was and what his family did for a living, and two men sitting at the next table spoke up, too, and Mrs. Walker came over and asked who he was, because he reminded her of Caleb King. Four men came in from Jacob's and said Jacob's had got lonely after Collins and Beth left. They sat down, and some poor old mountain man came in who didn't have a decent set of clothes; at least, the ones he was wearing were in shreds. But Collins made a place for him at the table and Beth felt perfectly at home with him almost at once. That was part of Collins' power, that everybody felt natural around him; there were no pretenses around Collins. He would never think himself to give this man money for a new shirt, but what he gave him at once was his respect as a human being, and he offered that to everybody in the whole wide world, which to him was a most remarkable place, a most intelligent dream, created by a mighty mind, and it could not possibly be improved upon.

In order to escape the crowd, he and Beth soon left this beer hall, too, and went to the one next door, Mitch's Place, where Collins found a secluded table. They talked for a while, Collins inquiring informally about the problems of the family. "Mama Lotti seems to think the world of that little towheaded boy, doesn't she?" he said.

"I know," Beth said. "I worry about her sometimes, should something happen to him."

"If I'd known Mama Lotti wanted a preacher so much, I'd have preached a sermon before I went away last time. I could have taken a sermon from some book, couldn't I?"

"Maybe in a library you could. But I think it would be difficult to fool Mama Lotti."

"If you get me a book, Beth, we'll see."

Beth laughed.

"Get some bishop's sermons and tomorrow night I'll go out on the lawn and speak out of the darkness, just when supper is over. I'll speak like a spirit and preach about the devil coming to get the King family if they don't get to praying more and loving one another."

Beth shook with laughter and she got choked on a swallow of beer. He patted her back until she got her breath, and she sat back in the small chair and shook her head in wonder. "You'd better never try that."

"Whatever you say, Beth," he said. "But you tell that little Johnny to do it in a few years."

She took another sip of beer. "I'm beginning to like it better," she said.

"Are you?" He laughed, delighted with her. "Cousin Beth," he said fondly, smiling. "You're the little girl I used to hold on my knee. I wouldn't dare do that now, even though it would be a pleasure. No, I see that fire coming into your eye that says not to try anything with you."

He had a big grin on his face, and Beth couldn't help but smile.

"I sure would like to hold you on my knee, though, Beth."

Five of the people from Mrs. Walker's came swaying in and found Collins. He began to get stories out of them about the mountain country, and he told them about the oil rigs in Texas and about a friend of his who borrowed money for a rig and a beat-up truck. This friend was driving the rig to the place where he was supposed to drill, when the truck broke down, so he just started drilling where he was. He brought in a gusher inside of three days right beside the highway.

Collins told other such stories, and people gathered around and listened and commented. Time passed on slippery feet for Beth, who had never been part of such wonders before. A prostitute came in and sat down beside her, but Beth felt uneasy for only a moment; one simply couldn't be bound to considerations the least bit petty with Collins, she realized. He admitted everybody into his confidence, he loved the world and every person in it. Even at one o'clock, by when as a rule the men had long since wrapped themselves in blankets down at the lot and gone to sleep, most of them were still holding out, singing and talking. The man who ran this beer hall, Mitch Cummings, a grievous fellow who had suffered ill health since his wife died, got a battered banjo out of a locked compartment under the counter. He hadn't played since New Year's Eve, but he began to strum the strings, going faster until his fingers blurred, and he commenced to sing in a cracked, foggy voice one of the songs of the mountain people, singing with clear enunciation, so that each word stood out, underplaying the story as he told it, which was the way the people liked to hear their ballads.

> Come all you kind people my story to hear,
> What happened to me in June of last year,
> Of poor Ellen Smith and how she was found,
> Shot through the heart lying cold on the ground.
>
> I saw her that morning, so still and so cold,
> And heard the wild story the witnesses told.
> I choked back tears when the people all said
> That Peter Gegraff had shot Ellen dead.
>
> Half crazy with sorrow, I wandered away,
> And lonely I wandered for many a day,
> My love in her grave and her hands on her breast,
> While bloodhounds and sheriffs would give me no rest.

Ellen sleeps calmly in the lonely graveyard,
While I look through the bar, and God knows it's hard.
I know they will hang me at last if they can,
But God knows I die an innocent man.

Beth clapped as much as Collins did. The beer was beginning to have effect on her. At each beer hall she had ordered a single mug of beer, not very much actually, but this proved to be enough to give her a glow. By now people were coming in from the street to hear, and she saw that Paul was among them. He stood near the door, gloomy as before and ill at ease.

Mitch strummed the banjo harshly, and abruptly his aged crackly voice rose and filled the place.

A little girl sat in a log cabin door;
The babies were crying outright.
The mother said, "Susie, don't wander afar;
I'll have to be gone half the night."

"Oh, Mama, don't make any liquor tonight,
Sheriff Slack may be watching the still;
I seen him today pass by on the road
And drive in the woods by the mill."

"Hush, young'un, hush," the poor woman moaned,
"Your paw ain't never worked none;
We ain't got nothing to eat in the house,
And the baby's got croup in his lung."

She went to the wood between midnight and dawn.
The woman didn't hearken to Susie's advice;
She put on her man's shoes and pants
And was shot through the heart by the spies.

As they tenderly took the body back home,
A poor woman in men's overhauls,
They stopped at the door and the tears flooded down
As they heard the poor orphan child bawl:

"Oh, why did you make any liquor tonight?
I begged till my heart's nearly wild.
Paw brought meat and flour within half an hour
And now I'm a poor orphan child."

Collins bent double laughing. Sitting beside Beth on a table, he led the party singing the mighty last stanza again, singing so loud the window glass rattled and shook.

It was 3 A.M. before at last the party broke up and he and Beth started the walk down the hill toward home. The music was still in her mind, ringing there full of laughter and good nature, and when Collins slipped his arm around her, her life caught for a moment. She guessed she would never forget this night.

"Cousin Beth," he said proudly, "you sure can sing. When you got to going on that Jessie James song, you almost silenced twenty men."

She laughed. "I didn't sing loud, did I?"

"Loud and pretty," he said. "Mitch has a weak heart, you know; that's what one of the men told me. He's not supposed to play any more, and he doesn't except once or twice a year."

"He's the best banjo picker I ever heard."

"He's like lightning with that thing. Wooow! He goes, doesn't he?" He laughed out at the stars and the night. "It makes my blood run fast just to think about it. I wish I could play like that, but I just have time to do the things that come naturally."

He drew her closer to him then, and she protested slightly, but he showed no sign of noticing it.

He glanced back over his shoulder.

"Is Paul following us?" she asked.

"Oh, I don't know," he said. He took her arm and hurried her along. "Paul never does anything except talk, anyway."

"No," she said softly, "that's not so, Collins."

They passed the store and entered the lane.

"You're about as nice a person as I ever met, Beth," he said.

"Listen to that. I was told you had a way with flattery."

"Who said that?"

"Everybody knows that who knows you."

"I'm just stating facts. You're pretty, you sing loud—"

"I didn't mean to sing loud. You embarrass me, you know it?"

"You stomp your feet on the chair."

"I do not, do I? Did I do that?"

"When we were sitting on the table you did. And you look so soft and appealing sometimes."

He stopped. He turned her to face him and took her in his arms, and he kissed her. She pressed back from him for a moment, then her hands touched his shoulders, and her fingers grasped his shoulders, and she pressed against him.

She could hardly stand it, for his hands were roving over her and the pressure of love had built up in her, threatening her. She pushed herself away from him and stood there on the lane facing him, staring at him. "It makes me weak to kiss that way," she said breathlessly.

Gently he drew her close again and bent to kiss her, and this time he didn't touch her with his hands. Warmth and wonder went through her like waves coursing on a shore back and forth, again and again.

He smiled at her and laughed softly. "Pretty Beth, little Beth," he said.

"We'll go home now," she said, backing away.

"Oh, Beth, hell, what's life for if not for love?"

"Yes," she said breathlessly. "I know. But I don't want to be swept away."

He bit at his lip and studied her, frowning like a disappointed boy, then suddenly the warm grin came on his face. "Every woman knows her own heart best, I guess."

It was so simply put, so kindly said, that she felt relaxed again with him at once, and grateful to him. "Come along, Collins," she said, and she led the way down the trail to the house path.

He said good night to her on the porch. "Cousin Beth, little girl and pretty as can be," he said. He kissed her again.

And as she left him and went, as quietly as she could, up the stairs, she held to the pleasure of his smile and of his deep voice. In her room she fell across the bed and held her face tightly in her hands, tyring to hold in the joy which possessed her and throbbed through her.

She turned over on her back. The world was beautiful, she knew then. All that was in it was right, and she was passionate and part

132

of it. All was right, for she knew that he found her attractive, that he, the best judge of women, found her attractive. She felt secure, for this was comfort for part of her doubts. And she knew now that he did exist, that the prince lived, that all the stories were true, and that there was even a prayer of a promise that he would belong to her.

10

Paul had followed them up the street like a whipped dog. He had seen the eagerness in Beth's manner as she had looked at Collins, he had noticed at the supper table that she laughed when he laughed and smiled when he smiled, as if under a spell to him. He hated that weakness in her. It was obvious to him that Collins was trying to get even with him for old wrongs, and was using Beth. Collins was trying to even up the score of the early years, Paul thought, and was trying to get even because Paul, who had stayed at home, had gained control of the store; it was Collins' nature to be vindictive, and he was seeking to gain revenge by dating Beth, misleading Beth, perhaps impregnating Beth, before, light-footed and with light cares, he left once more on the train for another place, another girl, another conquest—that was it.

"Cheap," Paul murmured as he hurried up the street. "Cheap."

He saw them go into Jacob's beer hall, and he stopped on the sidewalk and waited to see what would happen in there. Beth's being in the beer hall annoyed him. She should know better than that, for no woman went into Jacob's unless she was a prostitute taking the night off from bed work, or a simple-minded country girl who soon

134

would learn the ways of the city world. Not that anything was ever done in Jacob's itself that could be considered out of the way, but there were places in the world women went and places they did not.

He saw Beth and Collins when they crossed the street to Mrs. Walker's beer hall, and a few minutes later he saw several men come out of Jacob's and ask where Collins had gone. They were talking about him, speaking highly of him as they crossed the street.

Paul went into Jacob's place and ordered a beer, then ordered two more and drank his fill, even though he had had a big supper shortly before. Around him he heard people talking about Collins, what Collins had said, where Collins had been, how much they liked Collins.

He left the place and crossed the street to Mrs. Walker's, where he peeked inside through the front window to see where Beth was sitting. She was gone. Collins and Beth were gone. Paul caught a man's arm, asked where Collins had gone. The man told him that he was next door in Mitch's place.

Paul turned away from him, not even thanking him, even irritated with him. Ask where Collins was and people knew, they seemed to keep track of him, to remember passing him on the street, they seemed to tell each other where he was and was going. It had always been that way.

He went into Mitch's. It was crowded, but as soon as he got the door closed he saw them. Beth looked up at him guiltily, realizing now the error of her judgment in coming to this place. Upper King Street wasn't for her. He could have told her that, if he had known she needed telling.

He was aware of Mitch's playing, and he liked Mitch's playing above most of the others on King Street, but it was raspy and harsh now.

> Who will shoe your feet, my love,
> And who will glove your hands,
> And who will kiss your ruby lips
> When I'm in a foreign land?

135

He left the place and went back to Jacob's and had two more bottles of beer, but he kept his eyes on Mitch's. Jacob's was almost empty now. Everybody was over at Mitch's listening to the music. "He promised me not to play that damn banjo," Jacob said, scowling. "I planned to get little Sally Waters to sing in here if he ever wanted to start another music duel, and he promised me not to play again, but he's doing it."

"Collins starts trouble wherever he goes."

"It doesn't help to have music in a place. These people listen to the music and don't drink beers. I've known men to come in here when Black Taylor was playing, and they didn't drink beers." He gazed off sadly at the crowded beer hall across King Street. "That brother of yours is a happy man."

The beer filled the glass to the top with white foam which spread out over the sides. It had a strong smell and taste to it. "He's a damn pig. You get to know him, you'll find that out." It swirled inside his belly and soothed him. "A pig." He went out into the street. He went back to Mitch's place and looked through the window. Beth was there. She was clapping and singing with the others. He turned away and went back to Jacob's.

Jacob wanted to close, but he wouldn't close as long as Mitch stayed open. "They're over there paying Mitch cash money for beers," Jacob said, "when every one of them owes me money for beers drunk months ago. They're shelling out coin to Mitch, though."

A lumberman named Jessie Sims came sauntering into Jacob's and ordered a beer. He stood at the counter for a few seconds, then went out with it, telling Jacob to put it on his bill, that he was going back to Mitch's. Jacob sprang to the door and shouted after him, "Don't come into this beer hall in the future!"

He slammed his door to keep out the worst of the noise of music from across the street.

> O don't you see that turtle dove
> Flying from pine to pine?
> She is a-weeping for her love
> As I am for mine.

136

It was three o'clock before the party broke up. Paul saw Collins and Beth come out of Mitch's place, calling back thanks and saying goodbye to everybody. They started down King Street. Almost in a moment the spirit of the street changed from noisy merriment to solemn, sleeplike quiet. A drunk, accustomed to the noise and music, came out of Mitch's, shouting out his good feelings. He stopped, teetered on his toes as if he had caught himself on the very edge of sound; he peered around, seeking a reason for the quiet.

The night had belatedly moved in to take over. People spoke softly as they walked toward their wagons and trucks.

Another man shouted out. "Hey, Ernest, bring me that young colt when you come in on Saturday."

A man walking near Paul waved his arm at him. "Yi," he answered.

Paul followed Beth. She and Collins crossed the street to the east side and walked along the front of the store. He's not going to try to take her to a hotel tonight, Paul thought. No, by God, he knows he'd better not with me here. He'll never touch her.

Jacob, closing up his place, yelled across the street to Mitch, who was closing his, "I'm going to get little Sally Waters singing in my place, Mitch. I'm going to have her here tomorrow night."

Mitch locked his door and turned to face him. "You'd better fasten her drawers on with a length of rope, then, or she'll be screwing waiters behind the counter."

Paul grinned.

"She's going to be perched on my beer counter singing songs tomorrow night, Mitch, if I hear another note out of that banjo of yours."

"I have a right to play if I have the will to."

"The doctor said you'd kill yourself. Is that what you want?"

"You'll never see my funeral." He went stalking up the street toward his room, which was above one of the stores on Market Street, not far from where Jacob lived.

Paul heard Jacob shout, "I can't afford to lose money to your singing, if that's what it is, and you know it sells no beers."

Paul couldn't hear what Mitch answered. The two men were far

137

away, up at the corner of Market now, each one on a corner denouncing the other for the way he ran a beer hall.

Four mountain men were coming along the sidewalk, talking about the music and whether they had enough money to buy a woman for an hour. "There might be a free one hanging out down at the lot," one of them said. "No need to pay for it if it can be got free."

"They got pretty ones at the houses, as a rule."

"You can bag her head if her looks don't please you."

Paul saw Collins and Beth enter the sycamore woods. No telling what Collins might try to do with Beth there. Try to strip her down maybe. She was innocent, of course, pure as snow, no doubt of that. No telling what she might yield, though, to a charmer.

He entered the woods quietly. Not fifty feet away from him, the silhouette-like figures of Collins and Beth were moving along the trail. Then they stopped. Collins put his arms around her. He kissed her. And Paul almost cried out in soul pain and anger.

Beth stepped back. But Collins drew her close again and she yielded; Paul saw her yield, her body arch toward his, toward Collins; he kissed her so tenderly that Paul's eyes filled with tears.

They talked. What were they talking about? God knows, kill him, kill him. So softly they talked.

They went on down the lane. He watched them, a tremble in his legs. A nervousness came over him and he sank down on a rock at the side of the road. He tried to get control of himself and to clear his mind.

This wasn't that Hun, Morris Kraft, this was the old enemy come home. He had to be stopped. Somehow, damn it, stopped.

He got up, went on down the lane, hurrying, and he reached the path to the house. They had disappeared again. He hurried up to the porch to see if he had dared, if he had dared go to her room.

"Hello, Paul."

He swung around. Collins was sitting in a rocker, his feet up on the banister rail. He calmly lit a cigar as Paul watched. "You're out late, Paul."

Paul felt the trembling again. He moved to the porch rail, still

138

staring at Collins, and took hold of a post. "What do you want?"

"Nothing from you. Why?"

Paul was breathing deeply. "You want money, Collins?"

"Why? For what?"

"Is that it?"

"I expect I have more money than you, Paul."

"You're going after her, then. You want her?" He stared down at him, his lips working nervously. "I'm not going to beg you to let her be, Collins, not to hurt her."

"Hurt her?"

Paul couldn't talk any more. He couldn't stand steady. He was scared, not of Collins but of himself. He could crush Collins, right there; he knew he could.

He moved to the door and went inside. He stood in the dark hall, his hands pressed to his face. If I touch him, he thought, if I touch him I can't stop.

He went upstairs slowly, and in his room he lay down clothed on the bed. God, God, God damn him. Stop him. Stop him, he thought.

At breakfast he ate what Beth brought. When he was done, he sat there until Lotti and Cal were gone. When Beth brought in a new pan of biscuits, he caught her arm and held her, and he looked up at her face and she looked back at him unflinchingly. "Beth—" he said, "don't hurt me, Beth."

With her free hand she loosened his grip on her arm and put the biscuit pan on the table. "I've got to eat my own breakfast, Paul, if you're done."

He left soon. He went up to the store. Got to do something. He went to the market stalls and bought a handful of flowers and took them to the store and hid them behind the harnesses. Almost at once he got them out, though, put them in a paper bag, and went down the street with them. He entered the house through the kitchen, opening the door quietly so as not to attract attention. Beth was there, at the sink, working.

She heard him. He was almost to her when she swung around, and she gasped.

"I didn't—I didn't mean—" Why was she scared? God, why was she scared? He held out the poke full of flowers. "Here," he said, when she hesitated to take them.

"Are they for me?" she said, taking them out of the bag.

"Yes."

"I don't—know what to say, Paul."

"I wanted to talk to you." His voice cracked when he spoke. "I want you to tell me what I'm to do, Beth, and I'll do it, but don't go out with him. He's only going to hurt you. He's just trying to hurt me, Beth."

She looked at him strangely. "Don't say that."

"It's so. He's just trying to get at me."

"No. I don't believe it." She backed up against the sink. The flowers dangled in her hand. "I won't listen to that, Paul, do you hear me?"

"God damn. You take up for him, don't you? Beth, don't drive me down."

"I'm not trying to hurt you, Paul."

"Drive me down." He backed away awkwardly from her. "Jesus Christ, why do you hurt me, Beth?" he said.

When Collins came down for breakfast, everybody was off to school or to work except Beth and Lotti, and Lotti was in the kitchen baking. She had so much flour on her hands she didn't want to stop work right then, so Beth waited on Collins and sat at the table with him. She felt a delicious feeling of lightness and warmth, being with him, and she felt at peace with the world, seeing him smile. "I never tasted blackberry jam better made," he told her. "Beth, did you make this?"

"Mama Lotti made it."

"Listen, Beth, you come to California with me, and we'll open a restaurant—you and me and Mama Lotti. And that little Johnny can wait tables. What do you say?"

Beth laughed. "I can't believe that." It was funny to hear him talk so casually about little Johnny, to hear him joking. "I'll never leave these mountains," she said. "When you get to the lowlands, you get the croup, they tell me."

He laughed. "That's true," he said. "You believe that, Beth." He drank a cup of coffee and broke two biscuits in two, put fried ham on one and preserves on the other. "You could make country hams in California, too. Nobody can make hams like you."

"My father made that ham," she said proudly. "It's one of two he sent us last fall. It was smoked as well as cured."

"I know. He's got a knack for it," Collins said.

"He's been making hams all his life. When he was a boy, they had to have hams because the beef wouldn't keep. He told me about it once. Leastways, beef didn't taste good when it was salted so much. So they had a meathouse full of salt pork, which would get better as the winter went on, and was better still in the spring, like now. That ham is right now the best it's been."

"It's something." He chewed on a piece of it. "I want to meet your father soon," he said, "and see if he wants to go to California."

She liked to see him eat and talk. He kept his eyes on his food mostly, but sometimes he glanced at her.

"I'd like for you to meet him. I want to see him again, too." She hesitated, not sure that she should be so forward as to suggest a time for a trip to the country, but, after all, he had suggested the night before that they go. "Maybe we can go to see him this week, or next."

He nodded as he swallowed. "That's what I was thinking. You and me." He gulped down his coffee as Mama Lotti came in. "We were just sitting here talking about how pretty you are," he told her.

"Law, listen to him lie, Beth." She sat down at the table and dried her hands on her apron. She reached over and patted Beth's hand, one of the few signs of affection Lotti had ever shown her in Beth's memory. "Well, how did you like going out with my boy last night?" she asked. "Ain't he a sight?"

"We had a wonderful time."

"And did you treat her courtly, Collins?"

Collins laughed. "Mama, you should have seen Beth stomping the chair seat." He winked at Beth.

"It's not right to tell such tales," Beth said. "I don't know why in the world you want to tell Mama Lotti that."

"You sure were pretty when you did it, Beth," he said.

He told Lotti all about the night and the singing, and even remembered the words to the songs.

The fact that Collins had invited her to go out to the farm, or had, at least, wanted to go with her, gave Beth new confidence in herself, and the idea of being with him for an entire day, off to themselves, was enough excitement to rule her thought. That morning she was feverish, wondering what he might say, where they might walk, what they might see and do. They were going to be with her father for part of the time, of course, and she wanted to see him, but the day was to be spent with Collins, that was the secret meaning of it, the solemn promise of goodness in it, to be with Collins for all of that day, alone with him for most of it. The day was almost too burdened with promise to think about.

Her life, she thought, had certainly taken on new prospects all of a sudden. She had been in the lowlands for a long while, waiting on the Kings and loving them in the way a woman comes to love those who look to her for service and to depend on those who depend on her, but never had she been one of the Kings, though always she had been included in their thoughts. Still, she was apart, a cousin living in the house, not a servant any more than Lotti was a servant, but not blood kin in the close way. Now Collins had accepted her in closeness, perhaps had even desired her as a lover.

The very word swept longing through her. Lover. She was a member of the family now in a special way, for he, the most auspicious of the sons, had found her attractive. And the sameness of the world, which was the aspect the world had come to have for her, had been taken away, and her life had become a fairyland of wonders. She could not permit herself to dwell on the hope she felt. Every dish she planned for supper was for him. When she made his bed that

142

morning, she was lighthearted with thoughts of him. She wondered at the moods of the heart, of her heart, which pined so feelingly for him whom she had just two days before met after years of growing up, and who, because he had touched her and kissed her and wanted again to be with her, had given her confidence in the rightness of life and in her place in it. He was a reward, a beneficent gift from nature; he was proof beyond doubt that the old sayings were so, that those who have pure hearts and work and serve others will have their just rewards.

Collins sat around the house for half an hour that morning, then he went up the street. Several men saw him approaching the store and hurried to greet him, and he stopped and talked with them for a while. When he finally got to the store, he waited on a farmer who had brought in half a dozen chickens and hoped to trade them on dress material.

"Hens for dresses? Doesn't seem possible," Collins said, winking at the men standing nearby. But he led the farmer over to the cloth counter, where big rolls of gingham in eight patterns were hung on pipes. "Let's see here," he said, speaking to one of the store assistants, "you'd better measure off a good five yards of that for this man, for he has six hens."

"I can't trade for just five yards, Mr. King," the man said anxiously. He was a long-faced fellow and seemed to be eternally sad and discomfited, as if the world were playing untidy jokes on him constantly. "My wife's too big for five yards. My wife's too big for seven yards, but I don't expect you to go beyond that."

"Can't go to seven," Collins said solemnly. "Might go to six. How big is your woman?"

The farmer made a hoop out of his arms to indicate her size.

"It's going to press me to cover her for just six chickens," Collins said. "What else have you got?"

The farmer shook his head. "Got no money."

"It'll take eight yards to cover her to the ankles. You want her covered proper, don't you?"

143

"That's why I brought in the best of my hen flock. She's got to have a better cover on her, for what she's got is ragged as a horse blanket."

"I'll give you six yards of your choice of prints," Collins said, "and I'll give you two more yards if you'll bring me a gallon pail of thick molasses next week—now, I don't want watery molasses and I don't want molasses so thick they won't pour when room-warm. You've got molasses, haven't you?"

The man nodded. "That might be, but I don't want to run short and deprive myself." He rubbed his face and thought it over. "All right, I'll take six yards now of the red and yellow, and I'll bring you a pail of molasses for the two more yards come next Saturday, for I know six yards won't do."

Collins was about to turn the six chickens over to Prime to slaughter when a farmer offered him two hounds for them. Collins suspected that the hounds were sick, but he made the trade and pinched the dogs. One of them began to look spry. He took the other one behind the patent-medicine counter and fed him a saucer of tonic. When he had both dogs bright-eyed, he began to explain to a group of men that these dogs had come from bear-hunting stock and were willing to attack a bear even though they were pure hound. He talked them up and managed to trade them on a black calf with a lame hoof. He fixed the calf's hoof with a pocketknife and half a bottle of iodine, and though the calf bellowed for fifteen minutes, she was in better shape. "Who wants her?" Collins asked, peering at the grinning faces of the farmers. "I see at least five men anxious to have her right now. I guess they've come to like her voice."

About twenty men had gathered around. "Who wants the calf? Anybody want to trade a horse for her? You can't milk a horse, you know."

Nobody spoke up. Collins took an old man by the arm. "Think of getting your hand on this calf's tits, Grandpa," he said.

The man was startled at first, then a laugh erupted out of him. "Haw, haw!" he roared, and everybody laughed, and somebody bid twenty dollars for the calf.

"Not enough," Collins said.

Then a farmer from Chuns Cove, whose white hair was down over his ears and was thick on the back of his neck, allowed that he had a fine horse.

"I hear you," Collins said. "Let's see her." The group, Collins leading the calf, went across the lot to where the horse was tied. "Is this your fine horse?" Collins asked, studying her. "Did you bring her in on a wagon?"

The mountain men grinned and nudged one another.

"Here, somebody help hold this horse up," Collins said. "She's going to fall—look out over there, get the children back."

The man who owned her flared up. "She's in sound shape, same as me. I rode her in."

"Cruel, cruel," Collins said. He moved to the other side of her and tilted his head, as if trying to get a true perspective on the animal. "You rode her in?"

"I did."

"Well, you ought to let her ride you back."

He walked around the horse, twitching his face and clucking his tongue. The truth was, she was a reasonably sound horse, but he made out that she was on her last legs, and he got the horse for the calf.

Magically, as soon as that was accomplished, he began to find excellent traits in the horse. "Gentle as can be. A pretty thing for children. And see here, see here, she's patient. She's not the kind of horse to raise a rumpus if put upon to plow a heavy-sodden field. You couldn't get a complaint out of this horse. She's just the right size for the little woman to work, too." His arguments multiplied, and he traded her for a mule.

The mule he traded for six sugar-cured hams, average weight twenty pounds. He had come up in two hours from six yards of gingham cloth.

That was known in the King family as "trading out"; that is, trading for items not connected with the store. The big advantage the store had over "outside" traders on King Street was that the store had a wide range of items to bargain with and could wait until each of them was in demand, whereas the "outside" trader had to get rid of what he had just traded for. Collins had made his gains of the morning without trading inside except at the very beginning. He had put on a fine display of old, country powers, a competent exhibition, even the elderly men said.

That afternoon, farmers who were through with their own work and in no hurry to get back to the place gathered close to the store and waited for Collins, and when he got his dinner settled he came up and started in again. He began with a twenty-dollar harrow, and three hours later had two cows which were worth about a hundred and fifty dollars. The elderly men were as impressed with his prowess as they had been that morning. "You've got the touch, boy," one told him. "My lord, boy, you've got the old touch!"

Beth wasn't surprised when Collins didn't invite her to go up the street again. She had hoped he wouldn't. Seeing him too often would spoil expectancy, she thought, and she knew instinctively that she didn't have enough variety in her personality, or have laughter enough or smiles enough to match his wit each night. Usually he went up the street with Matthew, and one night they took Kin. The next morning Kin could talk about nothing except the night before and a girl singer named little Sally Waters.

For the next week or two, Collins traded heavily up the street, traded up in four hours one day from a bushel of seed to five acres of bottom land. He traded in chickens one afternoon in the damndest display of craftsmanship and salesmanship that the street had seen. And before the week was out, farmers were trading with Collins, coming in from miles around to trade with him and with each other, so that the street on the second Saturday was as busy as it had been before the depression hit. "Where've you been, Zeke?" one man called to another.

"Howard, I heard you'd died, but you ain't died, Howard." It seemed to be reunion week on King Street.

Paul swore it was all going to end in catastrophe if somebody

146

didn't tell the mountain people that it wasn't time to get prosperous again. "They'll all be in after loans inside of a month," he told Cal.

But Cal was having the time of his life. "Prosperity's pretty much a state of mind anyway," he said.

The boom continued. It continued even after Collins tired of the trading and came to spend most of his time swapping stories. He would sit near the water trough in the sun and listen and talk. He never forgot a story once he heard it, and he knew several hundred from all over the country. Now he was collecting all he could find among the mountain people, and the men on King Street were vying with each other to think up the biggest tales.

"My grandpa ain't got clear eyesight," one man, a sallow-faced, wrinkled man, told Collins. "He's rheumy-eyed, and my brother Henry told him he had some new chewin' tobacco, and Grandpa wanted to taste it, of course, because he's the devil's own for anything new. He took a bite off it. Well, it weren't nothing but cow dung broke off a dry pod in the pasture. And Grandpa chewed on it, and my brother Henry stood there alooking on, and finally Henry said, 'Grandpa, does it taste good?' And Grandpa said, 'It tastes all right, Henry, but it don't seem to gather none.'"

Hoarse voices laughed. "Hey, did you hear that!" one man called to another.

Before long, with mountain people swapping stories and trading heavy, with the beer halls competing with entertainers, a boom had hit King Street the like of which nobody had seen in years.

"Ain't there nobody out in the hills working?" Paul demanded. "Are they all here talking and getting drunk? Who in hell is going to put the crops in this year?" He took Matthew aside and talked sternly to him. "Listen, the world's gone crazy. You'd better get hold of your twenty per cent and get out, sell out of here, as I'm about to."

"Sell out?"

"We're losing money ever day in this store."

"With all this good trading going on?"

"It don't add up," Paul said bluntly. "It don't show on the books. This place is in a bad way. I'd get the twenty per cent and let me sell it for you. I know a man who'll buy it."

"Yeah," Matthew said, "I expect you do."

Later, in private, Matthew asked his father why the store wasn't showing a profit. Cal didn't want to talk about it, but that afternoon Matthew heard him talking to Paul, asking what was happening to the money. The question made Paul so furious that he couldn't talk in an orderly way; his words tumbled over one another getting out. He seemed to have no explanation to offer, either. "There's the books; you can check them if you don't believe me," he said.

Cal turned away from him, annoyed with that prospect and disappointed in Paul, and went out to stand on the street and peer about at the farmers and their women, and at the few sheep and goats and mules that had been brought in that day, and at the chickens and coops of fighting cocks, and at the guinea hens, and at the cloth-covered red roasts of deer and bear meat.

"Hello, honey," he said to a little girl.

She smiled up at him, her pretty face, with its perfectly drawn sharp features, reflecting sunlight.

"You're pretty as a calendar picture, honey," he said to her, and patted her head. "If your papa and mama don't want you, tell them to bring you to me."

She giggled and twisted around to find her father, who was nearby, watching proudly. "She's my sixth daughter, Mr. King," he said, "and ever one is pretty, just like her."

"Well, you must be a God-fearing man," Cal said. "You must pray many a prayer of thanks. Look at the innocent face on that child."

"She's sweet-tempered, too, Mr. King."

"She appears to be. With six of those, a man can marry his family into wealth."

He crossed the street, studying the faces of the people and nodding to this friend and that, for he knew almost everybody from times past. He stopped to hear a story told, then joined Collins near the water trough, and they sat there speculating about the weather and the state of King Street until it was near suppertime.

To Kin there was nothing finer than the new spirit of the street.

148

At long last, the austerity was broken and exuberance had taken control. Matthew was pleased, too, but he talked with Kin about the books' not showing a profit. Kin said he couldn't get worried even about that, any more than his father seemed to be able to, because he suspected that the time would soon come when Collins would get around to the problem of the books. When Kin mentioned this possibility to Matthew, a big grin came over Matthew's face, for he recognized the reasonableness of it, and when Paul next came out of his office, Matthew said he had heard that Collins was wondering about how the books were being kept in the store.

Paul stood in the center of the main room of the store considering that problem for a long time.

Kin told Beth about this, and about the activity that was enlivening the street. And she in turn told him about what Collins said at home, telling it word for word, it seemed to Kin, including what he said one afternoon on the porch when he and Beth talked for well over an hour, just the two of them. She told Kin, too, how the angel boy now would follow Collins around and ask him to play with him. "Mama Lotti permits him to play with Collins. She told me Collins wouldn't hurt a soul, that he wouldn't hurt little Johnny or make him any less of a preacher. And he won't, will he, Kin?"

Kin grinned. "No telling what he'll do."

"But Johnny follows him and waits on every word. He's the only person Johnny will talk to, outside of Lotti."

Kin felt keenly his own defeat in this matter, for he and Johnny had never come to know one another, and here Collins, inside of three weeks, had arrived out of the West and had awakened the boy, had broken open the severe isolation Lotti had imposed on him, and had done it in such a way that Lotti herself favored it.

Sometimes Collins would sit on the porch and talk with Lotti for an hour or more. Kin noticed this, too. And she would get to laughing more than she used to. She even took on an interest in the world and happenings in it. "Well, I don't know what you mean when you say you went from Texas to Oregon, Collins. Ain't they the same thing?"

Collins laughed. "No, Mama, they're not the same."

"Well, you know I can't keep track of everything. The West is just the West to me."

Collins never tried to explain the West to her. "It doesn't matter where it is, Mama. It's on beyond, that's the thing. A long piece beyond, Mama Lotti. And sometimes I get to thinking about Alaska while I'm sitting in the sun up there in the market. I'll catch a thought of warm sunlight on the cold plains, and I'll get to wondering about friends I have there, or I'll get to thinking about Arizona, where the sunlight is golden and the days are cool on the high plateaus, or South Dakota, with a stand of yellow and gray mountains. I get to reviewing the far reaches of this country, Mama Lotti, all of it hopeful and located beyond . . ."

It was talk like that which tore at Beth's soul and made her quiver. It panicked Kin, too. Neither of them could bear to think of Collins ever going away again.

11

THE TRIP TO THE COUNTRY WAS PLANNED FOR A
Sunday. At first only Beth and Collins were going, but when Mama
Lotti heard that they were visiting the old homeplace, she wanted
to go, and nothing would do but that they invite her. She wanted
to take Johnny, of course, and Kin wanted to go. Then Matthew said
he was going. And Lotti said it was time Cal got out for a trip. And
Paul said he would go, too. He had in mind that he must be with
Beth.

Since the whole family couldn't get into Cal's Ford, Collins on
Saturday borrowed a car from one of his friends. Kin intended to go
in Collins' car, as no doubt Paul did, but early on Sunday morning
he was roused from bed by the noise of a motor starting, and when he
got to the window, he saw Collins and Beth waving up at him. Collins honked the car horn and yelled out, "You going to sleep all day?"
Then, still honking the horn and waving, he drove the car down
the drive and into the lane. He and Beth were gone.

Paul came out of his bedroom at once, frantically pulling on his
clothes and calling for everybody to be up. He was in a frenzy. The
idea of Collins being off with Beth was near overpowering to him. He

hurried the family through breakfast and to the car, and he urged Cal to drive faster as they made their way over the curving mountain roads. The rhododendron was in bloom, but he didn't notice it. Once, when Cal drove the car over a pass, the world opened out before them, purple flowers framing it on both sides, but Paul was intent on the road. The car radiator began to steam, the motor chugged erratically, threateningly, but, even so, they pushed along fast until they reached the clay road which led to the gate of the old farm.

Cal brought the car to a stop but kept the motor running. "If we don't get some water, we're going to boil out completely," he said. "Get a hatful out of that pasture spring, Matthew." A branch ran across the road before them. The spring was off to their right in a patch of laurel.

Matthew brought a hatful of water and sloshed it into the radiator. "Why do you reckon Collins parked his car in the pasture instead of at the house?" he asked.

"Huh?" Cal and Paul turned to look. The borrowed Essex was parked over to the side of the road, all right, a good hundred yards this side of the house, in a grove of bushes.

"Now, where do you reckon that fellow is with that girl?" Cal said, glancing at Paul. Paul stood as in a trance, staring at the vehicle. He moved toward the Essex, still staring, then he looked off at the mountain looming tall before them.

"He's out courtin' her, I'll bet you a bent penny." Cal scratched at his face and frowned. He walked up the road past the pasture gate and peered at the house. He saw nobody. He looked out across the wide pasture, which fell gently down to King Creek, where the base of the mountain range was. The mountain rose with pastureland for a quarter of a mile, then forests took over and covered the land right up to the peak, which was black with conifers and expanses of heathland. The clean-smelling breezes blew down from them.

Lotti and Johnny got out of the car. Kin and the others followed and stretched their legs. Lotti walked up to where Cal was kicking at a clod of clay. "I tell you," he said, "Beth is going to get herself in trouble if she don't watch out for it coming." He glanced down at Paul, who was brooding, staring off at the huge mountain, where no doubt Beth and Collins were. "Collins is asking for trouble, too," he said softly, wondering about it, wondering about the power of Paul. Paul had been holding himself off, but he wouldn't now, Cal thought, not today. Back here they used to fight, he thought, and I guess they'll fight here again. He dreaded it; the worry made him sick and weary. "Can't raise a family without a storm of trouble," he said.

He turned once more to Paul. He probably feels cheated, he thought. Paul has always lost. He dreamed big, but before he ever got a dream in motion, he was cheated out of it, or lost it himself.

Lotti came up to stand beside Cal. She breathed in the flower-laden scent of the air, the clean freshness of it. She loved this place. It made her feel young again. She had spent forty-two years of her life on this farm, more than twice as long as she had spent in Asheville, and the country was dear to her. The country was intimate; she felt that she possessed the land. Never had she felt that she possessed the city or any part of it. A city had a way of taking control of a person, she thought, but a person possessed the land he worked and depended on.

"I don't want any bastard young'uns," Cal said. "Did you ever talk to Beth about matters of births?"

"I talked to her some," Lotti said hesitantly. Actually she hadn't, and she hated to lie. She had meant to talk to Beth a time or two, but not the first complete idea had been spoken on the subject. She got embarrassed. But she supposed Beth had learned somewhere else, for surely there were always brash people willing to talk about private matters.

Cal told everybody to get into the car who wanted to ride the two hundred yards up the road to the house. "No need to stand here and fret."

Only Paul and Matthew returned to the car. The others said they would walk. Paul had a harried, tense look about him.

Cal put the car into gear and drove forward slowly. Fortunately the house, which was at the very foot of Black Bear Mountain, wasn't any higher in elevation than the pasture gate, and there were no hills to go over, so there would be no more strain on the car. "They get us to this damn outing," Cal protested, as the car lurched over the eroded trail, "and a new set of worries entirely."

He remembered his own young days; that was one reason he knew to worry about Beth being with Collins. He had been a romper of the countryside himself and had followed many a skirt as far as it led. Every time the church met, he had arrived late for service, but in plenty of time to find a girl to "talk home." Cal had no idea that Collins was any less interested in women than he had been. He figured Beth and Collins were somewhere up on the mountain, with the world opened out beneath them, where they were possessors of it and not a soul could find them.

He was right in that, though Collins and Beth had made slow progress in their walking and were now only at the top of the rim of pastureland. But even from there they could see the farm stretched out below with its red-road vein, and they had watched Cal's car approach, and had even been able to see the steam rising from it. They could see the farmhouse, too, though not well because of the oak trees around it, and far out before them big cumulus clouds were hanging over the great Black Mountain range and the massive side of Mount Mitchell, where a professor had died, the one who proved it was the highest mountain in the East; he had fallen one night in a pond and his body later had been carried by mountain people to the top and buried there. A lonely place to rest. And cold in winter.

The wind was blowing in the hickories and elms and sourwood trees above them. The air smelled so sweet that Beth was almost beside herself as she and Collins started on toward the peak, Collins talking about the wonders of nature and asking her what she thought about flowers, and what butterflies were, and laughing with her and touching her every once in a while as if by accident, and holding her arm when they had a log to climb over, so that she became more and more elated.

Wild strawberries were ripe, and they came to a path at the edge of the pasture and stopped to pick a few. Collins sat down and gathered berries from around him. "We used to come up here and pick a pail of these, to make pies with. Mama Lotti would bring Paul and me and little Matthew. The three of us would pick and eat and pick, seemed like all afternoon, with Matthew eating more than he picked. They're so little, there's not much to be said for them."

"In a pie they're good," she said, sitting down beside him and eating the small horde of berries she held in her hand. A hawk was sailing in the clear sky, as if testing his wings and the strength of the high breezes.

"She fried pies back then, Mama Lotti did," Collins said. "I never did see that way of cooking done as well anywhere else. She would sweeten the strawberries, then flatten out the dough and put the strawberries in, cover them over, flop the pies into a frying pan, and when the pies came out, they were so hot inside you had to drink a pint of water to keep from burning your mouth."

"She ought to fry pies still," Beth said. "People often bring in wild strawberries. I expect pails of them are on the street now. But Mama Lotti won't go to the street much any more, you know, because she hates it so, and Papa King never thinks about food. Wild strawberries are expensive."

"They ought to be," he said, looking for more of them, swiveling around and turning over leaves, and finding a few. "There's a blackberry patch up by the fence," he said. "You like them?"

"Yes, but I'd rather walk on up the mountain, to see the flowers blooming."

"Would you? I told people when I left this place last time about the flowers blooming, but not many believed me. When you tell a man in Montana that the top of a mountain range turns purple with twenty-foot bushes blooming, he knows it's not true."

He stood up, then helped Beth up. She stood close to him for a moment and was nervous because of it, so nervous that she turned abruptly and hurried up the path.

They passed stands of galax, also in bloom, the small waxen leaves shimmering in the shade of the heavy trees, and they found a dozen kinds of wild orchids, purple and green and red, and came upon passion vines. It was a fairyland; it was just as Beth had remembered it from childhood, and she stopped from time to time to catch her breath and remind herself that it was the real world she walked in, that it did exist around her.

They looked above them higher on the mountain to see shimmering purple rhododendron blooming, covering the heathland so thick that a man could not make his way through.

She led the way along the path, always conscious of him near her and of his eyes on her and now and again of his hand touching her, and aware, too, that they were walking farther from the world of people below them and into a world which existed for themselves alone. The gray rocks were slippery where spring water crossed the trail, and he caught her as she almost fell. His face was close to her for a moment, a precious moment she thought, then she scrambled on. "I'm clumsy," she said. "I'm sorry." She led the way still, she being the one who wanted most to go on, who was not satisfied to stop yet, or was afraid to stop because she wasn't at all sure what might happen, what he might try or suggest, or what the place might seem to tell them to do, or even what she would permit under the dizzying spell.

They walked more slowly as the slope steepened. He talked about his boyhood on these hills and about searching for the cattle in the fall at roundup time, when the herd had to be driven down the trails to Asheville to the freight yard. "A world of work," he said. "Every fall we drove them off this mountain and down the valley to the creek, drove them along the creek to the river road. We had to drive them all the way in, because there wasn't much hope of a wagon containing them. People drove swine and sheep, too, even drove turkeys. As you walked along the river road you might see almost any sort of sight of animals and fowl, and drovers yelling at them. But Papa just drove cattle, and sometimes a mule or a colt."

"How far is it to town?"

"It must be about twelve miles. That sounds like a long walk to me now, but back then it wasn't thought to be anything. To these people, to walk twelve miles is a morning walk, that's all. And sometimes Paul or me would be sent in to Market Street to get something

156

Mama or Papa needed, be sent to pick up some item or other, and we thought nothing about going and coming that day. In fact, I liked to go on such trips."

"You liked to see the town, didn't you?" she said, smiling at him.

"To see the town? I'd say so. And the whole world. I wanted to see everything. I took courage in the number of people and happenings. Look at all there is to do, I would tell myself. I would get to the river and cross that on a barge if one was ready to go over, ride with a pack of cattle, or I'd walk across the railroad bridge or the road bridge and walk up the hill from the river valley, walk up to the tall town, set high where the river murkiness wouldn't bother anybody. The narrow, winding road went past a hundred little houses, where I used to think people would surely suffocate from living so close together. And dogs would come at me, because everybody had a dog, or a pack of dogs. And I would remember where the prettier girls lived and would whistle a tune as I passed their houses, and sometimes one would come out."

He was caught up in his story, for it had carried him back to his younger days. "But they weren't as pretty as you," he said.

"I wish I were pretty."

"You don't think you are? You're shaped like a charm, Beth. And your face is perfect, with that little chin and the high forehead, and I like the way your hair sweeps back here at your ear and the brown color of it."

"You'll never convince me I'm pretty," she said. "Or convince yourself, either."

"I think you are. Pretty beyond a man's powers to think straight, Beth." He squeezed her hand.

"I think I am some prettier since I've fixed myself up, I will say that," she said, and tried to smile.

"A little coloring on your cheeks and your lips, that's good. They stand as more open invitations now."

"Listen to that," she said, laughing. "Listen to him." But she wasn't criticizing him.

They walked on. "We're coming to the black forest now," he said.

157

She looked up the path and saw it then, dark before her, a solid forest of balsam. She stopped in awe of it, the black forest, opening like a cave. The wind rose in gusts and shook the heavy tree limbs and rumbled like music.

She turned and saw far below a silver river flowing toward the northwest, and on a distant hill sheep were grazing, white specks of life on the steep green hill near where the gray rail fences met. She felt his hand touch her waist and a gentle pressure as he turned her to face him, and she knew he was going to kiss her; she was afraid for herself and stepped back, and turned and moved on.

She heard his footsteps as he followed her.

The trees closed out the light. The only sunlight that came was filtered through the thick branches of dark-green needles, and occasionally there fell, as through a stained-glass window, a shaft of light. The forest floor was dark with ferns and moss and it reflected almost nothing, so that these long columns of light, filled with pollen which looked like dust, alone offered illumination for the path.

She looked up, trying to see the sky, and saw only specks of blue. All else was moving black branches and the interlocking limbs of the trees.

"A miracle," she whispered.

"Yes," he said. She turned to see that he had stopped back a way on the path and was looking about him into the depths of the secret place and at the shafts of light, and at the floor of moss so soft that his feet sank ankle-deep into it. About the forest was the heaviness of moisture and the smell of pine and the low, somber voice of the wind.

The centuries-old mystery of the place lay about her. She wasn't frightened, but she felt herself drawn to Collins. She stopped near him and he took her hand. He looked at her, his gaze soft like the light. It wasn't fear she had felt, but a sense of loneliness, and he led her upward along the path again, toward the top of the dome. He led the way, and she held back not at all. She closed her mind to thoughts about it. He led her, and there seemed to her to be no end to the path. The darkness was closer about them, and the trunks of the

158

trees, black and slightly tapered, rose for a hundred feet above them and closed out entirely now the other parts of the mountain world. Only this existed. This was reality now, and the noisy man-made world below was a distant crass image. There was no view now, there was no wide opening for the sky; there was only the world of black trunks and the canopy of black branches, and beneath them the moss and ferns and about them was the clean smell of the moist forest.

They walked on. A long way, she thought.

He stopped. She stood on the path and didn't turn from him. He came close to her and she let him hold her body against his. His face touched hers.

He picked her up, and she closed her eyes as he carried her away from the path through the moss. He stopped and laid her down.

She opened her eyes and watched him as he undressed her and kissed her body, and undressed himself. She watched him move; the whiteness of his body also was like a column of light. He came to her and lay down beside her. She sought him. And he was with her. Her body and his were one body, and her body swelled toward his and her arms were his, and his hands held her and caressed her and his tongue touched her and warmth spread through her in a lengthening opening of consuming beauty.

They lay stretched out, not moving. She comforted his head on her breast and watched far above her the branches sway in the higher winds. She rested in a daze world. Thoughts slowly formed of the wonders of her life in that moment, the wonder that her life would lead her to that moment, when every doubt about herself and living and her place in life, and her power to love and be loved, had ended in the stiffening of muscle and a cry unvoiced, in the wedding of breath and movement, in the softness of tissue. Her life had come to a peak of ecstasy which it would not surpass ever, she thought, and that moment would be remembered and would be part of her life from that time on; repeated with him or repeated in memory, it would not be washed from her life.

And always for her, life to come would be soft on her breast his head resting, and in her ear would be for all her life the sound of his voice speaking and the moaning of his breath. All beauty was in this time with him. It turned her thoughts within themselves and upon themselves. And she watched the branches high above, swaying and twisting. And only in long time passed did the worshipful feeling end.

He stirred. His hand moved up her body to stop near her neck. He touched her chin, her cheek, her hair, and entwined there. "Precious Beth," he said.

He sighed, then sighed again. He lifted his head and kissed her shoulder.

She was conscious then for the first time that he could see her naked. It was a funny worry, she told herself, for he had undressed her himself and she had not minded, but the sense of shame returned to her, now that the quickening, protecting need for him was gone. She reached out at once for her clothes, which he had piled to one side, and put on her underthings quickly, seeing him smile at her haste but hurrying all the faster. She slipped her dress on, and finally her stockings and shoes. Her hair, she knew, was a sight, and she laid the hairpins to one side on the moss and combed it, trying to get it in order. She combed the long brown strands while he watched, proudly she combed them, then rolled the hair into a bun at the back, just as she had fixed it earlier that morning, and fastened it with a comb.

He slipped his arm around her and pulled her tightly to him, then he released her. "Come along, dear," he said, and he led her down the hillside, not following the path, not even knowing where it was. There was no sense of direction now. They walked between the lanes of trunks until they saw a break in the dark arbor, and they followed that patch of light to a cliff from which they could look out over the waving tops of millions of wind-touched trees. Eagles flew nearby, holding close to the rocks, and they heard a wren noisily criticizing the ways of the day.

They rested at a spring. Worry had begun to come over her—not a shame for what she had done, but worry because she knew that she had been taken high into love and she knew also that Collins held the key to that love and to her future, and she was unsure how important that was to him. She knew that she was important to him. He had loved her in a way that proved this to her. She had no doubt at all but that in the forest above them for those moments he had loved her. Perhaps he loved her still, and the problem of her mind was what she might do to insure that or to elicit insurance of that, for it had become the most important consideration of her life.

She sank down on the grass, her thoughts erupting before taking form, so that she felt fear and had no plan to alleviate it. A baby, she thought—perhaps there will be a baby. No, please God no, she thought. But I want his baby, she thought.

What's he thinking? Why doesn't he speak? Men are cold after it is over—who once said that? But he could say something.

The trees, the tiny leaves turned below them. Then he spoke, as if he had heard her, and his voice was part of the wind in the caves nearby. He spoke quietly. He told her of her beauty of face and body. He told her intimate thoughts which he had had, which made her blush but which made her feel that she again was part of him, joined to him, her mind and his. He talked about her innocence and gentleness and compassion, and frankly about the quivering moment when the two of them had become part each of the other in that dim, old strange world of trees which had closed them in. "Not even God could see your body on the moss of that place," he said. "Only I could see you there, the curved beauty of your shoulders and raised breasts, while you waited."

He took her in his arms, and she put her arms around him and sought his lips with her lips, and for a long while they loved and held once more to each other, high on the cliff near where the birds nested, near the spring cold with water. And when they started down the mountain, she was weak with love for him.

The cabin of the first King homestead was only a chimney and a few scattered rocks near a deserted apple orchard of twenty trees now, and was located about a mile below the cliff, though it took them more than an hour to walk the steep path down to it.

The apple trees had finished with their blooms; the white and silvery blossoms were brown cups of husk. The oaks at the homesite were fat, since they had had sun room from the clearing to spread into, but they were dying in their lower branches, and no doubt the wind of the ice storms would tear more rocks from the chimney each winter, until at last the place would be covered by plants and vines; Nature would reclaim it.

On down the cove was a house built by Caleb King's father fifty years before, a frame house now deserted, which Caleb had used before moving his family to the city. It had a tin roof cover over the main part of it, and this glimmered in the sun, so that they saw it from a long way off. When they reached the farmyard, they found that the back sheds still had the wood shingles on the roof which had been put there decades before, but the shingles had buckled and given room to a light-green moss.

The house was damp and the fields were growing up in sedge and bushy trees. The blackberry plants at the fence corner were choked with vines. The scuppernong arbor had rotted through at the northeast post and part of the tangled old vine was piled on the ground. The chimney, never securely planted in the earth, had sunk in its own foundation site so that it no longer matched the house opening. Windows were cracked and two of them were open, and no doubt wild animals came and went as they chose.

"We used to eat on this porch," Collins said. He stepped carefully onto the frame timbers of it, for the floor boards were rotting. "You see that old well bucket with the bullet holes in it?"

"The hunters have used it for a target, I guess," she said. She accepted his help and stood beside him. He moved across the porch cautiously and pushed open the kitchen door.

"There might be an animal in there," she said.

He went on in and she followed. The door was broken, she noticed; it had not been opened in a long while, and the hinges were rusty. Inside the room was the odor of wood rot.

162

"Look at this place," he said over and over, as he went from one room to another, searching into his mind for old incidents. "Right here we ate our meals in wintertime, when it was too cold to eat on the porch, or in summertime if the flies got so heavy we had to eat in the house heat. We had a table right here, a round table on a pedestal base."

"I guess Papa took the furniture down to his place."

"And we had benches for us children, and two chairs for Mama and Papa. And a cupboard there for Mama's plates. And she had only enough for us, so if we had company—I remember one day your father and mother came to see us, and Paul and me had to soup from the same bowl so that there would be enough bowls to go around." He stood in the middle of the room, remembering that, seeing the images come back again. "Way off I see that," he said, "and I can even see Paul's white-haired head, and Matthew was little more than a baby then. And I can think back even before that, Beth, to when Mama hung a piece of fatback from the table leg, and I with my dirty little hands would grab hold of it and shove it in my mouth and suck on it. I can see myself doing that."

"Don't remember, don't remember any more," Beth said, suddenly sensing the hurt he had come to feel because of the old thoughts, from realizing that all the old was gone, and that the present would go, too, and he might look back a long while later and think, Yes, in that old room where I lived as a baby I stood thirty years later beside a girl named Beth, and both the baby and the young man are gone.

She touched his face. "It never happened," she said softly; "it never really happened, did it?"

"No," he said. "Whatever you say, Beth."

Outside he stood in the shadow of the house and looked out into what once had been a cornfield, and at the creek where once had stood a hand mill where corn had been ground into meal. "Those apple trees were the pride of this valley," he said. Now they were wrapped in age and their crooked limbs were entwined so closely that fruit wasn't likely to form. "It's all changed. Like a magic thing, it's all worn out and torn down and age-crippled, and it brings back such a memory, such a flood of thoughts."

"It's wearisome for a body to see the past," she said anxiously. She didn't want him to think any more about it. "It shows how far we've come and marks our days too clear."

He started on down the path toward the newer house, Beth's father's, which was hidden around the bend and was below them on the valley floor. They went past deserted pigpens, which were vine-covered and fallen in at the corners, past the branch where it washed across the road and where the horses once had stopped to drink before pulling the wagon on up the hill to the yard. They hurried along the stonebound paths until they came in sight of the newer house, and he put his arm around her and squeezed her close. "Now, don't you let them worry you with talk about where we might have been or what we might have done," he said.

"No, I won't. Don't worry."

"I want this to be a good day for you and me, Beth."

"It is," she said. "Yes, please, it is."

"Don't worry about anything," he said.

"No," she said.

They walked close together slowly along the trail. He stopped at the upper pasture gate and let down the top rail so that she could climb over, and she noticed then that he was studying thoughtfully the house below, as if there were something strange about it.

"What's the matter?" she said. She looked down at the house, too. Out in the yard, Cal, Lotti, and Johnny were walking back and forth near the springhouse. Cal had his hands behind him and his head down. Lotti was still and contemplative. Kin, she saw, was sitting motionless on a rock near Matthew.

She saw Paul. He was in a cleared place in the front yard, scanning the mountain behind the house, watching, waiting, standing as if poised, anxious for movement.

"Wonder where your papa is," Collins said.

"I don't know. I guess he's in the house cooking dinner." She still watched Paul, who looked up toward where they were. For a moment she feared he had seen them.

"No chimney smoke coming from the kitchen."

She considered that. "Well, maybe we're too late. Is it after time to eat?"

"It's almost time, about noon," he said, still studying the house and the family. "They don't walk about much, just stand there and stare out."

"Waiting for us, maybe."

"It's not that."

She glanced up at him. "What is it then?"

"I'll go ahead," he said. "You take it slow coming down."

"Is it Paul—something about Paul?"

He started on ahead, running toward the house.

"Collins!" She began to run, too. She ran fast, her dress billowing out behind her. She saw the family turn to watch Collins approach.

"No, no," she said, as if they could hear her. "Please God," she said, running fast.

She reached the yard fence and stopped. Collins was entering the house, and Paul was not following him. Paul was standing at the fence corner, looking at her.

"No need to hurry now," Lotti said to her.

"What do you mean?" Beth said.

"Now, don't you worry, Beth," Lotti said.

She saw sadness in Paul's expression, pity there. "What is it, Paul?" she said.

He shook his head.

Kin got up from the rock near the chimney where he and Matthew were, and there was little energy about the way he moved and he appeared to be anxious about her. "Kin?" she said.

He didn't answer. She bolted for the house, ran with all her might. She reached the door, but Collins met her and stopped her and held her. "No, Beth, no," he said, his voice deeper than she had heard it before, as if coming to him from afar. And she smelled the odor of the dead man, her father.

12

THE SHOCK OF THE DEATH FOLLOWING SO CLOSELY
hours of elation was all the more sharply distressing. Beth had left
her father years before, and even though it had not been of her doing,
for she was only eight years old at the time, even though it had been
his wish, for her mother was dead and he had admitted he didn't
know how to care for her properly, she had felt keenly the separation
and had felt responsible for having refused to go back to him five
years later when he had asked her to. That was during a visit to the
farm. For three days she had stayed with him. She had found the farm
lonely after living in town. She missed Cal and Lotti and the others.
She missed the noise of King Street; here there was no noise at all,
only isolated sounds—the horses moving against the rails, the rooster
crowing every three hours during the night, sending out his minor,
proud "all's well," the cows lowing of an evening when their udders
were full, the creaking of the wagon on the road, passing slowly by.

Her father had been of a mind that she should stay with him and
tend his needs, for he had no woman care except that of an elderly
relative who came once a week to clean house and wash and pound

his clothes clean. She lived three miles away and walked to and from his house on Tuesdays. She was a gnarled, clever woman, fast with her work. And strong. She could handle alone the heavy black iron pot in the back yard where the water was boiled.

He had told Beth about his loneliness and had asked her to stay with him. And terror had come to the girl. She had fled from him and had hid in the woods until it grew quite dark and she heard a wildcat cry off somewhere. She had gone home then, and she had told him, in the way a thirteen-year-old girl speaks, with tenseness and trembling lips, that she missed Papa Cal and Mama Lotti.

He had been stung by that, and even though it was evening, he went at once to the barn, drew the team from the stalls, and hitched them to the wagon. He told the girl to get up on the seat, and when she did, her small body alive with fear and caution, he whipped the horses into motion and drove down the clay road to the valley road, and along that to the river road, and along that to town, without a word, nothing said to her, no glance, either, his face stern as if cut from mountain granite, his eyes glistening like mountain mica.

But she had a hard face, too, and cold eyes, too, for her father was trying to come between her and her family.

Since then she had lived with forlorn memories of the three days at home and of the journey back. And now his death came to her with the slash and reminder of them, and brought out the guilt she had felt in leaving him; his death crushed out the hope she had nurtured those years that there would someday be a reconciliation between them. She had believed that the time would come when they might soothe their differences. She would, in that case, go to visit with him in the bare, gently creaking house, and would seek a close friendship with him, and perhaps would come to love him. That belief, which had held her firm in her childhood determination not to return to him, was shattered now by his death. He was gone, and except for Collins holding her, there at the door of the house, she might have fallen. "God help me," she whispered, a plea from her heart and a hope for forgiveness.

Collins led her to the shade of a patch of dogwood trees. She sat down on the chopping block. He knelt beside her, his arm around her.

Paul was standing nearby, watching, tears in his eyes, and he came to her, too. "Beth, for God's sake," he said, "don't cry, Beth."

She wept softly. He knelt beside her. "Beth, stop crying," he said, as if she could stop, as if he thought she could stop any more than he could keep the tears from his own eyes.

"I tell you all," Lotti said as she walked about nearby, "I tell you," she said, "he was ill for a long time, and we might have known he would be gone when we got here. He's been sick, and he stayed up here when he should have followed you to town, Cal."

"He had too much pride to follow me. But let's not talk about it."

"I don't see what's to be gained by weeping, Beth, for he's safe now. Death is a serpent, but we have the victory. Ours is the victory."

"Beth, don't cry," Paul said piteously.

She couldn't stop crying. She couldn't speak, and she was thankful for Collins' strong arm around her and for Paul near her; and she disliked the hateful words of hope from Lotti. She wanted no words of hope. She wanted to be punished for her failures of her father, for what victory was possible for her and him now, for her father, whom she would never in this world come to know well enough to be at ease with?

"Just leave the child alone," Cal said to Lotti. "Stop the racket."

"No better time to find comfort than now," Lotti said. "If Jesus doesn't mean anything to you in a time of need, then what good is He to you at all?"

"I don't find no comfort at this moment," Cal said. "I should have forced him to come into our house, and I meant to do it when I heard he was sick. I worried over asking him then. Some of us should have come out here to get him. A man can't live alone; no man can do that and be a safe person. Out here in this forsaken cove, this damp creek bottom—better to stay up in that first location where my grandfather built than to come down here where every mist is a mourning to the window glass."

168

He looked at the paint-flaking, tall house, two stories on the front with a kitchen wing behind; a window glass was broken in the second story and a rag flapped from the hole. Inside there his brother had lived, a man apart, brooding about the old days, wondering still, no doubt (for how could he stop wondering when he had spent all his early life at it), if his father had preferred Cal to him, and if he could manage to hold to the whole of the farm, which he had done. Yes, he had done it, and what a shame, Cal thought, that he had shriveled down to so little at the close that his was no fit ghost to join his father's.

"Well, somebody's going to have to get him out of there," Matthew said.

"Let go of that worry, too," Cal said. "Let's have no more complaints about his going."

"Well, we're not doing anything," Matthew said. "I might as well go find a box for him."

"Then go," Cal said sharply. "Take a car and see if you can find a casket. Do it, instead of looking at me. I don't know what to tell you."

Beth wept. Her body bent low in mourning. She sat on the wood-chopping block, the only place her father had worked for that past winter, though she didn't know that, and wept. He had had enough food in the house, salt bacon and beans, corn meal and apples. He needed no food, but he had had to chop wood. He couldn't seem to get warm. He had stuffed wood into the stove until the chimney was red all the way to the chimney opening, then he had put pine into it so that it would burn fast, but he never got warm. His aged cleaning woman, when she was there on Tuesdays, would have sweat on her from the heat, but he was cold. He would go out and cut new wood, and each fall of the ax on the block was a blow, but at what enemy he was never able to say.

Matthew didn't find a casket, but neighbors, when they heard the news he brought, began to gather, and they said they would box and deliver the body to Cal in town. Cal offered them money, but they refused it. There were some tasks a countryman did for which he rarely accepted pay, Cal knew, and death was involved in most of them. The people were awed by death. They could ignore every teaching of the Church concerning their lives. "Ah, he ain't got no right to preach about how many women a man needs to serve himself with," a man might say. But Death, the creaking-boned and groaning form, the mournful face, socket-black and eyeless, the cold, black-gutted, speechless, soundless member, Death they could not ignore.

Neighbors promised to join together to get the body out of the house, and Cal thanked them. A young second cousin said, "Maybe you'll come back out here to live now, Mr. King."

"Maybe," Cal said. But he could not return, he knew; he could not with good spirit awaken now to challengeless days.

No man can live here now, he thought, for death is everywhere about the place, even at the chicken lot, where foxes have broken in and eaten the fowl, except for those two hens huddled in the elm where they will surely die. The pigs are killed in their pens.

His mother had died here, too, of consumption, in a downstairs room. His father had died of a stroke which had cut him down in the prime of life in plowing season and left him bellowing like an animal in the south field. He had almost finished plowing the long rows and was working toward the crook of the field when it happened, and he never got enough of his senses back to know the time of day.

Cal turned away from the staring kinfolk and old-time neighbors and walked apart, seeking relief from the heavy thoughts. Was there nothing to be said of goodness here? he asked himself. The hunts, yes, that had been good. The nights camped out with a fire and the talk of other hunts and of possums and coons and dogs. The feasts on the church lawn, that had been good, with tables laden with fried chicken, deviled eggs, and chess pies. Laughter, singing. Life was rich then, wasn't it? The old way had cheer. The warm rooms of the house, his father's laugh, the smell of breakfast in the kitchen of a morning, of hickory and pine burning in the fireplace of an evening, the smell of oil lamps, the heaviness of quilts in the cold room where he and Clarence slept. The pasture, crisp in fall mornings with the leaves turning. The horses and cows waiting impatiently in the shed, turning and rubbing against the wood, wanting to be outside, following him now down the lane to the pasture gate. "Eat your fill, Cary, eat your fill, Mae," he, a boy of twelve, would say to them, to the two big brown cows which paid him no mind until milking time, when he would lead them to the barn again, where his mother or a sister waited.

"You come on out and live here, Mr. King," the young cousin said; he had sought Cal out. "It's a good house."

"Tear it down," Cal said quietly.

"Sir?" The cousin was startled, not having believed what he heard. He was about twenty-one, clean of features and sandy-haired.

Cal looked at him, hesitated on the verge of speech. "You want it?"

"Sir?" the cousin said, again startled.

"You can buy it from Beth. I'll loan you the money," he said, and walked away from him. Let him have it, if he liked it. He who likes a grave should have one, for they're not dear to find. On this rocky soil, let the boy work. But don't let him aspire to anything.

He walked to the spring, where he got a pail of water. He brought it back and filled the radiator of his car. He turned the car around, so that it faced downhill, and got its tires in the road ruts just right. Matthew brought up Collins' car and filled it to the cap, too. Lotti was still talking and walking about under the cover of the oaks, little Johnny hanging onto her hand and acknowledging first one introduction, then another. She was visiting. Cal didn't see how she could rise out of the slump of such a day and visit with people contentedly.

He honked his horn for her. Collins and Beth walked to the other car, Collins' arm around her, Paul nearby, not able to touch her, deep in his grief for her. "Hey, Kin," Cal called, "you coming with me?"

Kin shook his head.

"Yes, you better come with me," Cal said.

Kin stood by the other car, shifted anxiously from foot to foot. Cal walked back to him. "Come on now, boy. Let them be."

Beth was weeping on Collins' shoulder. They were in the back seat. Paul was sitting on the other side of her, his face a mask of pain, his hands knotted in his lap. He was awkward with emotions. He had been a servant to emotions all his life, Cal knew, but he had tried to keep them secret, for to him one's emotions were as personal as the organs of his body and should be treated with privacy. But he could not do it, he could not hold his feelings secret.

Cal turned away. "Come along, Kin."

Kin followed him reluctantly.

"You stop thinking about all this, you hear?"

Lotti still wouldn't get into the car. Cal honked his horn for her. "Lotti, damn it," he called, "you and your boy get in here, if you're going with me."

She moved closer, but she went on visiting, talking over the holy meaning of the evening, speaking to first one, then another, not at all anxious to leave this natural place which was the choicest setting for her life. In the next house up the cove she had lived safely, had had no worries about the souls of her children; she had known they would grow up to work the land and tend to stock and live a natural life. No woman could ask for better assurance for herself than such knowledge about the future. "I think little Johnny needs to see things like we've all been hearing about today," she said to a second cousin, Sarah Ross, "for death brings us all closer to Him, even though it pains us."

She eased nearer to the open door of the car, and finally, with a few lingering words of friendship to the women gathered around, she told Johnny to get into the back seat and she got into the front seat, but she wouldn't close the door, not until Cal let the car start slowly forward; then she at last waved goodbye to the people.

Matthew was already driving the other car down the road. Cal followed. "You hold us up all evening," he said. "Now we got the road to go in the dark."

"Well, you've got lights, ain't you?" Lotti said.

Kin and Johnny sat in the back seat, watching the lights of the other car as it sought out the twists of the road.

"Death don't bother me," she said. "It is appointed to us to die." She spoke on about it, her voice low, so that sometimes the noises of the car motor would rise above her. Her words came and went: a time

172

to die . . . turn to dust . . . raise from the dead . . . once to die . . . the power of death . . . the last enemy . . . destroy the enemy . . . the last enemy is death. . . .

Death, Kin thought; she talks on and on about it. Better, he thought, to be in that other car and hear the words of mourning. "Hush, Beth, hush," he had overheard Collins say to her when he had stood beside their car. "Hush, dear, hush, Beth." Better to be with them and even to weep with them than to listen to the ancient words which spoke themselves of victory but came far out of the past, the musty odor of death even on them.

"Victory over death . . ."

Beth, Kin thought, dear Beth, your father's dead.

"Ours is the victory . . ."

"Hush, Lotti, hush that talking," Cal said.

"Well, I thought you'd like to know the hope."

"Don't you care that he's dead?"

"Why, he's with Jesus, as sure as we're here in this car."

Like bugs, Kin thought, we travel like bugs on the back of the ridge. Perhaps from another ridge or from a house afar, a mountain boy is watching us, two black bugs with white-yellow eyes moving along the ridge.

Cars of mourning, he thought.

And in the other car Paul held her hand in his hand and patted it gently; it pained him to hold it, and perhaps she didn't know he held it, for she was weeping and Collins had his arm around her and she was nestled close to him. But he held her hand and comforted her. She wept, and Collins said, "Don't cry, dear. Dear, don't cry." And Paul was ill with agony and frustration, the agony for her, whom he comforted.

During the several days which followed the discovery of the dead man, a change came over Beth. She had come to grips with a brutal antagonist and had grown stronger almost overnight. She was harder in mind, more thoughtful before she spoke, less sure she could soothe another person's pain or solve his problem. She was less anxious

173

to change the opinions of others, realizing no doubt that her rightful place in life was not at the helm of the vessel of all humanity but at the helm of the vessel which was her own, which was more, she feared now, than she could handle rightly in dangerous seas.

The heavy weight of life had settled on her for a time, and she had changed because of it.

A change, too, came over Collins. Several times before in his life he had encountered death. He had known a woman in Plainsville, Ohio, who had died of cancer, and he had seen a man die on the street in Denver. The police had roped off the sidewalk to keep the curious back. To both of these incidents Collins had been an on-looker; he had not been emotionally involved. At another time, he had been a friend of a family in which a child had drowned, and he had known for an hour the intensity of their suffering. He had been able to escape only by moving on. But he could not escape now, not Beth's grief.

He had liked Beth very well from the beginning, no more perhaps than he would have liked another girl who was fresh and pretty, and close at hand. He had liked Beth as well or better than any girl he had met for a while, but when he had realized that she loved him, when they were out under those damn balsam trees where everything was so holy, he had come to care for her more than he wanted to. And when he had comforted her in the car, her grief had seemed to melt into his own heart. As the car wound over the expansive mountains, he had felt that he was a small item indeed in a mighty cosmos, and it seemed that he and the girl were in league together, companions in suffering.

Also, the dead body of Clarence King had been a sight to shock him, for the man not only was dead but he had been dead for several days and was decaying and varmint-bitten. It was as if he had been buried and weeks later dug up. And though Collins had seen the corpse for ten seconds, at most, the sight had gone through him. It had stunned his sense of laughter. It had burrowed into his secure concept of life. The man dead was a man partly devoured; he shuddered before it, and he could not dismiss the hopelessness which

174

attached itself like a leech to his forward-rushing life. The world was, he realized, a land of terrors. Perhaps it was also a land of beauty, but it was a land of terrors, and a cold promise waited at the end.

He tried to shake off the idea; he had been able to in the past, but this was no casual or historical incident; this was life around him, and he could not do it. He found himself then seeking sympathy, and he offered sympathy to Beth, and his sympathy, he knew, was also meant for all others in the painful march of humankind. The sympathy he offered Beth was also sympathy for himself.

He found now that he was comfortable only when with her. He was lonely of a night in the coldness of his own bed; he was lonely for her. It was not that he had a need for a woman, for any woman, but that he had a need for the woman who had come to be meaningful to him in a serious way, one beyond his own will and control.

One afternoon he was lying on his bed upstairs when he saw her go into her room across the hall. He got up slowly, stretched; the upstairs was hot, but the hall window was open and a breeze stirred the curtains lightly. He approached her door. He stood there watching as she sat down on the edge of the bed and idly began playing with the tassels on the counterpane. She was not weeping; she had not wept in several days. But she was pained still; the shock had not fully left her yet.

He went in and closed the door.

"Beth," he said softly, sitting down beside her. "You stop being so sad, will you?"

"I would if I could," she said, smiling gently.

"You let me worry." Then he said guardedly, "I do worry, too, Beth, since that day at the farm. I get to thinking about people dying."

"Do you?" she said. She ran her cool fingers over his face. "Hush," she said. She lay back on the pillow and held her arms out to him.

He leaned toward her and rested his head on her body. "It's not like me to worry," he said. "I get to feeling lonely, thinking about life ending someday."

"Nothing's to be said about it, except what we all know," she whispered. "Hush." She rubbed the side of his face with her fingers.

"Like a lost tribe, we are all part of a lost tribe," he said, "and we wake up one day and realize it. We see that we'll die."

"Yes," she whispered.

"I could go through half the continent and tell myself that nobody suffered, for I had found a way to live above it, to move on past it, to keep changing myself to better times."

"Maybe all of us should seek better times," she whispered.

Her hands moved over his body comfortingly. She soothed him, and she seemed to be an answer to his fears, and even to the challenges of his thoughts. He wondered if perhaps a woman was an affirmation of life, if union with a woman was an answer made to the lostness and challenges of coming death, a tribute of sorts to the life source, a will to start again; even though the coming generation would be marked with the tribal curse and would be doomed with the tribal doom, even so, it would continue.

There on the bed, with the curtains fluttering nearby, he found in her touch and in her arms an experience which was meaningful to him in a deeper way than any he had known before. It had no gaiety to it, it was not the enjoyment of a union of a man and woman, but went beyond enjoyment. He grasped her and held to her; he heard himself whispering words to her, to this one who had come to have special meaning in his life, the child-girl-woman whom he had always sought. He sought oneness with her now in the face of life and death, and he heard coming from his lips words of devotion for her. Even as he spoke he realized, wondering at the marvel of it and the mystery of it, wondering if ever he would regain sole control of himself, he realized even as he spoke the words of love to her that they were coming from his heart.

13

THE DEATH OF CLARENCE KING BROUGHT LOTTI TO consider the possibility of Caleb's death, and she came to wonder about his will. "What's for Johnny in it?" she wanted to know.

Cal told her the boy would get a proper listing, but she feared the will would be challenged after his death, and she much preferred for Cal to provide for Johnny now, so that none of the other children could possibly get what was supposed to be his. "You know yourself, Cal," she told him, "you put money out anywhere in this house, and all your children come running to grab it from each other. Johnny is the only one who doesn't want more than his share. So you have to provide for that boy and insure that he gets it."

Her sole concern about the will was for Johnny, which Beth thought was unfair, particularly to Kin, but Lotti said Cal would take care of Kin all right but who would protect her youngest? She believed that she must do this herself, and just as everything which got past the wall of her isolation became an obsession with her, so this became one, too. Fanaticism overcame her, and she dedicated herself to securing for Johnny complete security.

On the Monday morning following the funeral of Beth's father (a dreary affair at the Methodist Church for members of the family and two funeral directors), she dressed herself in a lace blouse, a fresh woolen skirt, and a pair of low-heel oxfords that Beth had given her a year before and which still had their first polish on them. She combed her hair back smoothly from her face and took her change purse from her apron pocket.

"Where you going, Mama Lotti?" Beth asked.

"I like to get out, same as another," Lotti said. She drew a blue shawl over her head and about ten o'clock left the house.

She negotiated King Street without incident, turned left at Market, and walked up a slight rise to the Square, which seemed to her to be frightfully large and active. She passed in front of the bakeries and linen shops, doctors' offices and restaurants, and by the tall building put at the spot where for many years a tombstone cutter had run his shop. Down the hill from it she stopped at a small red brick building which housed a number of law offices, one of which belonged to a Mr. Jeff Bailey, an ambitious man, balding at thirty-five because, as the mountain people said, of his heavy scheming. He had come out of the mountains when he was eighteen and had worked and fought his way to an education. He was from Bailey Cove, a long, narrow indentation where over a hundred members of the Bailey clan lived in eleven houses; a baby was always sticking his head out of a womb there. And mountain preachers sometimes set revival tents right at the mouth of the cove, for the Baileys were known to be an active, hard-living lot.

Lotti had known Jeff's mother from the church meetings in the country, and she remembered Jeff as a boy. At least, she remembered the pack of Bailey boys which was always roving about and creating devilment, and she knew he had been one of them.

He seemed to be pleased to see her now. He was a stocky, ugly man, but was neatly dressed in a heavy woolen suit. He took her into his bare inner office, where he listened patiently as she told him about Johnny. When she was done, he began to outline for her the possible forms of trust funds, but he noticed that she didn't appear to be attentive to what he was saying. "You seem to be interested in your questions but not in my answers, Mrs. King," he said at last, smiling.

"I didn't come for the answers," Lotti said bluntly. "I know what I want to know, and I came to ask you for the loan of a law book so I can study the matter out for myself."

Bailey sucked at a tooth far back in his mouth. "Ma'am?" he said. "You want a book to borrow on the law?"

"I read the Bible with understanding, so I can manage to make out the laws themselves."

Bailey sucked at his tooth some more. He peered at her thoughtfully. "Ma'am, God didn't write the laws," he said. She didn't seem to be impressed by that. "He didn't write them, and even lawyers who have read them can't usually figure out what they mean." He smiled at her, but she didn't smile at him. She was as solid and serious as ever. "Ma'am," he said then, "the law's a terror and none too clear. You can't read it."

She returned his gaze. "I'll pay you five dollars for a loan of a law book," she said.

Bailey protested still, but it got him nowhere, so at last he selected two books and suggested she look them over in his outer office. She took a chair by the window, where the light was good, and opened the first of them. It was a bulky work and contained hundreds of laws, and she realized from the start that no reasonable person could hope to twist his mind around to accommodate them. They were beyond meaning.

With a sense of defeat she lay the book aside and opened the other one.

This was a collection of stories and descriptions of court cases pertaining to inheritances. It also had been written by men of little talent, but the stories could be made out, and Lotti saw with rising satisfaction that the book was not beyond her. She read all morning, sitting stiffly in the chair, recording in her mind the catalogue of terrifying incidents and happenings which had befallen women who had permitted their husbands to die without wills, or without wills which would stand up against the onslaughts of their families. The book chronicled the plight of hungry children, suffering for a crust of bread, described the suffering of widows who had been left without covers for their beds. It was a fear-inspiring collection, and Lotti pressed assiduously into the study of it, her lips firmly met, her eyes narrowed in concentration.

At dinner, scarcely was the family assembled before she began to share with them her horde of stories about disappointed heirs. Every bite of food was accompanied with words about the law. Many errors had been made in the last wills and testaments of people over the centuries, and Lotti seemed to be intent on reciting them all.

After ten minutes Cal left the table. He carried his plate with him and ate by himself out on the front porch.

The best solution to Johnny's problem, as Lotti came to view the matter, was for Johnny to inherit his twenty per cent of the store now, just as Paul had. Surely in this way there would be no doubt about his owning it. She pestered Cal with this view one night, elaborating on the reasons for it.

"Lotti," Cal said to her finally, "the child's not hardly out of swaddling clothes and you've got him in business."

Lotti closed the door for privacy; she didn't want Paul to know what she was about. She spoke quietly but with emphasis. "I'm trying to protect his rights. We don't know when you might leave us, Cal, and maybe you trust Paul and Matthew—"

"Lotti, I can't by law give stock to a child."

"What's that? What did you say?"

"I said the boy is not of legal age, and he can't inherit nothing yet."

Lotti was nonplussed. "I've been studying of the law," she said.

"Well, have you read about any little seven- or eight-year-old children in town owning property? They can't own nothing, 'cept in trust, and their parents are the ones who supervise the trust, so where do you gain?"

She became quite nervous because Cal had called upon the source of her own authority, the law.

The next day she persisted, but to no effect except that Paul came to know of her intent. "The twenty per cent of the store I got," he said at supper, "is in exchange for my services to the store in holding it together, and now you're acting like it was my inheritance."

"It is your inheritance," Matthew said, surprised. "Isn't it his inheritance, Papa?"

"That's my understanding," Cal said. He had discussed the matter with Paul before giving him the twenty per cent. "Paul and me discussed it that way," Cal said simply.

"But he's denying it," Matthew said bitterly.

"It's payment for my sacrifices to the damn place," Paul said.

"No, it's not, is it, Papa?" Matthew said.

"You stay out of this," Paul said to him, and stormed out of the room into the kitchen. "I'll not be taken advantage of, even by my own family," he shouted back.

Collins left the table, deciding not to get involved in this, or perhaps knowing that, no matter what Paul said, the power to designate heirs rested with Cal, not with him, and that his words had no more meaning than wind in rafters.

"I'm the one who has sweated and strained to keep that store going," Paul shouted, "I'm the one who has worked for it, and now I'm to get the same percentage as that angel boy, who doesn't know a head of lettuce from a bushel of apples."

"Now, watch what you say," Lotti replied heatedly.

Paul appeared once more in the room. "Has he worked at the store? Has he turned his hand over to save the place when we faced closure? Has he traded for anything?"

"He's just a child right now," Lotti said.

"Well, what's he trying to inherit the place for if he's just a child?"

"He was born for a part of it," she said heatedly.

"Was born for it? And you think he's got a right to as much of the store as me, even though he's done nothing for the store at all, and I've given ever thought in my head to it? You think because we was born of the same kind, we get the same part, is that it?"

Lotti's lips worked nervously. "I don't like to be shouted at," she said.

"Hell!" Paul stormed out onto the front porch. "I'll not be cheated

181

by my own family," he called back.

It was a hectic night for the family, full of charges and pleas. Paul had now openly revealed that in his mind the store was, in large part, his by rights. The fact that he and Cal had once had another understanding was of no weight with him. Cal objected firmly to this, though he knew a mark of the mountain trader was that he sometimes forgot what he had agreed to; Cal had suspected when Paul had taken twenty per cent of the store that he would later insist on getting more of it.

The next morning at the store, Paul spent over an hour in conference with Matthew, and at noon, just as the family finished dinner, Matthew asked his father for a meeting in the parlor. The men, except for Collins, who said he didn't want to attend, filed through the hallway. Collins sat in the dining room with Beth, Kin, Lotti, and Johnny and listened to that part of the conversation which could be heard. Evidently Matthew was demanding that his father give him his twenty per cent of the store. Otherwise, he said he was going to accept an offer of an office-work job in a trucking company in Winston-Salem, a firm which sometimes shipped merchandise for the King Store.

Cal came out of the parlor, drawn and aggravated. His life was dedicated to holding together his family, and he knew Matthew had a right to his part, for Matthew also was working hard in the store. Still, Cal wasn't at all sure Matthew was able yet to represent so large an ownership. The boy wasn't on his feet. Also, this loss would mean that Cal controlled only sixty per cent of the ownership of his own store, and if Collins got the notion he wanted his twenty per cent now, that would leave Cal with forty per cent. His boys would have the store.

For days Cal mulled over the possibilities, debating with himself about what he should do, and he grew more and more aggravated, especially with Lotti, who had created the commotion in the first place. All Paul was doing through Matthew was blocking her in her effort to get Johnny his twenty per cent now. Paul had seen this way and had taken it, and in doing so he had left the family with a number of problems.

Cal decided that he would, in all fairness, have to give Matthew his twenty per cent, but he said the gift wasn't effective for two years. It was his hope that in that time Matthew would mature. He was taking a gamble, he realized, but he had confidence in the basic soundness of Matthew, in spite of present signs of nighttime weakness. As for Collins, Cal reasoned that he would leave town again soon. Collins had spent too many years free from home worries to abide them long.

At supper one night Cal informed the family of his decision and gave Matthew a signed paper. Collins seemed to view the matter casually. Kin was upset by it, and so was Lotti, who watched tight-lipped and pale of face.

Beth told her she had better let the contest drop right there. This was when they were in the kitchen washing dishes. "You ought to be glad Matthew got twenty per cent of the store, instead of getting so angry about it," she said.

"What? Glad?"

"He's your son, too, Mama Lotti."

Lotti stared at her defiantly, then all of a sudden a tremor came over her.

"It's all the one family," Beth said.

Lotti sank down in a chair, sat limp and still, the dishrag flopped over one knee, her lips pursed. "I do get to ignoring them," she said. She got up, struck by the knowledge and embarrassed because Beth was aware of it, and left the room.

"Mama Lotti," Beth called, following her. She tracked after her to the bedroom, where Lotti was sitting on the bed. "What's the matter?"

Lotti shook her head. "Go on, Beth."

"You don't feel too good?"

Lotti inhaled deeply, sighed with weariness. "I can't fight them all, can I?" A Kodak picture of little Johnny, its corner stuck behind the door molding at the head of her bed, was close by. She looked at it tenderly. "And it is true, the others are my boys, too."

Beth sat down on the bed beside her. "I know you love them, same as Johnny. Maybe they are a disappointment to you, but they're your own."

"I've had hopes for each one, each in his day."

"And now they're growing up so well. Matthew is a tall, handsome man, and he owns part of a business. That's good. And Collins is home."

Lotti nodded. "I understand," she said, as if there was no need to speak further about it.

For days after their discussion, she lived in a world of calm, and was polite in a studied way to Matthew and Paul. She watched them at mealtimes and on the porch and in the parlor, as if coming to terms with what they were, as if discovering them, defining them. She asked Paul about his plans for marriage; she asked Matthew if he didn't know a girl he would like to have in for dinner, a suggestion which so startled him that he sharply blurted out his refusal.

She began to fix favorite dishes for different members of the family. Often she served lamb, which Cal liked immensely but which the family had not had for years. She made pies and cakes and cookies. She made fresh light bread. She fixed herself up, too, threw away the man's straw hat she had been wearing, and got out the old, colorful bonnets which she had once worn and which Cal preferred. And after seven years of sleeping in the room with Johnny, she returned to Cal's bed.

A kindness, a desire to be friendly, came over her as if in apology for the aloofness which had held her before. But after a while, the excitement went out of the new part she played, and she began again a somewhat more chilly service.

To Cal, this struggle over the inheritance had already proved costly, with only one benefit emerging, and that was the change, even though tentative, in Lotti and the resulting change in Johnny, who had begun to participate in the affairs of the family. Cal suspected

184

that soon the boy might even venture onto King Street and would awaken to those natural hungers to rule and trade which Cal considered to be basic to healthy life. The boy needed to be hardened up. Collins was helping, but Paul and Matthew only terrified the child, seemed to be willing for him to be sacrificed if they could obtain more wealth because of it. Their desire for wealth and power was all right. Cal didn't object to that. But they seemed to know little about how wealth and power should be used to benefit the family or the community, or even themselves.

They would not help Johnny, but the one to blame for the boy's weak lot was Lotti, he felt, for she had no understanding of wealth and power at all, but only of beneficence, so she became not even an effective critic of the masculine-type world around her. She had withdrawn from the actual world, and she attacked it blindly, striking out where evil did not need to be attacked at all, it seemed to him. She was rearing a boy not for the real world; he was being given too many woman notions for that. She was creating a distortion, in Cal's view—not a dangerous creature, for he wasn't likely to have much will for authority, but probably a nervous person who would always yield a harvest of criticism of the world about him. It was not Johnny's fault; it was Lotti's, for she so much wanted a world which was given over to goodness that she wanted her child to be unable to create evil, not realizing that a child without the power to create evil was without the power to create at all.

One night they lay in bed, and as was her habit, now that she was once more with him, she talked a good deal about the day, about what she had done and what one of the boys had said about it, about Collins urging her on to cook apple dumplings soon, about Beth asking her to walk with her up to the Square to see the sights. "You ought to get out more yourself, Cal, get off the street," she said.

"They got too much glass up there," he said.

"Glass? What about glass?"

"Reflects everything, wherever you look. They got cars moving on the street, and they move in the glass. People are on the sidewalks and in the glass." He spoke slowly, sleepily. He wasn't accustomed to lying awake at night and talking.

"I don't know what you mean," she said.

"Revolving doors, got those now. Glass. I was up the street not more'n two weeks ago, and two country people got in one slot. They didn't know how to do it. They didn't know which way to push."

"I don't know what you're talking about."

"That little Johnny is the one who needs to get out more."

He heard her gasp, and he suspected he had made a mistake by referring to Johnny so abruptly.

"What you say?" she said. "What was that? Johnny?"

"Well, he might come up the street sometime, at least."

"To the store, you mean?" A fever suddenly was in her voice. "So that's it, is it?" She sniffed irritably, nervously. "I see it. Like a plot you've made against me, all the talk about what I cook for dinner and what I wear and how nice we get along. I see it now. You give Matthew his twenty per cent, you give Paul his part, and then you won't give Johnny a bit of his, and in spite of it you expect me to be a mother to this family—"

"Now, Lotti, you better keep from excitement—"

"Take him to the store, that's what you want to do, is it?"

"Lotti, you know you still keep him off to himself too much."

"He plays with Collins. I never saw you play with him."

"If he would come up to the store—"

"The store, the store? What's wrong with right here?"

"Well, I don't have no mercy here for playing. My lord, Lotti, I ain't a nursemaid. If he wants to be a man—"

"He is a man. Don't you tell me he's not."

"Now, Lotti, listen to me, he's got to develop his strength, for he's going to need it later to protect himself."

She began to weep. "You're unfeeling. You don't know," she said.

"You want that boy to be so out of step with the world and so unknowing that no power on earth can protect his estate, for it can be taken from him by any woman or man who has the will to do it."

"Now, you keep your voice down. I don't want him hearing such talk."

186

He lowered his voice. "You've got to get over the notion that whenever somebody leaves his prayers, he's gone out into the ways of evil. It's not so. That little fellow is going to be so tenderhearted that he won't be able to bring himself to eat a bite of meat once he finds out where it comes from."

She began to sob, and he sighed heavily. He was hurting Johnny and himself more than helping, he knew, but he was trapped by his own first error. He patted her shoulder, sorry for her. Maybe that had been so when they were back in the mountains, when he had married her before he had made love to her. He had never even kissed her except with a fence between. She had insisted that there be a fence there. She had been a fearful girl, even then.

He stroked her shoulder, stroked her head, and spoke softly to her. He knew how lost and lonely was her heart now, and that a woman growing old would cling to her last child. "It's going to work out all right, Lotti," he said. "Life heals many a wound that we don't plan for."

She sobbed on.

"I know the boy means more than half your life to you. But he's got to be a man when he gets grown, Lotti, not a doll baby."

"If you'd give him his part of the store now—"

He gasped. "Don't say no more," he said bluntly.

"What's the matter with you?"

"I don't want to hear another word about his inheritance for ten years, if I live that long."

She blurted out suddenly, "No, of course, that hurts you to think about, don't it? You've got that pack of boys so cruel they'll steal the shirt from his back, and then you blame my boy for not being cruel like them."

"He's got to learn to fight 'em off, Lotti."

"You've got my own sons so cruel they'd steal from one another. Well, what's to be said for you, Cal, for them, when they have no heart inside them?"

"They have, ma'am."

"That Paul—"

187

"Yes, and him, too, for he's got more emotion than you and me both—"

"Don't protect Paul. He's mean, he's mean to his bones—"

"I think not, if conditions pleased him more. I thought you saw that, I thought you had come to help out here—"

"Help? Help you take my boy to your store, steal him apart from me—"

"Steal? Ay, God, I don't steal, ma'am. And you listen; you needn't think I'm going to turn over part of the store to that boy, so don't talk about it, and stop feeding me and pawing over me of a day and night—" A tide carried him and he could not escape it; he moved away from the trust he held for her and she for him, broke the close union they had shared.

"You don't want me to touch you now, is that it?"

"Lotti, let's say no more."

"Do you want me to leave? I'll leave, if I have to, if that's it."

Suddenly, furiously, helplessly, he said, "Ay, God, leave, then, and take him with you." It was too much to consider, it grew and had no sense to it, it caught him from too many different directions at a time. Break free, he thought, knowing she would not leave him. "Ay, God," he said, "I never knew it was such pain to raise a preacher."

He got out of bed and sought the chest, pulled open a drawer, and sought his underclothes.

"You leaving?" she said tensely. She sat up in bed. "Going to the store?" she said. "Yes, you go on to the store; run it day and night."

"Hush," he said, softly, deeply. "Good God, Lotti, let's not talk any more now."

"Go on up there and open them big doors, let the noise go out. Get the farmers up in the market place to trade. Take Paul with you. Take Matthew up there, if he's come in from the whores."

"God damn, shut up, shut up," he said, and stumbled into the parlor, where red ashes lay in the hearth. "Ay, God," he called back to her, "Lotti, don't say no more."

"What a pity," she said, and she came to the bedroom doorway, "what a pity this has happened, Cal. You've taken them. You've stole them from me."

"Ma'am, I never stole. I do not steal."

"You have such honor, is that it? My father was a man of honor."

"Your father is an old song with you. Ay, God, I never heard when I was a boy such high praise of him."

"You hush!" she said fiercely, moving to him, leaning toward him. "You hush!"

He stared at her, stunned, weakened by her. "I didn't defame him," he said simply.

"No," she said, deep in her throat.

He turned from her. No more, he thought. God, no more now. He moved to the door. He still had the underwear in his hand. Where was he going, he asked himself.

"You won't get him, Cal," she said. Her face was red with the firelight, and her eyes glistened as she strained toward him. "You and your money ways."

"Lotti," he said slowly, softly, his voice husky and breaking, "Lotti, all I've heard from you for so long has been money. Money and the store. I go to the store in the morning to work and I think little about it all day, except the work, but the store to you is alive, like a beast. You are the one who lingers on thoughts of the store. You talk about Paul being selfish in his interest, but he's no more selfish than you are for that boy of yours, for I never saw a body who was more dedicated to money than you've been about him." He looked calmly at her face. "He ain't put upon, Lotti. All he needs to be a preacher is a pair of brogans and a copy of the Bible. He can go out to the nearest farm road and start appealing to families. Why does the store matter so much to you?"

Stiff of face, she watched him. "Hush," she said. "You hush, Caleb."

"You want a boy who is going to be a preacher, don't you? Is it for God he's to be a preacher or because of the store?"

"Hush, I said."

"I'll give his twenty per cent to the church if you want me to, Lotti."

Sternly she looked at him. "Cruel, you're cruel, you hurt me. But you listen. Ain't nobody living without a stained hand, and maybe I think money, too, since it's the weather in this house. Maybe so. But the stain on you, Cal, is that you've shut me out. That's the stain on you, and God will meet you for it." She wept. She bowed her head and wept, her hands over her face. "Cal," she said weeping.

He touched her, and she drew back from him. "Cal," she said again, needing him.

But she stood apart from him, her head bowed still, her hands covering her face, rejecting him. Close by she was, and a long way off. Needing him from a long way off.

14

For days after that, there lingered, shadowing them, the memory of their argument. Each sought to curb the illness. Tentatively, guardedly they approached one another. But there appeared to be too little they held in common except the others of the family, on whom they both depended and for whom each had a sense of ownership and obligation. Lotti still slept in the room with him, and though they didn't talk before sleep, as before, it was a comfort to them both to lie side by side, knowing the other was there.

More and more each came to look for comfort to Collins, the one about whom there was the least tension; coming from outside, he was in some ways a stranger to them and brought fewer entanglements. Lotti sought him out in the daytime, and Cal whenever he could, day or night. Often of an evening he would sit down in the swing on the porch and Collins would pull up a rocker, and they would talk not about matters of the store or the family but about Collins' travels. Beth would listen. Kin would hang around, too, and often Matthew would. Lotti might come out onto the porch with Johnny for a while, but nobody said much except Collins and Cal.

These sessions were a healing balm to Cal. The porch was dark and restful; the breeze would settle in on the hot city, moving down from the peaks as the sun set. The talk was easy. The open porch contributed to that. There was informality about coming and going, and the rockers made a soothing background for the slowly forming thoughts, the chuckling laughter, the words of far-off people, fat and slender, tall and proud and fearful and loving—Collins had known a world full of people.

At nine, Lotti and Johnny would get ready for bed. At nine-thirty, Cal would get up, stretch, yawning, and go inside. Lotti usually was lying on the bed in her nightgown by then, staring at the ceiling, working on the dreams she was piecing together. He would put on his nightgown and climb over her to his side of the bed, and he would wonder about what Collins had said, about the long-ago, the faraway, and the carefree, about the springs of other lands. To be gone, he thought, to be without care, to shake it off, the worries of the mountain people, the fitful workings of the family as it revolved on itself, slipping over itself as it pulled forward, grew older, twisting and turning, one person on another testing each other, forcing each other to struggle and to grow. Yet what a coarse, hard way it was, he thought. In a field a tree might grow well in the sun, and in a forest it might be crooked in the shade. The family was in the shade, he thought, and the trees grew twisted, seeking light, and only one or two would likely reach it.

During the day Collins spent little time now at the store or swapping stories at the market place. He could be found at home, talking to Lotti and Beth, or at the back of one of the beer halls, which weren't much frequented during working hours. Occasionally he would even disappear entirely for a day or two, evidently going away on a trip. He never took his luggage, never took so much as an extra shirt, so far as could be told. He didn't say when or where he was going, and he talked little about these trips when he returned. It seemed that whenever he began to brood secretively, soon he would be leaving on one of them.

His coming and going staggered each time the habits of the family.

Cal would grow moody and despondent. Paul would move away from his caution and burst out with orders, instructions; he would dominate table talk. "Come in here, rule the roost, change the street around, steal what he wants," he would say, staring darkly at Beth and Lotti, "then go, steal again from those who took him in. My God in heaven, he's not a fit man." Darkly he would hint, "Well, this time he won't come back."

Beth would shake her head. "He'll be back. You always say that, Paul."

Lotti would draw the angel boy closer to her of a day and night when Collins was away. Matthew, at the store and house, once more would listen obediently to Paul.

Then Collins would appear again, go to his room. Later he would come downstairs and laugh with the family, tell stories as in times past.

The ever-changing climate of the home so distressed Kin and, it seemed to him, Beth, too, that he determined to ask Collins why he went away so often and if he were going to leave permanently. One afternoon he sought him out at Jacob's, but Collins must have sensed the seriousness of the mission and said, "Did you ever discover the facts about women, Kin?"

"No, sir," Kin said, putting the "sir" onto his answer for some reason—insecurity, he guessed. Whenever women were mentioned, or, rather, whenever knowledge about women was mentioned, he thought of himself as being inferior to everybody else. At sixteen he knew not the first thing about that subject and was painfully conscious of it. "I asked Papa about it several times."

"What did he say?" Collins asked, a big grin coming over his face. "Did he know?"

"He said nobody had ever been sufficiently sure of his knowledge about them to make it known."

Collins laughed. "That's almost true," he said. "Oh, my. No, I tell you, boy, there's such a thing as an understanding of the nature of a woman, and that takes study. But knowledge about a woman—

that is, how they're made in body and what gets them stirred up around a man—that can be set down. I can tell you about it now, if you want to know."

Kin's throat went dry in a moment. His eyes widened as he leaned across the table. This was a subject he had a considerable interest in.

"But you probably wouldn't want to waste your time this afternoon talking about such trifles, would you?" Collins said, and turned away as if his mind had gone on to seek another subject.

"Well, I—want to know," Kin said awkwardly, not wanting to commit himself enthusiastically because he didn't know what the knowledge was. It might be something he didn't want to know after all. Grown people needed to know it, of course, but he wasn't sure he was ready to accept it yet. Many of the childhood fantasies had been missed sorely once knowledge had been acquired about the truth of them, and it might be the same with this matter. "I saw a birth once," he said.

"Did you? Kittens or pups?" Collins asked casually.

"Little Johnny."

Collins blinked and leaned across the table. "Your brother?"

"I saw it all. Mama on the bed with her knees folded up and the baby coming out, all watery, and the way her muscles got hard."

Collins stared at him as if he couldn't accept what he heard. "No, you didn't see that," he said quietly. "You dreamed it."

"No, Collins, I was under the stairs—"

Collins held up his hand and Kin got quiet. "You dreamed it," he said quietly. Then he leaned back in his chair and thought about something for a while.

"I wouldn't mind knowing about the women," Kin said flatly. He might as well admit it.

Collins smiled, a low, languid smile, and took out his pencil and picked up a piece of paper from the floor. Holding one hand to block Kin's view, he began to draw something. Kin waited, his pulse throbbing, wondering what the paper would reveal to him. Some monstrous organ attached to a woman's body, perhaps. Some box—he had heard a box referred to—an appendage which swelled and

194

hardened like a man's, he suspected. Whatever the secret was, which was locked so possessively among the adults of the world, he resolved to accept it staunchly.

Jacob came over to the table and started to sit down, but Collins shook his head at him. "Private party," he said, "family matter," and Jacob went away, glancing back testily.

Kin moved a cigar butt around on the floor with the toe of his shoe. He imagined he was making a road through the dirt on the floor with it. It was a big fat cigar and made good roads.

"Now this is a picture of a woman," Collins said finally, proudly, as he flattened the piece of paper on the tabletop. Kin peered at it anxiously, hoping to see at once the box, or to see whatever the secret was, to find it out and be done with it. But the woman's thighs were smooth, her stomach was smooth right down to between her legs; only her breasts poked out, and Collins had drawn big breasts on her, too, but Kin knew about the breasts already.

Collins made a few erasures and drew in steadier lines for the contours of the shoulders. He had one leg too long, and he fixed that. Then he peered at the drawing, leaning back from it. "It looks all right, doesn't it?"

"It looks fine to me, Collins."

Collins changed one arm before he was satisfied, then he began explaining about the breasts. He spoke casually, as if the subject were of no particular consequence to him, but Kin's face got hot as a poker.

Kin wondered when he was going to say something objectionable. He now knew that the baby was formed inside the woman, and that the man fertilized an egg in there, through the same opening that the baby, months later, would appear, assuming that there was to be a baby, which Collins said happily was only infrequently the case. Collins said one didn't need to take a chance on that, anyway. He told Kin how a rubber fitted on. It was simple enough.

Collins was thorough and talked half an hour. And he kept changing the drawing of the woman all the while. He just couldn't be satisfied with it. He went to work trying to redo the breasts, and he drew them six times, so that now the woman's chest was charred with erasures. "I'll tell you, Kin," he said, admitting defeat on that, "you can find a hundred different kinds of breasts on women. They run from flat to pear-shaped to cone-shaped; some are firm and some floppy, and the thing to do is to get familiar with them all."

He talked for a long time about breasts, making sketches of different shapes around the borders of the paper. Kin's mind absorbed everything he said. Collins talked about positions for love-making, too, and he tried to draw them. On his third try he drew a reasonably representative male figure, but he couldn't seem to get the two figures, the man and woman, together, so he gave up on it. But he did much talking and drawing and erasing, and Kin followed what he said.

Then in one corner of the paper, the only corner which had not been marked up and erased over, he drew a five-petal flower and put a stem on it. "That's about the only thing I'm able to draw," he said, chuckling. "I just want you to know I can draw something well."

He crumpled the paper in his big hand. "I remember when I first found out about women," he said, leaning back in the chair and peering out the front plate-glass window, a fond smile on his face. "Papa never told me anything, nor Mama either. They thought it was their secret, I guess. I was a young boy and was working at the store one summer. We were building it up then, just getting started."

"You didn't know about women out in the country?" Kin asked, finding that his voice was hoarse from tension.

"I knew about the differences. A boy learns about the differences quicker in the country than anywhere else, because he finds out how a stud horse gets into a mare and a bull into a heifer and a male hound into a bitch. And he knows this results in colts and calves and pups being born. But I hadn't transferred that knowledge to people. I thought people would be altogether different. So I was on King Street, ignorant as could be, when I was about fifteen or sixteen, about your age, and I sure was anxious to know about women. Well, sir, this farmer drove up in a wagon loaded down with pumpkins, big, golden-colored ones, and he had a pretty daughter with him. I guess she was about my age, and doubtless she had known about sex for much of her life, because you take a one-room cabin, Kin, back in the mountains, with maybe six or seven or eight children and a man and wife living in it, everything in there is common, and it's all common knowledge."

The idea that children might see their parents engaged in love-making so startled Kin that he shook his head at Collins, denying the possibility. It seemed to him that every effort would be made for privacy. "I thought they put the children in the loft."

"Some cabins do have a loft, but it's got so many holes in the floor that the children can lie on their bellies and have a clear view of everything going on below."

"They can't see in the dark."

"There's a fire going day and night right there in the fireplace."

Kin wouldn't accept it. "They put the children outdoors," he suggested.

"In the cold?" Collins asked incredulously.

"I heard they did," Kin said emphatically, though he had heard no such a thing.

"Hell," Collins said good-naturedly. "Listen, boy, those young'uns learn fast in those little cabins. Hell, they all sleep in the same pallet themselves, share the same coverlets, and they're likely to come in contact one with another and get excited, brother and sister and the like."

Kin was shaking his head again.

"What are you shaking your head for? Everybody doesn't grow up the way you do."

"They don't all sleep together."

"Well, where do you think they sleep? You think they have private rooms. Listen, it's a one-room house."

"I never even saw a one-room house."

"Oh, well, hell, there aren't many of them left, but that's now; when I was a boy your age, there were quite a few, and this farmer might have come from one of them."

"Which farmer?"

197

"The one with the daughter."

Kin sulked. He didn't like the idea of the one-room cabin and the big family.

"She was pretty, too, Kin. I still remember the flashing black eyes on that girl, and she was dark-haired. Not many brunettes back in there, you know. She got to helping her father unload those pumpkins. Well, I didn't have anything to do to keep me away from this, so I lent a hand. I noticed that the shoulder strap on her dress kept slipping down. The dress wasn't made for her, anyway; it was way too big. Probably was for an older sister, but she had to wear it when she came to town. I guess the sister sat in a bush and waited to get her dress back."

Kin laughed, in spite of his seriousness.

"I got to looking down her dress, of course. Every time she moved, I moved. And since we had a wagonload of pumpkins there, and since her pa and Papa went into the store to talk, this view I had amounted to a good deal of excitement before we ever got down to wagon bed. She knew what I was doing, too, and it stimulated her to have me looking at her like that. Well, I was beside myself. That girl and I were there alone in the pumpkin shed, and she just stared at me, Kin, with those black eyes, and I decided they were a challenge and an invitation. She had left her shoulder strap down, too, from that last time round, so there she was in that over-big dress with part of one breast showing. I put my hand on her shoulder, and she didn't seem to mind. I let it move around a little bit, and she didn't say anything. I just let it take its natural direction then, and when she didn't stop me, I got hold of her and took her over to one side, behind where a service cart was parked, and got her back in there to as private a place as I could find, and I discovered as much about women as I could in the five minutes I was allotted—discovered it first-hand."

Collins stared off reflectively, remembering fondly the happy occasion.

"Did they catch you?"

"No, no. Her father and Papa came back in, of course, but we heard them coming, and that girl just let that big dress down over herself and went to the wagon and mounted it without a word to anybody. She sat there, sawdust in her hair, as calm as if nothing had happened at all, and looked down at me, her eyes so wonderfully provocative, smiling like the Mona Lisa. And when her father drove that girl out of there, I followed like a hound halfway up the hill, loping along after her, trailing sawdust."

Collins wiped his forehead with his shirt sleeve. Perspiration had come out on his face. "Lord a' mercy," he said. "I'd walk forty miles right now to get a look at that girl." He shook his head in wonder. "Say, you ought to try to find yourself one like that sometime."

Kin bit his lip. "I don't know. Who do you think?"

"That little Sally Waters. You might try her." He tapped the sketch he had made with his fingers. "She's got everything I drew on this piece of paper, you know."

Kin blushed. "How do you—get to know her well enough?"

"Now," Collins said, leaning across the table and tapping Kin's arm confidentially, "every woman is different as to that. You take that Waters girl; I believe you just might suggest to her that you've watched her around and you'd like to spend some time with her, get to know her well. Say you're interested in her."

"Well—just say it?"

"Just say you think she's fine and wonder if some place and time you and she could meet."

"I couldn't do that, Collins."

"Why not?"

"Well, where would we meet?"

"She might think of a place. I'll bet she knows of one or two."

It was too much for Kin. It was one matter to remember what Collins had told him about women, but the idea of applying that knowledge terrified him. And being with little Sally Waters, holding her, taking liberties with her body, was such a marvelous and panic-ridden study that he couldn't hang on to it.

"That's enough lessons for today," Collins said abruptly. "Except for one thing. All I told you is facts, Kin, and they don't rule this subject, or this world, either. Being with a woman gets a man's emotions stirred up, and anything can happen between them. It intensifies a person. Their lives can be changed, their hearts can be broken, they can be drawn closer together or split more apart. Sometimes you'll be with a girl you'll forget ten minutes later, and maybe she's already forgot you; another time you'll be with a woman you'll never forget. You might forget her name, but you won't forget her. I can remember right now a hundred women who just cross my mind one after another. I get a glimmer of their face in my memory, the image of a face lying on a pillow somewhere a long time ago. I remember an impression of their meanness or their gentleness or their coarseness or their humor, or what one talked about, or what another one said as the tension built inside her and overflowed. It's a tremendous idea God had in setting the thing up the way he did, and some of your most memorable experiences will be had with the women you settle with. Or if you're like me, the women you leave behind."

Kin stared at him, a terror slowly building inside him. "Beth—" he said, "what about Beth? Are you going to leave her, too?"

The question brought Collins up short. He watched Kin for a long moment, then inhaled deeply. "I love Beth, is that what you mean? I love her more than anything."

Collins was embarrassed about love, Kin noticed. He could talk easily about women, but not about love. "Is she like the others?"

"What do you mean by that?"

"You love her like you do the others?"

"No," he said, "not like the others. Why?"

"Is she different from the others?"

"I tried to tell you that with some women love-making is investigation for a man, and with others it's deep-felt. I love Beth more than I've ever loved anybody else, if it's any of your business."

Kin swallowed. He was flustered, but he wasn't going to stop now. "You're going to leave Beth, like the others, though, aren't you, Collins?"

Collins stirred about in his chair for a moment, aggravated. "I

200

don't see how I can," he said.

It wasn't the answer Kin had hoped for. It was better than an announcement that Collins was leaving, but it wasn't a declaration in Beth's favor. It wasn't an answer saying that he wanted to be with Beth always. It revealed that there was a force pulling him away, as in times past.

"You want to leave, though. I can tell that. You say she's different and you love her, but you're not going to stay."

"What makes you think that? I never said that."

"You act like love is so important, but you throw it away. You don't care if Beth is hurt." He trembled as he talked. "You want to just take off on the train, just leave."

Collins stood abruptly. He stared down at Kin, stood there and looked at him sternly, his face knitted and worried, then he walked over to the front window and looked out at the street, his back to him.

Kin sat at the table, wondering if he dared follow him. He waited for a long while, then he got up and went over to stand near him, and he saw that his face was drawn up in sorrow. It was almost funny to see; Collins was childlike and awkward with sorrow.

"I'm sorry," Kin said. "Collins, I didn't mean to hurt your feelings. Collins, I wouldn't hurt you."

Collins smiled at him, a slow, easy smile. He ran his hand over Kin's shoulder. "Let's not worry Beth about talk like that, what do you say?"

Kin nodded. "All right, Collins."

"Hell, no need to take life seriously, is there?"

Paul was always around Beth now. He had a need to be near her. One morning he grabbed her arm, pulled her onto his lap, and she tore her apron getting away, but not before he kissed her hard and possessively. She went into the kitchen, so upset that she cried.

Through the spring and summer, she dated Collins. Twice they went out to the farm. They walked up to the balsam forest, where they were together again for hours. Once he took her to a supper club high on Beaucatcher Mountain. He was always bringing her gifts, too, a few flowers or a pin of cut garnets milled and polished by a mountain craftsman. When they were together, life stood in perfect form for them, but when alone he became every week more somber.

As fall approached and he had been in the house for five months, the family speculated each week on his tendencies. And one hot Saturday afternoon, Beth asked Kin to come to walk with her. Collins was not about; he had gone off the previous afternoon and had not come home since. She and Kin walked uptown.

She sat down on a stone bench on the Square, near the fountain, and Kin sat down beside her. The water of the fountain was misty and white, and two small children played in it, splashing it out on passers-by. It was a sticky day, not a breeze was anywhere about. The bits of paper in the gutter were motionless.

"I want to talk to you, Kin," she said, "and I thought perhaps this would be a good place."

He suspected he knew what she was going to say to him. "I don't know that I can tell you anything, Beth."

She smiled at him. "Do you know where Collins is right now?"

He shook his head.

"Do you know where he goes when he leaves on these trips?"

"I don't know, Beth."

"He's never said to you?"

"No."

The movie house let out and people came onto the sidewalk, blinking in the sunlight. Parents reached out for their children's hands.

"I've tried to talk to Collins, but I can't make him discuss this matter. He doesn't want to leave me, Kin. He says he can't leave me, that he gets depressed when he's away. But he can't be happy with me, either, it seems to me. He is unhappy, isn't he?"

"I don't know, Beth. Really, I don't know."

"Yes, he is." She stared before her at the playing children, but she didn't seem to notice them. "I love him, Kin. Do you know what that means?"

202

"No," he said quietly.

A child broke away from his mother and ran into the street, and the mother dashed out and pulled him to safety.

"I love him in a deeper way than most women ever have a chance to love at all. And I tell myself, what if you lose him, how will you live? And I say I can't live if I lose him."

"Well, he won't go, Beth. I don't think he'll go."

"Well, what should I do? Fight to hold him here, is that it?"

"Yes."

"Even if it pulls him apart?"

"He won't be pulled apart, Beth. He doesn't want to leave you."

"You don't want him to go either, I know."

"No."

"And Mama Lotti needs him, and little Johnny. And Papa King needs him here, and Matthew is doing so much better. Have you noticed that?"

Kin shrugged, unwilling to compliment Matthew.

"But I do worry about Paul. He gets so deep in jealousy. It preys on him. I don't like that."

"You worry about Paul?" Kin said.

She watched the streetcars unloading and the faces of the busy people, and the two children, whose mothers were trying to make them come out of the pool. Cars crept by on the streets.

"It's beautiful here on the Square," she said. "It's a private place, with people all around. There are so many people that nobody is ever noticed. And the fountain is here, and there are benches for resting."

She was quiet again, and he scarcely moved. "You've got to hold Collins somehow," he said. "Nobody else can hold him."

A man came by selling peanuts, and several children gathered around him. A lady came by in a scarlet dress that looked like velvet.

"Kin, when he gets back from this trip he's on, I'm going to tell him he must go away."

Kin for a moment refused to admit to his mind the full meaning of what she had said. The words had not come from Beth, he told himself, the warm, possessive Beth, who always fought for what was her own by rights.

"You're not going to let him go?"

"Yes," she said.

"But it will break."

"We must think of Collins. Don't you know that?"

"You don't love him."

"Don't I?"

"Beth, please, Beth."

She stood and brushed her dress down smoothly, brushed it as if she had just risen from the dinner table and it was wrinkled and had bread crumbs on it. "We'll not be weak about him," she said. "Love isn't weak, Kin."

There was no sign of a break in her firmness that he could see. She looked at him without a smile, and then without a word led the way across the Square.

It is not so, he thought, it is not so. And to himself he said, "Yes, she is right. For Collins was born to be free."

15

Collins returned from this trip to find a tenseness in the family somewhat different from before. He sensed it at once in Beth's and Kin's attitudes, but he asked no questions about it and permitted himself to be caught up in Lotti's enthusiasm. A recital was to be held that night at the school, and Johnny was, she said, to perform the leading part. She was so excited about it that Collins suggested that the family go, too. The idea was a novelty to her which seemed momentarily to panic her, but then, somewhat sternly and resolutely, she agreed that this was a good idea.

They talked to the family about it at supper. There was some complaining, especially from Cal and Paul, but Collins won his way.

After the meal, he retreated to the porch, lit his pipe, and took a rocker. Kin watched him from the hall, then he went out and sat down in the rocker next to him. It was a fresh night, not quite dark yet.

"You know, Kin," Collins said simply, "I take little trips off to myself to try to get a view on what I'm doing now, and I always manage to get my mind clear. Then I come home, and as soon as I walk through that door, the clarity disappears and I'm muddled, with all the old family ways."

Kin watched him warily. "You've decided you want to go away for good?"

"What? No, I'm not going anywhere, I told you. I always decide not to go."

"But it gets harder every time, doesn't it?"

Collins was unsettled by the question. He shrugged. "They trap us every one, every damn man of us, before we're done."

Cal came out of the house. He had on a fresh shirt, a string necktie, and wore his brown suit coat. He sat down in the swing and started it to creaking. "I wish we didn't need to go tonight," he said. "Go running up the street, when we could get the boy to say his piece right here on the porch."

"We might enjoy getting out, Papa," Collins said easily.

"No. At night I like to sit here and swing and talk. I think a lot about what you tell me, Collins, about the flatlands and the new ways. About what a man can see and do if he's not tied down."

"Uh-huh," Collins said.

"Collins is leaving soon, Papa," Kin said.

The swing stopped. The chair Collins was rocking in stopped, too.

"Didn't I tell you at the beer hall, and didn't I tell you here tonight that I wasn't going?"

"Yes, sir." Kin didn't look at him. Quietly he said, "Beth told me that she wants you to go, too."

Collins didn't move. His expression didn't change, either. He began to rock again. The thumping of his chair was the only noise.

"You've got to leave, she said."

"I heard what you said," he said softly. "Did you think I didn't hear you?"

Cal got up from the swing. He stood still for a moment, then quietly walked to the door and entered the house. Kin got up and backed away. "I'm going in," he said.

When he got inside the house, he found his father standing in the dark hallway. Cal appeared not to notice him. He was standing there looking at Collins on the porch, his hands gripped, his expression twisted.

206

"I had to, Papa," Kin said.

Cal said nothing.

"I don't want him to go, either."

He went into the kitchen and washed his face and hands. He put on his jacket. When he was ready to go to the recital, he went back to the porch and stood by one of the posts at the steps. Collins was still there. He was huddled in the dark, and Kin saw that he was weeping. He wasn't weeping tears, but he was weeping. His muscles were drawn tight and his body was quivering with sobs that made no sound and had no tears for themselves, but which took shape and came out through him, through his body, his whole body, for all of him was weeping.

Kin was drawn to him. He touched his arm. "Collins, it's all right," he said. "Collins—"

It was as if Collins didn't hear him at all. And Kin turned from him and walked out into the yard and walked back to the chicken lot, where he stood, getting control of his own emotions, where he stood until he heard the car horn honk and knew the family was leaving.

Every single child in the third grade of the private school was to recite something, as the family soon discovered, so Johnny's appointment was no special honor. This, however, did not dim the enthusiasm. Having prepared themselves to celebrate the honor he had received, having washed and polished and traveled to the place, they were going to celebrate his distinction anyway.

"All of my children have good memories," Lotti whispered to Beth as the event was about to begin. "They're all of them able to out-remember most children. When little Johnny was still a suckling, he seemed to know much about what was going on in the room where he stayed."

"He was bright," Beth admitted. He was, too, she knew. The child had shown a lively interest in almost everything, it seemed, except the family, and with them his participation had been guarded and tentative. He had accepted Lotti's love, and he did at once everything she told him to do. Never did he need to be scolded. But Beth couldn't get over the feeling that even in terms of his affection for Lotti, he was a person apart, observing even as he grew up, remaining objective.

Forty adults had come to the recital. Promptly at eight the teacher got up before them and stated her purpose, which was to discover talent at the beginning of the fall term. The children were in the hallway outside, and she introduced the first one, who came in to deliver a reading from Genesis. Another boy then delivered Joyce Kilmer's "Trees," shouting out the lines defiantly, his eyes tightly closed. He made only one error. Instead of "And only God can make a tree," he shouted out "And only God would make a tree," which left many among the assembly with a sizable idea to contemplate.

Collins showed little interest in the performance. Occasionally he would glance at the students, but his concern was with his own thoughts, and sometimes he would look at Beth, stare at her as if seeking comfort.

"What can I give Him, poor as I am?" one puckered-mouthed girl recited, holding to the hems of her skirt as if they afforded support. "If I were a shepherd, I would bring a lamb."

This was the type of poem which Lotti liked best of all. She licked her lips feverishly and leaned forward, better to catch the golden thoughts.

"If I were a wise man, I would do my part. What can I give Him? I'll give Him my heart."

A boy entered to recite a poem about a blacksmith and a chestnut tree, which seemed to Lotti to lack quality. The village smith, indeed. Her uncle Charles had been a smith for a while, and all it had meant to Charley was a pained back for most of his life. He had been trying one evening to shoe a horse, Lotti recalled, and when he turned around to pick up a shoeing nail, the horse kicked him in the small of the back. His wife had to get two men to come from next door to straighten him out. Better to tend to the field and let the smithying go, Lotti felt.

A boy who evidently couldn't learn a long poem recited "Fog," by

208

Carl Sandburg, to the consternation of many members of the audience. "What did that child say?" Cal asked Lotti.

"He told about the fog having cat's feet."

"Having what?"

Lotti shrugged. "Well, it sounded like cat's feet to me."

A poem which drew a fine hand was recited by a pretty little girl who stood up straight and proper and spoke without hesitation at any place. She told the moving story of a little toy soldier which was covered with rust, and she had Lotti and Matthew sitting on the edge of their seats from suspense.

She was followed by a frightened little boy who had been assigned the Twenty-third Psalm, the ancient sentiments about the Lord being our shepherd. The boy had made only one error; he had memorized not the Twenty-third but the Twenty-second Psalm, and his teacher had not known about it until too late to correct him. She did not know the Twenty-second, did not know it now, but she told him to go ahead with it since he had memorized it.

He took his place at the front of the room, turned to face the assembly squarely, and started out confidently and with vigor: "My God, my God, why hast thou forsaken me? Why art thou so far from helping me, and from the words of my roaring?"

Roaring he was, indeed, and Paul among others trembled with surprised chuckling.

The boy waded on into the ideas. "O, my God," he shouted, "I cry in the daytime, but thou hearest not, and in the night season, and am not silent."

Paul tried to control himself.

"I was cast upon thee from the womb, thou art my God from my mother's belly."

The teacher, who had heard this last line from the hall, appeared at the door, ashen and stiff-muscled. She peered disbelievingly at the child and at the rows of astonished parents.

"I am poured out like water," the child announced, "and all my bones are out of joint: my heart is like wax; it is melted in the midst of my bowels."

The teacher fairly dashed forward and grasped the child's arm. "Very good, very good, Harry," she said, as she tried to lead him away.

"I'm not through yet," he said, balking.

"Yes you are, Harry," she said.

After he was dragged into the hall, many conversations were started. Nobody was competent to say exactly what had happened. The boy had come upon them unawares and had assaulted them with a series of confessions. There was no explanation for it, unless a prank had been played.

"Now we'll hear from Johnny King," the teacher said from the doorway.

She stepped back to admit him, and she seemed to smile in a special way at him, Beth thought. He came to the front of the room, walking slowly and confidently. He turned to face the parents without fear, and began reciting calmly. His was not a serious poem, but it wasn't funny either; it fell nicely between the two. His voice was frail, but it offered promise. Lotti thought it had something of the same soul-stirring quality of her father's. The boy was, she told herself, becoming more and more like him, and when he got his adult nose and his hair darkened, the resemblance would be pronounced.

This was a moving moment for her, listening to this small creature of her own making recite words of such pretty sentiment about a spring day and the sunshine and a cow in a meadow. Such a pretty poem which rhymed so well. And Cal was attentive. Beth and Collins were listening appreciatively. And little Johnny, who had received so many hard words from Paul and Matthew, was facing them now and without a quiver was reciting a long poem, one of the longer ones, it seemed to Lotti, without a pause.

Perched on the edge of her chair, she listened, afraid she might miss a word.

Then he forgot. Other children had forgotten, but now Johnny forgot, and panic struck her. She was drawn to her feet, to intercede for him, but Beth caught her arm. "Sit down," Beth whispered sharply.

Lotti, pulling against Beth, stared at the boy, every nerve afire for him. She didn't know the poem; she could tell him the words if he had let her help him, as she had asked him to. There he was in front of all these people, looking at her, but she didn't know how to help him.

"Mama Lotti," Beth whispered huskily. "Sit down."

"Johnny," Lotti said.

Several parents turned to look at her.

Then he remembered. The words flowed from his mind again. His chirping voice came out, clear and distinct, and Lotti, close to tears, slumped back into her chair, her breath coming in gasps, her heart pounding.

"Well, I don't know whether anybody noticed him forget or not," she said later to Beth.

Beth and Collins didn't go home with the others. They watched the car leave and saw Kin looking back at them as the car went around a corner.

Collins hired a taxi to take them to the supper club on Beau-catcher Mountain, and from there, seated at a table at the front windows, they looked down on the city, a spangled display of white and colored lights, covering, like liquid settled in place, the floor of the valley and the lower reaches of the mountainsides. "It's no match for you," he said quietly.

"What isn't?"

"The lights. The city."

"It's beautiful."

"Yes, you are," he said.

He and Beth drank wine and looked at the view, where car lights moved along the roads, and he looked at her, as if considering the wonder of her.

"I declare, Collins, it certainly is nice up here. This is real linen, isn't it?" she said, examining the tablecloth.

"Yes. Probably from the mountains somewhere."

"And that chandelier is iron, isn't it?"

"Probably brass. Maybe from Europe, brought over here from a castle."

A servant came in carrying logs, which he put on the big fire in the fireplace at one end of the room. At a nearby table, a slim man, drunk and talkative, got to laughing. He fell into a fit of laughter, and his wife glanced about her, embarrassed, while two other men at the table got him out onto the terrace, where they began to walk him about.

Collins grinned. "He's happy," he said.

"Yes." She smiled. "Are you, Collins?"

"Yes, right here I am, right now, you and me."

"And tomorrow? You'll wake up and say, 'Where is this—is it California? Is it the Mark Hopkins again? Is it Nome? Is it Houston?' Then you'll see the cracked plaster and the string-pull light in the ceiling, and you'll say, 'No, it's only home. I'm still home. And I should be away.'"

"Don't hurt yourself," he said gently.

"I can't help it."

"Then don't hurt me, Beth. We mustn't hurt each other. Nowadays we're like two people who are never able to love the moments they have for worrying about losing moments yet to come. We defeat ourselves that way." For a while he looked down at the valley. "Look at the lights, like stars down there, moving stars like planets of old, like the star which sought out Jesus, maybe. Every star is seeking something, moving along the streets. Look at the mountains over there, black with the rim of blue at the top where the clouds are. Right now possums, fat and oily, sit in persimmon trees and listen to the baying of hounds far off, coming closer."

"Are they to forget it, Collins?"

"What?"

"The hounds coming closer."

He smiled at her, wistfully, considerately. "Don't you know," he said, "that there are no hounds, Beth, not for us. I'm not leaving you. How could I get along without you? It's very well to say that I used to, but that was before I knew you. I looked for you then. I was like one of those car lights down there, moving about all the time, but I didn't know what I was looking for, and now I know I can't go away."

"Hadn't you rather still be looking?"

"For what? I've got nothing more to look for."

"You didn't know what it was you were looking for before."

"No, but I know now. I've got no place else to go. It would be all empty now. But right here you and I can build a house, start a family—that's new experience enough. And I've got the street to trade in, to bargain in, to tell my stories and to seek out young men who haven't found their own life flow, and I can say, 'There's a man I'd like for you to look up when you go through Omaha.'"

Exuberance caught him up all of a sudden. "I'm not going anywhere, you hear me? This is my place. Hell, I was born here. This is mine, out there. Beth, there's no part of the world as beautiful as this land, and no people any better, any more stern of heart or life-simple. This is where I am. And when I wake up in the morning, I'm going to say, Today is for Beth and me. We're going to start a home soon, so we've got to start planning it, find a lot up on a hill with a view like this one, or on a spot down by a creek. Got to get going on my life, I'll say, Beth and me. You hear me?"

"I hear you," she said, tears in her eyes.

He took her home, went with her to her room, and kissed her good night. "Beth, you sleep quiet," he said.

"I will."

"Don't have too many thoughts, Beth. Let them lie. Too many thoughts fight one another."

"I guess they do," she said, smiling.

"No need to worry," he said gently, as she closed her door.

He stood there for a while looking into the blackness of the hallway, then he sighed. "Ah, lord," he whispered.

A light was on in his room. He crossed the hall to his door and pushed it open quietly. Kin was sitting on the edge of the bed, reading a book. "What you doing, boy?"

213

Kin smiled up at him. "Waiting for you."

Collins sat down on a chair near the window and pulled off one shoe. He held it in his hand and stared at it. "What do you want to say this time?"

"I want to go with you when you leave."

"Huh? Do you?" He gazed at Kin thoughtfully. "Well, I'm not going anywhere. I've been everywhere. Where would I go?" He took off the other shoe. "What the hell would I be doing trailing a boy along anyway, tell me that."

"I'm not a boy. I'm sixteen."

"If you're not a boy, you can go alone."

Kin blinked at him. His lips trembled, but he stiffened them.

"There are plenty of people who have wanted to travel with me, but not many who have had the strength to take off on their own. That's the test."

Kin's eyes were misty now. Collins looked up and saw this. He shrugged apologetically and held out his hand, and Kin took his hand, not knowing what Collins wanted, and Collins pulled him close and put his arm around him. "Don't listen to me tonight. I've got so confused with thoughts that I can't fight myself free. When a man like me falls in love, it tears him up."

He suddenly turned and stared out the back window toward the chicken lot, as if to hide his face. "I don't know what to say about myself. I've got so stretched out I can't seem to get control again."

"I don't want you to go," Kin said.

"I'm not going."

He was quiet for a while, then he turned to look at Kin. "The road's not for you, is it? Why did you say you wanted to go on the road?"

"To be with you," Kin said.

"Huh? Listen at him." He smiled, and he laughed softly.

"And to be like you," Kin said.

"Like me?" He was flustered by the thought and got up abruptly and crossed the room to the dresser. He took the change from his pocket and took out his handkerchief and his big brown leather

214

wallet, which was always crammed with money and checks on a San Francisco bank. He took his watch from his pocket and wound it. "The road's a dream," he said, "and I got on that dream while it was still awake for me and rode it, and it became the way of life I grew into. The dream and me, the road and me, it became the only way of life I knew. When a place got tiresome, I moved on. And every day was different, something new."

He laid his watch aside. He walked back wearily to the bed, his shoulders slumped, and sat down heavily beside Kin. "I don't want to leave here, boy. Listen, you can't know a girl like Beth on the road. Because when you know her, it stops being a good road for you. You can know hundreds of women. You can have a fine time with them, but you don't need any one of them for anything that the others can't provide. That way of life is worth living; it was for me. I love the road, and I went along it faster than any other man I've ever known. But when it ended for me, it rose up, boy, right there, bam, and I can't quite figure out where it went. Coming home, that contributed to it; seeing people I knew and feeling that I belonged, and seeing Beth, whom I had known when she was a child and had thought I loved as a boy. Do you hear me?"

"Yes, sir."

"And that day in the country." He stopped, as if considering it. For a long while he sat there, then he spoke quietly. "It's a terror," he said in a low, tight voice, as if he were afraid. "We've got to have one another. A man can't get old and not have somebody. You know that?"

Kin moved to him, touched his shoulder, and Collins put his arm around him once more. Collins was lost in his thoughts, deep and serious and lonely. Abruptly he blinked and smiled. "I got to talking, didn't I, boy?" he said. "Well, I've been going off to myself too much lately, trying to think it through. I've too few thoughts to work with, that's one trouble." He got up and paced the room. "Found a little inn up at Burnsville, good food, fire in the lobby fireplace, old wood beams, people to talk to. I go there and think, lie in my bed in the overheated room and think. But I just don't have the thoughts to work with."

He stopped at the back window and looked out, and Kin went to him. "Collins, it would hurt you more to go than to stay, is that what you mean?"

"Yes."

"Neither way is open to you now without losing the other, is that it? So it's easier to stay."

"That's what I think. Because when I stay, I take the pain of life, I take it slow, and Beth is with me and you're here, and Papa and Mama Lotti. I'll be with people growing up from childhood, maybe my own. Life is easier to take that way. Because life can be a terror when it hits you alone. And it's all so dreamlike and temporary, anyway, and Beth seems to know that better than me, and is able to make allowances for it. Like now, what we say now, it's all gone as soon as it's said. Life is all flashes, you see. Now is only a flash, a moment. Everything is dreamy and dying. Don't you see?"

Kin stared up at him.

"Don't you understand?"

"I don't know, Collins."

"Sure. So a person is some sort of total, added up sometime by somebody. Who do you reckon does it? A man's not what he is but what he has been; he's his past when the total is made and the man himself while he's going; he's the past and the future both, he's what he is and what he wants to be, and what he can be, and what he's ready to be. A man is what he is, but what he wants to be is part of what he is. You see?"

Kin stared at him. "I guess so, Collins."

"I can't say it clearly because I don't have the ideas to work with." He paced the room. "Pieces of things I understand. You've read books. Tell me what I mean."

"I don't know, Collins."

"You won't embarrass me to know more than I do. What is it that we are, will you tell me? What do the books say?"

Kin shook his head. "I don't know."

216

"Searching, wanting to get hold, that was me. Searching on the road. What for? Looking. Coming every day toward a grave, but not looking at that. Not being able to get hold of life, because it isn't, I mean right now it isn't. Even what I told Beth tonight is gone, it's the past now, it's dreamy. Beth and me in that room high on the hill, it's over now."

"Collins, don't try to tear yourself apart."

"Huh? I just try to think it through."

"I know a man who reads a lot, Collins, a tailor—"

"My mind won't turn loose. Hell, once I never asked a question; now I ask a hundred a day and can't answer two. Before, I just went. A woman and me. The day and me. The night and me and her. Good food. Good times. Stories to tell and hear. The smile of headwaiters and silver heavy on the tables. The day and me. The night and me and her, do you hear?"

"Yes."

Collins stood as if in a trance, considering it. "Hell," he said. "I think so many thoughts now."

"Maybe—maybe you'd forget us if you left, Collins, and find the old life again, and live easy again."

"You think so?"

"Maybe—maybe you would slip into the old way, and all of this would be just a dream that never happened."

"Yes," he said, "that might be. I could run from worry then, all right. That's the way I was born to be, Kin. I grew up being that way, and it's somehow the way my heart beats, and that's what Beth knows. She tells me that. I'm like a wild thing trying to be tamed now, isn't that so?"

"Yes. Yes, it is."

He caught himself in his new exuberance; it ebbed away, and wearily he turned to the bed. He sank down on it, stretched out on it, and closed his eyes. "But what of Beth, what of her, you see?" His eyes stayed closed. He sighed deeply, painfully. He sighed again, then was quiet. Kin waited a minute more before starting toward the door.

"Maybe it's not fair to stay for Beth's sake," Collins said quietly. "Maybe the only fair thing a man ever does is what he does for himself. If I stay for Beth, I might get to hating her for it. But if I leave her, Kin, I might stumble lost."

Collins said nothing else. Kin went out and closed the door. He went down the hall to the stairs and down the two steps to his landing. He opened his own door and was about to go in when he saw the light appear as Collins' door opened. Kin turned to see Collins standing there, a giant silhouetted against the yellow light.

"Kin, I'll tell you how it is out there," he said. "You ride the crest. It's as if a wave had formed and you let it catch you up, and you don't question it, you never fight it. You let it carry you down the wide road."

When Kin crept in between the cold sheets and closed his eyes, he couldn't get to sleep for the longest time, for he thought of Collins, and of the train arriving five months before, of the tall man getting off it, the second son of the family, with the air of the world about him. "Yes, suh, yes, suh, this way, suh" the porters had said, for they knew he was a man apart, rising above the rest, one who had escaped every net of life and stood free. "Yes, suh, yes, suh, this your stop, suh." And the ticket takers were proud he had stopped at the Asheville station. The people of King Street, Kin could see them watching him trade, listening to his stories of the faraway lands. All gone, all gone. And that first night at supper, the stories and throwing a chair at Paul. All gone. Not the stories gone or the night gone, but Collins, great Collins, lowered like Sampson cut of hair, was reduced to indecision and stumbled blind now in his own mind. For the nets had caught him.

At dawn Kin got up at once and dressed, unwilling to trust himself to further fitful thoughts. He went downstairs to the bathroom.

He heard his father stir in his room. "Cal, what time you think it is?" he heard his mother say.

He left the bathroom and went into the dining room and sat down at the table, rubbing his eyes. He sat there for a little while before he saw the letters. He stared at them blankly at first. They were right there before him, and one of them was left open. "To my dear mama Lotti, the sweetest little mother in all the world," it began. "I am going away for a while, Mama . . ."

His vision blurred. The thought seeped into him, Collins gone, great Collins gone.

"Papa," Kin said, trying to call to him. "Papa." But he didn't call very loud. He sat on the chair trembling and trying to hold back his tears.

Through his tears he saw that the other note was sealed and was addressed to Beth, and through the note Collins had stuck the stem of a single flower.

PART THREE

16

THE FERNS WITHERED WITH THE FIRST FROST OF THAT
year, and the hobblebushes turned red and orange and gold, and
dangled bright fruit clusters. The days in the fields were entertained
by the raspy voices of the crickets and grasshoppers, and the fid-
dling of the katydids.

The high mountains began to take on a wintry look, and down
the slopes, as if poured from a pot of lava, came the stream of color,
touching the deciduous trees, moving from the higher mountains
downward, and arriving soon at the Asheville plateau. Oaks turned
brown, sourwood trees purple, sumac red; the ash, the black gum,
the sassafras took on color. The hickories and tulip trees changed
from green to yellow and gold.

The sky and the earth awakened to the voices of the busy birds.

The country people herded their stock in from the mountain
peaks, drove many of the animals into trucks, and carted them to
the railroad-yard auctions. The white-faced cattle bawled in the
pens; the sheep huddled together.

Apples were carted in from the orchards and poured into bins
in the apple houses. Apple brandy and corn whisky ran from the

brook-cooled condensers of the stills, and farmers were testing their own and their neighbors' "pertnin' juice."

Fall also was butchering time. The hogs were knocked unconscious with an ax and bled, cut open, and cleaned out, and the white and tan meat was rubbed with salt in the meathouse. A few of the hams were rubbed with brown sugar, as well, about one part brown sugar to four parts salt. The hams would lie in the blanket of salt for six weeks, then would be washed and the sugar-cured ones would be smoked.

A steer would be slaughtered in first one community, then another, and the meat would be cut into roasts and carried by the children to the different houses. Occasionally a deer would be cut up, too, and sent around, or brought to King Street as roasts and sold from wicker baskets.

The coons, possums, and bears were fat on mast, and hunters were listening to the call of their dogs of a night. They had plenty of bear stories and plenty of bear meat, for they didn't much like to eat it. It was stringy and tough, strong tasting even when boiled all day. They didn't much like deer, either; it had too strong a wild taste. But they liked to hunt; they would hunt whenever a man wanted to chance his dogs.

Kin would listen to them talk. He would wander among them and sometimes he would drive with one of them to the big slaughterhouse auctions of stock. There he would sit in a stand that surrounded a paddock on three sides, a stand with steep steps on which the men sat. The place filled up quickly when a sale was about to start, and he would sit, jammed in among the farmers, and watch their faces. Solid rows of faces. Solid banks of faces. All looking down at the cattle, goats, sheep, and horses brought in for sale. The auctioneer would take the bids in a quiet way, but he kept the sale moving fast. The animals would come in one door and would be prodded to move about to show that they were well, then they would be taken out the exit door as other animals were driven in. Kin studied the farmers and buyers and their bleak, stern expressions, and listened to their talk about the way folks were getting on in the mountain country.

One sign of the year drawing near to a close was the pile of galax leaves that were brought to upper King Street. The galax was native to the section and was shipped to florists all over the country for use in Christmas decorations. It was a small waxen plant with leaves half as large as a man's hand, and galax pullers got twenty-five cents a thousand leaves, tied and delivered. There was no way on earth for most men to earn a decent wage, but it was one of the few ways they had of earning cash money. Families could be seen on the lower mountainsides and in the deep valleys, walking four or five or more abreast, moving into the wilderness areas, the briars cutting their legs and arms, the tree limbs swatting at their faces, the cold and dampness getting to their bones. Bent over, the bags of galax on their backs, a pack of food and sometimes a blanket with them, they moved like people half dead along the edges of the mountainsides and through the thick laurel of the valleys, where the creeks were. Twenty-five cents a thousand leaves on King Street.

In November, Indian summer came. Days were warmer than they should be, were so warm this year that the violets bloomed near the creeks. Hornets buzzed at the loft window and white-footed mice played in the walls of the deserted houses. The families took off wool and put on cotton clothes again, and they visited King Street in festive spirit. The street was colorful and sprightly. Girls wore goldenrod in their hair.

Then a morning came when the valley people saw that snow had fallen on the upper ranges overnight, and they drew their woolens on again. The women put scarfs around their heads and necks and tied on their bonnets when they carried the pails down to the spring for morning water. They built the cook fires higher in the kitchen ranges and talked to their older sons about the size of the pile of cut wood, which stood, shoulder high and twice the length of a man's body, double stacked outside the kitchen door.

"There's never enough wood, not when it gets snapping cold inside the house, when the wind cracks down with sharpness. Don't tell me there's enough wood cut."

The leaves choked the creeks and covered everything on the ground. The brook water disappeared under them, then reappeared near the brown ferns, then went under the bed of leaves again. The squirrel and the hornet nests were resting like clots of dead leaves in the trees.

The snows fell heavier on the peaks. The frost whitened the cornfields and the wind broke the remaining stalks at the ground. The black bear went into hibernation, the female heavy with her unborn young. The hemlocks were green at the top of the bare-tree mountainsides, and mistletoe clung in the oaks. Mountain boys climbed for it, swinging from grapevines and holding to tender limbs to pull it down, for it sold well on King Street.

The December winds came. Snow blanketed the valleys and closed the roads for a spell. A mountain woman threw more wood on the fireplace fire and put one dress on over another until she felt warm. "Will you close the door, Bert?"

Her words did little good, for Bert worked outdoors most of the time and it seemed warm in the house to him, even though the walls only buffeted the wind a bit.

"I like fresh air," he tells her, and squats by the fire, warming his hands and praising the way the hickory burns and seeing strange shapes form in the wisps of pine smoke. She slams the door and props it shut with a piece of rock. "Born in a barn," she says to him spitefully, but she likes his austere ways and shares them proudly, for she is his partner in this conquest of the harsh mountain country.

As he warms his hands, the children come inside the house to wait for dinner and listen to him, too. "Flying squirrels are in that dead sourwood tree, boys."

"I saw 'em."

"Maybe twenty-five in there, but let 'em be. I don't want to see no smoke going in that tree trunk; you let them squirrels alone."

226

He told them about where the bears were sleeping. "They'll come out and walk through the snow this winter, but you'll not see them. I showed you their tracks last winter, didn't I?"

The children nod.

"You'll see their tracks, but nary a bear. They're like ghosts in the winter. And I don't think they're looking for food, neither, for when I killed a bear last spring, his gut was clean as my arm. I don't know why they roam the mountains in the wintertime, but it's a contrary reason."

Hides were stretched to dry on the sides and doors of the barns, and were brought to King Street for trading, along with cane-bottomed chairs and baskets made of willow splints. Women brought in jars of preserves, jams, and jellies, and bottles of pickled beans. There were baskets of apples taken from the storage bins, and a few hooked rugs, and four men brought in pottery of mountain clay, which they had colored with bright dyes. Sometimes a farmer would come in with a treasure of gems he had dug for, or gold he had panned out during lonely days of work.

On the coldest days, the people who were around traded at the King Store, either with the store or with each other, for they could keep warm in there; Caleb King let them carry on their business near the row of six black stoves which burned oak chips and were kept red hot. The merchants of upper King Street also would gather in the store to warm themselves and to find out about what was happening in the mountains. "Is Arthur sick for a fact? Well, hell, he's the best one I got out afindin' herbs for me. I can't spare him for the whole season."

Another man said to Cal, "Hadley got married? Well, I knowed she'd need to soon, if she planned to give it a last name."

The store was the clearinghouse for all news about the mountain people.

"Sick or not, how does he expect to get medical help back up where he lives? A doctor couldn't get in there aridin' on a dog sled. He'll have to crawl out or die, I reckon."

The talk was rich with the feeling of the people in it. There was

227

nothing fancy about King Street talk. "She bore two children and her husband laid up drunk and complaining of a back injury. She bore them herself with her young'uns helping her. What do you think of that, Kin?"

"I don't doubt it," a man said, "fer her man never was one to stay sober."

"They busted up Jim Marshall's still last week, Howard."

"God knows, you don't say. I thought he paid enough to keep it safe, and ain't his cousin a deputy?"

"Been one for four year, but his wife and his cousin's wife don't get along."

"Why, he's had four busted in six years."

"He met the sheriff's men at the door, and they said, 'Jim, we hear there's a still on your land.' And Jim looked plussed out and said, 'Well, I wish you'd show it to me so we can get rid of it, then.' They took him to it. Course, it was his own still, with a copper boiler he had welded hisself to hold forty gallon of mash, and a copper worm that was twelve foot long. But Jim acted like a surprised fool over it. 'Can you imagine somebody putting that still within a hundred yards of my house, right on my creek, and not even so much as asking me for the favor of doing it?' He stomped around and cursed whoever it was had done it, and Wheensy Thompkins, that little son of a bitch that does office work for the county—"

Two men spat on the stove and the spittle sizzled there.

"That little bastard asked Jim to help him cart the still out of there. Jim got out his wagon and horses, and the men loaded the still up, and Jim carted it down to the road for them, and he helped them pour out the mash."

"That's why they didn't arrest him at the first and send him up to a trial; they wanted him to do the heavy work for them."

"It's a wonder they didn't arrest him nohow after he done it, for they're sneaky as henhouse dogs."

"Did anybody ever figure out how sheriffs get to be wealthy men?"

Eyes glistened and smiles appeared; heads shook knowingly. A

228

big man with the loose-jointed walk of the mountain people came in and sat down and began to rub his hands. "A fellow just drove by, said it was snowing again at Busick."

"It's always snowing at Busick, if it's snowing at all."

"Who gives a damn about Busick. It's at the end of nowheres."

"You shet your mouth about Busick."

"They had a baptizing about two weeks ago near there, Howard, in the South Toe."

"Good God, they must a' froze their buttons off. Did they have to chop ice to get down to flowin'?"

"No, not this time."

"I've heard tell of people taking hatchets to Baptist baptizings so as to get a place to stand in the pool. And one damn fool got to splashing around in an icy spot once and never was heard tell of agin till he flowed in to shore at the depot."

"They didn't have much ice this time, but it was colder'n a preacher's kiss. It was this young fellow from Morganton that had held a service or two in the church up to Celo. He had converted several, and they swore to bash apart their banjos and start living a songless life of right-eous-ness. Right away he was aimin' to baptize them while he could, in spite of the elements. He got the band of people assembled on the bank near the store, singing hymns in voices so froze that the air crackled, and after a song or two, he barefooted hisself and stuck one toe in the water, and right then and there he decided he was sick to his chest. And he asked one of the Moss boys to go into the torrent and perform the service. The Moss boy told him to go to hell, so he called on one of them twins that the big male gypsy spawned and went off without, left 'em in that Curtis woman, and one of 'em, maybe to outsmart the other'n, or maybe because neither one of 'em has sense enough to know cold from hot, splashed down into the river and went to neck depth and he commenced to yell like a skewered Indian. Well, they hauled him out and he rolled over and over on the ground, shouting out in hog bellows he was so near froze, and his brother went to the river to a shallower place and got in and stood it. Then the preacher called on the dutiful to bring the converts up. Well, sir, they was scared to death, and they was standing there in bed sheets atrembling so much they was almost knocking each other down, but finally one woman got so overtaken with her devotion that she splashed down into the rocky bed of the old South Toe, and she let out a scream that put so much fright in the other converts that they drew back to the road. This twin was shivering and not quite right in his head by now, but he had been listening to instructions from the preacher in spite of the yelling that was going on, so he had the information he would need. He got a grip on the woman and dipped her and bawled out, 'I baptize thee in the name of the Father.' She come up spraying water and trying to cry out. He dunked her under a second time. 'And in the name of the Son.' He let her up for another gasp. He sunk her for the third and final time, and then the damn fool looked up at the preacher, panic on his face, and he said, 'What did you say that other fellow's name was?' "

Laughter shook the counters and rattled the chimney pipes.

"Gee haw, listen to that one; hey, listen to that!"

"Good God, I didn't hear about that afore!"

"Get that young'un off the floor and pound his back afore he laughs his blood out of the top of his head."

"Stop laughing there, boy."

"Hey, Kin, throw a bucket of water on this boy. My lord, it weren't that funny, boy."

"They baptized twelve people out there that day. Put 'em under back first, like the Baptists do. I've heard tell most of the other religions of the world put a man under face forward, so he can bend natural, but hell no, not the Baptists."

"Baptists always do it the hard way. There's nothing easy about 'em."

"Those people at Busick come out of that river so froze they couldn't speak. You couldn't pound speech into them. They had to be helped up the bank to where the fire was going, and some of the menfolks made a blanket house so they could crawl in there

230

and change out of their wet covers. Then they would creep to the fire and shiver and pray."

"Well, I'll tell you, if it don't kill 'em, they'll probably go the winter without an illness. You get froze through good, and you just naturally don't need to worry about pneumonia or anything else."

"Is ary restaurant open up the street, Ed?"

"No, not yet. That old woman is talking about letting a body sit down in hers, but it's almost twelve and she ain't unlocked the door yet."

"What's she cookin'?"

"Those with eyesight fit enough to see said it was chicken stew today."

"Well, come on, let's go get some dinner. I've talked till I'm damn near starved."

Sometimes the men would get into an argument about a woman or about religion. Or about politics. "I've been a Republican all my life, right down to Franklin Roosevelt, and I'll brain with that there poker ary man that tells me he ain't a Republican."

"Well, Grandpa Sikes, he's running on the Democrat side of the slate."

"Huh? Listen, he ain't fer slavery."

"Well, the Democrats ain't for slavery nowadays. Ain't nobody running on a ticket for slavery today."

"Well, they used to. What happened to 'em, did they have enough of it? No sir, I'll not vote fer 'em. My people never owned a slave and never will."

"I don't see how anybody can claim Franklin Roosevelt to be a Republican. I can't to my soul see how that can be done."

"You can't, can't ye? I just explained it to ye. If you was listening and had ary brain in you head you'd a knowed by now."

The men thought nothing of gossiping about the King family while they enjoyed the comforts of the King store, though they tried not to let one of the Kings hear them. Kin overheard them only once.

"You take a man who owns a store like this and his son is

231

stealing from him, and the man knows hit, well, he has to make a choice, either to get his son out of the way or to learn to put up with the stealing."

"Paul's got money laid by, they tell me. And he's got money invested on the upper block, too."

"You can borrow money from Paul, but it's ten-per-cent interest."

"That's high."

"That's the way he is. But he's got it to loan."

"He was running low when Collins was here. That Collins talked to him. I heard him once myself. Collins told him to start putting all the profits in the bank in the store's account."

Kin listened, still and attentive.

"Collins told Paul in my hearing to let this store show a full profit or he'd call in the police on him. And after that, Paul was pinched for money for a spell."

"Collins is gone now, though."

"Well, there you go, that's what I mean. Now it's up to Cal, seems to me, and don't you think he won't skin Paul proper, too, afore he's done."

"If he does, he's just going to lose the boy."

"Sometimes a father is got to lose a boy to keep what's his'n, or he'll be left with one suit of clothes and directions to the poorhouse."

"Cal won't lose him."

"He won't? Well, hell, how's he going to skin him and not lose him? The boy'll leave town if he's skinned in sight by his own father."

"No, don't believe it. I know Cal, and he's slick as wet glass. He's got a scheme for ever change of the moon, enough to skin Paul and keep him to home, too."

"That don't answer me."

"Well, I don't know what scheme he's got. Do you think he takes me aside and whispers his plans in my ears?"

"No, I don't think no such damn thing as that."

"I know when it's over, Paul will still be here at the store, but he won't be high-stepping it."

232

"Maybe Matthew will get Paul in line."

"No, Matthew owes Paul too much money to break apart. He brays ever time Paul motions for him to."

"Well, that young Kin can't do nothing yet."

"Cal can, I tell you. Cal's got a plan and he'll work it. He's slicker'n a hog-greased pole in the sun when he gets riled up to take action. He keeps smiling, he keeps that smile on while he moves in to skin you. It's Cal, I tell you, that will do it."

17

AT HOME THE FIRST SHOCK OF LOSING COLLINS WAS bitter and intense and lingering. The family sought its new definition of itself and its relationships, and each person sought to compensate within himself, now that he was gone.

Paul sought control of family matters again, but he moved cautiously. Before, when Collins had gone off on his short trips, Paul had blusteringly assumed control; his action was mostly talk, and the family had tolerated it because they knew Collins would not desert them, leave them to be preyed on by Paul and to prey on each other.

But he had done it. And Paul sensed the depth of their loss and became respectful of their feelings. He made no charges against Collins. He spoke softly at meals, as if walking in a house where danger was on all sides.

It was a lonely season for Beth. Her life lacked color and brightness. She had little interest in what went on around her. She stopped dressing as tastefully as before. She became a rather plain woman again. The only appointment she kept during the day was

234

to meet the mail deliverer to see if there was a letter for her. One letter arrived from Collins soon after he left. Another arrived five days later. But in January, in February, in March, each day she brought in the mail and there was nothing for her. She expected nothing, so this was not a disappointment.

"Law, child, he'll be back soon," Lotti assured her. "None of us can do without him for long." She pursed her lips and frowned irritably. "Paul should shame himself for driving Collins away."

"He didn't drive him away, did he?" Beth said.

"If you ask me he did, always complaining around him, saying things about him."

"Collins didn't need to care what Paul said."

"I wish Collins was here again to talk to little Johnny. He used to talk to Johnny so pleasant of an afternoon."

When the spring of that year, 1934, came, Beth asked Kin, who had his driver's license now, to take her out to the old farmplace. She wanted to see it, she said, while the flowers were in bloom. She wanted to see it once more before she took Cal's advice and sold it.

They rode together in Cal's car, Kin driving carefully because he had never driven over mountain roads before. She asked him to park in the pasture, and she led the way across the field toward the mountain, not looking toward the house where her father had died. They came to a barbed-wire fence, and she was under it before Kin could even part the strands for her.

She stopped at the creek bank and took off her shoes, pulled her hose off, too, and waded across. He leaped across after her. She slipped her shoes back on and put her hose in her dress pocket. Without saying anything to him, she started up the hill, past the flowers and the bushes of colorful rhododendron, walking upward through a garden full of bees and butterflies and colored birds.

Kin noticed how pretty she was. Not with the obvious prettiness she had had when Collins was home, but with a naturalness and a pleasantness. She had come through the worst of her sorrow, and occasionally she would smile now.

She led the way far up the pasture to the rail fence. Wild strawberries were there, and they picked a few of them. "We stopped here," she said.

"You and Collins?"

"Yes."

"Did he eat any of these?"

"Yes."

"They're almost too small to fool with."

She smiled at him. "He said that."

Kin grinned, proud of being like Collins, and of being with her, like Collins. She mentioned that blackberries were ripening at the crook of the fence, and he walked up there alone and picked a few of them, then they walked together up the steep path. She stopped from time to time and looked around her, seeming to sense the memory of times past. At last they came to the border of the balsam forest, and she stopped there. Kin stood in awe of it and held back, but she walked far up and stopped, standing quietly, looking about.

"Beth," he called to her from down the path.

She appeared not to hear him. He went closer to her, moving slowly into the dark womb of the place. "Beth?"

She turned and suddenly seemed to become aware of him again. "You want to go back?" she said.

"Yes," he said.

She walked down the path, not hurrying, not speaking, until she was with him in the sunlight again.

There was a cliff nearby and she rested there. He sat beside her and looked far out over the waving trees, their spring leaves turning in the wind. He thought he saw a black bear, then was sure of it, a bear with two cubs, and he motioned for Beth to be quiet. They held their breath as the bear lumbered around the base of a distant rock, turning over stones looking for grubs. She was a grouchy bear, thin yet from the winter's hibernation, and grievously hungry.

When the bears were gone, Kin and Beth climbed down the face of the cliff, following a narrow stone path, Beth holding to his hand, and she led the way to a bold spring, where she sank down and drank from her cupped hands. She laughed and looked about in

236

wonder at the beauty of the flowering forest.

"Is this where Collins brought you?" he asked, embarrassed by the thought of what might have happened here.

"Yes. I wanted to see it again."

He knelt by the spring and drank, his lips touching the pool of water. A lizard slithered past and he jumped up, startled by it, then he laughed and sat down near her. At once he was closely conscious of her presence, aware again that he was there with her, as the year before Collins had been with her.

"It hasn't been easy to forget him, Kin. But I have. At least I can think about him now, so it's partly forgotten. For a while I wanted to break every present he had given me and everything else that reminded me of him." She smiled at Kin. "I did smash two things, and I burned one."

"I thought he might come back, Beth."

"Yes, I thought he might, too."

"He told me he wasn't even going."

"He told me that, too." She sighed deeply. "He changed, like a piece of glass in the light. He wrote me from Ohio. It was a pitiful letter. I burned it. He was lonely but he was still trying to find his old life."

Two birds began to squawk and fight. She smiled at them, but there was sadness about her. Sadness had become so much a part of her that Kin suspected it would always mark her ways. He touched her arm, then moved close to her and put his arms comfortingly around her. "Beth, don't hurt yourself."

She rested her head on his shoulder. "No," she said.

He touched her face. Gently he ran his fingers across her forehead and cheek.

He dropped his hand quickly and stared before him.

He started to touch her face again, but drew his hand away. He sat quietly for a while longer, then his fingers touched her, caressed her face, moving slowly over her cheek and chin and forehead.

He kissed her forehead gently. "Beth," he said, his voice breaking.

She sat up. She glanced at him and got up at once and moved to

237

the spring, not looking back. She got another handful of water, still without looking at him. He walked to one side of the glen and stood there, trying to gain better control of himself.

When he turned back, she was watching him.

"I'll take you to the old cabin site, if you want to see it," she said.

She led the way down the path. He followed close to her and took her hand.

"Isn't it good to be out here, Kin, away from everything?"

"Yes." He gripped her hand tightly. "Nobody else is around here, not for miles."

"I know," she said.

The remains of the old house chimney didn't interest him, for he was studying her, the sharp features of her face, the whiteness of her throat, how her breasts rose and fell under her dress.

She led the way on down to the other deserted house and showed him the place where the family once had eaten meals. He followed close, watching her. His thoughts revolved only around her.

She began to run as they approached the third house, and he ran after her, laughing as she was laughing, trying to catch up with her. He did catch her at the fence and held her.

Then instead of releasing her he pulled her close. Impulsively, suddenly, he kissed her on the mouth.

She pulled away from him, fought free of him. "Kin, please God," she said sharply, gasping. "My lord, Kin—"

She climbed over the fence, but he reached over at once and took her arm. "Beth—"

"Kin, this is crazy." She pulled free. For a moment she stared at him, then she ran down the hill, along the old road which went to the house where her father had died.

He got control of himself slowly, and when the passion was gone, he was left ashamed and afraid. What in the world had he tried to do, he wondered. What would Beth think of him now? Would she tell his mother and father about it? Or Paul? If Paul knew, he would kill him. Or Matthew? Matthew would roar with silly laughter and

238

beat his skinny legs, he would howl. Oh, lord, if Matthew found out it would be terrible.

He went down the old road. How twisted life was to trip him, he thought. And he didn't even know how it had all come about.

She was sitting in the front seat of the car when he got to the pasture. He was trembling so much he stopped at the rear of the car and leaned on the fender for support. She got out and slammed the car door as she came back to him. "Kin, what in the world has come over you?" She took hold of him and shook him hard.

Impulsively he grabbed hold of her, pulled her close again, felt one of her breasts with his hand, held to her for an anguished moment, then she slapped at him and pulled free. "Now enough, I tell you! My lord," she said. "Now get in the car."

"Beth, what's the matter with me?"

"I don't want to talk about it."

"Beth, I never—I don't know what's the matter."

"Well, I guess you're coming of age, but standing out here in a cow pasture's not the place to discuss it."

"Beth, don't tell Mama."

"I won't. For heaven's sake, I won't do that."

"Don't tell anybody, Beth."

"No, of course not."

"I don't know what to say."

"Well, get in the car, Kin."

"Beth, I never did anything like this before, not to anybody."

"No, of course not. It's—you come along now."

"Beth, you won't tell Mama?"

"I said I wouldn't, didn't I?" She got into the car.

He stood at the rear of the car until his breathing came easier, then limply he climbed into the driver's seat. He couldn't find the key in his pants pocket. He couldn't concentrate on finding the key; he was thinking about Beth beside him and what he had done, about his hand on Beth's breast under the cotton dress. He had the key somewhere, he knew. "Beth, do other people get to shaking like I do?"

239

"Kin, let's go."

He couldn't find the key. "I heard little Sally Waters singing the other night. I was on the street listening, and I got to wanting to touch her, and my body changed, you know. Do you know what I mean?"

"For God's sake, Kin. Are we going home?"

"And this—it—I wanted to hold her body and I couldn't stand it."

"We're not going to talk about it here, Kin. Can you drive?"

"Yes, I can drive all right."

As he drove home, he thought about the wretched incident. He had performed poorly, he realized; he had bungled everything, but at least he knew he was approaching manhood now. He had often lain in his bed and felt the new power when he thought of girls at school; he had dreamed grandly of his prowess. But today had been different. This had been real, it was part of a man's world. He was proud, just as he was also embarrassed and ashamed.

When he turned into the lane at the foot of King Street, Beth asked him to stop the car. He knew she was going to give him the devil for sure now, but he stopped, though he left the car lights on so that she would know he didn't plan to stay there long.

When she started talking, her voice was slow and soft. "Kin, we don't often talk about personal matters, even you and me. But we'd better talk now."

She was going to give him the devil, all right, he knew. He braced himself.

"After all, whatever dream I have for my life is for other people now, not for myself. And part of that dream is for you."

"You know I'm sorry, Beth. Do I have to say it?"

Perspiration stood out on her forehead and neck. "Well, you shouldn't feel that guilty. You weren't entirely to blame."

"I was to blame, Beth."

"No, I should have known you'd grown up. I wanted to go out there today, to be where Collins and I were last year, and I thought you were still a boy. But maybe it's just as well. Now we know you've grown up."

240

"Beth, you're not to blame for it. You always blame yourself."

"You listen, I'm telling you the truth. I shouldn't have taken you out there. It might have come over any man out there, that's what I mean."

"But—with—Beth—with you? I mean, we—"

"You and me? We have to watch our manners, that's all. Starting today." She smiled, a grim, small smile. "You'll have to do your discovering about women elsewhere. You and I know each other in a special way, and I don't want that lost."

"I don't either, Beth."

"I—don't want you to think I don't love you, because I do."

"And I love you, Beth," he said.

"I'm the first woman you ever came to trust, that's all. And I guess a boy as he approaches the time he needs to find out about women, well, naturally he feels he can find out easier with a woman he knows, an older person, who won't laugh at him, who will teach him."

"Beth, don't talk about it any more."

"Well, you needn't think it's so unusual, Kin."

He leaned forward against the steering wheel. "Isn't it unusual?"

"No." She breathed deeply. "No, I don't think it's unusual."

He took her hand. "Don't ever tell Collins about me," he said.

She squeezed his hand. "No," she said.

"He would kill me, I guess. I wish he would, Beth. And I wish you would get mad about it, too."

"No, you don't."

"I just love you so much, Beth. And I trust you so much."

"You'll find you a girl your own age soon. You're very attractive, did you know that?"

"Am I?"

"Yes. You're quite handsome. You have a fine bearing about you, too." She squeezed his hand again, then released it. She sat for a moment staring at the dashboard. "Do we have any more to say, Kin?"

"No."

"Things like this can draw people closer together rather than separate them sometimes."

"Beth, don't—don't let it separate us."

"No," she said gently. "It mustn't do that."

After a quiet moment longer, she got out of the car and walked down the road in the twin beams of the car lights, and he watched her, wondering about the toughness and the gentleness of her.

18

PAUL KEPT ASKING BETH TO GO TO THE MOVIES WITH him. The first night she went, they stopped afterward for a cup of coffee at a shiny-fronted diner on the Square. They sat down at a tiny corner table, much too small for Paul's big frame, and he sat erect and stiff, careful not to do anything out of the way. He ordered fried potatoes and two hamburgers, even though she didn't want anything to eat. "You might get hungry," he said.

He studied her with his feverish concern. "You see, Beth, he's not true to anything, he's unfaithful to everybody, he's just out for himself."

"Let's talk about something else," she said.

He put his big hand over hers on the table. "I tried to tell you," he said.

She drew her hand away. "All right, Paul," she said.

He watched her, hungrily, absorbed with his affection and his need for her.

He asked her out every night. She usually thought up reasons not to go, but sometimes she went. They always sat near the back of the movie house, and he would buy lots of candy and popcorn,

243

even leave the show to get more, if he thought she wanted it. He was polite and kind to her, tending every wish. "Paul, don't fret over me," she would tell him.

One night they got to the movie house before seven o'clock, when the next feature was to start, so they sat down in the lobby to wait. Blue-lighted water was bubbling nearby in a fountain. They could hear the music and the hollow echo of the actors' voices from within the auditorium. Myrna Loy was talking. But they paid no attention.

They sat facing the fountain, and he took a small neatly wrapped package out of his pocket. A ribbon was around it. He offered it to her.

"What is it, Paul?"

"It's for you."

"No, Paul, please. You've given me two gifts this week already."

He put the box into her hand. She stared down at it, wondering what she was going to say, wondering when the movie would end. "Paul, I don't feel right about taking more gifts," she said.

He gripped his big hands together and rested them on his lap. "You can't say no this time," he said.

He loved her, she knew, and his best hope for happiness was with her, but she didn't like to be with him. She was attracted to his dominance, to his masculine strength, to his identity with the King family, but she drew back from his sweaty possessiveness.

She stood. There was no quickness about her, no sense of elaborate meaning.

"What is it, Beth?" he said, surprised.

She put the small box on the seat beside him. "Paul, don't come with me," she said.

She stopped at the top of King Street. She could see the beer-hall windows from where she stood, and the men standing in front, slouching, arguing. She could hear a banjo playing and Mitch singing.

She saw Matthew come out of a beer hall, staggering drunk, and stop at the curb. He reached for his wallet and counted his money.

244

Every night since Collins had left he had been up the street, trying to act like Collins, talking big, gambling heavy, but he had lost money almost every night. He looked up toward where she was, and in the street lamp he looked older and pale, and for a moment she saw in him the ghost of Collins, as if the ghost were passing through Matthew, as if Collins now were a ghost, and she almost cried out.

He turned away and went down the street.

A mountain man stopped beside her. "You looking for somebody, ma'am?"

"Yes," she said simply.

"Can I help you?"

"No." She crossed King Street. She did not turn down it. She walked up Market to Haywood and along Haywood until she reached the tailor shop of Morris Kraft.

She stopped before his shopwindow. He had changed the counters around, she noticed. The place had been strictly a tailor shop before, but now it was also a clothing store, with ready-made, expensive clothes. He had mentioned to her once that he might be forced to go into the retail clothing business, since tailors could no longer compete profitably.

There was a streak of light under the curtain which closed off his living quarters. He was back there reading, no doubt. Would he like to see her, she wondered. She had not seen him for almost a year. He had come by the house only once while Collins was there, and he had sensed quickly that he had lost her. He could not match Collins, not in speech, in personality, in body. He was a man of thought, not a showman. To him an excellent idea was more interesting than a fine trade, or a story, no matter how well told. He had stayed on the porch briefly that night and had left, defeated by a man who had not bothered even to accept him as a combatant, and who was, by Morris's standard, an inferior.

She tapped on the window and waited. Far off a church clock struck seven chords, which tremored out over the city and were turned back by the mountain walls. Where was Paul now, she wondered. Surely he had left the movie house. No doubt he had

245

seen her going across the Square. Did he understand? She had been rude, but she had needed to be clear, to break off cleanly. It was false pity to do otherwise. Collins had taught her that.

She tapped on the window again, louder than before. A shadow moved and the curtain opened. Morris peered out. He could not make out who was standing at the door, and he squinted curiously ahead as he came toward her.

She held her breath. It was, she knew, brazen of her to come here, but she had rejected Morris, so it was right to take the first step toward mending their relationship. Theirs was, after all, she thought, not a schoolgirl romance, anyway.

He saw her and stopped. He stared, not quite believing what he saw. He had been reading, evidently, for he had a book with him; his eyes were tired, for he wiped his hand across them. He came closer to the door until only a foot of distance separated him from her.

Abruptly he went to work on the latch to open it, working too quickly to be efficient. "Beth, I'll get it open," he said. He mumbled something in German to himself, perhaps a firm condemnation of all mechanical things.

The door opened and he stood before her. "Beth, it is you, isn't it?" Awkwardly he shifted before her. The book, which was in his left hand, his index finger at the page he had been reading, was resting against his chest. He had no coat on. His shirt had been made of linen he had imported from Ireland; his pants had been made of the best wool cloth imported from Scotland. "You've come to see me, Beth?" he asked anxiously.

"I've come to see you, Morris."

He stepped back. "Yes. Please come in."

He closed the door after her, locked it, once more mumbling at the latch, and hurried to the central light cord. The low-hanging lamp threw magnified shadows on the walls, blotches of heavy sewing machines, and bolts of cloth. She sat down on a workbench, but immediately stood. "May we go into the kitchen?"

"Yes," he said, still standing, smiling at her, the book still resting on his chest. "Yes, you come along."

246

He drew the curtain back for her. She preceded him, walking through the bedroom and into the lighted kitchen at the back, where he had been making a pot of strong coffee. A loaf of heavy German black bread and a wedge of Swiss cheese were on the table beside his reading lamp.

"Sit here, Beth," he said, offering her the only comfortable chair.

She moved to the stove instead and removed the pot of coffee, which she set by to cool. "It has almost boiled away, Morris."

"Oh, that doesn't matter."

"And it's black as an eight ball. Look how black it is."

"Eight ball? What is that?"

"It's used in playing pool."

"How do you know?"

He was always fascinated by every bit of information, she knew, and by how it had been acquired, by a word, phrase, term, idea he had not heard before. He lived in a world of new ideas, while his hands worked with wool cloth and linen and silk.

"You never cease to amaze me, Beth. Do you play pool? What is that, a form of billiards?"

"I think so. There's a pool hall on Market Street, and Matthew is always playing there."

"Indeed, you say he is? I've never seen that shop, Beth."

"Perhaps you haven't walked up the east end of Market very often. You probably walk up Patton."

"Yes, you're right. I prefer Patton."

She poured a cup of coffee for him, took the cream pitcher out of the icebox, and poured in quite a lot of cream, for he liked much cream in his coffee. "Morris, don't you want some food? I can cook you eggs and bacon, or something."

"No, Beth. I'm not hungry now."

Books were stacked in the corners of the room. There was scarcely a place for her to pull up a chair because of the books. She sat down on a crate, which also doubtless was full of books, folded her hands, and looked about. It was a small room, well used and full of contentment, she felt.

He sipped his coffee.

"Morris, I need to talk to you," she said.

"Yes. I want to talk to you, too." He sipped at his coffee again and blew across the top of the cup.

She sought to detect a clue in his quiet and guarded statement which would reveal his attitude toward her. He was a man of kind inclinations, but of purely objective decisions; he was, she knew, quite competent to think through a rejection of her. After all, she had brought him more misery than anything else. "I fear that I was swept off my feet by Collins," she said. "You met him, I know."

"Yes, I remember him." He gazed down into the depths of the coffee cup.

"He was like a whirlwind, Morris."

"That's exactly what he was, I thought."

"I loved him, Morris. I still do. I loved him very much."

"I'm glad you said that." He looked at her. "Yes, I thought you had come to deny or to apologize, and I can't see the need of apologizing for one's emotions. Mind you, if what a person does is rude or thoughtless, an apology is due. But if what one does comes from the heart, if it is not rude or thoughtless, then even though it might be painful to others, or even to the person himself, no apology is appropriate. It appears to me that it is actually inappropriate to apologize for the idiosyncrasies of the heart. I'm not even certain that it's a compliment to tell a person that he is able to control his heart's desires, for it suggests a coldness about him, don't you agree? I think it might suggest that. And after all, to love a person is good, it speaks well of the one loved and the one who loves. Nobody loves except with the better part of his nature seeking to control, though it might not succeed always; nobody loves without profiting from it, either, even if the love ends in separation." He was tense as he finished, as if the will to speak about the subject had cost him much composure. "He is gone, isn't he?"

"Yes. Several months now."

He nodded. "Was I clear in what I said?"

248

"You always are, Morris. And you're always so understanding, almost to a fault."

"I'm sorry," he said frankly, looking innocently at her. "I was trying to analyze the situation as I saw it."

"But don't you become jealous? Don't you have feelings for me?"

"Feelings for you? Oh, I should say that I do, Beth. In fact, I learned through this experience what love is, Beth. I did not learn it with you; I came to know it after you had chosen against me."

"I don't know what to make of that, Morris."

"Why not?" He pushed the coffee cup aside, occupied now with his thoughts. "While we were courting, I felt rather content. Our relationship was one I liked extremely well. Then, when I realized that you loved this handsome, energetic man, I came to recognize my own inadequacies and to realize that love for me was a concept more than it was a flesh-and-blood and living relationship between two people. It was not for me the relationship of people powerfully drawn together in a deeply emotional union, but a relationship between two people who liked one another well enough to live in the same apartment—which is no small accomplishment, of course—and who enjoyed physical associations. And I was badly shaken, Beth, because I recognized the inadequacies of my approach and the barrenness of my life in this regard. But what to do? What to do? I found several wonderful passages dealing with the nature of love and read them repeatedly. But they, too, were more analysis than experience and no doubt were intended to be enjoyed by people who were in love, or had been, while I, poor soul, was seeking love. I came to believe that love is not so successfully thought about as it is experienced, if one only can experience it, and without the experience, the thoughts are irritating challenges which pop prettily but meaninglessly here and there. I came to see that I would know love only when I had a person to teach me what it was and to experience it with me."

He fumbled awkwardly for a moment with the tassel on the hem of the table covering, then got up abruptly, embarrassed, and walked to the stove. He turned suddenly to face her. "But I knew, too, Beth, and this is the more serious point, that I could never really come to know love in a deep way at all, for I have lost the ability to lose enough of myself to my emotions. Of course, I would not change what I have learned for what that other man feels. I think I have found meanings to life which he could not even understand, and perhaps could not live with. But what I realized, and this is the better way to state it, was that the experience of love might require a self-subjugation which I could not abide. In my studies, I have gained new dimensions for my mind, but I have lost properties of my emotions. I fear that my capacity to love is shrunk to a size no larger than your friend's philosophy."

He fidgeted once more, irritated with the task of expressing himself in a complex personal problem, realizing that he was continuing the error of which he complained, that what he should do if he wanted to win this girl was go to her and reveal his love to her. But he could not go to her; he did not have experience enough to support that type of courage.

Beth left her chair and came to him. She smiled so gently, with such understanding that he was immediately grateful to her. "We shouldn't worry ourselves so deeply, Morris, about not being like everybody else."

"But I did so want your love, Beth. I want you, Beth. I can say that, but I don't know how to show you that I do."

She kissed him. He put his arms around her, then held her tightly.

When she drew away from him, he was dizzy from the show of passion, and from his wonder that she had come to him at last, and had offered herself to him. But he could not help but question how much of herself she offered him and how much she held back for the other man. "Beth, can we be married?" he asked, the words impulsively leaping over his own argument against them before the argument could be fully formed. He watched her anxiously as she looked up at him from her chair, her eyes soft and her face reposed, as if calmness were in her power to hold and to give. She was a strong woman with a good temper and a tough will, and he wanted her and knew he could love her. She was the only woman he had really wanted to be with. "Beth?"

"Yes," she said.

He knelt on the floor beside the packing case and took her hand and kissed it. "Don't trick me," he said. "Don't hurt me, Beth. God knows, if it's yes you say, then let's be married now, this minute; let's not permit laws of a strange state or of strange powers we don't understand give us a hesitant moment now, not now. Let it be yes now, and this minute let us say it irrevocably. I can't stand to think of having you and then find in a week that I've lost you again. Beth, is it yes? Is it yes, Beth?"

"Yes," she said, and drew him close to her, his head on her breast. "We will have a ceremony soon, but not in the city. There is the family—there are problems involved here." She hesitated. "In a town nearby, perhaps."

"Whatever you say, Beth." He squeezed her hand.

"Do you make enough for us to live on, Morris?" She rubbed his face gently.

"I suppose I must. I don't know."

"Do you make enough for us to rent a house, perhaps near the shop here?"

He thought about it. "I rent the upstairs for storage. Those three rooms we could use and I can store the cloth and books in here. I make—oh—I should think that I make enough to live reasonably well on."

"Do you have savings?"

"No," he said simply, then he smiled at her suddenly, warmly. "I've not dealt well with money, Beth, but I will, starting tomorrow. And I should think we can rent a house soon, if you want one badly."

"I have a farm I'm selling, so we'll have something from that, though it's mortgaged almost to its value."

"Whatever you say, Beth."

He was like a little boy in money matters, looking to her for direction, as he would in matters of love, too, she knew. She resented it, in a way, but this dependency would at least assure her of a contented house. She would find with him an escape to the quiet life. She was, she supposed, retreating now from the Kings, from Paul and Collins, from the turbulent emotions of that strange clan; she was retreating even from the store, and its big responsibilities and powers, to this small shop. She would find contentment now, at last.

There was no wind in God's power which blew as cold on Paul as this deed. Beth's marriage released inside him a well of hatred for life, for the twisted actions of other people, not only now but in the past, for the trembling insecurity of the human being tossed to the world and deserted. His hatred bubbled like liquid in a flask, boiling faster until it spewed upward, and from him came a sort of filth, an anguish which propelled him from the house and ended in an alcoholic stupor, deep and fierce, that even the whores stood in awe of. "Tear it all down!" he roared at one woman in one of the houses, ripping half of her banister rail from its sockets and hurling it against the front door. He tore down drapes in her living room, and not a whore or a male visitor dared stay his hand. He broke windows, he shattered the marble mantle, he broke vases and scattered flowers, turned on its side the baby grand piano, and caused to flee in panic, some of them half clothed, the men who were spending their evening there. Two women finally succumbed and seduced him. Like a giant he lay sprawled on the floor of a bedroom while both tried to vent his fury. He sprawled there like a fallen idol in a temple, without further power.

Drunk still, disheveled, his shirt unbuttoned, his pants open, two girls supporting him, his beefy arms around their shoulders, he stood at dawn on the street. "Take him to a hotel, for God's sake," he heard somebody say. "Get him away from here."

He saw dimly the frightened faces of the two girls. "Whores," he said. "I end up with the whores."

"Now, Mr. King," one said, not daring even to call him by his first name.

"Here, let me get you straightened out," the other one, the older

252

one, said, also furtively glancing back toward the closed door of the house. It was chilly, and she wasn't dressed for traveling around. She and Barbara had brought him outside to walk him in the air, that was all.

She buttoned up his pants and stuck his shirt inside his belt.

"You whore," he said to her.

"That's right, Paul," she said firmly, simply. "Now, you and me are going to a hotel, and we're going to play like your mama and papa used to."

He leered at her, tottering on his shaky legs.

"Come on, honey," she said. Barbara was scared, she noticed. "You get hold of him, you hear me? We can walk him to the Langren; it's the closest."

"Will they let us in?"

"Well, if they don't, I expect they're going to lose the best part of their lobby."

They got him registered. The older girl, Margaret, who was about thirty, registered with him. The younger one, about nineteen, stayed near the front door, as if she wanted to leave. But Margaret motioned for her to help get Paul into the elevator.

They got him into bed and Margaret told the young one to get in bed with him. She went into the bathroom and sat down on the commode and swore softly to herself while she waited. When the young one came in, her hair stringy and her face blue at one eye, Margaret got up and, slowly, sadly, lethargically, cursing softly still, went out into the bedroom and closed the door.

The younger one left later on that day. She was weeping and said she wouldn't yield to Paul again, so Margaret told her to go home and to send somebody else.

But nobody else came. Margaret ordered food for Paul and more whisky. He drank steadily. He got sick and threw up and drank and ate and threw up. She kept the tension down inside him, watched him with the skilled eyes of the practiced woman.

On the second day, she phoned the house and insisted on relief, but none came. When she found out they were leaving her there with him, she got stone drunk, too, and the two of them lay on the bed naked and Paul hurt her and she didn't care and didn't feel much anyway. She could just lie there drunk and do again the old, old comforting, somewhat silly act, for so it was to her now, silly after a thousand, ten thousand, how many times, flesh to flesh and wearying.

"Paul, you better eat something today."

"You go to hell, Maggy."

"You keep pouring that whisky down, and you'll burn your stomach muscles."

"I'll burn yours, if you don't shut up."

"You ain't ate a bite since yesterday."

"I ain't going to eat. I'm going to lie here and starve. When I die, you lie right where you are. You lie there, even if I get to smelling bad."

"Sounds like I'd be better off at the house," she said. "The great generous Paul King. Such a great man, like his father."

"You shut your God-damn whore's mouth."

She twisted on the bed and licked her lips. They were dry and coarse now and feverish. Her face pained her where he had hit her. "Well, I want something to eat," she said.

On the third day she stopped worrying about the food. They were both sick half the time. She drank and cursed softly, but not him; she didn't dare curse him. She cursed the ones who had left her alone with him. Her hair was matted with sweat and her throat was clogged. She hated Paul, she guessed, but she liked him, too, because he was what she had come to think men were like, all men were like.

Late on the third day she thought about leaving him, but he wouldn't go to sleep. She had to get out of there, she figured. He had stopped drinking so much, but he was still whisky-soaked. His bones were, she guessed; his skin was, his sweat was, for the sheets were wet with it. He hadn't let the cleaning woman come into the room. The floor was cluttered with napkins and parts of sandwiches from the day before, or the day before that—she didn't remember. It was a muggy nightmare now, that was all.

254

Night came. Somebody would be singing at the house now. It wasn't so bad at the house, but this hotel room was pressing in on her, stuffy, hot, steam-hissing. Go home, that's what she should have done, go home to the country and marry that simple bloke, what was his name? Marry him and watch over his three young'uns and salt down the pork in the winter and keep him comforted. Comfort one man, my lord, she could comfort him proper, she thought. She could make him feel well handled, all right.

Somebody knocked at the door. She didn't believe it at first. "Paul," she said, "somebody wants in."

"Naw," he said. He had been moaning in his sleep.

"Maybe it's relief."

"Huh?"

"Come on, will you? Answer the door."

"I ain't dressed."

She yelled out, "Who is it?"

There wasn't an answer.

"Paul—"

"Shut up," he said. But when the knock sounded again he pulled his underwear pants on. He found the door before getting quite awake and pulled it open a few inches. Kin. It was Kin standing there. "Jesus Christ," he murmured, "what the hell do you want?"

"I want you to come home."

"Yeah? You worried about me?"

"Mama and Papa are, and other people are."

"Other people?"

"Beth is."

Paul moistened his lips. He peered at Kin suspiciously, then pressed his lips tightly together. "Is that your message?"

"That's it, I guess."

"Yeah?" He stared vaguely at the boy. "Well, wait a minute. I want to talk to you."

He closed the door. "Maggy, you get up and get dressed. What the hell you still doing here?" He wiped his eyes with his fat hands.

255

"Nobody told me I could go, or I would have," she said. "I ain't been so well treated I sought to stay." She sat up in the bed and looked for her clothes. They were wadded up with the bedclothing somewhere.

He went into the bathroom and poured water on his face. He rubbed the sweat off his chest as he came back to the hall door, which he threw open. "Come on in here out of the damn hall."

"Close that door, Paul," Margaret said. She was naked, and was still trying to find her clothes on the bed.

Kin closed the door.

"Come on, get out," Paul said to her.

"Well, Christ, Paul, I can't go through the lobby naked."

Paul went into the bathroom and closed the door. Kin stared at her. He couldn't stop looking at her as she knelt on the bed.

"He's drunk, boy," she said to him. "I wouldn't stay around here if I was you."

She was pretty, though bruised, he saw, and her hair was twisted up. Her lips trembled as she talked.

"You're the little one, ain't you?"

"I'm Kin."

"Well, I hope you have an easier hand on you than he does. And don't get so big. Jesus, he's bad."

Paul was cursing in the bathroom. The water was running. He stuck his dripping head out of the bathroom and saw she wasn't dressed yet. "You get out of here, I said."

"I'm leaving," she said, pulling her dress over her head. She grabbed up her shoes and went to the door, her hose dragging from her hand. She closed the door, and the hose caught in the door, so she had to open it again. Kin was standing in the room, staring at her. Paul had closed the bathroom door again. "Don't stay here," she said. She got the hose free and closed the door.

Kin listened to Paul cursing in the bathroom. "Did she go?" Paul called.

Kin didn't answer. He walked to the window and looked down at the Square, at the people, small creatures maneuvering at the

256

corners, and at the cars stopping and starting. He could hear the cars grinding gears and honking horns.

When he turned around, Paul was standing in the bathroom doorway watching him, drying his hair with a towel. His eyes were red, and he was ill yet. "Sit down, make yourself at home," he said.

There was a chair near the writing desk. Kin slid into it.

Paul belched. "You keep your damn mouth shut about that woman being in here, you hear me?"

"Pa knows you sleep with all sorts of women."

"Huh? He does, you say? Well, he's not so damn holy, is he?"

Kin braced himself to reject whatever Paul was about to say.

"They always act so holy. Like saints. St. Lotti and St. Cal, ain't that right? And St. Matthew and St. Kin. And that angel boy saint, St. Angel Boy. And St. Beth, her with the God-damn pure manners, when she's not whoring with Collins."

Kin stared coldly at him.

"All angels except one. Just one. One little boy ain't no angel. It's that one little sorry dirty-assed son called Paul. Paul is a bastard, he's a snotty-nosed bastard and nobody wants to fool with Paul. Everybody else is part of the angel band, but not Paul. He's the one they expect to operate the store, to trade at the store, to support the family. But what the hell, they don't respect him for it. They don't look up with any smiles when he comes into the room, do they? Did you ever see anybody glad to see him?"

Kin glared at him.

"You're God-damned right you never did. Because they're perfect. They're angels." He nodded heavily and bowed low, as if saluting the family. "Well, where's Beth? Who's Beth sleeping with tonight?"

"She's at home."

"Home?"

"She's living in the rooms over the tailor shop. She bought some furniture."

Paul studied him as if testing him. He tottered on his feet as he watched, and couldn't seem to focus on Kin now, or on what Kin had told him. He belched and turned back to the bathroom and closed the door. Kin heard him throwing up what was on his stomach.

When he came out, his eyes were partly closed. "You still here?" he said.

Kin shifted in the chair. "I want you to come home," he said.

"Why?"

"Because we have to hold it together somehow. Matthew was gone all last night, you were gone for two or three nights. Collins is gone. Beth is gone."

"You get lonely about old Paul, is that it? You and me friends?"

"No. It's not that."

"We better not be. You'd better watch it or you'll be thrown out of the angel band."

"Papa's worried about you, too."

"Doesn't he know where I am? If you know, why don't he?"

"He knows."

"If he's worried, why don't he come up here, stead of sending a boy."

"He didn't send me."

"Well, why don't he come, I said?" Paul shouted.

Kin waited for the sound to die down in the room, then quietly he said, "He won't do that, not for anybody, Paul."

"No?" Paul said. He paced the room. "I can rot in here, is that it? You know what this room is? It's a casket." He stopped before Kin. Sweat glistened on his bare chest and fat legs. "And I'm the corpse. Look at me. See my arms, my chest. I'm for this coffin here, left alone for it." He studied Kin with bleary, misty eyes. "He likes you the best," he said.

Kin shook his head.

Paul laughed, a sharp, brutal laugh. "You say no? You little liar. He thinks you're great. He even likes that little nothing Matthew. But not me."

Kin inhaled wearily. "Paul, aren't you coming home?"

"Home? To that God-damn factory of misery down there? Is that a home? Is that a name it's got still? With nobody speaking to nobody else, and everybody trying to hurt one another?"

"Mama is worried sick."

258

"About me?"

"That's right."

Paul laughed, a broken laugh. "She don't care about me. She don't love nobody. She ain't never even kissed me. I'll bet when I was a little bastard baby she never did dust my ass even, just changed my diaper and let me squall, for she don't care. Her idea of cooking a meal for that family is to warm over the beans. God, what we going to eat now that Beth's gone, huh? Huh?" He got to snickering. "My God, boy, she'll kill us all!" He laughed out and shouted in a great drunken voice. "Mama'll kill us all!"

It was an hour later before Kin got him into a cab.

19

Now that Beth was gone from the house, Paul spent even more time than before at the store, working, insisting on his way; all his energies went into the store. So bothersome did he become that Cal seemed to grow more resentful each week, and he even showed signs of illness, though he denied that he was ill.

Paul was concerned, of course, and each symptom of weakness in his father brought from him a sincere statement of pity, along with equally sincere advice that Cal stop working so hard around the store and leave its management to Paul. Paul also noted and discussed freely his father's recently developed tendency to talk at length about the golden days of his youth. Whenever three or more elderly men assembled, Cal would soon be there, listening and talking, and Paul took this interest to be a sign of senility.

Kin refused to believe his father was at all sick, but on the colder days of fall, he noticed that Cal sometimes would leave the store in late afternoon and walk, even in the sharp bitter wind, up the hill to Market Street. Since such trips were kept secret, Kin was suspicious of them. He followed Cal one afternoon, but lost him in the crowd on Haywood Street.

Since he was near Morris's shop, he stopped by Beth's apartment to talk to her. He mentioned his apprehensions, and she made light of them. There was no reason to believe Cal was ill, she said. She said she had seen him on King Street the week before, and he had seemed spry to her.

The next afternoon Cal left the store again. Kin lost him in the crowd this time, too, and again stopped at Beth's apartment. Since it was unlikely that he would lose sight of his father twice unless his father had intended not to be followed. Beth became concerned now, and she and Kin walked down Haywood Street together, toward the place where Kin had last seen him. They had reached the corner of Market and Haywood, when they saw him come painfully, grimly out of a four-story building across the street. Even as they watched, he turned down Market, hurrying along as best he could, but limping, favoring the left leg.

Kin started to follow, but Beth caught his arm. "He's just going back to the store now, Kin."

"But where has he been?"

"Dr. LeClair's office is in that building, on the second floor," she said.

The illness seemed to Kin to come and go in spurts. Sometimes he would find his father unable to move except with pain. On another afternoon, after a long, hard day, he came upon him unawares and found him working in the apple shed, sorting efficiently and with considerable agility. Sorting apples was Cal's favorite occupation at the store; for years he had done all of it himself, even refusing hired help to assist him. Quite obviously, the work had rejuvenated him and Kin commented on his good health.

"Winesap—look at that apple, Kin," Cal responded good naturedly, holding up a purple apple, large and firm. "It's pime blank right, as my father would say. Nowheres else grows apples pretty as that."

There were a dozen or more different kinds of apples in the shed, and different grades of each. Cal knew the entire stock. He was personally involved with the apple harvest more than with any other. When the grape harvest came in, he was interested, and he bought

261

grapes at the store, traded for them, ate them himself, sucked the sweet pulp out and threw the hulls in the sand boxes beneath the stoves, where they sizzled for hours and filled the air with a sweet smell. When the tomato harvest came in, he was interested in the yield and the prices; he took all that were brought to him for sale. But his greatest personal interest came with the apple harvest and with the affairs of the apple shed. He would usually have an apple in his pocket ready to take out and polish while a child watched speculatively—polish brightly to a sheen. Then he would give it to the child. He never ate an apple; he seemed to have no interest in them except in polishing them and giving them away, in buying and selling truckloads of them, in sorting through them by size and color and kind: Stayman Winesap and Stark's Delicious, Virginia Beauty and Grimes Golden, Rome Beauty, red and green and one of his favorites, and the old mountain apple, Winter John, the striped apple, Limber Twig, the big dark crimson Hoover, the red Winesap, the green Sheepnose. On this afternoon when Kin was there, Cal said that a man could do worse than spend his life sorting apples.

Fall passed with pumpkins, with shocks of bittersweet. Their red berries decorated the stalls. With ears of Indian corn and with the green-glass and white-glass jars of canned chowchow, hot green peppers, and pickled beans, with cabbage heads, white and yellow, with sweet potatoes, turnip greens, mustard greens, and sacks of brown chestnuts. Cal stayed that fall in medium health, but when winter came, he seemed to respond with illness again. One morning —on Kin's seventeenth birthday—he evidently couldn't get to the breakfast table without Lotti's help. He leaned on her as he walked through the parlor and down the hall, and she helped him to a chair. Neither she nor any child he had, nor the cookmaid whom Lotti recently had hired, dared ask what was wrong. They knew that to him illness was an enemy. He had always thought of himself as being above it. He would not receive it civilly, they knew, or admit it existed beyond an absolute need, and certainly he would not discuss it.

But even after Paul and Matthew left for the store and Kin for school, Cal sat at the table, his body tense. About nine o'clock he forced himself to his feet and walked toward the store, but he stopped on the way and stood in place for ten or fifteen minutes.

When he reached the store, his face was damp and contorted. He slumped into a chair near Paul's office and stared before him dazedly. Customers gathered around, but he ignored them, and only when Paul came up, pale and drawn, did he show interest. He motioned for Paul to come close and spoke hesitantly, his words drawn out and awkward. "I want you to get—with Matthew—and figure out—about the store," he said.

The mountain people who were standing there felt as helpless as if they stood on the porches of their houses or under the shelter of their sheds and watched a storm move up the valley to drown their crops. The illness of Caleb King was ominous, and it was mighty, and it struck at the welfare of their families.

"Do you want to sell out, Papa?" Paul asked.

"Oh, you don't have the money for the store, Paul."

"You don't expect me to run it if I don't own it, do you?" He watched his father's face, waiting for a flicker of expression. "I can borrow the money to buy you out, borrow on my twenty per cent and the sixty per cent of the store I'm buying. And I have some other money I can use to fill out the rest. I can do it."

"No. You just run it like I tell you to, Paul."

The mountain people watched, first the old man, then the oldest son, watched for signs of strength. It made a difference to them which one of these men controlled King Street.

"I'll want to buy the store, Papa, if I run it. You can count on that." Paul spoke without threat. His voice was controlled and his manner deliberate, for he had thought this through. He spoke not angrily or anxiously, but with assurance.

Cal was taken home in a cart, and four men carried him into the house. Dr. LeClair came at once, running down the hill, although he was up in years himself. Before he left the house, he gave Lotti a bottle of medicine which she was to dose Cal with every two hours.

Cal was laid up in the front bedroom, which opened off the hall downstairs, where there was a brass bedstead and a thick feather mattress. The furniture was upholstered and comfortable. It was the sickroom, where a person could be nursed conveniently, for it was the room down the hall from the dining room and kitchen, and where the patient could be visited without disturbing the home routine, for it was located just to the right of the main entrance of the house.

LeClair called the family aside on the second morning and spoke firmly to them. "I don't know what's the matter with him, except he's worked out and nervous. He admitted as much to me this morning. Just let him rest, give him that tonic, Lotti, that I give you yesterday, and don't worry him none about the store or anything else. Don't worry him, you hear?"

LeClair left, shaking his head as if depressing thoughts rested on him. Lotti went into the kitchen and started mixing biscuit dough. "No need to worry till we find out what's to be worried about," she told the cook.

Matthew went into the parlor. Kin left for school. And Paul went into Cal's room and closed the door.

He went to the head of the bed and touched his father's forehead, waking him. "Papa, I ain't going to run the store for you," he said.

"What?" Cal said.

"I'm going to sell my twenty per cent and get out, if I have to."

"Sell it?" Cal tried to sit up in bed.

"I'm not running it if I don't own it."

"You have to run it. I can't do it from here. Kin's too young." He got red in the face and began to cough. "I built it for all my boys, Paul."

"Let 'em run it then."

"You're taking Kin's part, you're robbing him of it, do you know that?" He sank back weakly on the pillows.

"I don't owe him nothing."

"He's your brother."

"He'll get the money."

Paul went twice more into the sickroom that morning, each time to make his charge to his father, and each time he felt a pain of old

264

times remembered; a weakness would threaten to come over him for the wrong he was doing. It was a crime, he guessed, one within the family. He could not justify it, except by saying to himself that it was for the store that he did it, to keep it from the weak ones, who would squander it and give it away. Something had to be said for strength, even when it was ruthless, he told himself, and for the good cause.

Each time he came to the room, Cal sat up in bed to talk with him. He tried to bargain with him, but he got nowhere. Paul was stern and staunch; he gave no ground at all. "You're tough as steel," Cal told him. "You had no pity on the poor people, now you have none on me."

Paul absorbed his father's charge. "I'm doing this for the store, Papa."

"The store, the store," Cal murmured. "Is the store more to you than flesh and blood?"

When LeClair came that night, Cal was worse. When LeClair left, Paul went into the bedroom and closed the door. He turned, once more to begin the argument, but he stopped short. Kin was sitting by the bed in a straight-back chair, was just sitting there.

"You going to be here long?" Paul asked.

"Yes," Kin said.

"Well, no need my staying in here then," Paul said, and left.

LeClair came back the next morning and said the night's rest had done Cal good. "He can gain on this thing, if he's kept quiet and easy," he said.

Kin went to school, Matthew went to the store, Lotti went to working around the kitchen, and Paul took care of his father.

For three days Cal lay in bed, and every day he listened to the insistent demands of his oldest son. "I can borrow money; I've found a man," Paul told him. "I can pay you eighty thousand dollars for the sixty per cent of the store."

Cal would not agree. "Don't you feel guilt, any sense of evil in you for what you're doing?" he asked.

"You can't stop me, Papa. Words don't stop me."

265

"What does stop you? No man ever swayed you except Collins."
Paul flinched.

"No woman except Beth. And they loved one another, and that was your biggest hurt, I guess, that she loved Collins."

Paul watched him coldly.

"I used to defend you. I swore by you, Paul. I said you were a steady worker, that you had sound emotions in you. I said it, but you were born at a bad turn."

"I'll not give in, Papa. You've got to sell, Papa, do you know it?"

They argued the week out, Paul unwavering, but on Monday morning he entered the room to find Cal standing by the front window. He was out of bed. "I feel much better," Cal said. "I think I can get around all right."

Paul was stunned.

"Yes, I tell you, Paul, it's a pleasure to be well again. The sickness is passed."

Paul, speechless, watched his father dress and walk out of the room to the bathroom. He stood where he was until Cal got back.

"I've licked this thing, Paul, I do believe."

Paul moistened his lips feverishly. "I saw a rich man last night and he said he could loan me even more than the eighty thousand."

"No, I don't want to sell the store. I'm well now and can run it myself."

Paul swallowed. "I'll go to one hundred thousand dollars, Papa."

Cal buttoned his shirt to the neck and took his coat down from the headboard post of the bed.

"It's not worth that, Papa, and you know it. You're holding me up."

Cal left him standing in the room.

Kin was so relieved to see his father well again that he courted Paul's irritation fearlessly. He didn't care. When he got out of school each day, he ran to the store to be sure his father was all right. He would listen for hours to his happy words and listen to the mountain men laugh with him again. They had accepted Cal's leaving with

266

the same stoic attitude with which they accepted a loss of yearly crops or other unfortunate acts of nature; they were accustomed to calamities. But they accepted him back with rejoicing, much more rejoicing than had been seen of late on the street. "My oldest daughter had a baby while you was gone, Caleb."

"Did she? Boy or girl?"

"A boy. We named him after you. Caleb King Fletcher."

"I'm proud to hear it. I wish him wealth and the help of a good woman," Cal said, pleased.

Paul was in misery. His days were spent in speculation about what he was to do. He was up the street every afternoon, trying to find a rich man to give him a bigger loan. He would return to his office and brood, usually alone, though sometimes he would call Matthew in. Kin went to the door once while they were talking and listened, even though the store attendants could see him.

"I met with Fulcher," Paul was saying. "He'll loan a hundred and twenty thousand. I had to make every promise he could think of to git it, though."

"I'll borrow half and you borrow half," Matthew said.

"The hell you will. I'm taking this loan myself."

"I get half, Paul."

"The hell you do. I've done this, and I'll get it all. And don't you push me none."

Matthew's voice trembled so much he could scarcely speak. "You're cutting me out, Paul?"

"You got your twenty per cent. Hell, what do you want?"

Kin went to the front of the store and waited on customers, and when his father came inside, he told him what he had heard. Cal listened, expressionless, wary, nodding slowly as if he had known about it all along.

Kin suspected his father would speak to Paul, but that afternoon Cal went home early from the store. He seemed to have too little strength, and he went to bed. LeClair came to the house and told him not to exert himself. "Those tests I made don't show what it is, Cal. I just don't know. It's new in my experience."

267

Cal smiled at the old man. "I thought you could diagnose a case of fever like this."

"No, it's hid somewhere. I can call in a doctor from Duke, if you want to spend the money for it."

Cal shook his head. "You'll figure it out before long."

The next morning Cal went to the store and traded for a few items, but he came home before ten o'clock and sat in the parlor until dinnertime. He stayed at home that afternoon, too. Paul stayed with him for an hour.

Cal was well enough to come in to supper, but he ate nothing much. He drank a cup of black coffee, and strangled on the grounds, and he breathed so deep with weariness that there was despair about him. When the cook took the food back to the kitchen, he told Lotti to close the kitchen door.

She closed it. "What's the matter with the door?" she asked.

"I want to tell all of you something private."

Kin, Matthew, and Paul also were at the table; everybody got quiet.

"Paul and Dr. LeClair tell me I'm sick," Cal said. "I'm not sick, but they say I am."

"You're getting old, Cal," Lotti said. "We both are."

"I'm not getting old. I want to stay on as head of the store, but Paul tells me to retire and just come up the street to trade when I want to. And he has backers who will finance the purchase of the place. Now, what all this means is this, Lotti: if we sell for a great deal of money—"

"Not the store," she said.

Kin was relieved; for the first time in his memory he looked to her for help.

"You can't sell the store," she said.

"I won't enjoy selling it, that's a fact."

"Why, that store is a hope of a livelihood for little Johnny—"

"Lotti, he isn't going to need the store. And the way to improve his chances of getting his estate is to establish a trust, as we once discussed, and you and me will just live off the income till we die. Do you understand?"

268

Kin stared at him, shaken and perplexed, but Lotti seemed to be cautiously receptive. She trusted Cal, she knew he never made a bad trade. "How much will we get?"

"A hundred and forty thousand dollars for the sixty per cent. Paul offered it." Quietly, firmly he added, "And I've agreed."

Kin stood. He faced his father across the table. King Street was gone. The farmers, the old life were gone. What he had hoped for in his own life was sold. His right to King Street was bartered for money by a man turned ill, but the store meant more to him than all the money in the coffers of the earth. "No," he said sharply.

His father looked up at him, shaking his head anxiously, beseeching him to understand. Kin saw the weakness and sickness there, and panic there, and the hurt. "It's done, Kin. It's signed."

Kin stumbled to him, stared at him, at the aged, lined face which once had held dignity and strength but so quickly and soon had come to the start of its failing. He stood before his father, an anger striking him; his senses were jarred and twisted, and suddenly his fist lashed out and struck his father's face.

A gasp came from Cal; his eyes closed tightly.

Lotti grabbed Kin, pulled him back, swung him around with surprising strength. "Strike your father?" she hissed at him.

Cal's eyes were wide. "Kin, why did you have to do that? Why don't you trust me, boy?"

Kin stood totteringly before his parents. He turned almost blindly and, hurtlingly, moved forward down the dark hallway to the door and outside and away from the house.

It had been unexpected. It had come counter to his knowledge of his father. It had been a tidal wave unannounced, tearing all that stood before it. The moment of truth had come and he had found his family lacking. His father had failed him. Beth was gone and his father had failed him. Collins was gone. And a sense of loneliness, so intolerably deep, came over him that he stopped on the street, his loneliness becoming dizziness, so that the lampposts became black spears hoisted toward the sky and on the upper block of King Street the buildings twisted and seemed to writhe, squatting behind open mouths through which people came, laughing.

He turned away. "Beth," he said. He shook his head frantically. "Beth," he said aloud again, needing her beyond need, wanting to see her beyond want. "Beth." In the dark road he asked for her, then stumbled on up the street, the dizziness coming back again. His father had failed him. His father had cut him off. Collins was gone. Beth was gone. And now Paul was in command of this street, of the store, and of the people.

He left the street. Mile after mile, hour after hour, he walked.

"You strike your father? You strike your father?" He remembered the hissing of his mother's voice as she said that, and the look on his father's face—disbelief, the expression of suffering. "You hit your father—"

He sat down on a rock wall in front of a little house, somewhere, maybe not far from the store, he didn't know where it was. What does it matter, he thought.

He saw the past leading logically, painfully to this unknown place, leading to now, when he had no future to this life. His life had ended at the age of seventeen.

He went on down the hill, he guessed toward the river. Where is Collins, he wondered. Where is Beth? He needed Beth for himself, and he needed Collins to right the wrongs just done. Collins could do that. He had the power of old gods, didn't he, lifted in concrete, arms missing, strong and stern. He was more strong than stone.

At the station house he sat down on an oak bench and got hold of his nervousness. He was scared. The shock had left him, and he knew he had no friends left and nobody to look up to, or to ask for help. He didn't have much money with him. Somehow he had walked all the way to the train station, by what route he wasn't certain. The station had drawn him to itself, for it was the only inviolate place in which he had known a sense of security. He sat beneath the great dome, hunched and afraid, like a worshiper who finds in a certain place a sense of peace.

He sniffed. He scratched his neck. He straightened and looked

270

about him. Nobody else was there except a clerk. He felt in his pocket and found he had a nickel and a dime.

With profound weariness he stood. He approached the counter where the clerk, tall and skinny and yawning, waited beneath the wall clock. Kin noticed in surprise that it was midnight.

"Yes?" the clerk said. The sound of his voice rumbled briefly in the hollow chamber.

"How far is it to California?" Kin said.

"Five days and nights." He paused. "Why?"

"I want to go there."

The clerk pulled a roll of tickets from a wall peg. He yawned and began to write with a stick pen, but after a moment he stopped. He laid the pen aside. "Where in California you going?" he asked.

"San Francisco."

He nodded. "It's a sight of work to make out a ticket to a place that far. You have the money?"

"Can I borrow the money?"

"From who?"

"The railroad?"

The clerk wound the tickets back up and hung up the roll. He settled back on a stool and paid no more attention to Kin.

Kin finally, awkwardly, went back to the bench.

Soon that clerk left and another one came in. He was not as sleepy as the first one, but he was grumpy, too, Kin saw. A train arrived and he went out to the platform and watched the people get off. He edged close to one door and thought about getting aboard. It would be easy to board her. But he allowed his chance to go by. The train left; he watched it move out toward the West. Then the station house was even more lonely.

He sank down on a bench on the platform and stared at the black roadbed before him, divided into ragged parts by the shiny rails and the edges of the boardwalks. Seth, the Negro porter, came by and went into the baggage room, where he worked for a while. When he came out, he sat down on a pushcart near Kin and rolled a cigarette.

"You working tonight?" Kin asked him.

"One week daytime, one week nighttime. The nighttime is the easy one and the long one. I work from four to four."

"Why don't you work better hours? From seven to seven?"

Seth licked the cigarette and lit it. "That's a good question. Why people tell people to do as they do is a good question."

A freight train arrived somewhere in the yard, maybe half a mile away. There was the heavy swish of steam brakes, then the dry squeal of the wheels as they stopped, then the clanging of the boxcars as they bumped into one another. "Can you get on one of those and ride it?" Kin asked.

"Yes, sure can."

"Does it cost anything?"

"Don't cost a cent. But you don't want to do that."

"I'd like to travel out of here."

"Would you? I always wanted to travel, but never been far from this town. I've ridden to Biltmore, just got on the train. They don't take up the tickets before Biltmore, did you know that?"

"That's just a couple of miles, isn't it?"

"That's right. I've been there."

"That's no traveling at all."

"That's what I say. It's not much to it. I've sometimes meant to jump a freight and fly out of here, but if they catch you and you're a colored man, you get bad treatment."

"Do they give white men bad treatment, too?"

"It depends." He scratched his neck and inhaled on the cigarette. "It's two things to think about in terms of that. One is that the railroads don't want to make it too easy, 'cause then everybody be riding freights. That's dangerous, and the railroad might not care if a man wants to risk his life, but they're left with the death on their hands, don't you see? They think o' that. And it don't do good for their own workers to be always finding bums on the trains, some of them maybe drunk, use dope, some of 'em mean. So they consider that and they don't make it easy. Then there's the reason that some people just do to other people what they please."

"What you mean?"

272

"Well, if you give a man a stick and maybe a gun, and tell him to keep the bums off the trains, he might come to like to use that stick and scare people with that gun. Come creeping down the line o' cars, flashlight in hand, hear breathing, creep up on it close, close, raise that stick. Then that light goes on. That stick comes down. Crash!"

Seth shook his head savagely. "Damn, damn. Get you, get you!" He looked away. "They might nigh kill a colored man."

"Can you hear them coming, Seth?"

"Oh, you learn which yards are tough, which yards easy. If you was to go from here to the big river, why I guess you'd meet ever kind of yard there is."

"But I'd get there, would I?"

"Most likely."

"Could I get to California?"

Seth considered that. "You might get there. It's a long way."

"What would I eat, Seth?"

"What people gives you, people along the way, railroad people, other men bumming. But these men are of all sorts, and some of the men feels they deserves favors for what they do, especially from young boys."

"Favors?"

"That's right."

"What—what do you mean?"

"You don't know?"

"I—guess I don't."

"Then you better not try to go to California without money." He leaned back against a pillar and stretched and yawned. "Some men like young boys better'n women, didn't you know that?" He stretched again, languidly, powerfully, his arm coiling. "Four to four," he said.

Down the track the freight train's funnel was smoking. It was getting ready to leave, maybe. Seth got up and went back into the baggage room.

Kin went inside the station house and sat down near the clerk.

Then he went up to the clerk's desk. "Can I send a telegram to California?"

"Yes, you can."

"Can I send it collect?"

"No."

"It matters to me."

"It don't matter to me," the clerk said.

Kin went back out to the platform; Seth was standing in the middle of the nearest set of tracks, staring up the line, waiting for a train to come in. He was singing low to himself, weary singing, keeping himself company. Kin stepped off the platform and walked northwest along the rails. It was difficult to walk on the ties, so he walked in the roadbed. He walked to within a hundred yards of the freight train. He stopped there, then he went on. He got to within a few feet of the engine, close enough to hear the engineer and the fireman talking, close to the smoke and the spewed steam. Its eye was white, now that he was close to it, and bright as the sun. The inside of the engine was yellow from the coal fire.

Down the track he saw colored lights burning, and a light moving as a man walked home, or maybe signaled. The roadbed was black from the fallen pieces of crushed coal and the coal dust.

The engineer put his head out of the engine cabin. His face was coal-streaked. He spat on the ground. "That's for us," he said.

He drew back his head. The engine groaned and steam rose from it. It churned on the track, caught hold, and started forward. Kin saw a man bent to the work of shoveling coal.

He watched it leave. He watched the whole train pass and leave. He was left by himself out in the big yard, with the black ground stretching on all sides of him, and the silver tracks leading into the West, away from him.

He waited for a long time, but a streetcar didn't come, so he started up the hill, walking along the narrow, unlighted street. The houses were rented shacks the Negroes lived in, and he could hear them snoring. He even heard one man whimper—something about his mother, it sounded like.

There were dogs, too, and two of them began to growl at him from their yards.

He heard a man cursing and saw him sitting on the steps to his porch. "Say, rich boy, white—" He was too drunk to stand. He sank back down on the steps. "You looking for my sister?"

Kin backed off from him. A woman was sitting on a porch. "I'm right here, over here," she said.

He backed away from her, too.

"Just wonderin' when you was comin', for I got an itchin' only you can cure."

The gutter struck his foot.

"If you have the time, I'll make it worth your while." She laughed low, the laugh rumbling inside her. "It itches so fine and deep."

He started walking faster.

She spoke louder. "You afraid your white skin will turn to lard if it rubs mine?" She laughed. "Lard skin, lard skin, if it strikes mine!"

A man laughed. Two shapes rose before him on the street, and he swung away from one. It was a postbox, and the other was a person who lit a cigarette, and the light of the match flared up and Kin, startled, stopped, staring at the Negro, a big man with a flint-like face, his lips holding the white cigarette, the whites of his eyes bright in the match light. "Better look out, boy," he said quietly, "or the devil will get you." He blew out the match.

Kin turned and ran. The man laughed, and Kin heard him beating his thighs.

Somebody else was running. Faster. Black faces, people running, black night, black ground, black porches yawning, people laughing, moving.

"There he is."

A hand grabbed him. He pulled away. Hands came toward him.

A body before him. "I've not hurt you," he said suddenly, as something struck his head.

He was falling now, through a world of ice, past walls of ice. He tried to call for Beth but could make no sound. He tried to call for Collins. He tried, finally, to call for his father, but there was no sound, except that he heard coming back from the canyon walls the dry echo: Don't you trust me, boy? The words got jumbled as they reverberated: Don't trust me you boy trust me boy. . . . Jags of ice ripped at his side.

When he awoke, he was lying in bright sunlight in the back yard of a bakery. He could smell the heavy yeasty odor even before he saw where he was. A truck delivery man was kicking lightly at his ribs to awaken him. "Move it, will you? I have to fill up the truck."

Kin stood. A pain throbbed in his head, and other pains went through his body. He slumped against the wall of the loading platform.

"You're a bit young to be laying one on like that, ain't you? What was you drinking?"

"What time is it?"

"Ten-thirty, maybe."

Kin tried to shake his head clear. "What is this? Is this Asheville?"

The man went into the building and came out pushing a cart loaded down with bread. He slammed the door. "Don't you know where you are?"

"Is it near those colored houses on the river hill?"

"Why? Did they get you last night, is that it?"

Kin nodded.

"It happens now and then." He began loading the crates of bread. "They probably thought you had money on you. You better stay out of there at night, if you ask me."

Kin went inside the bakery and found a men's room. When he came out, the pain was so acute he had to lean against the wall to keep from falling. The driver of the truck came inside to ask him how he was.

276

"Dr. LeClair's office—" Kin murmured.

"Sure, sure," the driver said quickly. "I know him."

They drove uptown. Kin got out at the corner of Market and Haywood and went up to the doctor's office, where he was treated and fussed over and at last told to go home and get some sleep.

He felt much better when he left the building and started down Market past Fulcher's. He had got to feeling pretty good again. At least he knew nothing serious was wrong with him. He noticed that King Street had changed from the agonized shapes of the night before. It was itself again, plain houses and shops. The people were talking to one another, or staring off at the ranges as if seeing a sight from an old age. They weren't laughing at him, he noticed.

"Hello, young King," Mr. Porter said from the door of the herb shop.

"Hello," Kin said.

"Your father really skinned him, didn't he?"

"What?"

"Your father. He skinned him."

Kin nodded. "I guess so." He walked on down the street.

A man called to him, "How big's it going to be, young King, when your pa gets it finished?"

"I don't know," he said, puzzled.

It was when he crossed to the lower block that he saw it and stopped in his tracks. From there he could see that workmen were taking the roof off of the Tumpkins house, the house his father had rented out, which sat between the market place and the Kings' own house. Heavy machines were crawling in the yard. A machine was scooping up earth and filling trucks with it.

"What is it?" he asked a man standing near the store, but he didn't wait for an answer. He ran until he stood near the machines and could hear the men talking. Mountain men and women stood nearby, their arms folded, considering the marvels of what was going on. "What's happening?" Kin asked a fellow.

"It's your pa," he answered, grinning. "You know, don't you?"

He saw Paul then. Paul's face was drained of color, was drawn and aged-looking. He saw his father come out of the Tumpkins house, two men with him, and walk briskly down the walk. Paul charged across the yard to Caleb and stood before him, blocking his way.

"You knew all the time you was planning to skin me, Papa. Ever farmer on this street knows this morning that you skinned me."

"You go on, Paul," Caleb said, as if weary of him. "I've got my own work to do, and you've got your store."

"You skinned your own oldest, before the eyes of ever man in this part of the world."

"Paul, you built a gallows and roped it, you put your neck in the noose and sprung the slot, and now that you're dangling there, you blame me. I never claimed to be sick."

"Claim? Claim? I seen you standing in that road there one day for near half an hour. You couldn't move."

"Yes, and I saw you watching me from the store window. I was listening to a bird sing."

"You laid in that bed—"

"I was tired, Paul. Hadn't been getting much rest."

"You strapped me with a debt I'll never be able to get rid of."

"Yes, you and Fulcher are in trouble. You've got poor Matthew in there with you, too. But you'll make a profit on that old place, if you trade liberal and try to build a loyalty."

"Papa, you listen to me—" He was in tears.

Caleb stepped past him. "I've got no more time," he said.

Paul grabbed him and swung him around. "If you build a new store with my money, that I borrowed and give you, I'm damned if I won't take revenge."

Caleb chewed on his tobacco and peered at Paul, and the twinkle came in the corner of his eyes and mouth. "Paul, who do you think I am?"

Paul stared at him, perplexed. "I know who you are, well enough."

"No, you don't. I'm the man who came to this town at forty and gambled all he had on beating out Fulcher and Market Street. And I did it. I took Fulcher for a second licking yesterday. That's who I

278

am. And I'll skin you and him again if you get in my way. You're no match for me."

Paul backed off from him. "I'll get even, Papa," he said.

Caleb walked past him, the two engineers with him, one on each side, both talking to him about what needed to be done. Paul stared after him, his lips mumbling low-voiced words, his face contorted with hurt.

Kin tried to hide behind a woman who was standing at the lot, but Caleb saw him. He stopped and stared at him. Kin stepped back out into view. He guessed he looked a sight, being bruised and his clothes being torn. He had just been away the one night, but he looked like he had traveled all over the country. Most of what he thought about, though, was having hit his father the night before. Now his father stood before him, not sick at all, and taller than ever in the history of that street, a legend for a second time in the story of the people of that country.

Several of the mountain people were watching now. Maybe they knew he had run away. Maybe they even knew he had hit his father. They stood by respectfully, saying not a word, keeping out of the way.

"Kin, you'd better get on home and wash up, or you'll miss dinner," Cal said. He wiped his mustache smooth at the edges, and a smile appeared on his face. "Who you been fighting?" he said.

"I didn't see them too good," Kin said.

Cal studied him thoughtfully, curiously. "You sleep in a coalbin?"

Kin swallowed hard. "I've been down at the train station, resting."

"Uh-huh," Cal said. He smoothed his mustache down again. "Well, I'll be home directly to eat with you and your mama."

He walked on, the engineers with him, talking with them again.

The men of King Street stirred their minds for weeks about what Cal King had done, how he had skinned his oldest son and at the same time had fixed it so that the boy couldn't leave home, and how he had solved his other problems with this single move.

"Cal's got a mean streak of justice in him," one of the old men

279

said, giving his summary of the event.

Some reasoned that Paul would have changed with more gentle treatment, but those who knew him well, who had traded with him over the years, didn't think so. Besides, he should have known not to fool around too much with his father, for Cal had a reputation for decisive action.

Kin had no doubt about the rightness of what his father had done, but he was curious about how much he had taken from Paul in the trade, and one Sunday afternoon, when they were sitting on the porch resting, he asked him.

Cal peered off at the lane and thought somberly about the matter before he answered. "I figured Paul had taken about twelve thousand from the store, and had doubled it by investing it, so that money was mine. And since he had thought it was just to balance the books that much in his favor, I didn't see that he should mind if I balanced them that much in mine. So I took him for about fifty thousand dollars." He peered at the lane and chewed on his tobacco, as the swing creaked gently.

Having settled the account with Paul this way, the matter was closed so far as Cal was concerned, and when, after a week or so, Paul started coming around the house again, taking his food at the table and sleeping in his room, Cal appeared to welcome him. But there was no hiding the fact of the change. Two stores now existed. Each had its heirs. And Cal was the head of the family.

Kin trembled whenever he considered all that his father had accomplished in one swift move, and when he considered the godlike strength of his father, "the mean streak of justice in him."

20

MATTHEW KNEW HE HAD BEEN FOOLED ON EVERY TURN, tricked more often than benefited, and that at the age of twenty-five he was left with his inheritance severely crippled. The store, the magic place of his youth, was in Paul's care, and only modest profits and rewards could be expected from it.

He did not feel that he had been wronged by his father. Paul's maneuvers were responsible for bringing him to this end. He listened apathetically to Paul's enraged charges, he watched, mildly interested and detached, as the earth-moving machines lengthened King Street. He listened without comment as Paul stormed through their own store and pointed out the need for work on the tin roof, on the walls, on the stone foundation columns, as he banged his palm against the smoke pipes of the wood stoves and called out in wrath, "He leaves us with these damn things, while he builds proper!"

How much he had personally lost, Matthew wasn't certain. His twenty per cent of the store had been cut in value, perhaps in half. If he stayed longer in business with Paul, he suspected he would suffer further losses.

At night he drank heavily and forgot about it. But of a day he watched from the front of the old store as the workmen hammered and sawed, constructing a long, low, single-story building with two main entrances, one from the new extension of King Street and the other from the farmers' market. There was a parking lot to the west; that is, to the rear of the store, down next to the King's chicken lot, and Matthew noted that customers parking there would be close to the new store and to the market place, but not to his and Paul's store.

Matthew, in watching the new place being built, the gallows for his high personal hopes, had cause to consider also his failures in personal life. He had dropped out of high school, and he hadn't learned anything while there. That was a loss he could not easily correct. He simply hadn't known the value of knowledge, so he had done poorly in the pursuit of it.

He had no family. He had spent ten years of evenings on upper King Street. They were not wasted; he had found much pleasure there. But he had not profited from them. At twenty-five he had no wife, no child, no home—not even a room he paid rent on. He had, he decided, played the fool.

Casually, objectively, he reckoned with this, stoically he thought it through, and stoically he decided that he must mend his ways and get going with his life. At twenty-five he had not yet lost all his chances, surely. He was prepared to admit that the old course had produced nothing of value, and he was willing to try another course, if he could just find out how to go about it.

The dimension of his business and personal problems was determinable only when Cal's store was finished and he could estimate what part of the mountain people's trade would go to him. Almost every day Matthew made a tour of the new store, and he watched with particular interest while it was being stocked and readied. He noticed that Cal had ordered little of the old-fashioned merchandise; largely he was using new stock. The store was, then, an expansion of the old one, rather than a replacement of it. Cal was putting in a display of inexpensive wrist watches, a counter for school supplies, a shelf of new Bibles, an assortment of reading lamps. The patent-medicine case had been expanded to include modern remedies. Whereas in the old store only two styles of dishes were stocked, one solid white and the other white with red roses, Cal had stocked seven different patterns; even so, he retained the sign which announced, "Cup and saucer sets interchangeable." He had a section of the store for hardware. He had fewer harness and saddle displays. He carried seven different types of electric motors. He had four different-size pumps. He had two lines of plumbing fixtures.

Matthew discovered other curiosities on aisle after aisle, and when he returned to his own store, he was, each time, struck by the contrast, the dimness of it, the rambling, chaotic displays, the lack of departmental order. The store was homey and inviting, but it was dated. Whether it would compete or not was the question he asked himself.

When the new store opened for business, thousands of people a day came in from the country. They overflowed it and the old store, too. For six days the sweep of business continued, then it relaxed. The next weekend it swept upward again, but on the next Monday Matthew knew it would fall heavily.

That morning he went among the store attendants and pepped them up, told them to stay on their toes. Paul arrived, bustling about, bubbling over with enforced good cheer. He knew that his customarily glowering face was not going to gain much business, so he was trying to improve. "It's going to swing our way," he told Matthew confidently. He peered at the store attendants, standing anxiously near the counters, wondering if they should have gone to the other store, as had many of their peers.

By eight o'clock the stalls across the street at the market were open. A few of the mountain people came to the store to warm their hands, but most of them went to Cal's place. By nine o'clock, however, those who had gone to Cal's place had also dropped by Paul's. Maybe from force of habit; Matthew didn't know and dared not guess.

The buyers for the restaurants and hotels were on the premises by nine-fifteen. Paul had a contract with most of them for vegetables and fruit, and he served them this morning with good spirit. Those he didn't have a contract with, Matthew noticed, went to the new store.

Tourists came down at ten o'clock, peering around, pricing the saddles, asking how much the jars of honey were. They bought wicker baskets, as a rule, or hooked rugs, or clay pots. With them and following them came the flood of uptown folk, who marketed on the street. Many of them, perhaps by force of habit, Matthew decided, came to the old store.

In late morning, and into the afternoon, the mountain people, who had laid by their milking that morning, arrived, parking their trucks and wagons helter-skelter on the street and in Cal's new parking lot. Most of them went to Cal's store, but there were more of them than usual, and much trade came to the old store. Maybe not for long, but for now, at least, the activity of the new store had attracted additional business, and this might result in better sales on the street as a whole. But it was too early to say.

Matthew stood at the door of the building and looked across at the glistening face of his father's new building. What to do, what to do, he wondered. His father had a knack for change, that was the truth of it. He understood progress, he had a grasp of the times. Matthew knew that he did not, that the present state of affairs had always seemed to him to be the permanent one. He even still thought of himself as an adolescent boy, though he was twenty-five.

At four-thirty, the day's activity began winding down. Parking places were once more available in front of the store. Soon the businessmen, on their way home, would stop to pick up a few pounds of vegetables at the market place or the stores. Paul came out of the room and walked across the store to stand next to Matthew. He was smiling. "You know, we've still got the advantage, I think; we're holding much business. I believe the trade'll shift even more toward us as we go along."

Matthew looked up at him. Paul was smiling, nodding. "You think so?" Matthew said guardedly.

"We had enough customers to keep going on today, did you notice? We've got most of the big accounts, and we can hold them, I think. And listen, those people going to Papa's store, they're going to miss this place and come back in here before long. You'll see."

"Uh-huh," Matthew said quietly.

"What Papa didn't realize is that people are creatures of habit, and these people's habit is to cross that street and walk right in through this row of doors. We're going to hold the tourist trade, too."

Matthew nodded.

"There's sanctity here. This place is holy when you think of the life that's been lived here. It's friendly. It's got it all over that other place, and it's got the goods the people need."

Matthew glanced at him. "You make a good case," he said. He coughed into his handkerchief. "We've got a big place here, solid stock; Papa has overextended himself in his new store."

"My thought, too," Paul said.

"A fellow asked me last night how much I would sell my part of this place for. He wouldn't have asked if he thought we might go under, would he?"

Paul squinted at Matthew. After a time he said, "You selling, Matthew?"

"I told the man I wouldn't take a full forty thousand dollars for my part of the store."

Paul was motionless. "If you was to sell, you'd sell to me first, wouldn't you?"

"I'm not going to sell. Why, the store's all I've got that I value; you know that." He turned away and walked past several counters to the other end of the big main room. He glanced back and saw that Paul was still standing at the door, hunched of shoulders, intent of expression.

A few minutes later, Matthew heard Paul approaching. He looked out the window toward the sycamore woods, as if he were watching a game several children were playing.

"Matthew," Paul said, "if you ever want to sell, let me know, for

I believe I can get together twelve thousand dollars for your part."

"I wouldn't sell for forty thousand," Matthew said.

"The hell you wouldn't," Paul said sharply. "That price don't reflect much loss at all for Papa's new building."

"I tell you, Paul, all my life I've wanted to own this store."

"You don't own it."

"I own a part of it." He turned and walked away, returned to the door where he had stood before, and now he watched the passing traffic, the people carrying bags of goods, carrying baskets full of vegetables and canned preserves and the like. He glanced back once and saw that Paul was standing motionless at the blanket counter, mulling, thinking deeply.

A man came in who knew Matthew, and Matthew traded him two sacks of wheat flour for a two-pound bag of dry goose feathers. He set the bag in a corner with two others, went out onto the sidewalk. It was five o'clock.

Paul came out about five-fifteen. "Would you sell for twenty thousand?" he asked.

Matthew stared at the water trough, where a farmer was cooling off his mare.

"Matthew, twenty thousand I say."

"Not at any price," Matthew said.

"The hell you wouldn't. I'm talking business now," Paul said heatedly.

"How much is it worth to me, Paul, to be able to stand here on the curb and look across at the market, look up and down the street which Papa made, and say to myself, I own a stake in this, right here at the old family store, it's mine. I'm owner of it."

"You're part owner, and not much part at that."

"It's my store, ain't it?"

Paul glared at him. "Well, I'm not too anxious to buy you out," he said.

Matthew folded his arms and spat into the gutter. "I'm glad you're not," he said. "I'd hate to think you was trying to get rid of me."

"God damn," Paul said, and stomped away.

286

Matthew went up the street at midafternoon and wandered about, asking if an empty store might be found for lease. He found shop space on the Square, a thousand square feet on each of two floors, which was for lease at two dollars a square foot a year, two years to be paid in advance on a ten-year lease. He paced it off, figured out where he might put counters for merchandise. A store selling clothes for women and children might do well here, he thought, for the Square was easily reached. He could stock low-priced, tough-quality clothing. He was certain the idea was a good one.

By Friday Paul had gone up to twenty-two thousand dollars, but Matthew turned him down. On Monday Paul went up to twenty-four thousand.

The idea of selling out on King Street and going into business for himself didn't terrify Matthew, perhaps because he saw himself getting the better of Paul after all the years. Just to do that was payment for much loss of status. Also, he had wanted to find a new course, and this was one, entirely new, entirely different. It was a complete break with the past.

He found a small house not far from the Square for rent, and he paid the first month's rent on it, only forty dollars. He told himself he had better get the house, for he wasn't sure what might happen. He went into a used-furniture store one afternoon and walked about, looking over the merchandise, not buying anything, just looking.

"You setting up housekeeping?" the manager asked him. "I never thought you would, Matthew."

"No, no. Just need a little table to work at down at the store."

"What you looking at the beds for?"

"Might need to lie down during slack hours," he said, a grin on his face.

Everything changing. A new life. Ride the crest. He told Cynthia he was seeing new possibilities for his life. He dated her sometimes. She was younger than he, but she knew how to take care of herself. Last woman on earth he would ever marry, he guessed, for she had been lively company for several men, to his knowledge. He did like

287

to be with her, though, better than with any other one. Not for marrying, surely. Just to be with.

"When you going to get married?" he asked her one night, just joking.

"When somebody asks me," she said, and spoke so quietly and with such feeling that Matthew was embarrassed. She had always been a jokester, not a serious girl.

"Nobody ever asked you?"

"I'm not saying nobody ever did. But I didn't marry, did I? Do you see a ring on my finger?"

"I didn't know you wanted to get married, Cyn."

"What you think I am, a tree?"

"Do all women want to get married?"

She shrugged, sniffing the air critically. "Do I look like all women to you?" she said.

She didn't. She was prettier than most, especially of body. She had many a curve on her, Matthew had to admit. She was a comfortable woman, but he wouldn't marry her.

He dated her, of course. It got so during the second week that he dated her three nights in a row, and once he walked her by the house he had rented and told her he had rented it. He hadn't meant to, but he told her. She didn't believe him, though, and he walked on, relieved that she didn't. Damn-fool stunt, telling her that, he thought. If Paul found out that he had rented a house, he might suspect something.

One thing he could say about Cynthia, she worked hard in the herb shop. She didn't object to work. Now, that had to be counted in, didn't it, by a man who was thinking about opening a clothing store on not much money? She could add fast; he had seen her. She could talk to customers in proper language, if she didn't cuss in the store. He had heard her once get mad and she had commenced on the English language with the "A" section and got done a while later with words Matthew had never even heard before, which he guessed might have started with "Z." She knew them all, every short word in the language. That one time she had proved it to him.

Rounded figure on her, comfortable woman. She wanted to get married, think of that. They would sure laugh on King Street, wouldn't they?

To hell with King Street. What the hell did he care what they said on King Street? What did King Street ever do for him except give him a jail to live in? That damn store, walled him in, cut off his seeing the outside world at all, hadn't it? Laugh at him on King Street? Well, he laughed at King Street from his house, and his store up on the Square. He looked down on King Street.

That's the ticket, he thought. Damn them all, he'd teach his boys to laugh at King Street before he was done. He would teach his boys to look down their noses at Paul King's boys and not to speak to them in school. To hell with that place.

"What we doing back here at this house?" she asked him. "Ugly house, if ever I saw one."

"Ugly? I don't think it is," he said.

"Set down there below the road. What you keep pointing out that house for, Matthew?"

"I told you I rented it."

A pause. "You rented it?"

"That's right."

They looked down at it for a while, neither speaking. Car lights swept past. "Well, it's got a nice big rosebush aside the porch," she said.

He showed her the house. He had had a few pieces of furniture moved in, and that afternoon he had had the utilities turned on. Why he didn't know exactly, for he didn't plan to live in the place. He showed her both bedrooms. There was a big double bed in one. She stood looking down at it. She didn't touch it, and he stood at the door, awkward about showing her the bed. He didn't want her to think he had brought her in here for love-making.

She was nervous, he noticed. He had never seen her nervous before.

Always a jokester. He was nervous, too, he noticed.

"You going to get married, Matthew?" she asked him, still looking down at the bed.

He had paid forty-five dollars for it. It was a new mattress. Nothing cheap about it. "I guess so," he said. He had been able to talk to her about the coarsest sort of subjects before, but now his voice broke.

"You marrying me?" she asked.

"I guess so," he said.

She turned around, shivering, it looked like, and scared, like a damn-fool virgin of a girl, like a damn fool, he thought. And something seemed to pull him to her, something he couldn't see or feel. But the first thing he knew they had their arms around each other and she was blubbering and so was he, both of them were blubbering like damn fools, as if they had never seen such a sight before, or thought such a thought.

He signed an agreement paper with Paul which stipulated that Paul had three full days in which to get twenty-six thousand dollars, payment for the twenty-per-cent interest in the store. Where Paul was going to get it, Matthew didn't know. Certainly he couldn't expect Fulcher to take another chance with him, and every other businessman had heard about Fulcher's experience and loss. If Fulcher took a loss, they knew it was a dangerous place. But Paul said he would get it, probably that very night.

Matthew sat in the parlor after supper and didn't move from his chair until ten o'clock. At ten, a car pulled up outside and he hurried to the porch, but it wasn't Paul arriving. It was Morris, coming to wake everybody up to tell them Beth had just told him she was going to have a baby. Morris had come all the way down from his tailor shop, and Matthew had to laugh just thinking about it. The idea of being so romantic, he thought, childish. And Lotti took on over the news and talked about maybe it was God's will for Beth to have a large family, as she had. "Maybe the first one'll be a girl," she said.

Cal pondered that critically.

"We've not had many girls in this family," Lotti said, "the men all being so potent."

Matthew paced the porch and cursed quietly and waited. Morris left.

At midnight he went up the street to see if Paul was anywhere about, but he didn't see him. He went home and stretched out on his bed, still clothed, and sometime during the night he fell asleep. He awoke at dawn and dashed into Paul's room.

Paul wasn't there. The bed hadn't been slept in.

That day at the store he wondered where Paul was. He traded with customers and talked to the attendants, but he kept thinking about Paul. He visited with Cynthia at the herb shop two or three times, and she noticed he was worried almost to illness. "He'll get the money within the three days, you know he will," she told him.

"He'll try, all right. But he might get drunk and spend his time in a hotel room."

"He'll turn the world over to get that money. Why, he must have had a scheme planned before he ever took that paper."

"That's what I thought."

"You've got to give him the full three days."

"He said he thought he could get it last night."

"Maybe he did, and just hasn't got home yet."

When Paul didn't get back that day, even for supper, Matthew told Cal about the proposed sale of the store. He didn't tell him about his house, though, or about his plans to lease the building on the Square. "He can't get that much money for your twenty per cent, Matthew," Cal said. "Why, he's got himself priced so high he can't borrow it."

Matthew went up to the beer hall and sat around. At ten o'clock he phoned the Fulchers' house. Some woman answered. "Is Paul King there?" he asked.

"No, he's not. Who's calling?"

"Has he been there?"

"He was here last night, yes."

"Where did he go?"

"I'm not supposed to say. Who is this, his brother?"

Matthew hung up. Not supposed to say? Not supposed to say? What the hell does that mean?

When he got home, Paul still wasn't back.

He slept not a wink. He paced, he thought, he wished he had said just twenty thousand, or even fifteen thousand. He had to get away from King Street. Twelve thousand. Too little but enough to start with. He had to leave now and get a start on his life.

He went into Paul's room every hour or so, just to see if maybe Paul had come in and he hadn't heard him.

At breakfast he ate very little. He was sitting there pushing his food from one side of his plate to another, when the front door burst open and he heard Paul come stomping back through the hall. Paul came into the dining room with a big expulsion of breath, as if he had been straining for a long while to reach this very spot. He took a banker's check from his pocket for twenty-six thousand dollars and placed it in Matthew's hands.

Paul had done it! Every single penny he had found. How, Matthew thought, how in this world had he done it? He stared down at the check. Get to the bank, lease the store, marry Cynthia, buy furniture —hell, buy new furniture, some of it!

"Who's she?" Cal said.

Matthew looked up. His father was staring at a woman standing in the hall doorway. She was skinny, about thirty-five, was dressed drably, darkly. A hard-faced, stern creature, she gazed before her as if she were standing at the doorway of her enemy's chamber.

Matthew recognized her by that gaze. Paul had married Fulcher's daughter.

Paul had not married for love, of course, as he well knew, or even because of his need for a wife. When he had lost Beth, he had dismissed woman-love, and such contact with women as he wanted, he paid for up the street. There was a girl up there named Lucy who said she liked him.

He had married Florence Fulcher because her father had suggested it. It was a business matter. Whatever hope he had left for a home was easy to trade for the bigger hope he had for his store. To own the store was his first love, and the only love he guessed he needed.

He had married her in Brevard, had spent a little while on what she called a honeymoon, and had come back to town as quickly as he could. They had spent two nights together in the bed, and he guessed he had been too hard on her, for probably she hadn't known exactly what he had been about, but she knew now, and he guessed they could carry on some sort of night life that would bring him four or five sons. He had told her the first night that he wanted sons.

Being around her was not like being with Beth, for the sense of the warmth and comfort he got from being with Beth nobody else had ever given him. He had lost her, though; she was with that damn Hun, living in the back of his tailor shop. She had chosen wrong, and he was left with this husk of a woman. But Florence would house babies, and they would be like him, he knew that, not like her; she would be the carrier of them for a time, the fertile body for them, but he would rear them. They would be his.

Others in the family also knew that money had had much to do with his marriage. Lotti called to mind other marriages which had been similarly arranged. There was a man named Sal Bowman back in the country who owned one of the finest bottomland strips in the county, with over three hundred acres in it. He had no fewer than twelve bold springs in the hills around his place. Well, he married a wretched creature who lived down the road, who was an only child, like this Fulcher girl was, and she had inherited three hundred acres of her own. Then within a month after the marriage, he and the girl went to take a trip to Morganton, and his car ran off the side of the road and carried the poor girl with it. Sal said he had yelled to her to jump out, but she must not have heard him. She went over the side and fell more than two hundred feet and into twenty-five feet of river water. They never did get her out of there, though one man dove down and said he saw her sitting in the front seat, her hair waving in the currents of the water.

There had been a number of weddings Lotti knew about in which wealth had held power over a man's will, but it did seem that Paul had given in to it too much, for Florence didn't know how to make a bed or knead a bread loaf. She didn't seem to want to learn, either. "My mother makes the beds at our house," she told Lotti.

Her mother must have done the cooking at her house, too, and the dish- and clothes washing at her house, and the bathroom-fixture washing at her house, and the fireplace cleaning at her house, and the floor sweeping and the window washing at her house, and the clothes mending and everything else. Fortunately for Lotti, Inez had taken a job with her to help out some. She was a hard-working woman who had come by the house soon after Beth left, looking for help and care. She had had to leave her brother's house because of his wife's tongue, and Lotti had taken her in for her room and meals, and had agreed to pay her three dollars a week in addition. If it hadn't been for Inez's help, Lotti would have complained more than she did. But even with her help, work was to do, and Lotti tried to teach the girl to sweep. It was Lotti's opinion that any woman who had the will to learn could learn to sweep. But the Fulcher girl didn't seem to know how to get her clawlike hands around the broom and wield it. Although Lotti suspected that the girl actually was trying to do poorly, she was impressed by just how poorly the girl did. She was incompetent for a fact, and Lotti didn't try to teach her to do anything else.

Even so, in spite of all the worrisome considerations, it was good to have Paul married and on the road to a family, and to have Florence around the house, for though she talked but seldom, she had a fine command of her own ideas. In a crowish way, she was handsome, too. Not pretty, but handsome. She seemed to like Paul well enough; at least, she stood sort of in awe of him. She was always surprised by what he did and said, as if she couldn't figure him out yet.

Lotti couldn't either, now that he had come into wealth. Payments on his debt to Fulcher must have been canceled out, for he was spending money on a new car and had bought two new suits of clothes. He was rising into class, it appeared, marrying into a rich man's family. Someday he would inherit buildings all over town, Cal told her, and stock in different companies. Paul would be a man of influence.

Beth went into grief for most of the day when she heard about Paul's marriage. It was wrong, she knew, it was wrong for him, and it was cruel for the woman. He was a tough man, powerful of body, and a stranger would not know how to deal with him. Whenever Beth thought of limbs being entwined in a bed struggle between those two, she cringed.

One morning about ten, she went to the house to meet Florence. She and Lotti were there drinking coffee in the dining room when they heard her come out of the bedroom at the front of the house.

"She don't get up when the rest of us do," Lotti said.

"Well, Mama Lotti, you've got to be patient. That doesn't matter much."

"If you had to cook for her, and wash her dishes—"

She appeared in the doorway. When Beth saw her, she almost gasped aloud, for she was pale of face, frail, and her eyes were dark, hid in sleepy sockets, her mouth was bruised.

Beth stood. She started to say "I'm sorry." The words were on her tongue, but she stopped them.

Florence nodded to her, suspicious of her, this other member of the enemy family.

"I'm Beth. I'm Paul's cousin."

"How do you do," Florence said simply.

"I didn't know whether you were going to get up this morning or not," Lotti said.

Florence shifted her shoulders slightly. She sat down next to Beth and stared before her.

"The rest of us have done had breakfast," Lotti said.

"I'll fix her breakfast," Beth said, getting up.

She fixed it and brought it to her. Florence hadn't moved at all.

She took the food and began to eat.

Lotti sniffed. "Beth, what are you going to call your baby?" Lotti was a great one for names, leaning heavily on Bible names for boys, though she liked Henry and Varlin and William well enough. This child, she knew, would be a girl, though. "I like the sound of Margit Mandy myself."

Beth watched the woman eat.

"It's got a nice style to it. I knew a girl named Margit, a pretty girl who was married to a young man and borne him six boys in less than six years. I sat in her doorway before we left the country and swatted flies and talked about the joys and sorrows." She sniffed again, enjoying the smell of the country ham. "I've got a Kodak picture of her in my room that—"

"I'd like to see it," Beth said simply.

"Huh? Well, I'm not sure quite where it is."

"I'd like to see what she looks like, if you can find it."

When Lotti left, Beth fidgeted for a moment with the eating ware, tin forks and spoons. Florence went on chewing her food, not looking up. She was frail, Beth saw, but there was a toughness about her, too. Her father's toughness, Beth suspected.

"He wants to be gentle," Beth said. She waited for an answering comment, but Florence didn't give any sign that she had even heard her. "It's like a fever in him; he wants to be gentle but he resents it." She couldn't talk easily about it. "So if you treat him gentle, he will resent it. And if you don't treat him gentle . . ." She stopped again, then said, "he might hurt you."

The woman chewed on her food. Her clawlike hands picked up her knife and cut a piece of ham. She chewed on it.

"If I can ever do anything for you, you must call on me," Beth said.

The woman looked up at her. For a moment the dark eyes met her eyes. Then she went back to eating.

She is in prison, Beth thought, in a deeper dungeon than those made in old countries.

"If he ever knows we are friends," Beth said, "he will hurt you all the more."

The family changed, and Kin watched it, not from outside it but from close in, surrounded by it, by taller people, bigger forces. He knew that Beth visited one day, then came back the next day bringing a gift to Lotti, but it was a gift too small for Lotti, a sweater that fitted Florence. "Well, I don't know how I got the size wrong," Beth had said.

Beth was going to have a baby, he knew. She would go through the agony, and he quivered at the thought of her being in such pain, her body stiffening as the head forced its way through. And Paul was buying expensive clothes and a car, he knew. And Matthew was caring not at all any more for the store or what happened on King Street. He laughed at the work of King Street, as if suddenly he were a long way off from what he had been. He was getting married to Cyn, who had stood beside Kin years before and rubbed against him and laughed with him, who had embarrassed him.

Matthew had a house to move into; Paul was looking for a big house to buy. Kin had thought about leaving, too. At least, Miss Martingale had told him he must go off to college. He had not wanted to leave, he feared the outside world, but she had insisted and had taken a cab down to the store, had come into the store and talked with Cal. "Well, ma'am," Cal had said at last, "all my boys are leaving the family right now, and I can't part with him, but he can go to the college here in town and get stuffed with more learning, if he wants it."

Miss Martingale had pled for a more distant school, but to no avail. So he would stay at home, he and Johnny and his parents. And the others would come and go as they wanted to.

21

AFTER GETTING MARRIED, BOTH PAUL AND MATTHEW seemed to feel free to talk more openly about women. They had repeatedly visited the houses up King Street, but never had they felt free to discuss this at home, or even at the store, but now that they had a right by law to a knowledge of women, they used this new-found freedom to bother Kin. "Going to get you a nipple at the five-and-ten-cent store," Paul told him, "and you can chew on that of a night."

"What do you suck on up in your room now, boy?" Matthew asked. "You suck on your pillowcase?"

"You know, that thing'll fall off of you if you don't use it like it was meant to be used," Paul told him.

They smiled when they talked to him, but there was no mirth about them, and Kin watched them coldly. When he was alone, he would come to terms as best he could with the pressure inside himself. He would lie in bed naked and think about girls at school, and about being alone out in the country with Beth. He would think of the diagram Collins had drawn, every detail of which he could remember as if he had just seen it the day before. Yet he knew no more at eighteen than he had known then at sixteen. And he knew he had to find out.

He was walking up the street one evening, trying to get up nerve enough to phone Cathy Raper, a girl he knew in school, when he heard the sweetest voice he had ever heard singing a beautiful song, and he stopped at the door of Jacob's beer hall and listened.

> Oh, love is sweet and love is charming
> And love is pleasant when it's new.
> But love grows cold as love grows older,
> And fades away like the mountain dew.

He hadn't heard little Sally Waters sing for a long while, had not seen her around for a year, and she was singing as sweetly as ever. He went inside the beer hall and there she was, perched on the edge of the counter, a guitar in her hand, her beautiful slender legs moving to the rhythm, her voice lilting its way over the words and melodies, while every man in the place watched her, stiff-faced in concentration.

> If I had known before I loved him
> That his love was false to me
> I would have locked my heart with a key of golden
> And pinned it there with a silver pin.

Kin sank down in a chair at an empty table. Every man in the room was staring at the creature. She was as pretty as a calendar girl, with a happy face and the rosiest cheeks he had ever seen. Her breasts filled out her bodice, and a yellow ribbon was in her hair. It was almost more than he could stand, just to look at her.

She sang four more songs before she bounded down from the counter. The men applauded and called for more music, but she tossed her hair back from her face and laughed at them. "More, more, more is all I ever hear from you," she said.

They laughed harshly, appreciatively. She smiled at them as she walked through the beer hall. They watched her move, drawing back from her respectfully as she passed. She walked among them and, to Kin's astonishment, stopped at his table. "Hello, Mr. King," she said softly, with a slight lilt to her voice. She smiled so sweetly at him that he almost died on the spot. "May I sit down with you?"

He nodded, seeking a word. His thoughts had panicked.

She plopped down in a chair, sighing. "It's fun to sing, but it sure does make a person thirsty."

He was awed by her. He stared at her openmouthed.

"Don't you want a beer, too?" she asked.

He blinked, realized suddenly what she meant, and jumped up. He brought back two mugs of beer, in his haste sloshing some of the beer onto the floor and table. She seemed not to notice, and when he sat back down, she once more turned her big innocent eyes on him.

"I tell you, miss," he said, his spirits soaring, "you sure are pretty and clever."

She laughed softly. "It's nice of you to say so." There was music even in her laughter.

He looked at her hungrily, intently. "If there's ever any place you want to go, I hope you'll let me know about it," he said.

She took a big swallow from the beer mug. Her face lighted up suddenly with a smile. "I guess that might be all right," she said, and shrugged her pretty shoulders. She crossed her legs under the table. At least, she did something with her legs under the table, and just the thought of it thrilled him. There she was, a human being with everything Collins had put on the piece of paper, as Collins himself had said, sitting within a few inches of him, within reach, and it just might be that she was going to permit him to get to know her, even in the way Collins had diagramed.

"Sometime maybe I won't be doing anything, some evening," she said, and she laughed, as if delighted with herself. "Where would you like to take me?"

He peered off at the bar. He cleared his throat. "Where would you want to go?"

She shrugged. Whenever she moved her pretty self it was more than he could stand.

"I don't dance much," he said.

"I'll bet you could."

"No, I couldn't, either," he said.

"Well, there's always the recreation park," she said.

300

"Yes, well—all right," he said. "When?"

She smiled, with her eyes mostly, it seemed to him. Her eyes stayed on him. When she took a drink of the beer, her eyelids closed, then she looked at him again. A little chuckle caught hold of her spirit, as if she had just thought of something very nice and funny, and she leaned across the table and touched his arm. "Why not now?" she said.

They rode out to the recreation park on a city bus, and all the way out there, she wiggled in her seat. It seemed to be nearly impossible for the girl to sit still, and her anxiousness was not from nervousness, or, at least, it wasn't from any feeling of inadequacy. It came evidently from a need to be wherever it was she was going, to be doing whatever it was she had been promised she could do, that she wanted to do.

Once, she sat back in the seat and began to chatter away about herself, flicking her tongue over her lips now and again. She told where she had been born and what her birthday was and how she had made out in the world. "I've had to work since a little girl, 'cause my father left us. He was a handsome man," she said. "He was more'n six and a half feet tall, and he had a square jaw and a sharp-pointed nose like John Barrymore. He was a loggerman back in the hills, but my mama lived in town, right up near the school in that brown house, and sometimes my father would come into town and stay for a few days. He was so broad-chested that he couldn't find any clothes in the stores to fit him, and Mama would have to piece his shirts at the shoulders. He was a wood sawyer, and he could saw down the biggest trees and hitch oxen to them and drive them off to the train stops, or to the slides. Sometimes he had seven teams of oxen yoked to a log, and they would pull them for miles, he told me once. He used to hold me on his lap and tell me about the work in the woods."

Kin was fascinated with the flow of language. The girl was enthusiastic about all she did, and she talked and squirmed in her seat and peered out of the bus to see if they were near the recreation park yet, and she glanced at Kin, smiling, and hugged herself and was off talking again, all in a series of anxious moments, as her eyes darted here and there, and her fleeting, ever-new interests changed.

"I took up singing when I was just a little girl, because I sang a song for my father. Mama said he was coming home for a visit, and she taught me the words to the song. The words were: 'May I sleep in your barn tonight, mister? 'Tis so cold lying out on the ground.' She taught me to sing that, and she dressed me up ever so nice, in a dress she had hand-sewed for me, and she stood me before the dining-room table, and after supper that night I sang it for him, so pretty that he cried and grabbed me up and hugged me till I couldn't breathe, and I cried out and laughed, with him holding me and tickling me and saying I was pretty as a picture on the wall."

She was sitting on the edge of her seat as the bus turned into the recreation park. "Can you hear the music?" she asked, "can you hear the Ferris wheel?" Eagerly she grasped his hand. "Listen," she said.

She was the first person out of the bus. "Oh, I just can't stand it," she said, stopping and gazing about at the world of wonders, with rides and shows, and the zoo high on the hill, and below them in a small valley a dark colored lake.

They rode a number of rides. Kin lost count. He had come to the park with almost four dollars in his pocket, and he spent all except bus fare home trying to satisfy her craving for excitement. All the while he was becoming more conscious of the chance he might have, and must take, when he would be alone with her. He kept holding her hand as they walked and as they sat in the dangerous rides, and pressing against her in the loop-the-loop, and even putting his arm around her in the car ride. On their fourth time on the Ferris wheel, she sat so close to him, and her hand held his so tightly that sweat ran down his face and neck.

When he told her he was out of money, she seemed to be not at all disappointed. "It doesn't matter," she said; "we can sneak down to the lake now." She took his hand and led the way, leaving the path at one point and darting along a smaller trail she knew. As soon as they were alone, Kin, unable to control himself any longer, stopped and pulled her to him, eager to kiss her, to break through the anxious challenge which possessed him. He held her possessively, an urgency

302

taking control of him, but she began to kick and push to be free.

She stepped back, her hair disheveled, breathing heavily. "Don't grab like that," she said sharply, trying to get her ribbon back in place. "Ask for what you want."

She was angry with him, a fury bubbling up in her. She turned and started on down the path. "Come along," she said.

She led the way to a six-foot-high metal fence which closed off the area of the lake, where she caught hold of a limb of a maple tree and pulled herself up. While Kin watched, she swung her feet over to the fence, pulled herself farther up, balanced on the fence precariously, gave herself a push, and dropped to the ground on the other side. "Come on," she whispered.

He climbed the tree and managed to get over the fence. He rolled to the ground with the impact of the fall, and she was next to him at once, like a pixie. "Now be quiet," she said, looping her arms around his neck. "If they find us, they'll put us out of here."

She was close and cuddly now, smothering him with attention. He embraced her tentatively. She wiggled excitedly and kissed his hand and touched his chin with her tongue, caressed him, rubbed her hands swiftly over him, clutched at him. He grasped her tightly, possessively.

She began unbuttoning her dress at the neck and kicked off her shoes. She began unbuttoning his clothes, too, and she smiled, warmly, playfully. "Why, I do believe you're almost nervous around me," she said.

He squeezed her as tightly as he dared. He was breathing heavily and his hands trembled, but he was not embarrassed, for he was dazed by the wonder of her and being with her. He felt her body from a world apart.

"I don't know what I'm going to do with you," she said, whispering to him, speaking his name, saying "Mr. King," which sent a thrill through him, "if you don't stop feeling of all of me at once." She took his hand and kissed it and slipped it into her dress and held it against her breast.

She laughed softly, breathing deeply, and pulled at his ear and

303

kissed him. She moaned and was constantly moving in his arms. Her body sought him, moved against him. She turned into his arms, her lips seeking him, and she pulled him on top of her.

He lost sense of place and time, and of himself, and of her as being apart from himself. He felt and sought and pinched and caressed, he discovered her, the body of her and her ever-quickening spirit. She permitted him the wonders of her body, moaning and laughing softly and wiggling and whispering to him and calling him "Mr. King," saying, "why, Mr. King, you do seem to move fast." Kissing him. "But you've got to stop doing everything at once, or I'll die."

He kissed and caressed her, carried into elation now, the moment blurred, carried off by longing, being part of desire itself and need itself, which he could not control, while she gasped and sighed her happiness and urged him on to still further and closer intimacy. The pressure of his love for her and need for her threatened to break, and he took her possessively, his body with hers, trembling from the sharing of hers, moving with hers, one with hers on the ground.

It was late when they rode back to the Square. He was withered and benumbed by his discoveries. He could see himself as if he had been transported out of himself; he could see himself cross the street by the hotel and the coffee shop, walking with her, light and competent, certain of himself, subject to her only, servant of her, this happy creature.

She and her mother rented three upstairs small rooms, she told him. "I won't be able to ask you in," she said. On the porch she waited for him to kiss her good night, and he kissed her passionately, confident of himself now, and she permitted it for a long moment before she wiggled free, laughing delightedly. She whispered, "My, my, Mr. King," and kissed him quickly and turned to the screen door. She looked back with a smile and a rippling laugh as the door closed behind her.

He kicked at the fireplug in front of the house and swung around a lamppost with exhilarated bounds. He was shaken with the glad tidings of the night's experience. This girl, this beautiful girl, had let him prove himself. He was in love with her and with all women, with the thought of women, with the idea that God had thought up, this rich experience. He favored it greatly, and little Sally Waters was, he knew, the choicest woman in that city, in that state, the most delectable, wonderfully exciting in love, soft and yielding, eager, caressing.

. Because of her—dear, he thought, dear woman, he thought—his life had turned, and he had arrived at last, after the fitful worries and the wakeful nights, at the place of the adult world. It opened now before him. He was awed and richly pleased and unafraid. It was luxurious, the night, the quivering moment.

At home he lay in bed and thought of her. His sleep was full of images of her, the childlike face and the round softness of her body, which now he knew so well and intimately. In his dreams she walked, he watched her walk. He touched her and she turned to him. "Why, Mr. King," she said. And he made love to her again.

He bathed next morning, thinking of her as his soapy hands slid over his body. He was tinglingly alert and caressed himself and poured water over himself and thought how marvelously powerful it was to be a man, to be able to dominate another creature and yield up the moist seed of life as he shared the intensity of life in the same exaggerated moment.

He dried off with two towels, dressed, and walked through the house, impatient for breakfast. He hung around the kitchen while Inez fried country ham and eggs, and he ate a big meal, barely able to restrain himself from talking in praise of all around him, of this fantastic and perfectly remarkable, rewarding, heavily favored world, this system of powerful urgencies which had been made for him to dominate. How perfect life was, how full of marvels, how cool and sharp its air on this morning, how exquisite the color and shape of the smallest petunia blossoms, the green leaves, the separate blades of grass.

Before school he stood at her house, longing to see her appear at a window, entertaining himself with thoughts of being with her at this moment, with her in the bed in the shade-drawn room, in the soft bed with the soft Sally Waters. He wished she would see him on the street and throw him down a kiss. What an arrow, a dart that would be, piercing him surely, he thought.

That day in school he heard little that the teacher said. He was called on twice and answered nothing correctly. He told himself that learning was nonsensical, an exercise engaged in by people who had lost their power to love, that it was an old man's and a cold man's world, that no one who knew the wonders of little Sally Waters could bear to spend time on facts of science or ancient happenings. My lord, he thought, where in these pages in this book is the account of the wondrous women and men who had loved and died loving? Learning was time-wasting; it kept him from her. He could be out under a bush with her. He could be with her slender body. What finer study could be made than of that body, the limbs, the smooth stomach, the breasts, the neck. How much more desirable that body than the silly facts and records. Oh, lord, he thought, it was torturous to be detained.

When school let out, he sprinted to her house and waited on the street, praying for her to see him. When she did not, he went to the porch, his body astir with memories of her perfume and the loving smile and the undulation of her body even as he kissed her good night. He paced the porch so that she might hear him walking. He stopped to listen. There was no sound from inside.

He knocked on the door. Tensely he waited, awkwardly excited. Sally, Sally, Sally, he thought. Little Sally Waters. Impatiently he waited. How perfectly made. To be held by her again. To be touched by her. To see her again. Dear, small hands eagerly holding him, little Sally Waters.

He knocked on the door again, louder, more insistently. And he heard a woman clomping down the stairs. "Hold your water," she called before her, and pulled open the door. "Yeah?" she said. She was about fifty. Her hair was stringy. Her clothes were smudged with grease and dirt.

"Is Sally home?" he asked.

306

"Not home," she said and slammed the door and went back upstairs.

He stared at the door, his mouth agape, shocked, rudely struck by the presence of a crude woman who evidently could live in the same house with this delectable daughter and be unimpressed. How could a girl who caused such buoyancy in his own spirit leave this person, doubtless her mother, completely unimpressed?

No, this wasn't her mother, not the wife and mistress of that lordly timberman who had had to have his shirts let out. This disarranged creature was a servant, and a crass servant at that, surely.

He turned from the house, dazed and confused. Life turned in a big prism; he could not follow all its changes of mood and color. This woman, was she related to little Sally Waters?

He walked the streets, looking in coffeehouses for her, walking the length of all the Coke bars. He asked at Jacob's four times for her. "Will she sing here tonight?" he asked.

"I hope so, if you don't take her off like you did last night," Jacob told him. "All she did last night was sing a few songs, then bolt out the door, and my beer business was soon gone to Mitch's place."

"Do you know where she is now?"

"How do I know? She just got back from Tennessee. She was living there with somebody. She came in here day before yesterday and asked for a job. I gave her a singing job, but she bolted off with you, with no more than a wave of her petticoat to me at the door. I haven't seen her today."

"What time is she due to come to work?"

"Seven-thirty."

Kin hung around the beer hall, asking others about her. Men smiled and winked at one another, commenting on his show of interest, but he didn't object to that. Let them know he loved her. Let the whole world know it. He was willing to stand up on one of Jacob's dirty tables and call out for them to hear, "I love little Sally Waters!" Let any one of them deny that he hadn't looked at her with interest himself, his own body yearning for her, leaning toward her, his thoughts revolving one on one, yes, let them deny it and he would laugh at him.

My lord, the agony, he thought. "Jacob, what time is she coming in, you say?"

"I said seven-thirty fourteen times today to you. Seven-thirty."

Kin backed off from him and left. What had made Jacob lose his temper, he wondered.

When he got home, his father wanted to know where he had been all afternoon. "I have a hundred things for you to take care of at the store. Where did you go?"

"The store?" he said.

Cal frowned at him, chewed his lip and studied him. "You don't know about the store?" he asked quietly, mildly stern of voice, solidly watching him.

At supper Kin ate little and he kept looking at the wall. Lotti noticed it. Cal watched him, waiting for a clue. Kin saw none of it. Little Sally Waters, he thought. Precious, dear. Could he call her precious? Would he call her that tonight? Precious, precious—

"You'll have to put in two or three hours tonight to make up for it, Kin."

"Huh?" he said, returning to reason sharply.

"The store. We got to itemize that load of salt bags; we got to price the new sets of Bible study books." He stared at the boy, "Kin?"

Work tonight? Study and work, was that it? How crazily the world revealed itself. Let it all go. Precious, dear. Where was she? At home with that crass woman now? Walking down the street, her hips moving gently. Moving, moving. He could see them moving. Precious hips moving, dear—

"You act like you burned down a barn today," Cal said to him.

Kin blinked. "What do you mean?"

"Are you going to eat?" Lotti said. "Are you sick?"

"Sick?"

"Well, he can't do nothing but ask the same questions he's asked by others," Cal said, exasperated. "What's the accident, Kin, that's got you so lost to sight?"

308

"What do you mean?"

"Will you stop asking me questions and answer one," Cal said, chewing on a bite of corn bread. A smile crept onto his face. "You look moonstruck, boy. I thought you'd not get moonstruck as bad as this, though."

"Moonstruck?" Kin said.

Paul came in, huffing and blowing and talking big. He and Florence had bought a house about a block away, down on Christian Street, and he could cut through the back lot and be at the dining room in no time at all. He was always coming in right after his meals at home and eating some of Lotti's food.

Lotti paid little attention as he turned over a plate and began serving himself. She sopped corn bread in buttermilk and chewed on the batter. She was a great one for buttermilk and corn bread, preferring that to meat.

Paul swept beans onto his plate, broke off a hunk of bread, and poured molasses over all of it. He never worried about his weight. "I saw little Sally Waters today," he said.

Kin's eyes snapped to him. Paul and Sally Waters? What did Paul have to do with Sally Waters? What did he know about her?

"She's a pretty little devil, you know it?" Paul said calmly, nonchalantly, cutting the corn bread and molasses with a fork, looking at his plate and at that only, not appearing to sense Kin's irritation and wonder, casually going on with his eating, his eyelids heavy, his mouth yawning open as his fork approached it. He chewed, and molasses bubbled out at the corners of his mouth. "I hear she's given to scattering her favors like scattering chicken seed, but I don't remember who told me that."

Liar, Kin thought. Liar, liar. He wanted to strike him, knock him to the floor.

"Well, she's not the first one," Cal said gently, understandingly. "Sometimes a girl gets that way. Is she the one that sings so pretty?"

"She sings like a virgin," Paul said coarsely, "but she ain't." He sopped corn bread in the sweet syrup. "No, she ain't," he repeated.

Lotti sighed. "How was the store today, Paul?"

309

"She was out last night with some fellow that took her to the recreation park," Paul said. He chewed and ran his tongue around the inside of his mouth. He licked his damp lips. All Kin could see were his lips. He concentrated on them, waiting for the next word, damnable, condemning, hateful word.

"This sure is good coffee, Mama," Paul said.

"You want some more? I got some hot on the stove." She got up slowly, moved her hands down over her apron to smooth it. "I get to tiring earlier than I used to, you know it?" she said as she left.

Kin stared at Paul's face; he hadn't stopped staring at him. His body was braced for the blow. Strike Paul. Strike him down onto the floor. Sprawl him there. Let him say just one word—

"The fellow that took her to the park hadn't never been with a woman before, she said, and it was a sight to hear Sally when she dropped by this morning and told about what took place."

Kin was limp in an instant, as if struck himself, his power gone; he sat back in his chair. The world of his life was split open now. Strike Paul? No, flee, that was all he could do, hear not another word, for Paul held the upper hand now.

"She told me this boy must have lost ten pounds in weight sweating it out when she touched him. She said she got him in such shape he couldn't hardly get over a fence, couldn't walk straight, neither." Paul wiped his mouth on Lotti's napkin.

Kin weakly wanted pity now. Surely Paul would have mercy now. He wanted mercy from Paul.

"You got that coffee hot yet, Mama?" Paul called.

"Directly," she answered from the kitchen.

The open mouth, the fork going into it, the lips moist and the mouth chewing, the eyes watching the white plate before him, casually looking. "Said this boy was so nervous he couldn't get his own pants undone."

"Looks like he could 'a done that, don't it?" Cal said disinterestedly. He swished coffee in his mouth.

Kin was afraid for himself now, and for Sally Waters. It was a moment terrible in anger and hate, deeper than any hate he had

310

known before, consuming his respect, making him want to tear down violently his image of himself and of her, that girl, and to tear down his brother, in some way tear him down and hurl him to the floor and stomp his face in, stomp his face . . .

"So she helped him get his pants down—"

Kin got up and fled from the room.

If it had been Paul's thought that he should crush the young man, he had devised an effective way to do it. The severity of the blow to Kin was painful beyond conscious consideration. He could not bear to fall so swiftly from the high place to which little Sally Waters' love-making had carried him, to fall from there to the debasing despair Paul had prepared for him.

The boy sought seclusion in the woods across the trail from the house, but the woods had been brush-cleared when Cal had extended King Street, and they offered little seclusion. He went up to King Street itself, to the farmers' stalls, where always before he had been able to lose bothersome thoughts in the variety of sounds and faces, but now it seemed that knowing smiles greeted him. That afternoon, the smiles in the beer hall, perhaps they, too, had indicated knowledge of his shameful ignorance the night before. He couldn't be sure. He didn't want to know. He would settle for uncertainty rather than know.

What a fool he had been in the eyes of the mountain men, he thought. What a simple-minded fool to have shown fear around a girl when he was eighteen, not by that age to have taken a girl, when the men had taken several by then. How easy to make him out to be a fool before them, this brother of Collins King, who was an unknowing, frightened child. Paul had done it, he had done it so solidly it could not be undone. By a crafty maneuver he had shuttered him from their confidence always, undermined the future of the competing store, of Kin's leadership of the Street. He had thrown him the net of little Sally Waters.

He wandered up Market to the Square, down Patton to a park, but he was drawn back to Upper King Street, and to Jacob's. He stood at the rear of a group of seven or eight men who were outside the beer hall, listening to a guitar being picked. The musician seemed to hesitate, then go on, to be seeking a melody that pleased the player.

She began to sing, her voice like a child's voice, light on the breeze, drifting through the door. The men nodded and licked the road dust from their lips. "Ain't she a sight, sitting there?" one of them said. The men could see her through the open door. "She's like a laurel flower."

"I'll bet she could love the poles right out of the bed," another man said.

> Oh, love is sweet and love is charming
> And love is pleasant when it's new . . .

Innocent, Kin thought, like a helpless waif in a picture of a storm. What was she that was not childlike and loving? To hear her voice a man's heart melted.

> But love grows cold as love grows older,
> And fades away like the mountain dew.

For money she had sold herself, her time and charm of last night, to bring him to terms, had sold herself to Paul. Kin had no doubt of that. Little Sally Waters, deceptive and a tramp.

One of the men turned to another. "I hear she got that young King boy last night and made a man of him."

"Weren't he a man yet?"

"She had to take his pants off for him, she says."

A lie, Kin thought. A bitch, a lie, she was a bitch, he thought. Strike her, he thought, strike her and fling her by.

One of the men said, "Look who's standing with us," and he nodded toward Kin.

Kin stared at the men as they turned to look at him. "Hello, young King," one of them said, grinning. "You come for a nip more of it?"

"It don't get any worse as you get older, boy," another man said, and winked.

Kin marked them down in his mind. He would remember them. One of them was a Cathy boy. He would remember the Cathy boy.

312

And their families, yes, every one of them.

He pushed his way through the group, anxious to avoid their stare, unwilling to turn from them, and stood at the door of the beer hall. Jacob looked up from the cashbox with a start. Kin moved past him and stood in the main aisle of the beer hall, looking at Sally.

Somebody snickered, but masks seemed to fall on the faces of most of the men. Their chapped, coarse hands rested folded on the table. They looked at him, then at her, then at him, wondering what was going to happen.

She saw him and a catch came to her voice. The guitar stopped for a brief moment. Then she went on.

> "Miss, will you have a mountain lad?"
> "Yes, yes, a mountain lad.
> He looks so neat and he kisses so sweet.
> Yes, yes, a mountain lad."

Kin stopped at the bar on which she was sitting. The men were intent as before, leaning forward now, lean faces waiting for the show.

Jacob touched his shoulder. "You better take a table, Kin," he said uneasily. "Come on now, boy."

Kin shook the hand away, but he was grateful to him. He wanted a way out, all right. He wished he weren't in that beer hall at all. To be outside again, that would be better. But he couldn't turn away now.

The song ended. Sally seemed to hesitate. Her fingers moved idly over the strings. Her dress was tied with ribbon at her throat, Kin noticed. A red ribbon was in her hair. Childlike, beautiful, innocent, he thought.

She winked knowingly at the men in the beer hall. "Look what little boy is here," she said.

Two men laughed. Kin looked at them and their laughter stopped abruptly.

Silence took over the place, and Sally shifted uncomfortably. The silence was unnatural. This was Cal King's boy; she knew it, she knew he held power.

The men were quiet.

313

"What you want, little boy?" she asked uneasily.

He said nothing. She strummed the guitar a few times. He moved closer to her, his eyes holding hers for a moment. He moved right up to her.

He moved to the other side of her.

Somebody laughed from the tension, and he looked at the man and the laughter caught in his throat.

Sally tensely, warily strummed on the guitar.

Kin moved behind the bar on which she sat. She didn't turn to look at him. She went on strumming the guitar, so she didn't see him turn to the gas burner at the back wall and lift the five-gallon tub of leftover tepid coffee, lift it high in the air, turn it, and bring the tub down over her head.

Her terrified shout was lost in the splatter of coffee. He held the pot over her head till it emptied, then threw it to one side, where it crashed noisily among the tables. She backed away from him, dripping and stunned and hurt. "God damn you!" she shouted fiercely, backing away. "You son of a bitch!" She was soggy with coffee. Her dress clung to her breasts and stomach and hips.

He moved toward her, his palm stiff as if he might strike her. She began to cry. "You let me be," she said, frightened and furious, backing away still.

He stopped, having won, he knew, having won in the eyes of the men and in her eyes, too. He felt a smile, the smile of his father and of his brother Collins, and he knew she recognized it, as did the men, for the mark it was on King Street.

He turned from her and, still without a word, left the beer hall.

He went on down the street, a swagger in his walk now, ignoring the commotion that made disorder in the place he had left, not even looking back to see the dripping girl who came to the door and stared after him, hurt and with fury in her eyes, looked after him, then turned to move through the flock of men who grabbed at her and fondled her as she passed, the dress still clinging to her, who patted her and pinched her and used her as a plaything now that she had been disgraced publicly, and humiliated.

She began to run up the street, two boys running with her. He didn't know it, he didn't look back. A coffee-stained child, she ran up the street, a child who wouldn't that night sing any more songs for her father.

22

My dear precious sweet mama Lotti,

How are you, Mama? I think of you night and day, and of my dear papa and of sweet little Beth, and Kin and Johnny, and of my other fine brothers, Matthew and handsome Paul, and I think I must go home to see all of you again once more, for none of us knows the day or the hour when his time comes, so do not be surprised to see me coming up the road, for I miss you, Mama, and the big house with those fine big meals you fix, but most of all I miss you and precious Beth, the sweetest girl in all the world.

I am here in San Francisco for a few days, then I will be off to Chicago, or maybe I will go straight home from here. Don't be surprised to see me soon coming up the road.

Your son,
Collins

THE LETTER SET THE HOUSE ATREMBLE. IT CAME THE summer following the birth of Beth's child, in August, 1937, and sent Beth's life into such complex patterns of feeling that she was dizzy and distressed with them, held prisoner, unable to free herself, not wanting to, wanting him to come home, hoping he would not, waiting anxiously for him, walking to the house each day to see if he had arrived yet.

The next letter came from Chicago. In it Collins said he might go to St. Louis before coming home, that he wasn't sure, for he just might come home and settle down permanently with his dear family. "I am looking forward every minute to being with you, dear mama Lotti, and with my dear brothers and with dear little cousin Beth, the prettiest and dearest woman in the world."

But there was no date to indicate the time of his arrival. Each day the family awoke, wondering if this would be the day. Every meal Lotti wondered if he would arrive in time to eat something. She made peach cobblers and tall poundcakes, hoping he would arrive to eat a bite of them.

August passed. Another letter came, this one from St. Louis, and in it Collins said little except that he hoped to get home for a brief visit soon. It was no more than a note.

In October letters began arriving at the house for Collins, addressed to him there, so obviously he intended to be home soon. Lotti put them unopened on the halltree, each week adding one or two to the stack as they came in.

By November the letters had stopped coming.

After that nobody spoke of Collins' visit. It was on everybody's mind, but nobody talked about it. By December the stack of letters had dust on the top of it. Only when Johnny's Sunday-school class planned a meeting at the house for a Christmas party was the stack tied with string and put in the top drawer of the high chest in the parlor.

Kin's letter to Collins in Chicago was returned. His letter to Collins in St. Louis was returned. A third letter, which he sent to San Francisco, was not returned, but it wasn't answered, either. In that letter he told Collins about the stack of mail on the halltree, and about how much they wanted to see him. He told him about the new store and that Paul and Matthew were married. He told him about every-

317

body except Beth. He couldn't seem to write down the right words to tell Collins about her marriage.

Collins' first letter stirred the old deep fears in Paul. He had been trading fiercely on the Street, ruthless in his determination to take over both stores, but when Collins' first letter came, he began to seek friends, particularly among the family. He and Florence invited Cal and Lotti over to their house, which wasn't far away, actually. It was a big two-story, old and rambling place, and Cal walked through it, measuring the rooms, estimating its value, while Lotti and Florence kept company in the parlor, Lotti doing all the talking, explaining about the old days in the country. More and more she longed for them again, she said.

Beth and Morris also were invited over. They arrived about eight one evening, and from the first everybody was uneasy. Florence had wine and cheese, but Morris didn't seem to like either one of them. Damn European taste, Paul guessed. And what could they talk about? Making pants, making suits?

Then, to Paul's irritation, Beth mentioned her baby. "Mama Lotti insisted we give him a Bible name," she said, "so we called him David."

Nobody said anything. Paul glared at the fireplace. Florence glanced at him uneasily. "Does he cry much?" she asked.

"No," Beth said, and she went on talking about him. Paul got more restless, until finally he went into the kitchen and got out a bottle of whisky and made himself a drink. Wine. She had wine, as if a man could live on wine. Good God, he thought. Baby did this, baby did that. Little David. Good God.

He drank heavily of the whisky.

Beth could see him from where she sat, and she knew what must be bothering him, so she started talking about Florence's decoration of the rooms, the colors and the placement of the furniture. It had a bareness to it, actually a bleakness, for there was no color to the walls, there were no flowers or pictures, but Beth commented on how clean the room was and how nice it must be to have a large house of

318

their own. "We hope to get one someday," she said.

Paul came back into the room. He sat down, a drink in his hand, and stared at Beth. He tried to keep from looking at her, or so it seemed to her, but he couldn't manage it, and she was in misery all evening. Shortly before ten she nodded to Morris, who had not talked very much, and they got up to leave. Paul didn't rise. He sat in the chair, his head wobbly because of the whisky, the glass, now empty, still in his hand.

That night he paced the floor of his bedroom, troubled by the failure of the evening, by his loneliness and his jealousy. By God, he thought, he wouldn't listen to any more words about that new baby of hers, at least he would be spared that. Was she the only one who could bear a child? Hadn't it been done before in the world? By God, he would have children of his own, he would have six sons by Florence, and every one of them would be taught sternness from birth. He would teach them to take their places in the world. Fight. That was the way they had to do it. A man fought for what was his and the best man won. The strong man won.

What else was there? You fought and you won. What else was there? Take over both stores, run a passageway between them, change the name to Cal King's Son. And in time let it be Paul King's Sons.

He sat down on the edge of the bed and pondered it. Beth thought she was the only one who could have children. Hell, he thought.

He had sent her a dozen roses when she was in the hospital. He hadn't gone by to see her. He didn't want her to think he missed her or had forgiven her. He sent a dozen red roses, and on the card he wrote one word. No salutation, no greeting. He scrawled one word: Paul.

Let her remember all she would. What would their life have been like together? He didn't know and he had wondered often. Happy? Yes. Satisfying? Yes. But she had sunk both their lives, and he had been left with an opening in his own which he had crammed full of money and the husk of a woman called Florence Fulcher.

Beth had had a son on her first try. Talked about it all the time as if he was the first baby ever born with a nose, two eyes, and a mouth. Probably turn out to be a little son of a bitch, but she thought he had wings to fly to heaven on. She probably tied ribbons around his dirty diapers.

Anger rose in him, and he turned on the bed in the dark room, turned to his wife on the bed and pounded her to awaken her. "All right, let's wake up, by God."

"Oh, God, no," she whimpered, moaning, turning on the bed away from him.

"I want a son, didn't I tell you?"

"Paul, let me sleep."

"I want a son. Beth already has hers born and you're not begun."

"I might be. I think I am."

"You lie." He shook her. "Tell me you lie."

"I lie," she whimpered.

He pulled the covers off her and pulled up her nightgown.

"Paul, for God's sake, please."

"I want her son," he said. He lay down over her.

"Paul. Please, Paul, please." He was heavy on her. Heavy on her breast, heavy on her belly, and full in her groin. He was the master and owner of her, brutal and seeking.

A husk of a woman, he thought.

An anger was in him, never to be washed out.

Nothing to her, he thought.

Seeking. Over and over, up and again, time after time.

A son, he thought.

Beth put the baby's mouth on her nipple, and he began to suck. The pops and smacks of his lips were the only sound she heard, except for the breathing of Morris, asleep beside her. The baby got heavy after a while on her stomach, but she didn't mind that. She wiggled her finger against his nose. She felt of his ear and his wet little chin. She squeezed him to her and took him closer into partnership with her own body again, and nourished him again with herself, with the milk she had made for him, this tiny piece of life

320

entrusted to her by God and Chance and the whims and happenings of Time, which was a sort of God, she thought, for Time was the healer and the bringer and was the one which aged and ended and survived. Time was the sickness which robbed men of their powers, but it was also the promise of those powers. Time brought death and was more heartless than a battle. But it was for the young, though the young would know after spending years swiftly that Time was not on their side after all, but was on the other, and that they were moving toward their own end. She had seen the end of time for herself approaching and had sought a child, through whom she would gain greater time. He would live longer than she and no doubt would breed, so that others would live, too, so that she would go on, and, through her and him, her father, now buried in a box seeping through, would go on, and her mother, who had once taken Beth's mouth and pressed it to a nipple on her breast, and had thought, perhaps—yes, this child is an answer to Time, as once she, Beth's mother, in turn had been the open mouth, the firm arms and shoulders, had been a heavy weight on the belly of her mother, who had in turn once been an open mouth and a weight, and so it was, an open mouth and a weight on the belly of a mother, generation after generation, back into time.

The sucking sounds were not like a calf makes, she thought. They were more of a slobbering sound than a calf makes, for a calf popped the tits when it sucked. No doubt a different sound was made by a bottle baby, she thought. She had thought of using a bottle for her own, up until they had handed the baby to her. Then she had decided not to do that to him but to treat him naturally, and it was not for his sake but for hers, she knew, but it was for his, too, in that she wanted to give him something more of herself. She had seen in Lotti's house that children did not love their mother closely, that they stood back and loved from a distance, but she would love the child herself closely and protect it from all harm. She would guide it in ways that were proper and would teach it. She would be his shepherd and his eyes, his ears and first voice; she would say to him, "Look at this flower, for it is beautiful. Beautiful remember,

321

remember beautiful. And listen to the birds. Do you hear them? The bird on the power cable above. Do you hear it? See it first, then hear it. It is beautiful. It looks beautiful to see and flies beautiful and sounds beautiful. Always see and hear what is beautiful."

She would never tire when he needed her. She would never grumble or complain when he annoyed her. She would never fail him. As a boy learning to walk, as a child going first to school, as a young man discovering the facts of his own existence, finding that he had a body which responded to other bodies and to thoughts of other bodies, she would explain to him herself the mysteries and wonders of life. And as a young man seeking a woman, she would tell him what was good for him to seek and to find, a woman who knew life and loved life and loved love and him, and the chance of love and the body, and the pleasure of being loved.

And when he was near-grown and found the woman, she would leave him then, withdraw from his life, and would suffer in the dark rooms, with Morris suffer in the lonely rooms, without him, her love, the child her love, suffer in the lonely life without him. For she knew she must let the boy go when he was able, not when he was able only but yes when he felt that he was able. To hurry him from the house even to make plans for their separation. She must remember that and start them early, even on the day when she would push him away from her and say, "You work that out for yourself, young man." And see the surprise, even the pain on his face. But the hurt would be in her heart, too. She could feel it tug now in her chest under the weight of him. She would remember to overcome the pain and push him out. Until he was his own person and was secure without her, and had his own woman and didn't need her care, a man apart from her, without her to guide to instruct to lecture to criticize. What pain, how many women could not stand that pain. The pain of birth was no greater than the pain of the second separation, the cutting off. It was easier, she could tell now, looking ahead, easier to lose him now in infancy than it would be over the years to cut him free of herself.

How to prepare herself for that? By never loving him. By never daring to yield her life to him. By retaining always such aloofness, such distraction at his questions and worries and tears, such personal allegiance to herself that she never permitted him to become part of her again, or to let herself become again part of him. Yes, no doubt there was wisdom in that course for her, but it would not be hers. She would go to the depths of love for him. She would crawl into the womb of love for him. She would hold him closer than the breast at which he clutched, and would bear him free that second time, her son.

Her son. How short the words on the tongue. Yet they encompassed more meaning than mother. They gave meaning to mother. Sooner were they said than father, brother, but closer was her son. Sooner said than husband.

Than lover.

Than lover. How sweet the touch of that word. How rich the sound in the mind was lover. How fluid in beauty and easily spoken. "My lover," she whispered.

"My son," she whispered and held him so close that the nipple slipped from his mouth. But he didn't cry. He was through eating, she supposed. "My son," she whispered.

She carried him to the moonlit window and patted his back, so that he burped. She held him up in the moonlight to see his face. "Hello," she said, and kissed his forehead, then his milky chin.

She laid him in his bed and covered him over. Moonlight was in his eyes, and he blinked at it. She lowered the shade and walked across the bare floor to her bed and climbed in beside her husband.

"Did he eat, Beth?" he asked sleepily.

"Yes."

"Why didn't you call me? I can help some with him, Beth."

"Thank you. It's all right now, Morris."

"I don't mind being awakened. I can keep you company."

"Yes, dear. Let's go back to sleep, Morris."

His arm fell across her stomach and his face nuzzled close to her. She patted his shoulder.

My husband, she thought.

My lover in some far-off place.

My son.

My son, my lover, my husband.

And all were far off, in the world each had of his own, each seeking the comforting, faceless moment of someday reawakening and finding close by a woman and a shaft of moonlight in his eyes.

Husband, son, lover.

Lover husband son.

Somewhere long ago, but someday coming; here and in a distant place; a letter, a vow, a presence on her shoulder; closer than her breath were her far-off possessions.

And Kin stood outside her house late of the night and looked up toward the second floor, where moonlight rested on the black shingles, looked at the darkened window where she and her mother slept. He whistled, thinking she might hear him. His body ached for her, this child of the winds, this mean-souled little child with the angel body, craving always a hand to touch her and to tame her.

"Little Sally Waters," he whispered, enjoying the sound of the name. He thought of the wonders of her as she had twisted in his arms. No other girl could ever do so well, he thought, as this girl whom he could not drive from his mind.

"Little Sally Waters," he whispered.

23

A FULL WEEK WAS SPENT IN PREPARATIONS FOR LOTTI'S
Christmas party, or, rather, for the party Johnny was having, which
Lotti was planning. She fixed spiced tea, three kinds of cookies, a
heavy black fruitcake, and she fried country ham, thick slabs of ham
which later she would pack between slices of freshly baked, warm
wheat bread. She quite exhausted herself, but she tried to look alert
for the party itself.

When the party started, however, Johnny pretty much took charge.
It was the first time since his first school day that she had seen him
with others his own age, and though she was pleased to find that
he was confident, she was surprised to find that he could decide
matters without looking to her at all. It was almost as if he didn't
need her.

"I don't know what's got into the boy," she told Beth, who was in
the kitchen to help serve. "He's in there telling them about the wall
clock, telling them it come from New York or somewhere, and I said,
'Well, let's go into the dining room and cut the cake,' and he said,
'Yes, by all means,' but he didn't move a foot. He went on talking
about that clock. Then he got to talking about the handwork on the

mantel." She sniffed and looked off distractedly. " 'It's not got a nail in it nowheres,' he said, as if this was a sign of value in it, and the children all pawed over it. Well, I didn't know the mantel was going to be of more interest than the cake I baked."

Beth smiled at her. "He's not a little boy now, Mama Lotti. He's growing some. I'd think you'd be proud of the way the other children look to him for direction."

"Well, he certainly does talk big for a child," Lotti said.

She was reassured when the group had finished eating and it came time for the devotional period. She was about to ask Beth to get the young people quiet so that Johnny could read from the Bible for them, but Johnny got them quiet himself, took up the book at once, and commenced to read, speaking clearly and loudly, so that he could be easily heard by those who had overflowed the dining room and were in the main hall. Lotti had selected the scripture for him, and she had found a poem for him to read. He had studied them with few comments and with not a single complaint. He had even memorized the poem. And he delivered them perfectly.

If Lotti needed proof that the boy would be an excellent pastor, she had it now, and after the party was over and the last guest had gone, she exuberantly made known to the household that the boy had a voice just like her father's, and the same way of cocking his head to one side while he listened, and the identical way of pressing his lips together after he'd done saying something, and his smile was like her father's. "My father was always of himself a popular man with folks, too, and after every session at the churches, there would be people gathered around to shake his hand and praise his ways. I tell you, Johnny's got exactly the same nature to him, and I expect he'll be the one to go on now beyond my father's work. He's even got my father's manner of closing his eyes tight just before the point of a story is made, then popping them open when the time comes to laugh. He's got a twitch in his left cheek just exactly like my father's."

Johnny listened from the secluded world of himself. He watched

326

her and his brothers and his father. And not a clue did he give concerning what was going on inside his mind.

Christmas was a festive occasion this year, more so than on most. Lotti baked two cakes, one of them a fruitcake and one a thick, heavy poundcake. She baked pies and cooked a turkey and fresh ham. But Beth and Morris couldn't come over for Christmas dinner, and Matthew and his wife, who said she was pregnant, went to the Porters. So Lotti had her big family meal on the next day. Everybody came then, and Paul talked a good deal about his prosperity, stressing plans for expansion and explaining to Matthew how he had got from his father's store the account of one of the big hotels in town. The family talked together, exchanged gifts, and Lotti told how it had been in the country when she was a girl. At Christmas if a girl got a china pitcher, she was happy as could be, and the small children were happy if they got a single orange. "We have so much now," she said, "but we don't appear to appreciate it any more than they did."

Dinner went on for well over an hour, and at the close of it, Johnny, at Lotti's instruction, read the story from the book of Luke about the birth of Jesus. Lotti sat on the edge of her chair and listened, pinned by every word. How precious a birth it was, she thought, how humble amid the animals, with an innkeeper little different, she suspected, from those of the hotels there in town.

And how pretty Johnny was. How proper he stood before the family and read in his fine, firm voice. At only fifteen he carried his head high, stood erect before the family. In time he would raise himself up as a staff is raised, and every stream would become a baptismal fount.

After the reading the family lingered at the table, picking at the bones of the turkey. Prime came in about two o'clock and said there was a long-distance call from Raleigh on the store's phone.

Cal told him he wasn't coming to the store that day. But Prime came back to the house a few minutes later and said the operator said it was important, so Cal and Kin went over to the store with him, Cal complaining about the bother and talking about how restful the day had been.

Prime held the back door of the store open for them. Cal walked slowly to the wall phone and put its receiver to his ear. "Yes," he said. "Yes, this is Caleb King."

He listened for fully a minute. Kin studied his face, where not a shadow of an expression was registered.

"Well, you do what you've got to do, and I'll be down there directly," he said.

Kin studied him still. Go to Raleigh? His father go to Raleigh?

"I'll come. You can say that." He stared straight ahead, his face set and unrevealing. "Yes, today."

He listened for a moment more, then slowly hung the receiver on its hook. He stood by the phone, thinking deeply.

"Was it a man from Raleigh?" Prime asked. Cal nodded, and the Negro grinned. "I thought he said Raleigh."

Cal nodded again. He walked to the main door of the store and stuck his hands deep into his pockets and looked out at the street. Kin walked up beside him and saw that his eyes were closed.

"Kin, you go home and get a change of underwear for the each of us," Cal said. "Your brother's down in Raleigh."

"My brother?" Kin said. "Who?"

"Your brother Collins." He looked out the door now, through the glass part of it, across the walk to the farmers' market yard, which was shrouded down in tarpaulins for the holidays, dotted with carts pulled over to one side, holding water in the corners of the cart beds where the wood had swollen tight. It was drizzling rain still. "We have to get down there, and I'd rather take the train than drive."

Kin nodded slowly, waited. Their talking and waiting were patiently done, like the pace of an old clock's tick. "Is Collins in trouble?" he asked, his voice tight and dry.

"He's near dead," Cal said briefly. "But don't tell your mama."

"No, sir." He stood there waiting, not knowing why or for what he waited. Perhaps to absorb what he had just heard, to let it be-

328

come part of him, and perhaps his father was waiting for the same reason. They knew now, but they did not accept it, had not absorbed it; it was not part of them yet. They knew they would have to accept it, but they had not accepted it yet. They did not fight it. They knew they could not fight accepting it. But they had not done it, that was all. They knew without knowing yet.

They stood waiting on the platform, nothing being said, Paul standing to one side fretfully. They stood waiting until at last out of the west came the train, its whistle sounding at a distant crossing, rising up from the hill beyond the bridge, clashing on the bridge, moving into the yard and to the station, stopping with steam gushes as men hurried forward with steps and cards and buckets and cans of grease. "Asheville," a porter called. Another called to people staring from the smoke-coated windows. "Asheville."

"You tend to the family, Paul," Cal said.

"Did they say what was the matter with him?" Paul asked, speaking over the station noise.

Cal stared before him, as if he hadn't heard, though he had heard, surely. "Come along, Kin," he said, "let's get aboard her."

They walked along the side of two cars to a place where the porter stood at a step. The porter nodded to Kin, but he bowed to Cal. Cal was old-fashioned in dress and manner, and the porter recognized that. He wore a string tie which he had fixed haphazardly, and he wore thick shoes. His suit coat hung long and was gray homespun; it had been tailored by Morris the year before to please him. His pants were from another suit and were dark brown and store-bought. There was about his clothes the look of tough quality; that was the look about him, too—strength and quality. "Yes, suh, you get aboard now, suh," the porter said to him, bowing.

It's as if he were Collins, Kin thought.

They sat near a water cooler, near where a fat man was sprawled out in a seat asleep, a copy of a Knoxville newspaper open and spread over his face. He was snoring and the paper was fluttering at one corner. In a seat behind him sat a pretty girl of about twenty-eight,

329

with the blackest hair Kin had ever seen, so black he knew she was not of the mountains. She had deep-brown eyes, too, and red lips painted carefully. He stared at her, drinking in the sight, the beauty of her, wondering about her, suspicious of her.

"I've never been out of this country," he said softly, as if to himself.

Cal shifted in his seat and peered sternly ahead. "No," he said.

In books Kin had read about the tough and beautiful creatures of the earth, roaming their own lands, and he had read that each one shared with all the others the basic hopes and workings of life, that each one wondered in the same way at the mysteries which so thrilled and dominated him at times that he could not drink enough in of life, or breathe enough of life, this heavy-scented spirit which gave him wondrous powers, this God-creation fashioned to embrace tears and goodness on a plentiful earth full of such marvels as sunrises and trees blooming and fall harvest and a long train moving out of the Asheville station.

No doubt all men did feel the pulse of life, he thought. Perhaps they all felt it alike, in all the countries and islands. But he thought not. Men living in Celo Valley were not the same as men living beneath Clingmans Dome. He knew that. But they were more alike than they or their women were kin to this black-haired, exotic creature sitting across the aisle from him. She was a far-stranger to him, as she was to them; he was grouped by history and culture with them. His world was the mountains and King Street. He had sometimes wanted to leave them and see the worlds outside, but he had always been afraid to go. He was afraid now, he admitted, and his father was tense, too, he noticed.

Collins would laugh at that, he thought.

A whistle screamed; the train shuddered as it abruptly stopped. The conductor came stalking down the aisle. "Don't leave your seats, please, don't leave your seats." He went on into the next car.

He came back a minute later as the train bolted into motion again. "I vow, can you imagine? When are these damn mountain people going to get the cows off the tracks?"

330

Kin was lifted from his seat by anger. Damn mountain people? He stared at the conductor as the conductor went on through the car and into the next one. Then self-consciously, red of face, he sat back down.

But he was still angry. What did he mean by damn mountain people? Who the hell was he, a rich prince? The idea of him speaking that way. Kin had heard his father say that when the train line was new, the trains had been stopped by stock at every turn, not just every ten or twenty miles, and not by cattle only, but by deer, too, for deer were inquisitive and liked to see the trains go by. They would gather near the track and wait for them. The train was a wonder to them, and sometimes in the meadows on snowy nights they would stand so long they would get ill with cold, but they would not seek shelter until the train had come by. Also the mountain people had congregated to see trains pass, and sometimes for devilment, or perhaps for serious purpose, the mountain men would fire rifles at the engines, ricocheting bullets off the heavy metal sides. So Cal had said.

And here, only fifty years later, this sour conductor was complaining bitterly about a single cow on the track, one lone cow, which no doubt a farmer and his sons and pretty daughter were at this moment seeking, wandering through the wet grass of the pastureland calling "Nell, Nell," for that might be her name, Kin thought. He could imagine the daughter's voice rising as she crossed a divide and went into another pocket, walking swiftly, a tall mountain creature with long legs and the bouncy walk that comes to women and men who live on the rolling, high lands. "Nell, Nell."

And who was this conductor in his box of a steam engine with rolling, clanking wheels, to speak so bluntly and in criticism of her who walked the meadows of another world? Which of them was thoughtless and unfeeling, the farmer and his cow, or this contraption which flooded the air with smoke and clamored at every curve and screeched and frightened birds?

The conductor came back through the car and Kin stared at him coldly, so coldly that the conductor stopped and blinked in surprise, then went on, glancing back twice before reaching the door of the car.

Cal sat erect, stiff and composed, none too comfortable. "We'll not need to be out of the mountains for long, Kin," he said.

The train roared down the valley, moving fast, and came soon to Swannanoa. How beautiful that name, Kin thought, how much more lyrical than Asheville. Swan-na-no-ah. It was an Indian word, he had no doubt. He wondered what once it had meant and if the name were beautiful to everybody; for example, to that exotic woman. Was it beautiful in England, in far off Tangiers, in Ceylon? Swan-na-no-ah.

The train pulled out and he strained to see the sights. There were cattle grazing near a stand of oak, near where the walls of mountains rose.

Beyond Black Mountain the train came to the edge of the plateau and he caught a glimpse of rolling clouds below. Off into the east lay old Carolina, the historic land of toil and trouble. The train began to curve downward among the mountains toward the lowland hills, and he caught his breath as it entered the first tunnel, the Swannanoa tunnel, and he remembered what somebody once had told him, the porter at the station house at the depot—yes, Seth had told him, about the men who had built the tunnels through the granite, blasting each other apart with homemade explosives and dying under landslides and working with sweat so thick no firm grip could be taken on the picks and sledge hammers, working with horses and oxen. Toil and labor. Work of men soon to die working, some of them to be buried by their own digging beneath the place on which the train now roared through the Swan-na-no-ah tunnel. Men buried in common graves, under clay and broken rocks which had been moved to make the Swan-na-no-ah tunnel, down the mountains, through the mountains, with a whistle and steam pistons pounding, giant wheels turning, steel moving on steel holding, the rocks of the tunnel leaking, the rails creaking and the train slowing, then bolting on ahead, with a ray of light opening, then the world again and

332

below and before them lay the great hill country.

His heart pounded with wonder. Ranges of hills undulated off across distances toward the Atlantic four hundred miles away.

Car-o-lin-a. Into the east, puff by puff, clinging to the edges of the mountain, moving slowly in the drizzly rain as the cars swung around the bend, making their way over the workers long since memory-forgotten, down to the next tunnel, creeping now to a third and to the next and the next, the smoke from the engines black now, not gray, banking against the closed windows of the train in the tunnels.

How long, he thought. Every minute pleased him immensely, not because it brought him to the hill country below but because it showed just how high indeed was the mountain country where he lived. The train still struggled, its oversized engine puffing to hold back the cars, overheated smoke exploding in the air, the train turning, braking, moving on.

Two small boys patted their palms on the window glass, and one of them spoke to the thick smoke. "I see you, smoke, I see you."

The fat man turned over. He blinked and wiped his eyes as the train bolted from a tunnel into the sunlight. There was no rain now, no drizzle even. It was as if the train had come through a wall. "Is that the last one?" the man asked Kin.

"I don't know," Kin said, uneasy in the new place. Never before had he not known at any time where he was in relation to places long known about. He watched tensely, ill-at-ease, as a moment later the train, bells tinkling, rolled heavily into the Old Fort station.

Cal shifted his body on the mohair seat. "Are we done with that twisting?" he asked.

"I think we are. We're out of them now."

"Can you smell it?"

Kin sniffed. "Smell what?"

"The lowlands. Ay, God, I can smell it. No lightness to the air. Heavy air. You smell it, don't you?"

"Yes, I think I do."

"It'll drive you crazy to live down here without lightness to the air. Heavy, heavy. I guess it just sinks down, don't you?"

333

"It has more oxygen in it."

"You say so? I think it sinks down. Air falls like everything else. Naturally it ain't as thick up where we are as down here, for it falls on this part of the world more heavy. And we ain't seen the worst of it yet, either."

"No, sir," Kin said.

"Old Fort, this is. They used to kill Indians here, to hear my father tell it about his fathers. Scalped 'em." He peered around, trying to see the place from his seat. "Did you know white men scalped Indians?"

"I never heard it."

"Just like Indians scalped white people. They scalped aplenty of them. It was from Old Fort that some settlers first come up to our part of the world. What a climb they had. My great-grandmother was sitting in her mountain cabin up home one early morning frying pork, when she heard a shot, and she suspicioned what had happened. Her man and six-year-old son were out there. She waited for a spell, and not hearing them call to tell her they were all right, she grabbed up the two babies and hid in a laurel patch. Soon seven Indians come around, slowly creeping in on the cabin, one of them carrying her little boy under one arm, aiming to take him back to the settlement. The boy was alive. Another one was carrying her husband's scalp. She recognized the hair on it. She kept as still as a scared animal, and when the Indians had done stomping around and were gone, she ran down the stream bed to the Starnes place, the only other house in that part of the world. From there she went with Ned Starnes back down to Old Fort and told her husband's brothers what had took place. One of them, Felix was his name but he was called different—I don't recollect what—posted their vows and brought her and the two babies back up the trail on horseback to that same cabin, and he started in where his brother had left off."

Cal shook his head wearily, considering the toil and work and care and death of the old days. "This here place," he said, "was the western end of this country then."

Presently the train jerked into motion, the cars crashing into their locks. He belched. "This air turns my stomach sour," he said.

The train moved through the hill valleys, by the thousand lighted windows of the lowland people, through a million acres of pine forest. Everywhere was forestland. There were no high mountains here to gather snow on their crests, no beauty of perspective, Kin saw; each man lived on his own land and no man could look out over another's. Each man had a fence around all he owned, as if he were suspicious of his neighbor, and his house stood near the road, not far back in the coves where he could be off to himself with his own.

A man was out pulling logs with two mules, Kin saw. His boy was looking on, twisting his brogans in the red moist soil.

The train moved by a long brick building with sides marked off by windows, and Kin could see women working at big looms, finishing up their work for the day. It was the first factory he had ever seen, and was no bigger than his father's store, he noticed with relief. Perhaps it hired a few more people, but it was no bigger.

What were those women like, he wondered. Did they get cotton lint in their throats and stomachs of a day and digest it of a night? What was that farmer like, working with two mules? What was red soil like?

Were people out there saying now, "Latch the door," as was being said in a thousand homes right then back home? "Latch out the night"? Were families gathering in the kitchen, or in the front bedroom, for talk and stories?

Lights were put on inside the train, and the windows reflected the world of seats and aisle and faces. Cal was sitting bolt upright, thinking no doubt of Collins. His face was stern and unfeeling; he was rigid with his thoughts, and he didn't even seem to notice when Kin stood and stretched and walked to the water cooler.

Kin moved on along the aisle toward the back of the car. He wondered where all these people were traveling and if any other among them had a deathwatch on his mind. His despair because of Collins was numbing him and his thoughts. Even when his thoughts were

335

about the lowland houses, flashing by like bits of light pulled out of place, the deathwatch lingered and numbed him. He wondered if any one of the passengers had known a person such as Collins, the roaring masculine life, the candle burning brightly as it burned itself quicker and quicker. Yes, he thought, each of them must have known Collins inside himself, often, or at least once in a while, the intensity of unshackled life.

In the next car he sat down near the door and leaned his head back on the towel cloth which protected the upholstery. He wondered why the tragedy of Collins had not come through to him yet. Was it because of the excitement of the trip, or because he did not believe and would not be able to believe that Collins could suffer for long? If Collins' laughter were a cure for the ills of others, then surely it would save him, too. How could Collins die? What death could grasp this vital man and strangle out his goodness? Death was a sneak and not an openhearted creature; it had no standing with Collins. Collins was the servant of life—no, not its servant. Its companion. Most men served life, Kin thought, or tried to tame it; Collins went along wherever life led. So could death fall on Collins? Certainly not, for Collins at the age of thirty-nine would break death's hold surely. With contempt he would hurl death aside.

A rain started. No doubt the rain had been at this place all along, and now the train entered it. The rain splattered, slapping on the windows, and a roll of thunder carried through and over the roar of the wheels. An elderly woman lay down a magazine she had been reading and peered about her suspiciously. She drew her coat closer around her shoulders. "Where are you going?" she asked Kin. "Back to school?"

"To Raleigh, to get my brother. He's supposed to be dying."

The woman looked at him as if she were still waiting for an answer, then quickly she took up her magazine and went back to reading.

She doesn't want to think about it, Kin thought. At her age death will come for her before long. He wondered how many years of life were left for her, the one who sat alive and reading before him.

336

Or for his father. Or for his mother. To think that they might die panicked him even more than to think that Collins might die. Collins' value was in what he left with a person; Cal's and Lotti's value was in day-to-day living with them. They were part of all that life was, they were involved and entwined with it. Without them what would happen to him, and to his brothers, and to the old house?

He would come back someday, he thought, like Collins, and find the house overgrown with vines, the porch pillars rotting, the doors swinging rustily on dry hinges, the rooms littered with broken glass.

He turned his mind sharply away from it.

But why had he seen himself coming back to the house, he wondered, as if he had gone away? Was he going away? Did he want to leave his father, leave the store, which had been built for him?

He tried to turn from that thought, too.

The store someday would be gone, he knew; it would rot away.

He stood up irritably and walked through the train and stepped out onto the platform, where it was cool and damp, and where he let his body fill itself with the rumble of the wheels.

He looked down at the rain-soaked earth, the arrows of water still falling, the streams of water flowing along the track beds and forming puddles between the ties; there was the sound of thunder far off.

The train door opened and he saw the conductor peer out quizzically at him. The conductor stepped out onto the platform and closed the door. "How you?" he said.

Kin murmured a reply, the words of it buried in the rush and noise of the train. The rain beat at his face as the train turned a curve; the current of wet air slapped in against him, then the train moved swiftly into a straightaway.

"Sometimes from this point of a night," the conductor said, "when we move into a curve, you can see the mountains behind us, young man. They rise from the valley floor like women's breasts." He smiled at Kin. "And they're just as hard to get ahold of." He winked heavily at him.

337

He was a rude man, Kin thought, an unfeeling man.

"Where you from?" the conductor asked.

"From them. From Asheville."

"Do you like these hills?"

Kin shrugged. "I don't see much."

"No, I don't either. It's not mountains and it's not the flatlands. It's got no smell, except of the factories. But it's got the most people in it. I guess the people have so little to do that they breed themselves night and day both." He laughed, a throaty laugh, and peered through slits of eyes at Kin. "Lint heads, they're called," he said, winking at Kin. "Branch-head farmers and lint-head textile workers. But call a textile worker a lint head and he'll try to fix you. They work in air filled with cloth dust. Can you imagine?"

"We're all different, I guess," Kin said.

The conductor folded his arms across his chest. "I'll say we are." He winked at Kin, then peered off fondly, thoughtfully. "No, I don't like the hills or the mountains, either, I guess, because it's harder to get a train through them. Where I'm from it's a long level straight track, and the train don't never stop at any station, just rolls on like something way off in your mind. I like the flatland for that, and because it's the sea nature in me to want to be home, where it's honest, simple and honest, and where the sea gulls follow a man as he plows in the fields, as once they followed me, and where a man can stand on the shore and look out over clean salt water to the ends of his sight and say to himself, It all changes except this, it all suffers change except this, everything in the world, everything except this, the rolling ocean, changes."

Kin looked up at him slowly, at the broad, coarse face peering now into the darkness which was lengthening behind them. The man did know. He, too, was able to respond as Kin to the powers of Nature and greatness before him. He didn't see in the stretches of mountains the strength and beauty which Kin saw there, but the same sense of strength and beauty came to him when he considered the vastness of water-filled space, the wrinkled ocean which washed on North Carolina and across the sea on ancient, weary Portugal, on Africa, on mighty England, the fatherland. This coarse, crude man from five hundred miles away from Asheville had something of the same soul, Kin felt, that he himself had, though it had been tempered by a different fire.

Kin stared at him and started to speak to him, but the man's mind seemed now to be a long way off from them.

His father still was sitting, facing the front of the car, when Kin came back. He sat down beside him. "I don't think I'll sleep, do you?"

"No, not tonight," Cal said.

Kin breathed deeply of the damp air. "I want to see Collins. I just want to see him, that's all, and talk to him again. What is it with him, that I want to be with him so much?"

"Every man has his way with life, don't you know that?"

"I wouldn't want to see Paul, or Matthew. But Collins. I want to see Collins. I can't seem to wait to see him."

"The man has goodness, has appeal. Every man is different."

The train whistle sounded, and the conductor came along the rows of seats. "Hickory. Hickory."

"I wonder if we're getting close to Raleigh," Kin said.

"It's a pity," Cal said softly, "that he dies so close to the time of his arriving."

That was all he said, and Kin sat for a while wondering what he had meant by it.

Children waved from the Hickory station platform, and the red-caps pushed wagons loaded with gray mailbags. The Earle Hotel looked down on the tracks from its prominence, and salesmen rocked in wooden rockers on the porch, studying the men and women getting on and off the train. The train shuddered and moved forward again, gathering speed as it passed two textile plants on the left. A furniture plant on the right had its black unloading door partly open, and Kin could see several men inside working in a single pool of light.

What is their work, he wondered; what are they like? How are

339

they different, and at what time long ago did they choose, or their parents choose, this other way?

Conover passed to the left, a textile mill to the right. Then other factories to the right and left. They were no bigger than the buildings back home, Kin thought. He put his face close to the window, shaded his eyes from the car's light, and watched as Newton passed and the fields moved in again. Here and there stood a lonely house and a stand of pine. Pastures, fields of corn and hay, trees which had the elderly warped shape of fruit trees stood near wood fences and sheds. A nameless town passed. A beautiful girl lives in that town, he thought, and I wonder who she is. A creek flashed under the railroad bridge, then a highway where cars waited for the train to pass, then a wide river with fields on its banks, then woods. Factories appeared and the houses of workers, tar-papered and closely placed. "Statesville," a porter called.

It's different from home, he thought, but it isn't any better or any bigger.

"You go to the diner car and eat your supper, if you've a mind to," Cal said.

"No, I'm not hungry."

"Just order what you want." He took out a big roll of bills which he had taken from the store safe and peeled off two of them.

"No," Kin said, not wanting to admit he didn't know how to eat on a moving train.

The train pulled out. Cal took out a train schedule and studied it. "Winston-Salem is next," he said, and yawned.

"Are we near to Raleigh?"

Cal said nothing. Kin rested his head on the back of the seat and closed his eyes. He felt the pulse of the train. "Not much down here to see, is there, Papa?"

"I don't see nothing worth while. Don't know why folks ever leave home to travel to see this."

"I don't either."

The train moved through black woods; for an hour it roared through the woods, and not a light shone that Kin could see. Then

340

it came to a suburb, and he sat erect expectantly and cupped his hands to his eyes at the window glass. He peered at the outskirts of the first of the big cities. There was a road and stores, then houses, then a filling station, a furniture store, all much as they were at home. It was not better, he thought, not bigger.

There was an Esso station. A highway was below them, they were passing over it. Cars crowded on it, their headlights gleaming, passing by. A big factory was to the left, bigger than the others, and Kin squinted at it suspiciously. A solid line of warehouses appeared, streets beyond. A factory to the left, and Kin saw that it occupied an entire block and was three stories high. He felt uneasy, for the buildings spoke to him of city strength.

The train rolled on. It moved swiftly by factories and warehouses. It rolled at thirty miles an hour over roads and highways. Kin caught his breath. A line of factories appeared out the windows to the right. Other factories to the left. Houses on narrow streets, people crowding at the corners. A highway was below as they rolled across a bridge, a whistle sounding from the lonely, thudding train. Then suddenly, opening up to the left, spread out on a hill, covering the hill for twenty blocks, were factories. The hill was covered with lights, and above the banks of lights rose tall buildings, shafts of buildings, the city.

He sat back in his seat and closed his eyes tightly.

"Winston-Salem," a porter said, as the train shuddered and stopped.

The exotic woman got up and put on her black shawl. Two businessmen moved through the car, walking fast, talking fast. A family hurried through. Other people were rising, putting on coats. "How big is it?" Kin asked quietly.

"I don't know," Cal said, glancing uneasily out the window. Above them could be seen the streets full of lights, factories still working, even into the night. The smell of tobacco was strong.

"It's bigger than Asheville, don't you think?"

Cal grunted. "I expect so."

Kin looked at the crowded platform, where people embraced

friends, hurried on, people neatly dressed, men in white shirts and tweed suits and polished black shoes, talking, always talking. Planning, Kin thought, making their schemes. "How big is Pittsburgh, places like that?" he asked. "They're bigger, aren't they?"

Cal shifted on the seat. "I've never been there."

"And New York?" He considered that, the wonders of such a place. What must New York be like if this was Winston-Salem? He looked up at his father, his gaze intent and searching. "Paris, France?" he said.

Cal turned away.

"All 'board," a porter called, "for Greensboro. All 'board for Greens-boro, Dur-ham, Ral-eigh!"

24

THE HOSPITAL SEEMED TO RISE UP OUT OF THE RAINY
street, its front windows reflecting the headlights of the taxi as they
approached. Cal got out and dug from his pocket the big roll of bills.
He paid the driver and led the way through the rain to the door.

The lobby was of marble and reflected light from a brass chandelier. They stopped in the middle of it and stared at the attendant,
who was asleep at a desk. A clock set into the wall said it was four-
fifty.

Cal took off his hat and shook it, spraying water on the floor.
He coughed to get the wet air out of his lungs. "It's still lower here,"
he told Kin.

"Yes, sir." The place was strange and had an echo of their voices.

"We can see Collins now," Cal said. But he stood indecisively,
he and the tall, lean boy, not at all pleased to wait here, but not
ready yet to approach the task at hand.

Kin looked up at him. "He's not dead, Papa."

"I don't think he's dead, either."

"No. It can't get hold of Collins."

Cal grunted. "You think not? Don't you know that every time a seed of life is planted, a seed of death is planted with it in the same hill? No, not in the same hill, for the death seed is inside the life seed."

"Are you saying he's dead?" Kin asked.

Cal looked up at the clock, then at the sleeping attendant. He appeared not to have heard the boy; then he said, softly, considerately, with more kindness than before, "I didn't mean that."

He hesitated on the verge of speaking again, then did speak, but to the attendant this time. The attendant woke with a start and glared uncomfortably at him and Kin.

"Collins King," Cal said.

The attendant sighed, murmuring, something like "Oh, gosh, oh, gosh," and leaned forward and opened a big book. He ran his index finger down a column, peering, blinking. His finger traced along a line. "Collins King?" he said at last, looking up at Cal.

"I'm his father."

"He's on the third floor."

Kin sighed aloud. Collins was alive.

"But it's not visiting hours till ten o'clock tomorrow," the attendant said.

Cal considered that. "What room's he in?"

"You can't see him till ten o'clock."

Cal slowly walked to the attendant's desk. Calmly, without threat, without need of it, he said, each word separate, as if each one were newly born and for the first time used, "What room is he in?"

The attendant glared at him, no doubt considering old explanations about hospital rules, then he bent over the book again. "Room 305."

The night intern met them at the head of the stairway. "You could have taken the elevator," he said.

Cal and Kin stood stiffly before him, out of sorts with the complicated, cold-walled place, irritated in that they sought in such an unfeeling house for one of their own, with strangers looking on, men of rules and systems, not men of heart. A nurse came up, and

Cal turned to her. She had a gentle face and seemed more likely to care. "I want to see Collins King," he said.

They followed her. She walked quietly except for the squishing of her shoes and the crisp rustle of her starched dress. She stopped at a wide door, which she pushed open. Beyond it was a darkened room. They heard him now, his breathing, a husky sound, raspy, erratic, loud.

They stopped at the door, held by the sound. Kin's face was touched with fear, as if fear had been painted there.

The nurse turned on a lamp, and they saw him, gray and white, a tall man lying under a white sheet, his face sallow and colorless, the face of an old man except that there were no wrinkles on it. His eyes were closed. His lashes, even from where they stood, glistened damply. His mouth was open and the breathing came from it. His face was sweat-coated, as if a film of plastic had been laid over it.

The nurse wiped his face with a hand towel and spoke to him. "Mr. King, your father and—" She glanced at Kin questioningly. "Your father and brother are here," she said.

No change came in the breathing.

"Mr. King," she said. She jostled him gently.

The intern came into the room and walked to the other side of the bed from her. He stood there studying Collins. "I don't know," he said sleepily, "he's doped up so much." He peered at Cal. "As Dr. Weatherborne told you on the phone, he has a bad illness. He has evidently been seeking treatment for it in Baltimore, and before that in St. Louis and Chicago, and perhaps other places. He came here on his way home, we imagine, or perhaps he was going to Duke at Durham, we don't know. But the pain overcame him at the Raleigh station, and he was brought here."

He studied Collins for a moment more, then he said simply, "There's little that can be done."

A sheet of rain washed against the window and the light of the

345

electric lamp dimmed. A rumble was heard somewhere way off, maybe of thunder.

The intern said, not looking at them, "We'll keep him here, Mr. King, and see that he's kept comfortable."

Kin wondered if the trembling would ever go from inside him, the shaky mellowness of his muscles. Collins, he thought, here in this white-walled room, in this death place, his strength cut down.

Cal breathed deeply. He stirred, as if awakening. He took out his handkerchief and wiped it over his face, his eyes, his mustache. He stuck it back into his pocket. "I've come to take him home," he said.

The intern murmured, "No, no."

"Can you make him painless for the trip to the mountains?"

"I wouldn't recommend such a trip."

"Well, what's your thought, to let him die here, away from those who care for him?"

"We can tend to him and lessen his pain."

"Can you help him?" Cal said.

The intern shrugged. He looked up at the nurse, wearily, as if admitting an everyday defeat. "Nobody can help him, sir. He has been dying for two years."

He must have known that he was sick soon after he left home, Kin thought, but he didn't come back.

"How long does he have?" Cal said.

"I don't know. I can't say that."

"Well, you say it if you have the knowledge. I want to know how long he has."

"Anytime. Any hour he'll go."

There was silence for a time. The nurse moved slightly; the rubber soles of her shoes squished. "If you try to take him home," the intern said, "you'll only make it worse for him."

"Collins," Kin said impulsively. He moved slowly to the bed, made cautious by his grief and wonder at his own impetuous action; he looked down at the gray face, was struck hard by the closeness of it, the open cells of the skin and the drops of slobber at the corners of the open mouth. He turned and sought the door, but his eyes

346

were blinded, closed and misty, and he didn't know where he was in the room, so he sought a wall and leaned against it, his legs about to give way under him. He turned his face to the wall.

He heard his father say, "Give him whatever he needs for the train. I'm taking him home."

When Kin turned from the wall, the nurse and the intern had gone, and his father stood near the bed. He saw Kin turn. "There's a train at eight o'clock," he said.

Kin nodded.

"He'll be at home tonight." He clutched his hands behind him and sighed heavily. "Let him die to home, where knowing hands will care for him, not in this place like a butcher's hall with a whiteness to it." He shook his head irritably, resentfully. "It's better to lie in somber rooms with portraits of his people on the wall, and go down gentle, with no hand touching him save those who knew him when he was above illness."

"Yes," Kin said softly.

"Collins, are you there to hear me?" Cal said.

There was no response.

"We'll be taking you back, Kin and me. We've come for you. We've come for our own." He paused, waiting for Collins to speak, if he had heard, if he had the will and strength to answer. "You are my own," he said, "for as much of me is in you as in any of my boys. And what will I do now, without you being alive and roaming in some far-off place? What will I do without the thought that I am somewhere far away in my next-to-oldest?" He patted Collins' hand, awkwardly, tenderly, and when he spoke again, his voice was lower, deep in tension and feeling, so that the words formed slowly on his tongue and were fused together. "Two times I've touched your hand and you not know it. That first time, you were red-skinned and newborn and didn't have much sight in your eyes yet. I touched you and said to you, though you heard me then no better than you hear me now, that you were a frail creature indeed to be let loose on such a twisting road, with so many sorrow and death

347

pits in it." He shook his head, as if the worry of the life journey had taken hold of him. "And what's the journey that lies before you now? I can't even tell you what dangers lie there, for you start on it before me, and before your own time, for you're not yet even forty."

He stopped. He stared at the damp face, the weight of the injustice heavy on him.

"What can I say to you?" he said. "What do I say to you when you are leaving and I am left here? It tightens my throat to think on it, that you are leaving, for you've not reached your best days. You are a crop cut down before it ripens. I have my complaints about the wrongness of it. Better for death to touch me, for I have almost lived out my time."

He stood motionless, as if waiting, perhaps waiting for Collins to speak, perhaps seeking proper thoughts to say. He shook his head, then once more patted Collins' hand. "We're born blinded into this world, and blinded we go out of it, and in between we seek ourselves; we do what work we can and enjoy the days, the sun and good weather and the smell of the earth when it's turned over, and the smell of corn being ground at the mill, and the chalky smell of fresh milk striking against the side of the pail, and the smell of hay just hoisted into the barn loft, and the smell of a pine house newly built and left to weather. We eat and enjoy it, we sleep with a woman and enjoy it, we raise our families and enjoy it, knowing all the time that it won't last forever, that it moves forward to the end, like a brook becomes a creek becomes a stream becomes a river, and I guess sooner or later gets to the ocean, some of it, maybe most of it, but the brook is dead and the creek is dead and the stream is dead and the river dies; it's all dead. But none of it dies like a man." He paused, seeking meaning, trying to grapple with his concepts and thoughts here in the shadow of death. "A man's life is like a steer with a rope around his head and his nose, his nose pulled down to the ground at the stump of a tree, and a hard blow falls on his head, then a knife opens his neck and the blood gushes out, hot and steaming in the cold morning air, so much of it that it sops

348

the ground. To think on it, to think on it being over. Nothing more that the body does. The body is dead. A man's life it goes on to heaven, I guess, but, God knows, I don't look forward to it. God knows, whatever it is, it ain't like this, it ain't like it is down at the foot of my hill where my store is, not like it is at the herb shop and the gun shop and the store Matthew has on the Square. It's not got that. And not like the house with the porch where a man can sit of an evening, where we used to sit, Collins, you and me, it's not the same up there, God knows, whatever it is, it's not real like the hallway and the dining room, and the food of a noontime, when a man can eat and rest and wonder what he better do that afternoon. A man dies. His life don't die; his body dies, but his life can't be the same, for a man is part of a place, and he has set a time for rising and for work, and for dinner and for sleep. That man dies, blinded again he goes. And his body is fertilizer for the ground."

He looked down at Collins' body, then backed off, out of reach of it, and shook his head, frustrated and thought-complicated. "We'll carry you out of here, boy," he said, suddenly stern of voice, firm, a hardness coming back to him. "We'll do that at least. You'll be with God's own, if your life holds, and you'll go down easy." He backed away and turned and wiped his face with his handkerchief. He wiped his nose and blew his nose. "You see they don't harm him, Kin," he said, and went out of the room and down the hall.

Outside, the city slept. Only the softly falling rain was heard in the room. A clock ticked, and Kin saw that it was on the bedside table. What time is it, he wondered.

Do they know, he wondered, all the people in the city, do they guess that he is dying?

How often does he die? he wondered.

He moved to the foot of the bed and gazed at him. "Collins," he whispered, "Beth wants to see you, Collins."

The husky breathing came from deep inside the body, as if the body were breathing from another body inside itself, so that he was a sounding board for the deeper body.

349

"Collins, Beth and Mama are home waiting for you. They've been waiting to see you for a long time, since you first wrote."

There was no answer. He moved closer to him but was afraid to touch him. "Collins—"

Collins moved on the bed. Slowly, slightly he moved. His head turned, he seemed to be seeking a way to regain sight, then his eyes cleared and his head stopped moving. He saw Kin and stared at him as if trying to recall him from among the thousands of people he had met over the years. "Kin?" he asked at last.

"Yes," Kin said.

Collins smiled. "Where is this place? Raleigh, isn't it?"

"Yes. Papa and I took the train down here."

"You say you did? I tell you, Kin, I've got a bad thing in me. It's more worrisome than a chestnut burr and it's about five times that big. It's lodged inside me, waiting for motion."

"Papa wants to take you home."

"Huh? Well, you'd better log me full of dope if you do." Seriousness came over his face, as if he were studying a pain that was threatening to develop inside him right then, but the warning passed and he smiled. "Go home, you say? That's right, that's the hope, isn't it?"

The nurse entered the room. "Is he awake?" she said. She gently pushed Kin aside. "You'd better save your strength, Mr. King." She straightened the covers on the bed and put a fresh pillow beneath his head.

"You treat me gentle, like a mother's hand," Collins said to her.

"Oh, hush," she said, smiling. She filled a hypodermic needle. "I suppose I remind you of some girl you once knew."

"Yes," Collins said.

She wiped alcohol on a spot on his arm.

"A pretty Eskimo girl," he said and winked at Kin. "But it would take me a little while to find out if you were related to her."

She pressed in the last of the fluid and withdrew the needle. "Just what does that mean?" she asked.

350

He smiled and looked at her. He lay there smiling, as if lost in pleasant contemplation. She smiled, too, finally. "You're crazy as you can be, I know that," she said playfully, teasingly, "whatever you mean."

"There was a girl in Denver looked like you," Collins said. "She had the same color eyes, same shape of face. Had a nice figure, too."

"You certainly can talk today," she said.

"Ten years ago. It's been quite a while since I stopped over in Denver."

"Better to keep quiet," she said, "and save your strength." She smiled at him and went out quickly.

"The Denver girl had a round bottom on her, Kin. It was shaped like a bushel basket with an ax cut in the center of the bottom of it. It was a marvel to witness when it was standing still, and a wonder to behold when it was in motion." He smiled. "Huh," he grunted and shook his head, caught in the throes of the memory. "She was the biggest-assed woman I ever saw, and it was all as soft as stomach fat."

Kin moved to his side. "Collins, did you find the highroad when you left home last time, when you left us?"

He didn't answer. It was as if Kin had not spoken at all. He exhaled deeply through his mouth, then wet his lips. "I want to go home. Tell Papa, will you? Where is he?"

"He's down the hall. I'll get him."

"Tell him I want to go to the big place again. I don't want to stay away off here in Raleigh."

"We'll take you home."

"I want to see Beth," he said, drowsiness coming over him, thick and deep. "I've got to see Beth," he said.

"All right," Kin said.

"A man goes off and plays the fool, lonely, lonely, God knows. I want to see her. He gets sick and loses his courage. I want to see her again."

"All right, Collins."

"Lord, Lord," he said.

He said nothing more. Kin waited, but he was asleep. "Collins," Kin said. There was no answer. He backed away and hurried down the cool hall toward where his father was.

At the train station, Collins was lifted aboard; a nurse, one hired to watch over him, helped the ambulance attendants. Kin watched them, hovered about, fearful lest Collins be dropped. Then he sought out a pay telephone in the waiting room and put in a call to the clothing store in Asheville. Morris answered and hurried up the stairs at once to get Beth.

Kin heard them come back down the steps. Beth answered, her voice so low Kin hardly could hear her.

"I'm in the Raleigh train station," he told her. "We're bringing him home, Beth." He knew she was standing in the clothing store, and probably Morris was watching, so he tried not to say anything abruptly. "He's bad sick. It might be wrong to seek much hope about his recovering."

She didn't speak.

"You might go down and tell Mama," Kin said.

"All right," she said.

"I don't know what else to say, except I talked to Collins this morning and he said he wanted to come home."

"What did he say?"

"He said he wanted to come home and see Beth."

After a moment she said, "Did he say it that way?"

"He said it just like that. He said he had to see Beth again. 'I want to see her,' he said." He waited to see if she wanted to ask anything else. "I thought I'd phone you, since you have a phone and Mama doesn't. And you can tell Mama what you want her to know, what she can take of it. I'll—be getting on the train now, Beth."

He hung up quickly and sat in the booth, staring at the phone, getting hold of his emotions.

Cal was standing beside the train when he found him. He was peering off toward the west, his arms folded, the heavy wind from the sea, over a hundred miles away, striking against his back.

352

"I called Beth," Kin said.

Cal frowned. "Might have been better to wait to see if Collins lives to arrive home."

"No, I think it's better for them to know and not have to imagine."

Cal shook his head. "He might die on that stretch of track."

"I didn't tell her he wouldn't."

"We might arrive with a corpse and nothing else, and his mama waiting to see him and talk to him."

A porter with a cartload of ice came by, singing to himself in a deep, guttural voice.

"I got us two seats in the pullman coach," Cal said. "You sleepy?"

"No," Kin said. But he was. His body was weak with the need for sleep.

He went on inside and found the seat. It was near the compartment where Collins slept. The nurse, about thirty, a girl with brown stringy hair and thin shoulders, a strong girl, sat near Collins reading a movie magazine. Kin saw that she had a stack of magazines, six or seven of them. She wasn't worried about Collins, she was worried about movie stars. Maybe she wanted to have her own picture taken, Kin thought, and shown to everybody in the world, so that she could be recognized wherever she went and be followed after by men, like dogs follow a bitch in heat. He had sometimes thought of himself as a movie star. It used to be that he was a cowboy, but of late he was a polished fellow with good manners who had girls clamoring around him because of the way he smiled and carried on.

He chuckled, thinking about himself as a movie actor. He wasn't much of a lover for a fact, he knew well enough. He had gone out with only a few girls since his encounter with little Sally Waters, and the one time he had stopped at her house and asked to see her, he had got the door slammed in his face. He still thought of her with anger and affection; he couldn't forgive her, but he couldn't defeat the happy memories of her, and he sometimes got scared when he thought she might leave, go back to Tennessee or somewhere.

The conductor came by and said the train was going to start in a minute or two. He was anxious about Collins, he said, and told the nurse to pay attention to her duties.

Cal came aboard. He stood at the compartment door, trying to decide whether to sit in the room with the nurse and Collins or outside with Kin. He went into the compartment and sat down across from Collins' bed.

A porter on the platform called, "All 'board for Dur-ham, Bur-ling-ton, High Point, Greens-burrrrrrrr-o. And points west!"

Kin rested his head against the back of the seat. Beth, he thought, she's waiting right now. Beth, so deeply moved to know Collins wanted to see her again. Beth, he thought, the gentlest one.

Why, he wondered, didn't he weep. He knew now that Collins was going to die. Was his mind able to withstand deep grief easier than it withstood a casualty? He would be more concerned to find that Collins had lost his arm than he was to find that Collins was losing his life. His emotions were listless, as if deadened by a drug.

"Westbound train. All 'board!"

Passengers were going up and down the aisle, seeking their seats, taking off overcoats and hats.

"Pull that shade down, nurse," he heard his father say.

Beth, he thought, closing his eyes and resting his head on the seat, we're bringing him home for you at last.

"Turn out that light and put them damn magazines away."

And Collins, imprisoned, unable to see or hear clearly or to think clearly, knew that he was on a train that was leaving a station somewhere. He felt the motion of the train, and he heard a voice say, "Westbound. Westbound. Westbound train."

How often had he heard that call, most often in St. Louis, where the West started for him. Twenty times or more he had heard it there.

He heard a man speak, and his voice sounded like his father's. "You watch him careful now on these curves, for this train might lurch," the voice said. It was like his father's voice, but it could not be his father, for he wouldn't be aboard a train leaving St. Louis, the city of rock walls and green gardens, passing over the Missouri now, three hundred feet wide with swatches of trees making deep

354

shade on the high banks, moving up the center of the valley.

He knew this land from many crossings. A rich black river valley, then hills rising to either side. The Missouri again after a while, flashing under, as, passing warehouses of corn and wheat, the train moves through the belly of the country into Kansas City, then over the Kansas River, brown with dust, across a flat valley which stops at the base of mountains near where a big brown cornfield lies. The train rolls through Abilene and through the tangles of farmland and trees, rolling at eighty miles an hour into the West, climbing steadily toward the plateau of Denver, past oil tanks and power stations, and moves on across the drier lands to Cheyenne and into Laramie, where once pioneers waited, congregated. The plains lie open here. How cleverly they hide their devilment. A water hole glistens. Distant mountains are blue and friendly. A small river, no more than a dozen feet across, rolls idly nearby. The fields are yellow green— always yellowish in color at winter sunset.

The train passes haystacks and sheep in the yellow-green fields, and a lake, and rolls faster over the prairie they crossed; they and their wagons and their women walking and their young'uns crying and their milch cows and their stumbling, heavy-headed oxen, into the dust, into the big hope, toward the mountains alive with color beneath the gold clouds and the amber clouds, with blue sky darkening as it rises to a black dome, and the horses flicking their tails at the flies. The train roars on, over bad land, high and level with mountains far off, past a dry water hole with pearl-gray earth at the bottom, into Hanna with its coal mines, and on at ninety miles an hour into Dana, treeless country, past cattle-loading places and across the North Platte at an elevation of a mile high, past the Ruby Hotel near the Continental Divide, where he once had known a girl named Ruth and they had made love in a tangled bed, past Creston, a few houses only, a place passed by in the rush of men to reach the riches of Oregon and California, past Robinson, which is only a sign beside the track, past Hallville, which is only a station house, rolling through an unreal land, empty, blistered and unused, like a castoff fleck of another planet fallen just lately to Earth and called, for want

355

of a better name, Wyoming. Trains passing from the empire of the Far West to the empire of the Near West, across Wyoming. Wagon trails once rolled here, a hundred thousand wheels, wearing out their rims, breaking through their ribs, dragging on, oxen tired, oxen dead, moving on. Wyoming. Across Wyoming, someday to be crowded with people, an empire here surrounded by empires, Collins thought, in the heart of America. Rolling past a three-story hotel near the train tracks at Evanston, on the banks of a little river, where a girl whose name had passed from memory once sat with her feet dangling in the water and turned her face up to him and her small hand touched him. Rolling on, rolling west at a hundred miles an hour into the night.

Kin got up from the seat and went to the door of the compartment. The light was off inside, the shades were pulled down, and the nurse was sitting beside Cal, who was sitting straight-backed in the same place. Neither the nurse nor Cal spoke to him, so he returned to his seat and let the rumbling of the train lull him toward sleep.

When next he awoke, a haze had settled over the world, an afternoon haze which filtered in among the straight pine trunks and clung to the fence edges. He went into the men's room and tried to wake up by splashing water on his face. A porter was there. "Your brother all right?" the porter asked.

"I think so," Kin said. He went back to the compartment, wearily, pensively. His father had his eyes closed, but he was still sitting up straight. Collins was breathing through his mouth, hollow bursts of air moving into and out of his sick body. The nurse got up to give Kin a seat; she went out, toward the women's room. Kin sat down beside Cal.

"I was thinking about Collins as a boy and stealing all my chickens," Cal said, his eyes still closed, his head moving with the sway of the car, "and the time he filled all my shoes with dirt 'cause I took a strap to him for his meanness." Cal chuckled deep in his throat. "He was a great hand for getting even. He stole the horse and buggy many a time and charged through town, cracking his whip like he

356

was an Italian soldier. I never did know how to control him, if there was a way, for he was given to his own experiences, and to temper acts at times."

Cal spoke so slowly and softly that Kin sensed his heavy weariness.

"I remember down on King Street there was a peach tree standing near where that young pear tree is, and he picked the peaches one July day, but he didn't do a good job of it and I told him to get them all, ever one of them and bring them up to the store to sell. He said he couldn't get out on the limbs to all of them, but I told him he'd better, and about an hour later he come by with a bushel more and said that was ever one of them. That was good work, I thought, and fast work, and I complimented him and told him his excuses obviously had been as shallow as a brook bed. He listened dutifully, and it wasn't till I got home that I found he'd cut the tree down."

He shook his head in wonder. The train noise sounded and he bobbed his head as the car swayed. Outside the dark compartment a baby started crying again.

"They ought to mouth-stop that baby with a handkerchief," he said, "if they ain't got a nipple."

"I asked Collins if he had got rid of his Beth notions when he left us last time," Kin said. "But he didn't answer me."

"Well, what if he did or didn't? Some men can forget a woman, some can't. What one does doesn't apply to anybody else."

"I hope he found ease again. But for Beth's sake, I hope he suffered first."

"Why do you worry about Beth? She has a good man. At least, he's pleasant and simple enough, seems to me. She has a baby and another one coming."

"Does she already—another one?"

"Oh, I imagine she'll have one soon. She says she wants to have three." He was so sleepy he could hardly talk. "She can think about Collins any minute of the day she wants to. Sometimes it's better to know a good thing, then to lose it before it sours on you. Maybe it was a good thing for Collins to leave when he did."

"Did you advise him to go?" Kin asked.

357

"What do you mean?"

"Did you come up to his room that last night and tell him he had better go?"

"Would I tell you if I had, boy?" he said simply, wearily, his eyes closed.

Abruptly his head fell forward and he sat up straight. He peered about him strangely, out of sorts. He settled back again, more awake now, but listless still. "I used to advise Collins before he ever left the first time. I advised him to stay and tend the store, find his place in the world. I told him life got thin-worn when it was used to roam hill shadows. I told him I had thought of doing that myself when young, and I admitted to him that sometimes I wished I had, for then I wouldn't have a family to worry about, no cares much, wouldn't need to consider about debts and farm families suffering, and illness in the country, with no doctors to speak of and some of them that's there no-count. We used to have one doctor near my home that never had studied medicine; he just got hold of some knives and pieces of white cloth. My Lord, when I think of him I get angry—"

"What about Collins?" Kin asked, interrupting him.

"Well, what do you mean? I told you, he didn't pay any mind to me, as I knew he wouldn't. So he left, ran off, and he's wandered."

"Collins is a good man, though, Papa."

"I'll say he's my best in some ways. He's got both manliness and decency, and plenty of folks have got one or the other but they don't have the pair. He's among the best, though Matthew might someday pass him, for he's coming along now that he has responsibility. I turned a farmer down for a loan two weeks ago and suggested he go to Matthew. I wanted to see what would happen. The man didn't have good security, but he had a holy need for cash. He come back later and said Matthew had loaned him two hundred dollars. Now, that's not much, but it's a sign, and word'll get around, and before long other men will be going to Matthew, not just to borrow but to trade. Have you seen his store lately?"

"No, I don't go around him."

"He's got five racks just of children's clothes. He's got seven racks

358

of women's house dresses. He's put in two racks of fancy clothes, bright-colored stuff. He's got counters mounded over with nothing except underwear. It's all good-quality stuff, made to wear well, and I'm proud of him. I wish him luck with the store and with his wife, though the Lord knows she's so nervous he's going to have to temper her with a sedative before she gets her baby born."

The nurse came back and leaned over Collins. She felt his pulse.

"Paul is trading fair now, too," Cal said, "maybe because he has to. I don't know that he will be for long, but he is now. And you're growing up reasonably well. I think, all in all, the boys ever one are going to match up."

"But Collins is the best," Kin said.

Cal peered off unhappily. "He's not leaving anything permanent, seems to me."

"We can't leave anything permanent; nobody can," Kin said.

Cal glanced at him, dissatisfied with him. He leaned forward and cleared his throat. "He's lived a lonely time of life, ain't that so? And that's a sickness, to be alone all the time."

"He never was alone," Kin said. "He couldn't get alone for five minutes."

"Well, I suppose if you're going to argue about everything I say, I might as well stop talking to you."

"For Collins his life was the way life should be."

"You sound like you're more than just mildly interested in his life for yourself. Are you?"

"I'm just saying that Collins has done a good deal for other people, that's all."

"You think so, do you?" Cal sniffed and cleared his throat and spat into his handkerchief. He lifted a shade and stared out at the passing countryside, deeply irritated, his back to Kin now, the conversation over.

The train wound its way through Hickory.

"He sleeps so sound," the nurse said.

They passed through Conover. He still rested, without stirring. When the train came in sight of the mountains, he began to stir, as

359

a wild animal might stir when it comes close once more to its home country.

The train ascended into the mountains, and behind them he knew was the lake and the desert where, in olden days, many of the oxen had gone mad and died, and where the men had first realized that they might die, too. Steeply they climbed, the trees folding back on each side, the engine coughing, a tunnel closing in around them, then ending, another tunnel starting. The sound of the rumbling of the wheels deepened. The engine was hot with power. The tunnels drew fire from the funnels, the smoke exploding in heat puffs.

So the wagon train had climbed, upward with oxen pulling and the men saying in low voices, "We might not get over the pass before the snow." Moving toward the place of death, where winter stopped them, catching them with a white, smothering, stinging softness. Upward they rolled toward the place of awful death, past the places some of the men and women had died, one here, one over there, through the tunnels toward Donner Pass, until now the long last tunnel and a life-shriek from the engine as it entered, and a pain struck at his stomach and he saw Death waiting; Death touched him and he met Death with a cry which clogged in his stomach and his throat, and he awoke in darkness, blood on his face from his mouth, and stared with clear eyes ahead, as the train bolted from the tunnel and, gasping with relief, he saw before him not the snows of the High Sierras but the green and welcome hills of home.

25

News traveled out that Collins King was next
to death. Mountain children heard about it in their cabins. Collins,
the next to oldest, Collins, of the broad smile and the mellow voice
and hopeful words, lay dying.

His death approached at thirty-nine, out of season, so it had a
special meaning. In punishment it came, the old women said, sent
by God for a sin too often committed, woman love too much ex-
ploited. For that sin and for leaving home, leaving his mother's house
and going away. They lectured sternly their own children to look on
him, to consider.

The men permitted such instructions, though they weren't convinced it was wrong to love such women as would permit it, or to
wing free from home. They had themselves heard both calls and
knew the magic that was in them. But they listened without comment as their wives placed the blame for the punishment that had
fallen on Collins. "God will haunt your journeys if you leave your
mother's hearths," they said.

The first morning Collins was back, Paul stood in front of his
store and stared down toward the house, then he peered over toward

the water trough where horses once had been tied, and dampened his lips and spat. Collins' illness touched a nerve in him which sent shivers through him. Paul had won now over Collins. Hadn't he won? He was free now of Collins, or near free, not by his hand or action, but by God's hand. The shackles of Collins King were let loose.

Paul didn't side with Death, of course, but he had no control over Death. Death had come; he couldn't stop it. He didn't welcome it, but it freed him, just the same. And it scared him. Normally Death was a far call away; now, abruptly, it was right at home. By whatever mystery moved its mind, it had struck Collins. Was it done, satisfied, satiated? It had a gluttonous hunger, Paul knew. Was it done now, once it had finished with Collins?

It chilled him to think on it. Should he die soon, what would he leave? To whom? His store would go to Florence? Lord, what a waste that was! To whom could he leave it, then? To his father? His father was the only person he respected, but his father had tricked him and would accept the gift as a sign of weakness. Give it to whom? In that town there was no single soul he could look on as his own close friend.

The more he considered it, the more angry he became. Where were his children? That damn Florence had not spawned a one. From where he stood on the sidewalk he could see fifty mountain women, any one of whom could doubtless be bigged in short order, healthy women, not even needing such frequent attention as he had given Florence. Any one of them could give him children, but he was left barren.

Strong women, handsome, of good stock, any of these women would do to breed with. He had heard tell of such arrangements being made by others. A baby would be dropped and fed and weaned, then taken home by its father.

My God, he was forty-three; there was no time to lose. It would take twenty years to get the first one grown, and he would be almost too old to enjoy his work, to guide him, to instruct him in business. She had done it to him, held back. Hadn't he told her night after night not to hold back on him!

Over sixty when my first one comes of age, he thought.

It was frightening. In fear and anger he considered it. My God, he thought, the treachery of it. Death was close by and he was without an heir.

They could tell old man Fulcher it was her child. They would go on a trip and soon after they returned, she would have the baby, and they would tell him.

It would be nice for Florence to have a plaything around the house, anyway, for all she did now was spend her time listening to the radio. She sat in the chair in the kitchen and leaned her elbows on the table and listened to the music and the jokes, and never so much as swept the floor, except for the passageways.

He crossed the street and walked about among the stalls. There was a pretty brown-headed woman with a fine body on her standing near the trough. She would do, he thought. He saw one with blond hair, pretty of face. She seemed to be a healthy person. She would do.

He saw another, also healthy as could be and laughing, a happy woman. She would do, he though. He saw another that he liked. The market place had many; everywhere he looked, he saw another one. The market place was overrun with them, and he could breed with any one, provided he could be sure the woman wouldn't make gossip, tell everybody that she had mothered Paul King's son. He didn't want talk to get to Fulcher, nor did he want ballad singers and storytellers to relate at fireplace times how Paul King had married Fulcher's daughter for her wealth but had had his children by Mae Smith over to Topknot way. They would tell how he would take the baby out of Mae's arms and go home with it to Florence, who had a steamed milk bottle waiting to feed the baby with, and would say to Florence, "Well, here's our next one."

No, it had to be a secret, or the sons would be marked to suffer for it. He had to find a woman who would keep quiet about it. Somehow he had to win the love of a woman; then she wouldn't damage him.

He peered around him. Blond and red-headed and brown-haired, smiling faces, openmouth and closed, laughing, somber, high fore-heads, a hundred women were at hand.

He walked up King Street to Jacob's place, ordered a beer and drank it down, then drank another one. Every woman on that street had a man she loved, or was seeking a man to love, so it shouldn't be too difficult to find one for himself.

But how did a man get a woman to love him?

He had to hurry up somehow and get a woman to love him and bear him sons.

He drank a third beer and went back down to the store. He felt better with the beer in him.

Brown-haired, red-haired, skinny, fat. It didn't matter, damn it. Somebody to breed with.

To love him. How did you trick a woman into loving you?

Buy a woman. A thousand dollars. That should be enough.

He went into the store and into his office and closed the door. He took a bottle of white whisky out of a drawer and took a drink. The Sikes boy kept him supplied; the old man owed money he couldn't pay, so the boy paid interest in whisky. Paul drank another long swallow of it. Well-made, pure whisky.

When a knock came at the door, he put the bottle away. "Who is it?" he said.

Nobody answered, but the door was opened slowly and there stood a lonesome-looking fellow. Paul couldn't place his name right off. The man owed him money, he remembered that. "What you want?" he said. He didn't like for anybody to come into his office.

The man stood there watching him, twisting his hat in his hands. He stepped into the room. "Mr. King," he said, and Paul was about to tell him to get out when he saw a woman come to the door and stop, this fellow's wife, probably, a woman about thirty or thirty-five, and she had a baby at her breast, nursing it while she rocked it gently. The sight of the woman and the baby stopped him.

"I need some money, Mr. King," the man said.

Paul couldn't stop looking at the woman, and she was looking at

364

him, at ease, comfortable, rocking the baby in her arms, glancing at her husband, then at Paul, the only one in the room who was relaxed.

"I need three hundred dollars, Mr. King, if I'm to get my taxes paid. The county's talking about auctioning off my land."

Paul leaned back in his chair. He wished he hadn't had so much whisky. It had got to be a problem of late. He was going to have to cut down on it. "What's your name?" he said.

The man stared at him, dismayed. "I'm Luke Isaac," he said. "You know me, Mr. King."

"Luke Isaac, do you need anything besides the tax money?"

The man shifted uneasily. He peered suspiciously at Paul, as if testing the intent of the question. "My mule's sick, as a rule," he said. When Paul only nodded, he considered his next step and said, "I need new fencing." When Paul only nodded again, he said, "My truck's broke."

"Do you have a valley farm?" Paul asked slowly, looking at the top of his desk.

"No, I have a hillside farm, Mr. King," the man answered guardedly, watching Paul. "You know that."

"It's better farming in the valley," Paul said simply.

"Yes, I think you're right about that."

"It's easier to work, more productive."

"Yes, that's true."

"You can get power put into your barn and house." He folded his hands on the desktop, then looked over at the woman, stared at her, and she looked back calmly, the baby still sucking at her. "You got a baby, I got none. Don't have a son." She knows, he thought; they all know right away. The only thing they do all know is when a man needs them. It's born in them to know that. "You and your woman go talk it over," he said.

The man was dazed. His eyes were narrowed to slits. He was vaguely aware of what Paul meant, but wasn't certain, had not focused on it yet. Perhaps he had not dared to, that was all.

When they left, Paul got the bottle out again and took a drink. He took another one then. That man, he might not come back at all, he or his woman. Well, nothing had been said. Let the man consider it. Let her consider it, too. They would probably take a week to figure it all out. Then maybe they would come back. Who the hell cares, he thought. There are others.

Matthew was so moved by Collins' illness that he left his clothing store in another's care and haunted the big rooms of the house, pacing anxiously the sickroom off the main hall where Collins was unconscious. Lotti also stayed in the room much of the time, pestering the covers and talking, rambling about for an idea. And Dr. LeClair spent several hours in the house. He was old now and tottery; he served only a few patients, and he served them carefully.

Kin stayed close to the bed, too, and Johnny often could be found leaning against the brass rails, his eyes bigger than usual, as he watched Collins. He was there on the second afternoon, listening to the torturous breathing, when Lotti whispered to him. Obediently he went to the stand where the family Bible was and opened it and sought a place that suited him. He read to her about Jesus being the victor over Death. He read slowly, and she rocked back and forth in time with the meter and the meaning, biting at her lower lip and frowning as if the words pierced her.

Cal stayed in the dining room mostly, drinking coffee and wiping the worry sweat off his face and listening.

That night, Inez fixed some supper—thick potato soup, boiled chicken, and biscuits. She put it on the table, along with pear preserves and coffee. LeClair sat with Cal at the table and ate a little something. Beth was in the house but was upstairs, in her old room. She had been there all day, except for brief trips downstairs. She had not wept over Collins at all, had only glanced at him a few times.

But when she came downstairs about nine o'clock, Kin took his father's car and, even though she protested, drove her home. He parked in front of the clothing store and walked with her to the upstairs apartment. When he came back down, Morris was waiting at the clothing-store door for him. "I had thought Beth might want to stay at the house tonight," he said.

"I don't know," Kin said hesitantly. "She has her baby to think about."

Morris looked away, then nodded.

"I mean, she has things to do here, doesn't she?" Kin said. "You and the baby are here and need her."

"I could watch after the baby."

Kin frowned at him. "I don't know what she wants to do."

"Will you go up now and tell her to go back to the house if she wants to? Do you think she would like to do that?"

"Morris, I don't know. Don't you care?"

"I'll ask her," Morris said and went up the steps.

Kin stepped out to the curb and waited, his hands in his pants pockets. Morris came back alone. "She'll stay here tonight, Kin. I'll bring her to the house tomorrow morning."

"All right," Kin said. He left quickly and without looking at him again.

That night Collins became worse. He began speaking crazily about the redlands of Arizona and a family he had lived with there, evidently twenty years before. The talking became a rambling stream of words. He talked about a River of No Return, and a green lake, about a cabin he knew of somewhere in a woods in Wisconsin. He talked about people he had known, mentioning their names, and sometimes seemed to be conversing with them.

The family sat in the room and listened, marveling at the accumulation of impressions; even Lotti was hushed much of the time. Cal didn't listen at all. He sat at the dining-room table, sat sideways to it, one arm resting on it, a coffee cup by his arm, just sat there, thinking, responding to questions that were asked him, but asking nobody anything, except about Collins.

At ten o'clock Lotti came into the dining room and sat down at the table, too. "It's time for bed, ain't it, Cal?" she said.

"Bed?" he said gently. "Oh, I don't know, Lotti." He hadn't slept at all the night before, except that sometimes he would doze in the chair. "Is he still talking?"

"Yes. He goes on and on."

"About his travels?"

"He could talk forever, I guess. His voice has got husky from it."

"Does Kin listen to him?"

"Why, I reckon he does. They're all in there listening, 'cept Beth. Where'd she go?"

"Kin drove her home a while ago."

"Well, it's hard on me to see him so sick," Lotti said. "I told Beth this morning that we just have to keep reminding ourselves that all things work together for good to them that loves the Lord."

Cal grunted. "That so?" he said. "Is he still talking about Iowa?"

"I don't know the states," she said, "except a few."

"You sure do take all this easy, Lotti," Cal said. "I hand it to you."

"I don't know what you mean, take it easy."

"I mean it don't seem to get through to you deeply."

"Why, I worry as much as I can."

"Uh-huh. You know, living with people is like walking through a hardwood forest in a deep cove. You find all kinds of trees on hand, all different."

"I don't know what you mean," she said, anxious now, upset because of him. "Why, I can't stand to think of him dying." Her lips trembled. "A mother feels for all her children, feels deep for ever one. I bore him, and that pain of Collins' birth I still remember, though Paul was the most pain to bear. He seemed to never be done getting born. Course, he was the first one, and that's part of it. You can't bear the first one as easy as the rest." She was rambling along now, but she stopped, and her lips trembled again. "Why did you say that about me, Cal, about my not caring so much?"

"Oh, I see that you do," he said calmly, not looking at her. "I'm so tired, Lotti," he said, shaking his head.

"You talk like I'm unfeeling."

"I didn't mean to bother you, Lotti. I'm tired."

368

"Well, come on to bed then. Why, they'll call us if he gets worse. He's just talking now."

"Uh-huh. I might come in to bed sometime soon."

She talked some more about childbirths before she left, as if she were afraid he might forget what she had told him. Then she went into the bathroom and later into the bedroom and closed the door.

Kin came into the dining room two or three times, but he didn't stay long. It was as if he had to go back and listen. Matthew was listening, too. Paul was somewhere, maybe on the porch, out in the cold. Nobody seemed to know where he was. But Matthew and Johnny and Kin sat in the room near the bed, and Inez stood near the fireplace, where a coal grate was, and listened to the wondrous words. The voice would be muddled for a while, then would come clear, ring true about somebody way off. Collins sometimes would be talking to this person or that. And it seemed like he was on a train at one point, going up a mountain through the tunnels, and when he was getting toward the top, he sat up in bed, his eyes open, the first and only time that day they had opened, and maybe he saw somebody in the room, she couldn't tell, but he said nothing to anybody. He lay back down on the pillows and went to sleep again, and said nothing more, even in his sleep, for a long time.

He was a handsome man; he was strong, too, she guessed. She had heard about him many a time back in the valley where she'd lived. Now she stood near the foot of his bed and watched over him.

Matthew went home about twelve, and Inez went to bed soon after. Only Kin and Johnny were in the room when Cal came in and sat down near the head of the bed. The boys felt uneasy at once, sensing that they didn't belong there now, and Johnny first, then Kin, left. But they stood in the dark hallway outside the door, not wanting to spy on their father, but being unwilling to leave.

"You still hold on, don't you, boy?" they heard Cal say, speaking slowly, heavily. "I didn't doubt but that you would. God knows, you've lived so much of your life, so high and fine you've burned it, taking chances and not caring much, that it's a sorry time when this

369

has to fall on you. Many another it could take, men who are older and more afraid of their lives. Not that we all ain't afraid sometimes. I am. Like on yesterday when I stopped by the store of an evening and a fellow come to me and told me something about Paul that was the strangest message I ever heard. Well, in strength or weakness, a man holds on to his life as best he can, I know, Paul in his way, every man to his own. And you fight for yours. I stay in there by the table, and I say to myself over and over, 'Hold on, hold on, Collins. It matters to hold on.' And sometimes I pray. God knows, the prayer probably don't get no more distance out in space than the walls of the room, for I've got no special sway with God. But I pray for you. I'd strike a bargain with God right now for you. I'd give him might nigh all I own and myself and not accept a word of thanks from any living soul. I'd be glad to do it. For I don't like to see you this way. It clobbers in me, it don't strike right. I want to shout out and say my anger, for who planned it this way? Whose hand? God damn, who planned this waste of life? It's not your time to go. Are we to mumble quiet kindnesses about it when a wrong is done? Hell! Damn! God damn! Your life shouldn't end now. Let Him represent Himself who takes it, for I'll not bow down to him this time."

No more words. Kin, in the hallway, could hear the old clock ticking. It bonged now, a single time, so he knew it was one o'clock. The sound of the bong died out. Before him was the bedroom where the fire glimmered. No light was on in there; the fire was enough light, though. Beside him Johnny stood as stiffly as he, gazing at that yellow-lighted doorway and into the room beyond.

"And yet, Collins, I pray to God for you," they heard their father say.

Deathly quiet again. No more words. Minute after minute. Then they saw him appear, suddenly loom up, and Kin thought of Collins when he had seen him before he went away, standing in a doorway, back-lighted, tall, a strong man silhouetted. Cal came out into the hallway and walked by the boys, saying nothing to them. And Kin heard him in the dining room. Kin knew he had sat down again in the chair, beside the table, his arm on the table.

370

Kin went into the sickroom. He sat down near the head of the bed. Johnny came in and stood at the foot of the bed. Where are the women, Kin wondered. They have all gone away.

Paul came in that morning after breakfast and said he had had a hard time getting to sleep the night before because he was worrying so much about Collins. When Beth and Morris arrived, he left at once and went out the back door and stood in the yard under a sycamore tree, kicking at the yard boards. Just seeing Beth always brought up old thoughts.

When he went back into the house, she was in the hall talking to the doctor about Collins. LeClair was explaining that the body always gave out after a while, that the illness would win inevitably, that the body deadened itself, so that it would stop fighting and would yield to it. His senses would not be really awake when he died, LeClair said.

He left, pulling his overcoat around him as he crossed the porch, puffs of heat mist coming from his mouth as he breathed. The pastor passed him in the yard and came up the steps and came in. He was a young man, just recently appointed to the town, who didn't know the Kings well, but knew that their names were on the books. He came in, talking softly, asking if he might pray for Collins. Lotti was called and she showed him into the room.

Beth turned from the door and saw Paul standing nearby, limp and saddened. "You'd better go into the bedroom and see Collins, Paul, while there's time," she said.

He stared at her with his searching, burning gaze. "You're hard now, aren't you? You don't really care about him."

"I don't want to talk about it, Paul."

"You and him. You once was hot on fire for him."

"I said be quiet, Paul."

"Did you stay here all night with him?"

"Paul, don't be such a baby about this."

"Don't be a baby, you say? Because of him I've got nothing."

"No," she said quietly, "it's not because of him." Then she said,

"He's dying, Paul. Go see him at least once."

"He's dying, but it don't matter; it won't help me now, will it? At any other time, it might have meant something, but this is the only time it doesn't, so this is the time he dies."

"Paul, do you think the world goes around because of you, that he dies because it won't help you for him to die, or that he did what he did when he was well because of you?"

Paul studied her anxiously, awkwardly. "He won you over, all right."

She turned away from him, softly turning, not in anger, not even in disappointment. She was above anger and disappointment now. He stepped closer to her and she felt his hand touch her shoulder. She didn't stiffen, she didn't react at all. He kissed her on the cheek, lightly, and waited, his hand still on her shoulder. She looked out through the glass part of the door, not tense at all, not moving, not reacting.

He removed his hand after a moment and backed off, and she heard him go into Collins' room, and she thought to herself, Well, it didn't happen, and if it did, it doesn't matter.

Paul went home to get Florence, and Matthew went home to get Cynthia. As dinnertime came on, the whole family, including Morris, gathered to wait in the hall and in the dining room. At noon Inez put food on the table, but nobody sat down except Cal, who was already there, and he didn't eat anything. Lotti came in finally. She sank down at the foot of the table, broke a biscuit in two, and chewed on the bread, not looking at any of her children.

Cyn came into the dining room. She sat down and ate a big meal. She didn't say anything to anybody, or act like she was sad when she wasn't; she just ate. She was hungry and was honest about it. Matthew sat down beside her when she was almost done and ate a few bites to keep her company.

Paul came to the table and stood near Lotti, and he chewed on a chicken back. He listened to Florence, in the hall, talking to Beth about her father's health, as if anybody cared whether old man Fulcher had the croup or not. Lord, he was one to hold on to life,

Paul thought. There was not much hope of his dying soon.

Beth finally got away from Florence and came into the dining room and sat down near Cal.

Lotti remembered that nobody had said the grace, and she asked that somebody say it. Nobody said anything. Paul called for Johnny, and he came out of Collins' room, his face distraught, and reported to his mother. He recited grace. While he talked, Lotti and Beth and Cyn bowed their heads, Cal stared at the tabletop as if seeking an answer to a question he had once asked, and Paul went on chewing at the chicken back.

Johnny went back to Collins' room. Kin came in and ate, then walked down to the chicken lot, where he thought about the loneliness of his life, and about Collins, who was going into the great night.

When he got back to the house, the family was standing in the hall again and in Collins' room, and Beth was standing in the parlor. Kin took up his watch near Collins' bed. Collins murmured on, nothing understandable until a time came soon after two o'clock when he spoke out clearly again. It was as if, in murmuring about old incidents, an incident of immediate importance had been reached. His eyes opened, though he couldn't see, evidently, and he said one word, simply and clearly. "Beth," he said.

She was in the parlor. Kin went to find her. "He wants you," he said.

"Yes, I know," she said, but sat in the rocker still, then slowly she got up. "Are they all in the room?"

"What do you mean?"

"It doesn't matter," she said. She crossed the hall.

Cal wasn't in the room, but everybody else was. Lotti, standing near the head of the bed, peered at her strangely, jealously. Beth went to stand beside her and looked down at Collins' open eyes, which were glazed and couldn't focus. She leaned against the bed, one hand holding to a bedpost, the fingers bloodless. She gazed down at him.

"Beth," he said again.

"I'm here, Collins," she said.

373

His eyes stopped moving and his vision came true, then flickered. It disappeared into softness again, then cleared. He saw her.

She leaned closer to him. "Yes?" she said.

"I was thinking about you," he said, smiling gently. "Way up in the clouds, the trees, Beth."

"Yes," she said.

"The way the light fell through the trees."

"Yes, Collins."

"Black trees, but the light was clear."

"Collins," Lotti said, "Collins, are you feeling better?"

"Hello, Mama," he said.

Lotti took his hand. "Collins, we've been expecting you for months, but I guess you had other plans. I had your room fixed and ready, and we was planning to feed you well. I kept waiting for you to arrive."

"I got to messing around, Mama. I wanted to come home, but I hoped to cure myself first."

"You've missed out on a world of trading and growing around here of late. My Johnny has growed as tall as you; he's so big he's taken for a grown person. And Matthew's married and his wife's expecting, and Beth's baby is pretty as a calendar picture, and is curly-haired, like his father."

"Your baby?" he asked Beth.

"Yes," she said.

"Yours?"

"Johnny, you come here and see your brother," Lotti said.

Collins was looking at Beth, tenderly and kindly. "Yours?" he said again.

Johnny came to the bed, and Lotti made room for him and gave him Collins' hand to hold. "Hello, Collins," Johnny said.

"Hello, boy. Say, you did grow."

"Yes, I'm six feet tall."

"Are you? You fight the girls off yet?"

Johnny grinned. "I don't have too much trouble."

"Don't fight hard, boy."

374

"No, sir," Johnny said.

"Some will tell you to let your chances go by, but I never missed a one. Don't you."

"Law, listen to him," Lotti said, flustered.

Collins smiled at Beth again. "Your boy?" he said. "I wish him well, too."

"I'll remember."

"And Kin. I want to tell Kin something."

Kin was at the foot of the bed. "Yes, Collins," he said, his voice choked up.

Collins didn't seem to hear him.

Kin pushed his way quickly to stand next to Beth. "Collins," he said.

But Collins didn't hear him. His eyes were glazed over again.

"Collins," Kin said, leaning close to him, knowing without touching him that he was gone, was dead, that it had happened just that simply and quickly. It wasn't like an arm being slit open by a knife and the bone exposed and the whiteness of the bone seen for an instant. The whole body died simply, easier than the body might lose a part of itself, and Kin knew it before anybody else, knew that he was not there any more, that he could not be reached by a message again, that he would not respond to any word, odor, or sight, neither of nature nor of men nor of what men have built nor of what men have thought nor of the members of his family, lovers, brothers, father. Nothing would reach him now.

The knowledge settled in among them all. Paul turned and went outside and into the hall. Beth hesitated, then started out of the room, but she stopped near the door and stood still, as if trying to remember something. She went on out into the hall, and when Kin got to the door, he saw that she had stopped again. She wasn't crying.

Morris and Florence were in the hall. Cal came in from the dining room and stopped still and stared at Kin. "Is it over?" he asked.

Kin nodded.

"God damn," Cal said. "God damn this."

"Yes," Kin said.

"Did he go down quiet?"

"In a moment. He was gone, that's all."

Beth was at the foot of the stairs. She started up them. She went up several of them before it came over her, and she went soft and bent over. She tried to climb up another step, but she couldn't. Sobs broke from her. She held to the banister rail and bent low in suffering, and the sobs broke through again and again. Her weeping sounded through the house, and Morris sank down on the halltree below her, his own body quaking with his grief for her, his wife who wept for Collins.

Kin went to her. "Beth, don't." He put his arm around her. He didn't cry, even though he touched her; he was a far distance from them all now, and he looked down at them as if from another time, as if he were older and were looking back. He could see them, his father, near the dining-room door, watching Beth, his face perplexed and caught in pain, in sympathy for her. Paul, looking up, his lips quivering as he watched her. Lotti, staring up, stunned, strangely looking at Beth as if Beth were of another, never to be quite understood world. Matthew, anguish on his face, leaning forward slightly, peering up questioningly, wonderingly, sorry for her, but curious, too, more curious than sorry. Florence, grim-mouthed, grim-gazed, standing behind Cyn, who was brushing big tears from her cheeks. Johnny, standing to one side, inscrutable.

All in a moment Kin saw them, and knew he would remember them looking up at her, and that he would look back on it and wonder about it, and would wonder why he felt nothing deeply now, even though she trembled under his hands, whom most of all he loved. "Beth, Beth," he said comfortingly.

She tried to go up another step, and he helped her. He helped her to the next. "Beth," he said, holding her tightly, helping her, "he loved you, Beth."

376

PART FOUR

26

THAT SAME WINTER, A MAN AT LUCK, CLINTON SILVERS, in order to cause his yule log to burn slowly, for no work needed to be done around the place as long as it burned, soaked it in a creek for two months, and it was so waterlogged that he had to haul it out with a mule. The mule dragged it right on into the house, too. When Clinton's wife saw the mule coming through the front door, she let out a whoop and said her husband was a damn rascal and had better, if he wanted to keep living, get that mule outdoors. But Clinton was so occupied trying to steer the mule through the hallway, and trying to get those children who weren't needed out of his and the mule's way, that her anger made no impression on him, nor did it have the slightest effect on the mule, which managed to get the log so close to the fireplace that Clinton and his two oldest sons were able to roll it in without backstrain.

The mule did knock over some of the furniture going out, and he took part of the parlor door frame off the wall. Clinton's wife went to bed with nervousness, and Clinton did a good deal of proud talking at the store that afternoon about what he'd done.

Since the snakes were in hibernation, and since it was possible to see a long way through the leafless hardwood forests, this was the time of year for forest cruising. One couldn't see far along the creeks, however; the laurel protected the banks and occupied every damp space available. One couldn't see through the dense growth even on the coldest days, when the laurel leaves would curl. They sulked that way, protecting themselves, and as the temperature increased, they would uncurl a bit, and when the temperature increased again, they would uncurl still more. Close to the creeks and in the high mountains, the laurel leaves were rolled much of the time, and some of the mountain men said they could tell the temperature by the leaves, which wasn't true, of course.

Occasionally a creek would freeze over and would look like cathedral towers, especially where the falls and slides were. Children enjoyed taking chunks of ice and sliding them down the creek beds, laughing as the ice crashed far below. The trees bowed heavily with ice, too, and sometimes a limb would break and occasionally a tree would explode because of the freezing. These trees were usually located in the icy region near the peaks, and most often on the mountain's shady north side. The layer of tissue inside the tree would expand until the tree would burst its own flesh, sometimes splitting all the way up the side, with such a noise that it resembled cannon fire. The report could be heard easily in the nearer valleys, though one could not always tell if a tree had exploded or if several tons of ice had fallen from a cliff. The sounds were approximately the same, though there was a longer rumble to an ice slide.

There was one man at Celo, Philip Harkness, who had spent much of his time in the winters walking the timberland and drawing maps. He knew nothing about contour lines and didn't bother to represent Celo Valley accurately; his interest was not in the peaks, even in the Black Brothers and the other giants of the Black Mountain range, or Celo Mountain itself. These he simply indicated with circles. His interest was in the way the springs fed water to form branches and creeks. He had spent much time following the streams and drawing narrow lines, which grew larger as they led to the

Toe River (Estatoe, the Indians had called it). He would show his map to anybody who wanted to see it, unrolling it lovingly on the table of his kitchen. One could see there the awkwardly made representation of the land, with the land appearing wrinkled because of the streams. And those who came to see were entertained by Philip, who told how at this stream he had met a white wolf, and from this other stream he had fished a trout that was four pounds by store weight. He would explain how Celo Valley was connected with other valleys. "This cross-mark is Joe Butcher's house. It's just this side of the divide and about the exact place old Sol Butcher, who was a drunk fool and everybody knowed it, was up on the mountain one night and hungry, so he snared a pig and cut a piece of ham off of it, then let her go squealing back into the thickets, and he ate fresh pork that night. You see where this stream starts here on the side of Wild Hog Mountain?"

The winter was Philip's favorite time of year, for he could more easily walk through the countryside, and it was easier, too, to follow the creeks. To him this was the mighty land, a nestling place which always bled pure water, cold and full of swirls where it swished around the creek rocks, and gentle in its flow over the flat beds of sand and by the roots of the bushes.

On December 29th a snow fell that closed in the valleys, so that there was no getting out or getting in, either. The lofts and cribs were full of food, however, and there was no hardship except for the ill, who had come to depend on doctors and commercial medicines. Several people died. It was wretched to die without such comforts as they had been used to.

The isolation and danger and deaths intensified the fear of spooks and evil spirits. One child near Franklin turned blue with a disease, perhaps a poisoning, and his parents, who had much fear of devils, set him outside on the front steps. He froze to death that night. Next morning they hacked a hole in the cold ground and pushed him in with a hoe handle, then burned the handle. The rest of the day they spent making up elaborate stories to prove that they were justified in what they had done, recalling stories of other blue bodies in olden days and what had happened to those who ignored the warning. The mother explained to the father, "Don't fret, don't fret, for God would a' kivered him with leaf mold to keep him warm, if he'd not been possessed."

Lordly people lived in the mountain country alongside the devil's own, and the tales of spirits moving about were so common that many people, both wise and not so wise, believed them. Murder and stories about murder, and stories about strange mysteries and magic and peculiar deaths, also crept across the mountain country of a wintertime. Collins King was talked about. The strangeness of his death occupied many brooding minds. He died for love, some said. For sin, others said. Killed by a woman who thrust a knife into his stomach, some said, for they had heard about it from somebody who had seen his corpse, they said. Poisoned by his brother. Poisoned by his mother for the hateful way he had done her. The poison was put in his tea before they brought him home on the train. It was put on a piece of pork they fed him. It was put in a biscuit and buttered over. It was put on her lips and she kissed him. It was put on the tip of a pin and she scratched his skin while he slept. It was put in the fire and the smoke smothered him. It was put in a flower and he sniffed the smell of it.

It was not a poison but a curse, some said, put on him by a woman somewhere far off who hated him because she had loved him. It was put on him by a foreign woman who had borne him two children and he had left her. It was by a woman somewhere near to home who had loved him and been left, whose heart had broken for him. When he died, they said, the white pine at her grave died overnight and its green needles turned brown and hard and would pierce the skin of anyone who touched them.

When Collins' death first was known, mountain people assembled every night on the lawn of the King house and burned fires to keep warm while they kept watch. Women sang old dirges, songs distantly remembered, the words lost but the melodies recalled, for the melodies, more than the words, were part of their blood flow and the inner worry and longing for life and death, the women more than the men; in the womb of feeling, not of birth or of thought, they protected them, songs composed by mourners in ancient Wales and Scotland, eerie and rippling with minor intonations, sung now by old women, toothless, as a rule, bent and shaggy, who stood near the fireplaces on the trail before the tall King house.

Each night Caleb King came out to look down at them from his porch. Three times each night he appeared, and on the third time each night he would come into the yard and shake the visitors' hands and accept their spoken sympathy. With him he would bring one of his sons, most often the young one, Kin. But one night the youngest, John.

The people also talked about Caleb, who was deep in mourning, and about Kin and John, about how the two boys, so much different, had both been stirred by the death. And about Beth, the niece of Caleb and cousin to Collins, who didn't come often from her apartment now except to walk each day, without acknowledging any face, to the tall King house, where she would sit, or so a cook named Inez said, in her upstairs room.

One day Kin came from the store to the house and threw his coat over the banister rail and sat down on a step, a feverish longing, not defined, coming over him again. He sat there for a minute, then got up and went into the room where Collins had died. He closed the door and listened, as if waiting to hear what Collins had wanted to tell him. He heard echoes of the raptured voice, the falling-waters of words. But no instruction.

What was the power of Collins, he wondered; what was his peculiar miracle? Each person was a miracle different from all others, but some were not big enough in themselves to make much show. Collins had stood out, he was triumphant. Maybe that was it. He was not in bondage to anything, but he had all the fruits which bondage promises. He had broken with routine, without knowing he had done it or knowing what routine was or without

383

hating it. He was so free in spirit that he didn't need rebellion to set himself free.

Kin noticed that his two yellow leather bags were under the bed. He dragged one of them out and opened it. He looked down at an assortment of clothing, the socks and underwear rolled tightly so that they took little space, the shirts rolled except for the collars. Everything was of silk.

He pulled the other bag out, laid it beside the first, and opened it. Before him were four suits made of expensive cloth. A small box of cuff links was there, a tin of shaving lotion, a shaving brush, a razor, and a strop.

He took out a pair of pants to see if they were wrinkled. He held them against his own legs. They seemed to be about the right size. He hesitated, then put them on. They fitted perfectly.

He put on one of Collins' coats. It fitted, too. Exuberantly he turned to the mantel mirror and studied himself; he saw that he looked very much like Collins.

The next afternoon he went into the room again. This time he put on another of the suits, carefully examining the coat lapels to see if there was lipstick on them, or a blond hair, or a brunette hair such as that of the dark lady he had seen on the train.

Each afternoon he put on Collins' things, and each day the thought of leaving home gained authority with him. He found chaffing faults with the idea of remaining much longer. Beth was in mourning, the store was a routine, his mother paid attention only to Johnny.

I could leave before spring, he thought. I could take money from the store and buy a ticket to San Francisco. I could take Collins' two bags and learn to be like he was. I could seek out his old friends.

He told himself he would never have another chance to equal this one.

He watched over Collins' death room, and each afternoon spent time there. Nobody else went into it, so far as he could tell, until on a Saturday morning, when he came back from the store to get a ledger he had been working on the night before, he heard a noise in there, a slight shuffling sound. He moved to the door quickly and threw it open, ready to pounce on the intruder.

It was only Johnny, standing near the center of the room, startled.

"I thought I heard somebody in here," Kin said defensively. "What are you looking for?"

Johnny studied him critically. "What do you want?" he said.

"You didn't like Collins so much, did you?"

Johnny looked at him with his big, searching eyes.

"I wish I understood you," Kin said. "You never are what I think you are."

Johnny watched him.

"You never deny you'll be a preacher, but I don't know. Is that what you want to be?"

Johnny said nothing.

"When Mama says pray, you pray. When she tells you to read the Bible, you do it. But you don't read it if she doesn't tell you to, do you?"

Johnny's expression still revealed nothing. "What do you want, Kin?" he asked.

Kin was embarrassed by the calm, superior manner, the maturity of the boy. "I don't know," he said.

Johnny was another reason he should leave, he told himself later. What sort of justice was there in a boy being born to take his name, his mother's affection, to be given every opportunity in private school, to be treated like a prince from his first breath?

Better to leave home and become like Collins while he could.

He set a time to leave, the coming weekend. There was a train at 11 P.M. on Sunday, and there was one early the following morning. He decided to take the early-morning train.

That Sunday night he lay awake on the top floor of the house, reflecting on his trip, which he dreaded but also longed for and deeply wanted. After he left, the second floor of the house would be empty, he realized. The family was breaking up as the children went on off to make their own way. Only his father and mother and little Johnny would be left. Only three of them would be left to inhabit these twelve rooms. The large talk and boisterousness of the old days were over. He remembered his fight with Paul, and he remembered Collins knocking many a time at Beth's door to take her out on a date, or to go with her downstairs to the porch for an evening of talk. He thought of the store, which he dearly loved, and the men of the street, and the beer halls, and little Sally Waters. He was leaving them all, and the Square and the Battery Park Hotel, which he had never entered.

He lay awake, clutching the store key in his sweaty hand. He would need it to open the door and take the money. He would leave his own clothes in the chest and on the hooks, just as they were. His father wouldn't be certain that he had gone until night. He would suspect the truth, no doubt, but not accept it. He would tell himself that Kin had not left. Then he would accept it, and, as the evening wore on, sorrow would flow over him.

He pitied his father, but he must win his own freedom; that was part of growing up for a boy. His father was trying to hold to him, just as his mother was trying to hold to Johnny, but he would win his freedom. It was time, and this was his chance.

At 4 A.M. he crept out of bed in the dark and went to the window. He could make out the sheds and the back corner of the new store, and the tall trees seething with limb motion. He dressed in his clothes of yesterday. He would change to Collins' clothes on the train. He crept downstairs, carrying his shoes, moving like a shadow along the wall. He found the light cord in the bathroom.

He heard his mother moan in her sleep. Perhaps she knew. Even though they were strangers, perhaps she sensed in the grogginess of slumber that one more child was leaving to try for his own life.

He left the bathroom quietly and made his way to Collins' sickroom, where he slipped on his shoes and tied the laces. It was dark, but he knew the room well. He knelt by the bed and reached under it for the suitcases.

He didn't find them, and he reached farther under, where they had been pushed back.

He didn't find them farther back, either.

386

He pulled up the shade at the window, but there wasn't much light, not enough to see by, so he pulled on the light. The bags were gone.

He sank down weakly on a small chair. They were gone. His father—had he known? Had Beth discovered his plan and decided that this time she would stop the traveling? Or had Inez simply put the bags away somewhere else in the room?

Yes, that was it.

But he couldn't find them. Perhaps they are under the stairway, he thought.

He went quietly into the hallway, leaving the bedroom door open so that the swath of light fell through. He parted the curtain and sought them among the trunks, but they were not there.

He heard his mother. "Is that you, Johnny?" she asked.

He waited for her to get quiet again, then he went back into the bedroom and looked under the bed.

He heard his mother's voice from her room, anxious and angry now. "Cal, did you hear what I told you?"

He went back into the hallway, his thoughts revolving crazily. He started up the stairs, anxious to get to his own room and try to think this out.

"Cal, what are we going to do?" Lotti asked.

Kin stopped on the stairs. Her voice had sounded as if it had pain in it. Why was she awake? Had he awakened her? Did she know? Did his father know?

He came back down the stairs and looked into the parlor. The bedroom door was open; the door to Johnny's room was open, too, and both lights were on. His father was sitting on the edge of the bed. Lotti was standing beside him, her nightgown caught at one knee, and fear was on her face. "My lord, my lord," she said.

Cal saw Kin and came out of the room, took his arm, and led him into the hallway. "Get down to the train station, Kin. Take the car and drive fast."

"Yes, sir. What's wrong?"

"It's your brother, that Johnny. He's run away."

27

THE POLICE FOUND JOHNNY IN ST. LOUIS AND
brought him home. They delivered him to the door, a wrinkled-
clothed, worn, and weary child who was near dead for need of sleep.
He came up the walk with two police officers, carrying Collins'
two bags, which were so heavy they slumped his shoulders. He set
them down on the porch, and when he saw Kin watching him incredulously from the other side of the front screen door, a frown
settled on him and he sighed; then the ludicrousness of his situation
won its way with him and he grinned. He was a ragged, bobtail,
weary traveler, for a fact.

Lottie was in bed. She had been under the doctor's care, but the
commotion on the front porch alerted her and she came out of her
bedroom, her nightgown clutched in her hands to keep it from
drifting out behind her, her legs wobbly in her haste. "Who is it?"
she called ahead, as she came through the parlor. "Who is it?"

Kin nodded to her reassuringly. She inched her way into the hall,
conscious of not being properly clothed. She started to speak again,
then hesitated, unsure, pitifully nervous and anxious. "Johnny?" she
said huskily to whoever it was on the porch.

The front screen door was opened, and one of the police officers stepped inside. Lotti cringed back into a corner, but Johnny came in, and her mind ruled out all else. She stared at him, studying him, seeking the reason he had left her, as if the reason might be marked on him, wondering where she might find a break in that armor she had so carefully constructed for him over the years. Was this the boy she had thought he was? No, he could not be, for that boy would not have run away. So it was a stranger in Johnny's flesh, just as all the other boys had been strangers in the flesh she had made for them, and strangers to the care she had shown them and to her ambitions for them. She didn't know how to receive Johnny now, or what to say to him.

"Hello, Mama," Johnny said.

"What you doing?" she asked, the question stirring no meaning in her. "Johnny, where were you?"

A policeman said, "We found him in St. Louis, trying to take a train, trying to sneak away."

"Sneak away?" she said. Red patches from nervousness marked her face and neck. "What does he mean, Kin?" she asked.

"I don't know, Mama."

"Well, don't come back here if you want to sneak away," she said to Johnny, but it was not a statement with severity in it. It was an appeal to him to deny that he had been running from her home, and from her. "Johnny?" she said anxiously, when he didn't answer.

"Mama, I didn't want to leave home," he said. "Why, Mama, I never would want to leave you, Mama, you know that."

Kin stared at him, astonished, for Johnny had never been given to making speeches about his feelings.

"Mama, I missed you," Johnny said. "I thought about you all the time, out on the road, and worried about you. Did you miss me, Mama?"

Kin was baffled. And even as he watched, Johnny held out his arms to Lotti, who was almost overcome with relief.

Lotti recovered from her nervous illness at once. She thanked the

389

policemen as they left, and, while Johnny went to the kitchen to serve his hunger, she dressed, talking all the while to Kin, who sat in the parlor near the fire. "I knew to my soul the boy couldn't have just decided to go, to leave home when everybody here loves him so much. Why, I said to myself that the world has lost its senses entirely." She came out of the bedroom, pulling her dress down into place. She plopped with a laugh of relief into a rocker and began to pull her stockings on. "I said, Well, what's the matter with the world, when a mother don't know her own children?"

Kin watched her speculatively. He could hear Johnny now back in the kitchen talking to Inez, who was giggling with throaty laughter. Hadn't Lotti seen at once, when Johnny stepped through the front door and said his first words to her, that he was no longer the boy who had slept in the back room, the child to be oiled and treated and nursed, the untidy schoolboy, that he had made a magic step from boyhood to manhood, had made it well before his years. Couldn't she realize that the image she had of the child was no longer valid for the man who had been returned to her?

"I knew he'd come back. I tell you, boys get a devilish fever to travel, and it's well that they get rid of it soon and come home to their mothers again. Johnny!" she called. "Johnny!" Then she said, "Kin, what's he doing back there in the kitchen?"

"He's eating, and talking to Inez, Mama."

"Talking to Inez? To Inez? What kind of sense is that? Why, Inez don't know nothing. Johnny, come here!"

"Here, here," Johnny said, coming through the hall, approaching them, "what's all the yelling about?" He came in, swaggering a bit from the wonders of his new-found prowess. He was eating a biscuit filled with blackberry jam. "Mama, this is the best blackberry jam I ever ate," he said. "I didn't get anything like this on my trip."

"It pays to stay at home," Lotti said, winking and nodding emphatically. "I tell you, boy, it don't pay to journey out like you done. Why, Johnny, you scared me to death."

He slipped an arm around her shoulder and nudged her to him. "Mama, you knew I'd get lonesome for you."

390

"Why, listen to that," Lotti said, gushing the words out happily, flushed with pride and good feeling. "Well, I hoped you would, Johnny. I was so worried I took to the bed."

"Mama, Mama, don't you ever worry about me."

"I want to worry about you. What do you mean, don't worry?" She was suspicious of him again at once.

"Well, everybody has to worry about himself, Mama," he said defensively, sitting down on the cot near the window.

"You expect me to bear you, to raise you, and then to hear you tell me not to worry about you?" She gazed at him anxiously. "Johnny, you know I care for you more than for myself." She sat down beside him and clutched at him. "Johnny, don't never leave me no more, you hear?"

"Mama, I wouldn't leave you, Mama," he said.

"You're for the Church, Johnny."

"Yes, ma'am," he said simply, flatly.

And Kin saw for the first time into the opinion of Johnny on that subject, too, and realized that the boy wasn't going to be a minister, that he didn't want to be one and perhaps never had, that he was a far wanderer, he would always be a far wanderer; he would seek God in distant places and with many people, would seek on his own, perhaps throughout the world, insight into the magic formula of man. He would be a minister in the sense that Collins had been a minister, a pastor of the little-known byways who had a strong sympathy for man's hungers. He would be a medicine to the ill in spirit, a soothing hand to the weary, a help to those who needed confidence and good spirit, testifying always, not in holy ways but in roadway laughter, to the basic worth of man's lot on earth.

"Mama," Johnny said, whispering to her, "I love you more than anything, Mama." He touched her arm. "You know that."

Deep-seated joy came over Lotti. "Well, I know it ought to be so," she said. "After all my work and prayers."

When dinner was over Kin walked up to Beth's apartment to tell her Johnny was home. She was feeding her baby Pablum with a spoon, and she welcomed Kin and gave him a seat in the kitchen. "It's gotten monotonous around here, Kin. Every day seems to be like another one, Sunday excepted, when we at least go to ride to look at houses." Her dress was splotched with baby food. She was weary looking, but the smile was the same as always, and the genuineness of her came through anyway, and the goodness of her. Just looking at her was like the day awakening for Kin. He still loved Beth the best of all, he guessed.

"Where had the child been, Kin?" she asked, as she spooned food into her little boy.

"He told us all about it at dinner. He talked so much Mama Lotti couldn't get a word in. He told about the train trip to St. Louis, about seeing the police in the train station, and about their trailing him and catching him. He talked about the food he was eating, telling Inez she was the finest cook in the world, until Inez grew so nervous she dropped a plate of hot bread."

Kin made the statements simply, then waited, watching Beth, who looked up after a moment, the meaning seeping through to her. "Do you know what you're saying?"

He nodded. "Papa noticed it, too, right off."

"Why, he's not but a boy."

"I know."

She finished feeding her baby and laid him aside. She wiped her hands off with a kitchen towel, which she flopped over a chair. "It does look like Mama Lotti could have gotten at least one preacher, doesn't it?"

"Maybe he can preach a little," Kin said.

"Trying to make a preacher out of one of the Kings is like making a steer out of a colt, I guess. They just don't tend that way." She smiled at Kin, but there was considerable sadness in it. "It makes me weary for Mama Lotti."

They went into the parlor and sat down near the front window, which looked out over Haywood Street. The radiator hissed steam, and she turned it off. "It's either too hot or cold up here," she said.

"You can't get the store downstairs comfortable without burning us up in the apartment. Customers keep going in and out of the store, and the cold air sweeps in, so the furnace has to work all the time."

"Aren't you ever going to move from here, Beth?"

"We have to, with the baby growing. We don't have room enough in here to swing a cat. But I do like the place, Kin. I like to look out and see people pass, and I know that Morris is close by downstairs. He's such a comfort to talk to and be with. When are you going to get married and start a family?"

"I'm in no hurry."

"You're about twenty, aren't you? Soon you can vote. If you can vote, you're old enough to get married, I say, and have children. Are you having a good time at college?"

"Yes."

"Any girls out there to go with?"

"There are two I like. And there's a girl in the library uptown, a pretty girl. But I tell you, Beth, they're rather tame people compared with those on King Street."

"Girls on King Street? You go with girls on King Street?"

"Well, I mean the people on King Street. Those girls I know would get to crying if they were to sit down and eat with Paul and he started talking big to them. They're gentle people; they don't talk loud or carry on all the time like him and Matthew."

"You'll need to find you a tough one, all right."

"That's what I think. Some woman who can throw a steer." The idea struck him funny and he laughed. Then Beth laughed. "Most women in Asheville," he said, "don't even know how to make corn bread any more. That's almost all we eat at home now."

"I tried to get Morris to like corn bread, but it didn't taste good to him. He likes black bread, which he orders from Washington, D. C. It comes in once a week in the mail, and it keeps forever. I don't think it would spoil in forty years. I can't digest it myself. It's like a knot in my stomach for a whole afternoon after I've eaten a bite of it."

393

"I've been looking for a girl with a lot of gumption. The only one I've found is the first girl I ever went with. I've not taken her out since, though."

"Why not?"

"I've seen her around, and I asked her at her house once to go out with me again, and she slammed the door in my face. I got to laughing, then she got to laughing and opened the door. But I got angry and left."

Beth scowled at him. "What do you mean? She slammed the door on you?"

"Yes, We had a misunderstanding once, Beth. I—got peeved at her."

"Uh-huh." Beth nodded briefly. "You want a Coke?"

They went back into the kitchen to get the cold drinks, but Beth decided she would rather have coffee, so she made that. She sat down at the clean table. She kept a neat kitchen, though the place was worn and old. "Morris is going to have to buy all new appliances when we move from here," she said. "He makes good money downstairs now, Kin, really fine money now that prosperity's come again, but we're like people caught in a rut. We settled down in these three rooms, and we came to like them. We're like mice in holes up here." She sipped at the coffee and blew on it. "What girl is the one you first dated, Kin?"

"Little Sally Waters," he said, watching Beth carefully.

"Who's she?"

"She's a—well, she's wild, Beth. She really is."

Beth took another sip of coffee.

"She's a wonder, though. I can't get her out of my mind."

"And it worries you?"

"What makes you think it worries me?"

"Because of what you say and the way you talk about her."

"Well, why shouldn't it worry me? She has more life, more energy, more love in her than—well, why not take her out? You know."

"What is she, a whore?"

394

Kin recoiled. He cleared his throat uneasily. "Not exactly."

"Well, do you feel degraded, is that why you don't see her?"

"Ah, Beth, you women talk about being degraded. I—I'm too pure, Beth, you know it? Women, when they get married, they don't look for pure men, do they? They go for the first waster who comes along."

Beth turned pale at once. Kin hadn't meant Collins, but she thought he had, and he didn't know how to amend what he had said.

"I didn't know you ever spoke so bluntly, Kin."

"I didn't mean you, Beth. Collins wasn't a waster."

"No, it's not the same, I suppose." She waited for a moment. "And it's true, what you say about women is true. I don't know. It's too complicated to talk about."

"Paul used to go with all types of women. No, I guess he didn't. He just went with the bad ones. And now he has a home, he has a fortune, he's married to a woman who's as pure as snow, I'm sure."

"Yes, and you can follow Paul's way, if you want to. Do you?"

"What do you mean?"

"Paul is suffering every day because of what Paul is. Of course, everybody has faults, but think of the suffering of Paul. Not that you could act like Paul if you wanted to, or suffer in the same way, or even understand how he suffers. You're not made so that you can treat people badly, as he can and as Matthew used to be able to. You can't bathe yourself in gutter water, like he can, either."

"My lord, Beth," he said uneasily. "I was talking about little Sally Waters, who is a pretty girl, an innocent-looking girl, who smells like rose petals, and you talk about gutter water."

Beth slammed her cup down onto her saucer. "Well, you know what I'm saying. Now, you think it through for yourself, then. My lord, Kin." She went storming out of the room, leaving him alone and miserable.

He found her in the parlor, sitting by the radiator, which she had turned back on. Steam was once more hissing from it.

"I'm sorry, Beth. I didn't mean to get you angry."

"Oh, I'm not angry. I just get worried about you."

He sat down across the room on a straight-back chair.

"Life is a gamble in which a good deal is at stake," she said simply, looking at the street below, "and so much depends on a decision. We're all involved, trying to make do and make out, and it's all different and crazy-quilted, and what's so for one person isn't so for another, and what advice you have for me doesn't quite hold for me, and what I say isn't quite right for you. I don't know. How can I know? Each of us is given a life to live, and we don't get very many second guesses. So we try to learn from one another as best we can."

"Can't you play it too safe, Beth?"

"I didn't play it safe, did I?"

"I guess not, Beth."

"I am now. Is that what you mean?"

"I didn't mean you, Beth. I mean, can't a person play it too safe?"

"Yes," she said.

He scratched at his neck. He rubbed his face and watched her. She was still looking down at the street.

"My hope is for my child, and for you," she said, "for I love you both and dream for you both. I hope my next child will be a boy, too, because I can't quite come to the place of dreaming for a girl. How can you train a girl for life and have any confidence? If she chooses wrong, she has lost her hope. A boy can choose poorly in love but still have his work. Life's problems are easier for a boy, and so every decision is more important for a girl. No one can be a woman very well, no one can be a mother or a wife well, be part of a family when that family is all she has without suffering the troubles which wait around the hearth. There isn't much clearness waiting there, is there, but pain's there. It's full of nice things and treachery; they're both there, and it's what a woman has. It's all a woman has."

She said nothing else. Her coffee was cold and she had drunk

396

little of it. He listened to the traffic from the street for a minute, then got up quietly and went to her and kissed her. "I'll be going now, Beth," he said.

When he got to the door, she said to him, "So what is this little Sally Waters? Is she a failure before she starts?"

That night Kin went to his room and stretched out on the bed to study for his classes. He had classes on three mornings of the week this semester, which gave him time to do his trading at the store. He liked everything he was studying, but he found he learned more from the books he read on his own than from those he read on assignment. It was a marvel to be able to lie on his bed in his room in his father's house in Asheville, a town on a raw, new, unfinished continent, and consider the lives and works and thoughts of men of other places, of other families, far back in time. He and they were part of a march of men, a march muddled and indecisive in motion, but, over the centuries, moving toward greater freedom and equality, the two not being the same, the two balancing one another.

The march wasn't over. He chafed whenever he considered his father's ways and wealth in terms of the poverty of the poorest of the mountain people. And although his father had earned his wealth and shared what he had, the paternalism involved troubled Kin's conscience, though he had never mentioned it to his father, who doubtless would only be irritated.

Johnny came upstairs. Kin heard him go into the back bedroom which Collins had used on his long visit home. Lotti came upstairs. "I don't see why you feel you have to move all your things up here," she said.

Kin closed his book and listened.

"That little room of yours downstairs is big enough, seems to me, even if you do have to keep all of Collins' things."

Kin sat up on the bed. He started to go out and protest the taking of Collins' things, but he didn't.

"It's so dusty in here," Lotti said, "and you'll be lonely on this floor, with nobody up here but Kin. Come on back downstairs, Johnny."

"I'm not afraid up here, Mama."

"You used to be afraid in the dark. I remember when you wouldn't go to the bathroom without somebody coming to the door with you."

"I don't remember that."

"I always used to go with you. Come on back downstairs, Johnny."

"Mama, I want to have my own space now."

There was a pause. "You seem to be growing away from me, Johnny, but I hope you won't grow away from Jesus."

"Mama, I never could grow away from you, you know that, Mama."

"Couldn't you? Well, I know you're upstairs now. I know that. I know it's unfeeling of you, of every one of my boys to leave me like this, and what am I to do? What am I to do, will you tell me? I can't bear no more. But you seem to be so set on it—"

"Mama, I'm not far away."

"I've never slept more'n ten feet from you, Johnny. I don't know that I can get to sleep tonight. When you was out West, I lay awake at night, I counted the cockcrows and prayed for Jesus to take care of you, and for my father's sake I knew he would, him who rode the trails and called on people and helped them. I always have hoped you would be a preacher, Johnny."

"Yes, Mama."

"For the world is in need of help. When I think of all the pain there is in the world."

After a while she went downstairs. Kin stared up at the ceiling of his room, his head resting in his hands, and wondered if all women came to old age so lonely. He guessed his mother had made the error of limiting her life to such a narrow interest, and divorcing herself from the ever-changing world so completely, that now the world and she were strangers, and the interest she had was petering out. She had lost her place. And Johnny, who was her arrow into space, the hope she had of reclaiming the world that she remembered from her childhood, had been set free. What if he had not gained his freedom, Kin wondered. A pity that would be. A deformed person he would have been if he had been the man his mother wanted. But she didn't know this.

There was a time, Kin knew, when the world was almost static, one generation to another. There was little change, and a father could shape his son exactly as he had been shaped, for the same work, the same house, the same shop, the same town. And a mother's hand would be steady then as she regulated childhood ways. But now each year brought new ways, and the old ways proved inadequate. Space and time and matter all changed.

Kin noticed the knob of his door turn. He held his breath watching as the door was pushed open a crack. It was Johnny, he suspected. The door opened farther, and he saw his father standing there, tall and tough, and the light threw shadows into the lines of his face.

He came inside and closed the door behind him. He stood looking down at Kin, then he sniffed and reached for the chair and pulled it under him as he sat down. It was the second time in Kin's memory that his father had come into the room.

"I tell you, boy," Cal said, rubbing his hands together slowly, as if warming his palms, "I've been thinking about something I want to ask you about. I want to know what you've decided about leaving home."

He said it simply and without looking at Kin, and when he received no reply, he said, "For it seems to me that Collins was a person to call a young man to travel, as was a brother of my father's, who was a traveler, too, and whenever he come back to home, it was with big news of far-off places. Back then, of course, there wasn't much of a way to get news, so everybody crowded around him, and the young men got the distant look in their eyes. Four boys left, following him one time, and other parents had to use strops and ropes and everything else to hold their families together. Nobody would even meet my uncle Charley at the train station, nobody wanted him to visit their homes, where their boys would get to hear him talk. So I know what the pull is and how it festers in a man, for once I had it, too."

He coughed and spat into his handkerchief, which he stuffed back into his pants pocket. He seemed to be asking Kin a question, but not one he expected to be answered.

"Oh, I know Collins was a great man in many ways, and I don't deny it. But I can't get over the notion that a man is a creature of responsibility, not of whims. Collins told me out on the porch one night that a man wasn't living fully unless he was totally free. Now, what does that mean, will you tell me?"

Kin licked his lips and studied him.

"It seems to me like a man that says that to himself is under bondage aplenty, for he's got to keep ducking and moving to keep from getting tied down to anything or anybody. Does anybody think Collins was free? He wasn't free from the first moment of his life to the last, but was under bondage always. In the country I was a backwoods man, and I was more free than I am now. I had two horses, a herd of sheep, a woods full of pigs, one good cow and one sorry one, a herd of beef cattle, a flock of chickens, and a flock of guinea hens. Well, I could leave that house just about any day I wanted to and go to Candler and visit, tilt back in the chair against the side of the storehouse and talk loose and swap knives and toss creek rocks at a line drawn in the dirt. I could go into Asheville or Canton and spend the day. I was more free of concern back then, and I spent forty years that way. And when I was forty years old I hadn't done anything, I wasn't worth anything, but I was free."

He peered at Kin as if challenging him to question it, then he sniffed and grumbled. "So Collins was wrong, you see." He rubbed his nose with the back of his hand and nodded, accepting what he said as so. "The only freedom I want is freedom to decide for myself what kind of harness fits me, and that's all any man gets."

He stared at Kin, his eyes as sharp as a young man's. Kin didn't move a muscle as he watched him and let his father's words seep into his own thinking.

Cal studied him. Kin knew it, too, but he didn't turn away from him. Then Cal inhaled deeply, satisfied with what he had said and with the manner in which he had said it. "The truth is you're not made like Collins, but like me."

He scratched at his face, his fingers trembling from tension and age. "You can sometimes tell when a boy's young what kind of person he is. At least, I can, so I don't believe we've got any more to say about this matter of leaving home, have we?"

Kin met his father's gaze. "No, sir."

"Now, if we do, you say it, because I get to worrying. I know you're steady, but it matters to me. Do you know that?"

"Yes, I know it."

"So speak up now. If you've got something I need to know, I want to hear it."

Kin looked off at the dark window, where a tree branch was scraping at a pane. "We've got nothing more to say about it, Papa."

Cal knitted his fingers together, moistened his lips, and peered at his son, satisfied with that. Then he sat back in the chair. He rested quietly for a minute. "Mark Coleman's family is after a loan. What do you think about it?"

"Is he the crippled one?"

"No, he's not crippled. He's got a limp, that's all."

"That's what I meant."

"Well, he's not crippled. The limp don't stop him or hold him up any. He's borrowed fifteen hundred dollars from me on his land already, and he's just got fifty acres, so I can't loan more than that with good safety. He's smart as a whip and an honest man. But now he's got a crop to plant, equipment to repair and some to buy, and he's got to get some cloth for his family, and salt and the like."

Kin studied his father.

"Now, you'll have your majority next year, and I think you should start to think about money matters and the making of loans. You'll be doing some of it at the store."

"All right," Kin said quietly.

"And you can start with it now, if you will, and take charge of some of these matters."

"All right," Kin said, still not showing any anxiousness to do it.

Cal looked at him sharply. "How much should we loan Mark Coleman?"

Kin stared back at him. "I wouldn't loan him anything," he said, "except enough to move into town with."

The answer came as a blow. It struck Cal and he blinked a time or two, then he turned from Kin and stared at the back window of the room. "I didn't know you had so much fondness for city life that you believed all mountain men should come into it."

"He has to make the move someday. It's not a favor to keep him in your debt."

"I never had him complain about being in my debt," Cal said bluntly.

"He's too smart to be wasted, Papa."

"Wasted? Is that what you think is happening now?"

"Yes. He's too much wasted now."

Cal peered at the black window, which the night backed against, and he said, "I see, I see," a murmur which escaped him. "Well, I didn't figure you'd have exactly my views." He got up irritably and went to the window and stared out. "But I didn't count on this." He shook his head erratically. "It's cruel to tell a man to leave his land, don't you know that?" He gripped his hands behind him and shook his head again, annoyed with the idea. "You'll have to be the one to do it yourself, if it's done."

Kin thought about that. "All right," he said.

"I'll be bound to send you others to decide about, for I expect that's where the future lies most heavily, in loans and money matters."

"I think so," Kin said. More than in the store, he thought. He knew the mountain region would change, was changing. The store on King Street was as busy as ever, but was a bit less important than it had once been in the lives of the people, for other stores were growing up in towns and at crossroads. And that was where the new challenge was, Kin thought, in the opening up of the territory, and in claiming the people for the productive world.

402

Cal opened the window. The room was too stuffy for him. He never liked tight places, or little rooms, either. He turned back to Kin and nodded, then he went to the door, but he stopped there and looked down at him. "If you ever have to break with me, you'll just have to do it, but I don't want you to leave. You're the only one I've got who has balance to him, like me. It's hard to find a man with balance to him. A father just gets one or two. I've got one."

"I'm not studying leaving; let Johnny have that way."

"It'll kill your mother early for him to follow off, but I guess he's bent to it. A woman sees her last one take on manliness and it blankets her breath down, for she knows she's had her last one, her last try. God knows what they're trying for; I don't know, do you?"

"Something better, maybe."

"Most likely. That or a plaything. God knows. Then they see death ahead, and they know they didn't get it."

"You afraid of dying?" Kin asked him, sensing in the way he spoke of death that he might be.

"No, are you?"

"Sometimes. Whenever I think about it."

"You'll grow out of that. An age comes when a man don't fear it so much for himself. A young man thinking about death is like a colt with a sore on his belly. But when he gets his flowering over and is sunk down in age, he'll go to meet it more willingly. He sees it's natural, and it's necessary."

"I get to thinking about it some nights. I get to trembling just thinking about my life being over and about being lowered into the ground, like Collins was."

"Uh-huh. Well, don't think about it, then." He scratched at the side of his face. "I don't know a subject that's more for old people and beyond the young than that one."

"How do you stop thinking about it?"

"Think about something else. It's just a stage you're going through. You grow out of thinking that way. When I die there'll be bonfires all up and down King Street, and on that yard out there, and in the farmers' market space. If all the people I've benefited stop by to admit to grief, they'll fill this territory. But so long as my interests go on soundly, I'll go down easy. I have no energies to waste fighting what's natural. I've come from way off, Kin, to this place. Twenty-five years ago, at an age when most men have given up, when I was forty, I bundled up my children and my wife and my things and drove in two wagons into town, and since then I've had to change myself all around, and I've seen the town change. And now I see in you that you're figuring on more change yet. Well, I don't know anything to say about that, except one season follows another, and a son follows his father, not to be like him any more than summer is like spring." He smiled grimly, and wearily. "Or maybe like spring and winter. Maybe that's better, for I'm now in the wintertime of my life."

"I don't think so, Papa. You're not so old in energy."

"I'm sixty-four, and I'm in the wintertime, so I'll go down soon. But I'm keeping my spirits up, because I see a new season coming on in you. And I just hope it's rich and full, as my life has been, not that I'd care to live it again." He was misty-eyed, but his face was strong, and his skin was parched and lined, the skin still of a man who has in his life worked a good deal in the sun and wind. He went to the window and spat.

He turned back, perhaps to speak again, but Lotti called to him from the bottom of the steps. "Cal, tell Johnny to come down here to his room. Cal, you can make him do it."

"Now, Lotti," he said, as he went to the door, "you just let him find his way."

"I can't get to sleep, Cal. I can't sleep when he's up there."

"Lotti, he'll be all right," he said, peering down the steps toward where she stood. "Don't hurt yourself thinking on it, Lotti."

"I worry so," she said.

"Go back to bed. I'll be down in a minute." He waited, watching the place she had stood; then he looked down at Kin once more. "I better go to bed now," he said.

"Good night, Papa."

404

"It's not easy," he said, thinking about it. "It's not simple. Do you know that?"

"What's that, Papa?"

"We're all in it; it's all about us. We make do. We make out. We get through somehow. It's a feeling more than anything." He scratched at his ear, then pulled at one ear lobe. He cleared his throat and coughed deeply. "You sleep good," he said.

Kin listened as he went down the stairs, moving slowly, walking in the dark, like an old man. Wintertime, he had said. His father dying, Kin thought.

He pulled the light cord and the light went off. He stretched out, even though he was still clothed, and listened to the branch scrape at the window and thought about his father, who had grown stronger with the years. He supposed he also had grown stronger in the past few years himself, though there was a way to go before he matched his father. At what age had his father taken on his full power, Kin wondered. At what age would authority come to him. Surely not, he reasoned, while he was still trying to determine the shape and size of his life. No doubt it would evolve, as nature worked its way; no doubt manhood did not come upon a boy all in a moment, or maturity arrive in the shell of a seed. Life felt its way along, growing as it found it was able, being shaped as much as shaping, and each day might bring him progress, just as it would give opportunity to Matthew, too, and to Beth, and even to Paul, who had lost in every move he had made in life and had ended up wealthy.

Kin smiled at the thought of that. By failure Paul had become rich, and no doubt Kin would be borrowing money from him someday, perhaps to open a chain of stores in the valleys, or to build a factory in Burnsville. Paul would own a world of goods, though Kin suspected he would not own much happiness.

He wondered if Beth would. He thought for a while about her and hoped she would have a baby girl next time, because that was what she needed most. She was trying to make too much of the boy,

405

he thought. She would have many problems with a boy, but she could rear the best girls in the world, if she let them follow their mother and take their chances.

He would have to find a girl for himself, he knew, a tough one, and soon. Maybe that summer one would come in with her father on a wagon loaded down with yellow pumpkins and would help him unload them in the shed. Kin smiled at that thought. But he would just as soon she would turn out to be less open-minded than the girl who had pleased Collins for a few minutes one afternoon years before; he would just as soon find more modesty to her. But whether she was on a pumpkin wagon or behind a desk in school, he would seek her out. He lay awake speculating on what he would say to her of an evening, how he would make love to her of a night and tell her the world of the mountain was hers, for he guessed it would be his someday, for he, the next to youngest, was the heir to his father's spirit and to his loyalties and friends.

He would make love to her and comfort her in the days of summertime and the falling away, and in that far-off season of coldness which would surely come. And she, this strong-willed woman with a pretty face and body, would accompany him on the journey he was just now getting under way, on this most remarkable, never really to be believed journey.

What an idea, he thought, this idea God had had. He could imagine himself a long time hence, a man unlike his father, but like him, too, walking slowly down a flight of darkened stairs from his own son's room, walking in another house somewhere, moving slowly down toward his wife's room, knowing that he had done most of what he in his life could do.

He hoped he would sleep that night in the far future as soundly as his father would sleep tonight in the feather bed on the floor below, where he and Lotti were left alone now.

He lay awake, wondering about himself and thinking about his father, and listening to the wind blow through the sycamore tree.

406

JOHN EHLE is the author of eleven novels and six nonfiction books and has won numerous literary awards, including the North Carolina Award for Literature, the Thomas Wolfe Prize, the Lillian Smith Award for Southern Fiction, the Sir Walter Raleigh Award for Fiction, which he has earned five times—more than any other writer to date—and the Mayflower Award for Nonfiction. His books have been translated into French, German, Swedish, Czech, Spanish, and Japanese.

Following service in World War II, Mr. Ehle earned his BA and MA at the University of North Carolina-Chapel Hill. He taught at the university for ten years before joining the staff of Governor Terry Sanford in 1962. He resigned from the governor's staff in 1964 to write *The Free Men*, a nonfiction account of the civil rights movement that took place in Chapel Hill, North Carolina during 1963-64. Mr. Ehle later served on the White House Group for Domestic Affairs and was appointed to the First National Council of the Humanities. He has been awarded honorary doctorates from Berea College, the North Carolina School of the Arts, the University of North Carolina-Asheville, and the University of North Carolina-Chapel Hill.

Mr. Ehle lives in Winston-Salem, North Carolina, with his wife, actress Rosemary Harris. The two divide their time between Winston-Salem and three other homes in Penland, North Carolina, New York City and London. They have one daughter, actress Jennifer Ehle.

CPSIA information can be obtained
at www.ICGtesting.com
Printed in the USA
LVHW022232280721
693949LV00002B/142